A Foreign Affair

Pamela Burton

A Foreign Affair

In memory of Clare

A Foreign Affair
ISBN 978 1 76041 129 9
Copyright © text Pamela Burton 2016
Copyright © cover photo © Jodie Johnson – Fotolia

First published 2016 by
GINNINDERRA PRESS
PO Box 3461 Port Adelaide 5015
www.ginninderrapress.com.au

1

Darwin, Saturday 18 November 1989

Had Miroslav Bozin not lingered over his coffee he might have lived beyond the next two hours.

The salty breeze gave little relief from the humidity of Darwin's wet season, though the table he was sitting at was shaded by she-oaks. He was sipping his double-shot coffee when, from his vantage point on the grassy parkland, he saw the fat Eurasian man peering out to sea through binoculars on the sandy inlet below. The man's crinkled cream jacket swung loose and his shirt came adrift as he turned suddenly and made to leave.

Bozin decided there could be only one reason for the man's presence here at Nightcliff. A cry from a woman at a nearby table confirmed it. Heads turned to follow her pointing hand clasping a take-away coffee.

'Look, boat coming in! It's heading for the beach.'

A fishing boat with painted blue and maroon stripes was edging its way into view. No flag, just flapping blue and white checked propylene sails giving some colour to the scene of forlorn wretchedness aboard the dilapidated wooden craft. Boat people were a novelty in Darwin. It had been decades since boats of refugees, then mainly Vietnamese, had arrived here.

A group near Bozin abandoned their Saturday coffees and croissants to stand up and watch. Others began running in the direction of the beach.

Soon media vans and reporters arrived; cameras flashed to capture the commotion. The sound of an engine appearing round the corner added urgency. A police pilot boat headed for the rickety craft as it putted into Nightcliff Beach.

Bozin decided that there was now no need to keep his two o'clock appointment with the fat man at the race course. He'd confront him here, instead, and tell him what he had to tell him. That decision sealed his fate.

People on the beach craned to see the tired and worn faces of refugees huddled on the deck. They told a story of hunger, trauma and illness; relief perhaps that they would soon have their cracked and infected feet on solid ground. Young men hung over the side of the boat as if to see for themselves what the Darwin they had heard about looked like.

The boat grounded in the shallow water and several of the young men slipped over the deck and into the clear water, turning, arms outstretched, to help women and children off the boat. The noise of the police boat's motor drowned the excited exchanges.

'Stay aboard. Do not move,' a loudhailer crackled from the pilot boat.

Two thin young men were already on the beach kicking up sand with their bare feet.

Immigration officers pushed their way through the growing crowd on the beach. The fat man, his brown leather satchel strapped across his chest, scrambled across the rocks to the foreshore to join the crowd. He removed his sunglasses from under his cream straw hat and wiped the drips trickling down his tobacco brown skin with his handkerchief. The sun caught his Rolex, sending a circle of gold flashing across the rocks.

The new arrivals were escorted from the boat up the sandy beach to the waiting vans on the road. Not even a child cried. An empathetic silence descended on the watching crowd. It was broken by a cry from the boat and shouting voices.

A young man, or rather a boy, barely fifteen, was protesting in English, 'I'm not crew. I'm child. No prison. No,' as he was being handcuffed by a customs officer. Another passenger moved to protect him before being restrained.

The fat man hovered at the top of the beach. A smartly dressed man walked towards him; navy blazer, clean white collar and a blue tie that spoke of officialdom. Asylum seekers came under Australian government jurisdiction.

'Afternoon, Ormandy,' the fat man greeted. 'Not often you escape your policeman's desk in Canberra, eh?'

'Too right. But can't say it's a pleasure to be here,' said the federal police officer, looking down on the much shorter man. 'You pushed the envelope using an illegal boat, you boofhead.'

'Well, it arrived. I said it would. You lot ought to thank me. No one else knew they were coming, let alone where it would land. It was me who rang Immigration to tell them a boat was likely on its way. Man called Pratt seemed pretty happy about my public spirit! Didn't tell him how I knew, just that I had contacts and heard…'

'I'm glad it arrived safely – for your sake,' Ormandy interrupted. 'But I hope there's not a stream following.'

The two men waited while a scrawny fisherman, the boat owner and sole crew, was handcuffed and marched to a van with bars on its rear window. When the van left, the crowd dissipated.

The policeman and the fat man watched while the pilot boat attached a hawser to the fishing boat and tugged it out of the bay. They turned and walked back through the park from which Bozin, now standing out of sight, had first spotted the fat man, and headed towards a small man-made harbour protected by a stone breakwater. Bozin kept his distance. The two men stopped at the top of the boat ramp and waited for the boat to be tugged in.

The policeman approached the customs officers stationed near the now cordoned-off fishing boat wedged between the pilot boat and the breakwater. 'Senior Detective Mitch Ormandy,' he said, flicking up the lapel of his blazer to reveal a badge. 'You can leave it to us now,' he muttered.

The Customs officers left their posts and walked off. The illegal fishing boat was now in the hands of the federal police.

'Come on,' said Ormandy, beckoning the fat man to the pilot boat. 'We have some cargo to check. Let's hope it's intact.'

The fat man placed an uncertain foot on the wobbly bottom strand of a rope ladder, trying to avoid wetting his patent leather shoes and, about to lose his balance, grabbed his companion's jacket. 'They're in the cargo hold,' he wheezed from behind. Heaving himself onto the police boat, he stumbled across its deck to the desolate fishing boat.

They tried to avoid treading on empty tin cans and cracked plastic bottles that littered the deck. A putrid stench greeted them from an open hatchway, and the fat man covered his nose and mouth with his handkerchief.

Crooked steps descended from the cut-away door to the small cargo hold. The fat man peered down and gagged on seeing faeces spilling over the top of several buckets in one corner of the hold.

Ormandy pushed him aside and lowered himself into the hold. The fat man squeezed down after him, took a screwdriver from his satchel and handed it to Ormandy. He watched as the policeman squatted to unscrew the clamp which secured a long box to the floor under a bench at the end of the hold. With much effort and little help from the fat man, Ormandy got the heavy box up from the floor and set it down on a bench. The fat man handed him a key and the other worked the padlock.

'Three dozen .22s,' the fat man panted, pleased and relieved. He plonked himself down beside the box on the bench.

Ormandy lifted a layer of felt to check the rifles, and shifted some of them to look underneath. 'What are these?' he asked.

'Berettas. Not for you – for another customer. I can get some next time for customs if they prefer them to the Glocks.' The fat man picked up a Beretta 92F and turned it over slowly in his hand to show it off. 'The Indonesian navy use them,' he said.

'Nope,' said Ormandy, picking up one of the guns. 'Customs use Glocks for front-line officers.' He looked at the fat man and warned, 'And don't you go boasting about that deal. Not a word. If the licensed dealers have proof we're bypassing them, you won't be selling any more firearms to us or anyone else.'

'Come on. The Glocks are legit. They're not black market,' taunted the fat man.

'Don't get cocky. They're grey market – only one shade different. You're lucky to be supplying Customs without going through the red tape. But it's crossing the line to use people smugglers to get these rifles in. Not to mention the Berettas. I warn you, they'd better not end up with Max, that ASIO rogue.'

'None of your business,' the fat man laughed.

'Don't go playing Mr Big with me, mate,' Ormandy snapped. 'Your only job is to tell us who buys the rifles. It won't be long before you'll have to shut your dodgy operations down. Do some honest importing. Got it?'

'I know the deal. Let's go. We need to get these rifles away. Then I have a race meeting to get to. And make sure your goons keep well under cover, or they'll blow it.'

'We know our job. You worry about yours.'

The fat man put the three Berettas in his shoulder bag and closed and locked the box of rifles for Ormond to lift. The policeman managed to slide the heavy box on to the deck with one foot on the ladder below, and then climbed out of the hold. The fat man followed, his satchel heavy with the Berettas.

'Oh, the matter of the boat,' the fat man said as he stood up, heaving to catch his breath. 'I have a buyer.'

'You've got a nerve,' Ormandy glared at him, 'Forget it. Tomorrow it'll be towed to Fishermen's Harbour for inspection and quarantining. Then it'll be burnt. It can't be used again anyway – it'd sink... What the...'

The noise of boards creaking caused both men to turn abruptly.

'Hold it,' a voice said from close by.

The fat man reeled, and gaped at the young man standing only metres away, holding a pistol at arm's length and pointing it at them, legs apart and feet firmly planted.

'Shit! What the fuck... Bozin, what are you doing here? I said the racecourse at two.'

The policeman went to whip a gun from the inside pocket of his jacket.

'Drop it,' shouted Bozin, his command hardly audible as a bullet hit the deck with a crack at Ormandy's feet, splintering the rotten boards. Ormandy jumped back and dropped his gun.

'What's a cop doing here?' Bozin asked with a thick accent.

Ormandy also addressed the fat man. 'This foreigner a friend of yours?'

'Cool it, both of you. Yes, Bozin's my buyer. We're all on the same side.'

'Not me. Not with cops around, crooked or not,' said the newcomer. He held his gun at Ormandy without taking his eyes off him. His nostrils flared and his chest muscles heaved under his T-shirt as if about to burst through.

'How do you expect me to get the stuff in?' the fat man quavered.

Without shifting his gaze, Bozin answered, 'Bribe a customs officer; that was the plan, but this…no way. I'm not here to help arrest my compatriots. Anyway, I saw you arrive, followed you, to tell you it's over. The Croats don't want any more rifles. I'm not surprised. Looks like this is a double-cross.'

'No, no, you've got it wrong…' the fat man pleaded.

'I'm done with you. Go sell your guns somewhere else. Deal's off.' Bozin lowered his gun, pocketed it and made to leave.

'Stop!' the policeman ordered.

Bozin turned around briefly, holding his palms up in a resigned gesture of 'Just leave off,' then turned back and kept walking.

The policeman retrieved his gun, and yelled again, 'Stop. I'll shoot.'

Bozin half turned and Ormandy fired. The bullet entered the side of Bozin's chest.

He fell to the deck staring up in disbelief and managed to spit out, 'You fuckin' bloody apes…' before his head lolled and blood gushed from his mouth.

'What've you done…?' the fat man turned to the policeman. 'Get an ambulance.'

'Bit late for that. Help me clean up this mess, and quick. We have to get the rifles back into the hold. Get his gun onto the deck, quickly. The place will be abuzz soon enough. I couldn't have him blow open the whole operation. Call it an accident. You saw what happened.'

'Oh, yeah? Accident? Sure.'

'Shut the fuck up, will you. It was self-defence.'

'And how do we explain me being here? "'Scuse me officers, just doing a bit of gun-smuggling, rifles for sale – all official of course"...'

'Stop babbling,' Ormandy yelled at him. 'You're up to your eyeballs in all this. Be grateful I'm here to protect you. You think you'd be safe after that scummy Balt reported you were helping the police?'

'Scum he may be, but not a murderer. Whereas you...' The fat man stopped on hearing the wail of distant sirens. He retrieved his handkerchief and bent down to remove the pistol from Bozin's jeans pocket and place it beside the dead man's right hand.

'Get this straight,' Ormandy directed. 'We tell it exactly as it is. A botched operation. Local cops won't contradict a federal cop. Not over an official operation run by Canberra's spooks.'

'And me?' the fat man asked.

'We'll stand behind your guarantee. Now, shut up, back me up and say this was self-defence,' the policeman said, looking at the now-still body on the bloody deck.

The sirens grew louder as two police vehicles approached the road above. The street was soon full of vehicles with flashing lights. An ambulance followed.

'You owe me now – big-time,' said the fat man.

2

Canberra, November 1990

She walked along the Griffith shopping strip as he had suggested. Her sleeveless black and beige linen dress showed off her tanned slim legs and her black sandals flapped noisily. 'Make it look like an unexpected meeting,' he had said.

And here she was in suburbia, using her lunch break to carry through their little plan. It was innocent enough, as was their affair, which she was glad he was happy to own. She didn't see a lot of him. They met, talked, made love when the spirit moved them; a relationship that suited them both. It was necessary, though, that she declare him a significant person in her life when she reapplied for a security clearance for her upcoming government consultancy. A secret liaison would invite suspicion.

As she passed the Minos Café, on cue, she heard a gentle knock on the café window. She turned and saw him and an involuntary thrill shot through her body. She cursed her failure to control the reaction, but felt the better for it. He beckoned her in.

Two business-suited men sat with him at the window table, backs to the door. They turned to see her. The spread of coffee cups and scrunched serviettes said that they had just finished eating. He excused himself and rose to greet her. She read affection in his dark, almost black eyes. He embraced her with a light kiss on the cheek, instead of his customary continental three pecks, and held her hand as he introduced her to the suits.

'Larry, Eugene, meet my special friend Dr Josephine Rowan,' he said.

'Jo,' she corrected, holding out her hand.

The men moved to stand but she bade them stay seated, still offering her hand, which they took and shook in turn.

'Join us for coffee,' one of the suits invited.

Mujo had told her that he wanted her to meet his spook friends. They worked for the Australian Security Intelligence Organisation, ASIO as it was called, though she would not be letting on that she knew. Her first thought was to challenge them for dressing like spies trying to look like public servants. Ludicrous, she thought.

Instead, she said, 'Thanks, if I'm not intruding. I only have a few minutes – due back at work.'

'Good to see you,' said her friend.

'How do you know this reprobate diplomat?' Larry asked.

'We met some years ago in Belgrade,' she replied, 'at an embassy cocktail party…of course.'

Mujo took a swig of whisky from the glass beside his coffee and slumped back into his chair, apparently confident about the pantomime being played out.

'What about you?' she asked Larry. 'Why would respectable public servants befriend my reprobate foreign friend?'

'Us? Public servants? No, Eugene and I are mixing a little business with friendship. We're in the export business. Mujo is always looking for good trade deals.'

She laughed, and sipped her coffee for a few minutes while joining in the chatter about nothing in particular. Then she said, 'I must go' (the shortness of her stay had been planned). Smiling her goodbyes, and after a special glance at her friend, she slipped out, slinging her bag over her shoulder and shading her eyes from the hot sun.

The phone woke her at one in the morning.

'Are you awake?' he asked in a soft deep voice.

'I am now,' she answered, and, far from being put out by the not unexpected wake-up call, that pleasurable sensation jolted through her again.

'I soon finish here at this over-long embassy function. May I see you?'

'I won't turn on the lights. There's a glorious full moon,' she said.

She rose, but did not dress. Her loose white cotton beach dress doubled as nightwear. She splashed her face with cold water, tugged a comb through her thick curly hair, and padded barefoot across the wooden floor to the kitchen. She removed two chilled glasses from the refrigerator and placed them on a small terrace table at the rear of her modern suburban town house. The air was breathlessly still.

Canberra, Australia's capital, was purpose-built to house the national parliament and a plethora of public servants. The garden city, with its tree-lined streets, open green spaces and national monuments, sits on a limestone plain surrounded by deep blue mountains. Its population of mostly newcomers had grown into a middle-class community of public servants, academics and scientists, not to mention the butcher and the baker effect. It had also become home to foreign diplomats who lived in ornate embassies, many of which were just minutes from Jo's home in Yarralumla, a prestigious suburb hugging the shores of Lake Burley Griffin.

Within minutes, Jo heard the purr of Mujo's small black BMW break the silence of the night in her driveway. Yarralumla slept on.

She was tall, though not a match for his six feet. Her black hair made a striking contrast with her white dress. His black hair and dark complexion merged with a dark navy suit.

He released his tie as he greeted her. 'My Snow White…' he whispered, touching her cheek for the first of three greeting kisses before she clutched the lapels of his jacket and brought him in, pressing her lips to his.

They drew apart and walked through the house and the sliding glass doors to the back terrace to enjoy the warm November night. She poured cold wine into frosty glasses. He lit a cigarette and passed it to her; then one for himself.

'Your "friends" knew what you were up to,' she said. It was a statement rather than a question.

'It doesn't matter,' he replied. 'What matters is that they see you and

I are not secret. They cannot, how you say it, hold it over you, or me, knowing we are open.'

'Yes, certainly I need my security clearance renewed if I'm to start work at the Immigration Department.'

'It's a silly game. But they can't hurt us, or my family back home.'

She was quiet for a moment, and then asked, 'And will they join you here?'

'I hope so. I'd like you to meet my wife and my little frogs. She is lawyer too. We met at university, though she is much younger. I hope she will come to Australia, but for moment we stay apart.'

His faltering English was easy enough for Jo to understand and it added to his charm, though he was lazy with his pronunciation given his fluency in the language and he made little effort to insert a 'the' or an 'an' before a noun to conform to English construction.

Jo struggled to respond generously. 'Of course I'll like her. But, well, if you get back together again, it has to be the end of this – us.' She leant over and picked up her glass, and stared into it, rather than looking at him.

He kept his eyes on her, watching. 'I know, I know. I would like us to be forever. But when my posting ends, we part anyway, so, rather we keep strong friends, you with my family, then I do not lose you,' he said.

'You don't want to lose either of us, you mean.' She smiled and looked up at him, not expecting a reply. 'Will you go back, though? How will you be treated by Milošević – a Serbian tyrant for a national leader? What with independence movements all over Yugoslavia, Belgrade seems the wrong place to be.'

Mujo laughed and shrugged. 'It must be. My colleague Marika, Serbian woman, is here to watch me, report if I show interest in defecting. But I watch her too, enjoying life here and I think she is the one who might stay. Not me. My old mother lives in Belgrade. There are other reasons. I must go back, make my marriage work and wait the chance for another posting. Then maybe.'

'I'll miss you – us.'

'Me too, but you will have other lovers. I have family…' He stood up, not taking his eyes off hers and stretched out his hand. 'Enough of this …' he said. She took it and he hauled her up. 'Right now…we are together.'

A squeeze of the hand, and she forgot the futility of their relationship. Her brain stopped reasoning and her body took over. They walked inside and sat down on a Persian rug. He leant against the sofa and stretched his legs out, making room for her to sit between them, facing him. She undid his belt buckle and loosened his clothes. He leant forward and gently rolled up the skirt of her dress. Whisky lingered on his breath from his earlier on-the-job drinking. She didn't mind.

Moonlight came through the living room windows, reminding her that she hadn't drawn the curtains. Too bad. No one was likely to be around at this hour. He brought her close with his hands around her waist and then rocked forward gently bringing her down onto the rug, as she raised her legs to rest her ankles on the sofa. He slid himself into her and his gentleness gave in to her hunger. She loved him at that moment; loved him for the strength of his body, and for everything it did to hers; for his whispered words; for being there for her.

Their excitement peaked and, still inside her, he guided her sideways on the floor. She clung to him and then let him go. He was an addiction she could break when necessary, she told herself. Meantime, she would enjoy the way that their lovemaking happened anytime, anywhere, as it did tonight.

He reached across her for his cigarettes.

'But why were you lunching with our spooks?' she asked as if the day's lunch had been the night's only topic of conversation.

'It's my job to keep an eye on what your spies are doing. It's their job to keep an eye on us. They watch and try and learn about KGB interrogation techniques. We want to know if we are seen as friend or enemy. At the moment, we are friends.' He lit his cigarette and looked up at the ceiling as he exhaled. 'Your Murphy's raid on ASIO in Melbourne years ago made that possible. Your government accused ASIO of protecting extremist Croatians. My Serb-led government was happy about the outcry.'

Jo remembered the publicity surrounding Attorney-General Lionel Murphy's surprise raid on ASIO's Melbourne headquarters in 1973, and his allegation that ASIO, by focusing on communist enemies, was missing threats by Croatian terrorists.

'The Communist bogey had faded,' Mujo continued, 'and your spooks needed a new enemy to keep growing their power. So they obliged Murphy and focused their watch on Croatian fascists rather than Yugoslavia's Communists. This is good for us. So I became "mates" with agents like Larry and Eugene. We now have mutual interest in finding Ustashi operatives who are training Croatian migrants to support the Croatian Liberation movement back home – "picnic camps", they are sometimes called. Though sometimes intelligence services get in each other's way. Your guys killed one of ours in Darwin a year back.'

'An accident, I hope? Bet we didn't get the real story in the press?'

'No, too embarrassing. I didn't enjoy telling our fellow's family either. We are cautious about sharing information now.'

What he said made sense to Jo. There had been some publicity about suspected Croatian military training camps in New South Wales and Victoria. She also recalled arrests of supposed members of the Revolutionary Brotherhood found training with rifles and the Croatian community protesting that false allegations were being spread by the Yugoslavian Serb-controlled communist government. She wondered where the truth and Mujo's personal loyalties lay. It couldn't be easy for a Bosnian Muslim to be a career diplomat working for Milošević's ruthless regime.

Mujo went on, 'All a game…' He then added, 'Sometimes, more serious things at play than game…' He stopped, gave her a squeeze, 'But for the moment, it's okay. I help your guys, and they give me something to keep Milošević happy.'

He did not explain further. And she did not, would not, ask him.

3

Canberra, May 1991

James Pratt straightened his silver and white striped tie and buttoned up the jacket of his light grey suit. He limped as he descended the stone steps of the Immigration building. His left leg had never fully recovered from that jeep accident during an army training exercise. He had good days and bad days. Today was a bad day. He wondered if anxiety increased his leg pain, like today, worrying if he was doing the right thing by Josephine Rowan. She'd been working in the department for nearly six months now. He didn't like blocking other people's work, especially that of a high-flyer like Rowan's, but nor could he put his section's project at risk.

He spotted Agent Alec Brown approaching. It was lunch hour. Public servants were leaving buildings, rugged up against the cold May day, criss-crossing roads to buy sandwiches and hot pies from nearby cafés, and hurrying back to the warmth of their offices, brown paper bags tucked under their arms.

'Hello, Alec. Can we find somewhere to sit, rather than walk as we talk?' Pratt asked Brown by way of greeting. 'Sorry, my leg…'

'My car,' Brown replied. 'It's over there,' he said, pointing to the asphalt car park.

Seated in the spook's black Ford Fairlane behind tinted windows, Brown asked Pratt how Operation Fishnet was going. 'Is that bastard Fish performing?'

'Well, yes,' said Pratt. 'He forewarned us of two boat arrivals. Both full of Indochinese refugees. But it's about keeping Operation Fishnet under wraps that I'd like a word. A little issue has cropped up.'

'Fire away.'

'We blocked the promotion of a woman into our section, as you suggested. But that's caused another problem. A woman has been sent to Immigration to prepare a report for Prime Minister and Cabinet on gender equity stuff.'

'The same woman we tried to stop getting the consultancy...?'

'Yes, well... Ah, did you? Rowan's her name, Dr Josephine Rowan, a university bird.'

'That's the one. We had no choice but to renew her clearance. Prime Minister's wanted her in there, and Furzer vouched for her. So what's going on?'

'Well, now she's specifically investigating why a senior woman, Annette Armstrong, lost a promotion to the youngest fellow in our section. She wants to look at our files.'

'What is she asking to see?' Brown asked.

'She wants to see the recruitment file on that appointment. Trouble is, well, you know, the selection process was, well, a bit rigged. It won't take long for her to pick up on, um, that, and uh, then, well, other embarrassments.'

'You mean concerning Fishnet?'

'Yes. Like using that dodgy Fish to suss out information on illegal boats. She'll conclude that we didn't want a priggish career woman questioning our methods. And we don't. Don't want either of them nosing around.'

'No, we don't.'

Pratt stared straight ahead and through the windscreen to watch a couple of pigeons squabbling over a crust. If they weren't careful, the sparrows would take it while they argued. Sparrows everywhere and never noticed. Just like ASIO's sparrows: a myriad of civilian informants infiltrating radical student groups, clubs, unions and the like in the hunt for 'subversives'. But Fish was no mere sparrow and Pratt had reason to believe that he was not just unreliable, but actively dangerous.

It had been Senior Detective Mitch Ormandy's idea to engage Fish to provide intelligence on owners of fishing boats carrying asylum seekers to

Australian shores. After all, Ormandy had argued, it was Fish who'd alerted them when the first of the recent wave of asylum boats was heading for Darwin. Pratt recalled the telephone call. He'd questioned the reliability of the caller's sources. What were Indochinese refugees doing in Indonesia, Pratt had asked. How did the caller know the refugees were looking for a fisherman to take them on the last leg of their journey to Australia? The man had told him that he did a lot of business in Indonesia, and that his wife was Indonesian. 'My networks are good. Maybe I can help you again,' he had suggested. Pratt had promised nothing but thanked him for his help. And then Pratt was flatly told that Immigration would be taking part in an intelligence operation run in conjunction with ASIO – Brown the contact – and the Federal Police – Ormandy as Fish's handler.

Evidence was mounting that Fish was not just informing on but involved in people smuggling. Was he manipulating Ormandy, his police handler? Or was Ormandy complicit? On balance, Pratt had decided against raising his doubts with Brown. The last thing he wanted was to be seen as short on commitment to the end game. Surely the federal police and the intelligence agencies involved in the operation knew what they were doing? Still, if only to protect the department from political embarrassment, and to protect himself, he had decided that he had no choice but to ask ASIO to help keep the lid on his section's project.

'Thought I'd better share my concerns. It's important that no one leaks details of this operation, especially if it goes off the rails. And Rowan being an outsider might do just that.'

'Off the rails?' Brown looked shocked. 'It had better not, James. Not on your watch.'

'No, no, of course not, that's why I'm here.' Pratt knew he had to be careful. He was fortunate to have secured a job with Immigration when he left the army. An eye for detail, being trustworthy and with a high level security clearance fitted him for the Special Projects Section. It was work he thought important for the security of the nation, just like the army. And he'd done well to rise to become the head of the section.

Pratt shifted in his seat and wiggled his leg to ease the pain. 'Surely

ASIO can find a reason to downgrade Rowan's security clearance? Don't want to make a big issue of it, or she'll smell a bigger rat, but, well, if her clearance were qualified somehow, we could keep her away from the files that matter. She could still interview people, look at job criteria and the interview process, say?'

Brown said nothing. He looked in the rear-view mirror, and patted down his already-slick hair.

Pratt tried again. 'Otherwise, we let her in on the details of Operation Fishnet. She's security cleared and sworn to secrecy, but, well, as a feminist, she would never accept that we couldn't have engaged a woman for the job. How can we explain that, well, we don't want a purist who might put our operation at risk?'

'No, no, you can't do that. We need to stop her poking around,' Brown said. 'We'll find something to keep her out of your hair.'

'I haven't raised it with Furzer, yet,' said Pratt. 'As he's department head, I should have, but, well, Rowan, appears to be very friendly with him. He told all section heads to cooperate with her.'

'Glad you told me first,' said Brown. 'I'd like to look at her last ASIO assessment and see what we can do. Meantime, talk to Furzer about it. You're more likely than we are to convince him of the dangers of an outsider nosing around your sensitive operation. Tell him you think she needs another ASIO assessment – you know – so that her access to material is restricted. Don't want to take him by surprise. And I'll call you when I find out more.'

Pratt was at his desk, steeling himself to talk with Furzer when Brown rang.

'James? That matter we talked about. It's in hand my end. Ask Furzer to arrange for Rowan to be available for interview by our ASIO assessors next Monday, if that suits him and her. If there's any difficulty, get him to ring me direct. Meantime, I need to discuss something with you. There's a small complication. I'll call by your office after work.'

Pratt took a deep breath and went downstairs to find Furzer. The head of department seemed to understand. He said that he'd let Rowan know about the interview arrangements. Pratt, relieved, went back to his office.

It was six o'clock and there were not many people around when Pratt met Brown outside the Immigration building. They walked around the building and talked. The clouds were purple-black and it was getting cold. Pratt was almost dragging his leg, and having trouble keeping up with Brown.

'Rowan's security assessment is that she poses no risk,' Brown explained, 'apart,' he laughed, 'from being an academic and female. Feminists are worse than terrorists, in ASIO's eyes – likely to blow the whistle if someone nicks some paper clips and a biro. As a radical feminist, probably a Marxist Leninist, Rowan has been a "person of interest" since the seventies. But we're in enlightened days! She was cleared to work with the defence forces, and having cleared her for working in Immigration, she's not due for a review until next year.'

'So you can't do anything?'

'On the contrary, we're going to cancel her clearance altogether.'

Pratt stopped still. 'You can't do that. She needs a clearance, at least to Protected level, to be here at all. She's a high-flyer, and she's been placed here by Prime Minister's, don't forget. We only need to restrict her access to our files. What's the problem?'

'There's a complication. A former agent of ours has partnered up in some business deals with your informant, Fish. Trouble is, he was running an operation in Darwin that involved Yugoslav nationals. We didn't like his methods. He sometimes acted impulsively and we cut him loose. He was never suited to our work. It's his knowledge of that operation and his current business dealings with your informant Fish that concerns us. We don't know what information they've shared.'

'What's that to do with Rowan?'

'We can't afford to have her near Immigration while she's bonking her Yugoslav boyfriend, Mujo Zukić. He's with the consulate here. With civil unrest in Yugoslavia, we have to reassess the risk of her association with him.'

'I should have been told about this earlier. Fish was hired to help our operation, not to jeopardise it.'

'Calm down. All you have to do is collect information from Fish about the boats, and pass it on to Customs and Border Control.'

'This is not what I intended when I approached you. It will have consequences. Anyway, Furzer will have a fit. He won't allow it.'

'We can square it away with him, don't worry. Even he has skeletons. We already have the interview arrangements in place now, for next Monday. Furzer will be there.'

'So what will be used to justify an adverse assessment just a few months after you cleared her?'

'We'll think of something. She's been seeing the Yugoslav, Zukić, for yonks and we had no reason to use it against her before this. Helpfully, our relations with his government are not as strong as they used to be. The Serbs are troublemakers. We could use that. The boyfriend's Muslim, a lawyer who rose through the civil ranks to diplomatic status. He probably would like to defect anyway, rather than work under a leader like Milošević, but he's made no move.'

Pratt looked at Brown, who was staring straight ahead. 'Are you telling me everything?' Pratt asked.

'Everything you need to know.'

'I need to know who Fish is associating with. We have to know our informants are reliable. How he became involved with a former ASIO agent that you distrust, I'd like to know.'

Brown turned towards him. 'The former agent is Max Peacock. He and Fish are in the importing business. You don't need to worry. Fish's handler, Ormandy, is keeping an eye on Peacock. He was angry that we let him go and he lost the plot for a while, but harmless enough so long as we leave him alone. You're to say nothing of this to Fish. Don't stir up a hornet's nest. Business as usual.'

'Still no reason to punish Rowan. We could just keep her away from Fishnet files.'

'Ormandy doesn't want her in your department. He has his reasons. Not your business why, or how it's done. Sorry if you like her.'

'It's not that. It's, well, I reckon she won't accept it. It puts her career at stake. She'll take ASIO on, I bet. And then what?

'Don't panic. There's nothing we can't manage.'

4

Friday 17 May 1991

'Damn,' Brooke shouted, looking at the chook muck on her shiny red patent leather stilettos. 'Why do I always do that?' she asked Rocky.

He looked up at her with the liquid brown eyes that melted her heart, and thumped his tail on the floor. He didn't care what she did, so long as he was part of the conversation.

She had hurried home last night. It was dark and cold, and the sensible thing to do would have been to go inside, put her bags down, turn on the lights, take off her shoes, and put on gumboots and an old coat before going up the stony hill to lock the chooks in. But, no, if she got the outside chores done, she wouldn't have to brave the cold again. She had stumbled up the hill in her fake fur (at least it kept her warm) and high heels, guided by the sensor light at the back door. Once inside, she kicked off her shoes and forgot them. Until now.

'I can't afford to be late,' she muttered, taking the shoes into the kitchen to scrape off the chicken dung, and wipe them with a damp dishcloth. She squeezed them on, gave her fur a shake to dislodge any stray pieces of hay, picked up her bag, patted the dogs and the cats goodbye, and left.

It was half an hour's drive to Canberra from her hilltop house, high above the small country town of Bungendore in New South Wales. But she was a Canberran, through and through. Apart from a few kilometres of dusty gravel road, the rest was easy highway driving. It gave her time to consider how she'd handle her morning appointment.

She pulled into the basement car park of Canberra House in the city, grabbed her bag and stilettoed her way across Hobart Place at a pace that made her gait awkward. On stepping out of the lift of the AMP building – Twelfth Floor Chambers, as her floor of barristers was known – she was relieved to find the waiting room empty. She had made it before her client.

As she sat down at her desk, her clerk, Jane, poked her head around the door to announce, 'Dr Rowan is here to see you, Brooke.'

Brooke re-clipped the hair that had sprung back to her forehead, and rose to fetch the eminent academic from the waiting room. She did not want to keep her waiting. Not just because she was high profile, or one of the country's leading authorities on gender equity, Brooke persuaded herself. Clients were generally apprehensive enough about seeing a lawyer and to be kept waiting implied that the lawyer valued their own time more than their clients. Not that Dr Josephine Rowan was likely to feel apprehensive. Quite the opposite. Brooke felt over-awed, and a little nervous, knowing something of this radical feminist's attitude to lawyers. She drew a deep calming breath. Indeed, Dr Rowan was sitting in the waiting room, exuding confidence and control with every draw on her cigarette.

'Josephine!' Brooke greeted her with a beam.

Her excessive friendliness was met with a curt smile that paid lip service to a necessary social grace. Dr Rowan stubbed out her cigarette and thrust her hand out to Brooke in a deliberate feminist gesture. Brooke took it and succumbed to a sort of handshake, disappointed that she had not been greeted with the spontaneity of a friend.

'Good to see you again,' Brooke said, as she led the way to her room.

Her client followed in silence.

Autumn in Canberra is spectacularly colourful. Brooke enjoyed the view through her floor to ceiling window, looking west towards Black Mountain and its tall telecommunications tower. The forest of trees on the nearby university campus formed a mosaic of red, gold and yellow-green running all the way to the base of the mountain. Despite working in the city centre, Brooke could hear nothing outside her room. Canberra was not a bustling city, and in any event, the window was double-glazed;

solid too, thank goodness, she had thought one time she had leant back and toppled her chair against the glass. If the glass had broken, well, thinking about it made her shiver.

'You do well, you lawyers, don't you?' challenged Dr Rowan, breaking her silence as the view drew her to the window.

Brooke winced and refrained from saying, 'Bet you earn more than I do.' Instead, she ushered Rowan away from the comfortable two-seater lounge and into the client chair at her desk. Brooke settled in on the opposite side of the desk, a barrier that offered the psychological protection she felt she wanted.

'Well, Jo, can I call you Jo…?'

Dr Rowan nodded.

'You mentioned the other night that you had some problems with your employment…'

'Yes,' Jo said.

Brooke felt that Jo's searching green eyes were studying her like an inanimate article she was about to purchase.

Then Jo said, 'I don't like lawyers much – as a profession, I mean. They slot so easily into the big end of town, making money, never really questioning the value of what they do.'

Another psychological punch Brooke tried to cushion. Jo delivered this extraordinary statement with the confidence of a person who knew the power of their personality. At the same time, there was something in Jo's demeanour which told Brooke that Jo knew she couldn't afford to antagonise someone whose help she needed.

'But you need a lawyer,' Brooke said, trying not to sound smug, but rather to show sympathy for Jo, who clearly didn't like having to seek help.

'Probably, but I'm not sure if anyone can help me, or if you're the right person to ask. I picked you because you're a woman.'

Ouch. It was not getting any easier for Brooke.

'Well, you never know…maybe I can. But if one of my male colleagues' expertise is needed, I'll be happy to refer you.'

Round one, thought Brooke, but her nervous smile belied her inner anxiety. She tried to tuck her frizzy red hair behind her ear, but the useless clip let it spring onto her face seconds later. She shifted in her chair and waited for Jo to respond.

Jo leaned back and unbuttoned her gabardine jacket as if considering this proposition. Brooke noted that Jo was wearing the same smart green top she had worn several nights ago when she gave a dinner talk. It toned well with her tailored brown skirt. The only thing conservative about Jo was her clothes.

'I'm carrying out a consultancy for Prime Minister and Cabinet at the Department of Immigration. I have leave of absence from the university to do it. It's about gender equity, what has to be done to address a culture that seems to block women being promoted into senior positions.'

'Ah, a big project, Jo. Needed too, I expect.' Brooke was genuinely interested.

'I've done this sort of work before. My gender equity report for the defence forces was well-received, and my recommendations were largely implemented. But in Immigration…something was happening that I couldn't understand. Then, before I could get to the bottom of it, ASIO withdrew my security clearance. Without it, I can't access the records I need to do my work.'

Brooke jerked upright in her chair. 'Whoo-ie.' She nearly whistled her exclamation. It was the last thing she expected to hear. How had Jo stayed so calm in the circumstances? It was reason enough for Brooke to stop thinking about how Jo had been treating her. 'Oh, Jo, I am sorry. That's a terrible thing to have happened. What a blow! You'd better tell me the story from the beginning.'

Jo explained that she had sought access to some files as part of looking into why a senior woman in the department lost a promotion to a male junior officer. The woman had applied for a position in the Special Projects Section of the department which was currently investigating the arrival of Indochinese refugees by boat. 'That is, so-called illegal immigrants fleeing from south-east Asia and looking for asylum here,' she said. 'A good deal of sensitivity surrounds the work, naturally. Next, whether a coincidence or not, I was told that I had to front up to an ASIO interview because the level of my clearance was being reviewed. Instead, it was revoked.'

That puzzled Brooke. She asked, 'Had you had any difficulties accessing other department files before this?'

'No. I had detected a general unease over my presence in Immigration… not hostility exactly… Well, obviously my being there to report on gender bias might be seen as a threat by the mostly male management. It probably is, and I can understand they might want to hide certain files, but almost everything? No – something much bigger has to be going on.'

'Did they give you a reason? Silly question. Of course they didn't. Too secret, they'd say.'

'Exactly. How did you guess?'

'I've encountered this sort of thing before. Did you talk to the department head about it?' Brooke asked.

'Mike Furzer was at the interview I had with the ASIO officers. There was nothing he could do. A couple of days before, when he told me ASIO was coming to interview me, I asked him what it was all about. He said, "Not sure – we'll find out," and scurried away. He pushed hard initially to get my clearance through so I could start work at the department late last year. But this time he acted strangely. I know him well – very well, in fact …' Jo's expression looked like she was about to allow herself a small smile as if fondly remembering something about him, but did not elaborate. 'He's been very supportive of my work. He says he wants to address obstacles to his female staff progressing. I trust him, but who knows what pressures he's under. I've heard nothing from him since.'

'Can you do any of your work there without a security clearance?'

'No. This action effectively gets rid of me. You need to have the lowest clearance level to even be there. Everything is classified these days. To protect public servants' arses from the blunders they make, I expect. So I'm going back today to get my things. With the material I have so far, I can write a report of sorts, but it will be pretty benign.'

How could she contain her anger, Brooke wondered. If this had happened to her, she'd be concerned for her reputation. To have a security clearance withdrawn suggested you were regarded as a subversive: a risk to the security of your own country. It went to your integrity. She asked Jo what it would mean for her future if she couldn't get the decision changed.

'Bloody disaster, of course.' Jo raised her voice for the first time. 'I think ASIO must have been put up to do this by someone in the department who doesn't want me to expose some boys' club business. You know, like trying to cover up their methods of keeping women, like Annette Armstrong, the woman whose case I was investigating, out of powerful policy-making positions. Exposing that agenda is the threat I pose, none other.'

'But you have your university position to return to?'

'Sure, for what it's worth. How can I obtain any more consultancies without a security clearance? I have to be squeaky clean if I'm to be trusted by both sides of politics, not just the current Labor government. Surely, I can appeal and get this mess sorted out?'

'Ah, Jo, we can talk about your right to have ASIO's decision reviewed. But sorting it out quickly, or at all, is not so easy. The hearing is secret. You mightn't know what they say against you.'

Jo stared at her.

Before she had time to respond, Brooke said, 'Look, I need to know a lot more before I can say whether you have a chance to get this changed. Can I get you a cup of coffee?'

Jo nodded a thank you.

Brooke left the room, glad for an opportunity to think the problem through. It was an impossible ask to beat ASIO at this game; no one ever won. She had to tell Jo the reality even though she would likely see Brooke as lacking fight. Well, she could refer her to someone else. But Brooke knew she was one of the few lawyers competent to handle such a case because she had previously fought ASIO for several clients. Most lawyers wouldn't want this brief, given the Kafkaesque processes surrounding reviews of security assessments, not to mention the time and expense. Brooke, though, knew she was a sucker for interesting and challenging cases.

She returned with a tray and some mismatching cups. 'Milk? Sugar?' she asked a now subdued Jo.

5

Brooke had met Josephine Rowan for the first time the previous Friday evening, at a Women's Electoral Lobby dinner at which Rowan was guest speaker. She was surprised to be invited, not being active in the feminist movement. She decided she should go, despite some reluctance, remembering the last time she had attended such a dinner. A collective anger had hung in the air like a thunder cloud ready to break.

Brooke entered the spacious wooden-floored and dimly lit restaurant in the Kingston shopping centre. She looked round for suitable shelter, relieved to find it in her lawyer friend, Deidre, sitting at the bar chatting with a group of women.

'Hello, Brooke.' Deidre greeted her warmly. The two embraced. 'What a surprise to see you here. I'd like you to meet Wilma. Wilma, this is Brooke Talbot.'

'Another lawyer?' Wilma enquired.

'Yes,' said Brooke, 'another lawyer! All two of us.'

'Ah!' was the response.

Deidre raised a sympathetic eyebrow towards Brooke, and turned to Wilma and said, 'A feminist lawyer!'

'That's an oxymoron,' grumped Wilma.

Nothing's changed, thought Brooke. A feminist had once accused her of 'joining a male profession'. Wilma's remark didn't deserve a response, but Brooke bit anyway. 'We need feminist lawyers. It's women who are most likely to push for gender equity reform.'

Deidre came to the rescue. 'Let's take our drinks to the table,' she suggested.

The women moved to a long table in a narrow room at the rear of the restaurant, curtained off from the main noisy restaurant area.

'We're in the back room?' Brooke queried.

'Jo smokes,' explained Deidre with a resigned smile.

'Oh,' sighed Brooke. Designated smoking areas were usually cramped and she knew the air would soon become choking and unpleasant.

Jo was holding forth at the head of the table, shaking an emphatic index finger that pointed at no one in particular. Equal pay for women, the application of the merit principle, equal employment opportunity, and the right of mothers not to be discriminated against in employment were policies she pushed. All had been topical since the mid-eighties when Susan Ryan had pushed gender equity after becoming a senator for the Australian Capital Territory in the Commonwealth Parliament.

There was barely room for the women to squeeze between the seats as they took their places. A buzz of conversation continued while meals appeared until a glass was tapped and Jo was introduced. When Jo rose to talk, a hush descended; only the noise of knives scraping china plates and the occasional tinkle of a wine glass clipping a piece of cutlery could be heard.

'I have been asked to speak tonight about whether affirmative action is effective as a method of achieving gender equity in the public sector – or is it an insult to capable women? Also, on how the concept of merit is working – why the principle of promotion on merit seems to be accepted in theory but largely ignored in practice, or, more to the point, mentioned only when women are applying for senior positions,' she opened.

Jo's grey-green eyes, together with her short black curly hair, and tall, slim figure, made her striking. She was well groomed, dressed in a black skirt topped by a simple green wool jumper; she wore no jewellery other than small gold studs in her ears. She spoke with persuasive conviction. Her speaking style was as intense as her gaze, and she had a presence that compelled her audience to listen.

She talked about the effect on women in the workforce of a culture of unconscious bias, a consequence of customs and conventions that favour the well-off, the powerful – mostly men. Then she moved on to talk about the law's ineffectiveness in addressing discrimination against women and vulnerable minority groups.

Jo had everyone's attention, and kept it, as she paused to light a cigarette and inhale. A deplorable habit in Brooke's eyes. Not just the smoking, but the way in which it demanded everyone to wait patiently for the speaker to indulge her habit. But it was a powerful technique. It held the audience in suspense. Some of Brooke's male colleagues were masters of it. Preying on the politeness of the audience, it gave them time to think. Jo threw her head upwards and sideways as she deftly blew smoke into the air.

'What, no smoke rings?' Brooke whispered to Deidre.

Deidre dug her in the ribs.

Cigarette between her fingers, Jo extended her right arm in a dramatic gesture and continued, 'Lawyers apply the law without question – the "rule of law" they call it – part of our revered democratic system. But there is much that is undemocratic about how our legal system works. Laws imposed from the top don't always recognise the needs of those at the bottom – the homeless, the poor.' She looked across to Brooke and Deidre, and added, 'We have some lawyers amongst us, so I must be careful. But one example is our punishment system. A wealthy person who commits a serious offence can afford a lawyer and pay a fine. The poor and the unemployed are not so lucky. If they can't pay the fine, they end up in gaol and lose their job – if they have one.'

Having made the point, she took her eyes off the two lawyers and started to talk about the way women in the workforce might act to improve their prospects.

'Riot!' This came from Wilma.

Jo didn't have all the answers. She made the point that without merit applying across the board, the men's club would keep working to appoint their stereotypes and make matters worse. 'The argument has to be framed around productivity,' she argued. 'The greater the pool of job applicants, and including women potentially doubles that pool, the greater the diversity of skills, abilities and ideas to choose from. By definition, appointing on merit must bring better outcomes.'

When she finished, there was silence, and then clapping. Jo answered a few questions from her sympathetic audience. Brooke had been warned that Rowan was known to respond quite aggressively if her views were challenged. She expected people to agree with her, at least her followers, and she had many in the women's movement. They were in awe of her; her world view, her passion; never mind the absence of a positive plan for achieving the vision. She was an advocate of radical change and that was enough.

Brooke felt like an outsider. She better understood now why feminists were scathing about lawyers. Jo had implied that they were propping up a flawed institution, 'the tool of the establishment'. Brooke didn't agree.

The women began their own discussions as they topped up their wine glasses. Many wanted to talk with Jo as she squeezed behind chairs to move round the table. Brooke could see that Jo engaged and showed interest in what was said.

In due course, she headed to Brooke, wine in one hand, newly lit cigarette in the other. She sat down. 'Well, Ms Lawyer, did you find that threatening?' she challenged.

'On the contrary, Jo,' Brooke retorted, determined not to be provoked. 'It's healthy to question existing frameworks, even though I believe our legal system works better than most. I suffer too, you know, from working in a stifling male culture. But the law is a useful tool for change…'

Brooke stopped. She had lost Jo's interest. Jo was looking around the table, keeping an eye on other people to whom she wanted to speak.

She turned back to Brooke and came to the matter she had wanted to raise. 'Brooke, I think I'm going to need you, professionally. Can you see me if I give you a call?'

So that is why I was asked tonight, Brooke thought.

'Of course. What about?'

'Much along the lines of my talk tonight. Faceless men in grey suits trying to undermine female employees. In particular, I think someone is trying to sabotage my work. But I won't go into it now.'

'Sure. Ring me and we'll make a time for you to come in to chambers,' Brooke said.

'Good. I'll call your office,' Jo confirmed. Brooke did not miss the jibe.

6

'Tell me what you can remember of the ASIO interview,' Brooke asked Jo when they sat down with their coffees. Before telling Jo she had no show of winning this case, she needed to get a feel for what might have prodded ASIO into action.

'The spooks went over the material in my original assessment, and asked questions about my relationships, travel abroad, a bit about my work. I answered everything. Then I was asked about past boyfriends, not just "foreign affairs" – they always want to know about those – but all my past liaisons.'

'How far back did they want you to go?'

'Oh, they asked me about the past ten, twelve years. And that made Furzer very uncomfortable.' Jo hesitated before going on. 'You may as well know. Mike and I had an affair about seven years ago, and I had to say so. Mike was not happy this had to come out. It was obviously done for his benefit. The crude subtext was a warning to him not to open his mouth in support of me, or…others might hear about it too.'

Brooke wasn't surprised. She had learnt not to be surprised by anything her clients told her, and anyway Canberra was a hotbed of indiscreet affairs between high-flying public servants, politicians, journalists and the like.

'What did he do?' she asked Jo.

'He just sat there stony-faced for the rest of the interview. It's the way of things, for married men – ongoing affairs don't stop their careers.'

'Don't I know it. Go on.'

'The spooks were mainly interested in my current boyfriend – a foreigner, Mujo.'

'Mujo?' Brooke quizzed.

'Yes, Mujo Zukić. He came to Canberra three years ago, end of '87, as first secretary at the Yugoslav Consulate. We'd already met in Belgrade, and our affair started soon after he arrived. But, Brooke, here's the idiocy of it all. One of the ASIO fools referred to Yugoslavia as part of the "Soviet bloc"! Last I heard Yugoslavia was independent of the Soviet Union. Can all this be happening because ASIO is ignorant of who our enemies are? Anyway, ASIO already knew about me and Mujo when they cleared me to work at Immigration. They didn't assess me then as subversive or vulnerable to blackmail or likely to tell secrets in the bedroom. And it's not as if there are secrets at Immigration that would interest the Yugoslavs. No, it's got to be a ploy to stop me writing my report.'

'Perhaps,' Brooke nodded. 'ASIO might be using your affair with him to justify its decision. They're not accountable to anyone really, so they can get away with making up anything about anyone if it suits their agenda. Did you ask them why ASIO cleared you and then changed its mind?'

'I tried to. All they said was that my clearance was only for the purpose of my work and didn't carry a right to access other departmental material.'

'Which seems to suggest that your asking for certain files triggered a reaction?'

'Exactly, yet the matter of the file I asked for never arose. They didn't ask what information I was interested in or why. The little pricks seemed more interested in humiliating me and Mike by fishing around in my private life. They'd already made up their mind that my clearance should be withdrawn. When I asked what this was all about, one said – get this – "We can't go into the reasons, as it would involve disclosing classified material. We can only say that we look at all the circumstances, and a decision has yet to be made." I told them it was all barking mad nonsense and that the explanation insulted my intelligence.'

'But not theirs, clearly,' Brooke said.

'Someone has asked ASIO to do this. Not Furzer, someone with more clout. They want to discredit me because my gender equity work is a threat. So they've fabricated reasons and can't reveal them as the lies they are. I can't believe Furzer would be complicit in allowing an anti-feminist conspiracy to grow in his department, and then concoct some story to get ASIO to help protect it.'

'How did Furzer explain it afterwards?'

'He didn't. He shrugged sympathetically, and when I showed him the revocation notice yesterday, her said, "Not much I can do about it, Jo. There are sensitive operations undertaken in this department, not solely under my control. And what can I do if you go crawling into bed with the wrong people?" I was angry then, told him he was a hypocrite. I also gave him a spiel about everything being over-classified to stop anyone seeing the stuff-ups. That didn't go down well.'

'Okay. So let's start with your work. What threat, and to whom might you pose it?' Brooke picked up her pen as Jo uncrossed her long slim legs and talked.

She was a university professorial fellow and lectured in sociology. She specialised in women's studies and had published several books in the area of gender equity. 'As you know, the government seems genuine in trying to make things fairer for women in the workplace – to make sure gender is no barrier to their careers. Easier said than done, though.'

'I can imagine,' Brooke agreed. 'So much discrimination is subtle.'

'And the boys' club is hard for women to break into – football talk, men-only lunches, and so on.'

Jo explained her earlier consultancies. 'I fully expected resistance from the generals and admirals when I was trying to turn Defence's bullying culture around. I didn't get it, yet here I am having trouble in a "soft" department like Immigration.'

'Was there something specific you were asked to look at?' Brooke enquired.

'Yes. To look into why only a handful of women in the department have made it to senior positions,' Jo said. 'My findings have the potential to embarrass senior management, especially if there's a covert agenda to stop women reaching senior levels. That would explain why they might want to thwart my study.'

Brooke wasn't convinced. Her experience was that even though men sometimes disliked an efficient female co-worker showing them up, they were mostly not ashamed of being labelled sexist. Perhaps Jo was overstating the importance of her work.

She realised she must have let her scepticism show when Jo stared at her coldly and said, 'Well, how would you feel? I'm the expert called in to identify discrimination, and I'm the one being discriminated against. I feel pretty stupid, having to seek legal advice on my own situation.'

'Yep, I understand,' Brooke sympathised. 'But do you mind my asking you about other possible motivations – like wanting to stop you stumbling on something embarrassing, their work methods, or corruption even? You know: something other than wanting to block women attaining senior positions?'

Brooke hoped she hadn't offended Jo. It seemed not.

'Sure. It's possible it has nothing to do with gender issues. Not directly anyway. The Special Projects Section, for example, might not want anyone knowing what methods they use to try and stop the arrival of boat people. Those poor refugees are forced to pay huge money to ruthless snake-heads, packed into rotten boats by desperate fishermen who're paid bugger-all to get them to Australia. Who knows how they interrogate the crew or boat owners. Perhaps there are smelly secrets that Immigration and ASIO wouldn't want a principled woman to discover and expose.'

'Ah, now, there's a thought.'

'They didn't want Annette Armstrong in the Special Projects Section, and this all happened to me after I sought access to the paperwork on her failed promotion.'

'They can't trust a woman to be corruptible? But would Furzer, as department head, be a party to such a cover-up?' Brooke asked.

'On that scenario, he wouldn't necessarily know. He could be told anything to justify getting rid of me.'

'So, perhaps corruption and conspiracy against women?' Brooke flicked her pen backwards and forwards between her two fingers, thinking.

'Either way, something murky is going on,' said Jo.

'We can work on that, but how to prove it, or use it to get your clearance back. That's the issue.'

'I'll try and talk again with Annette.'

'I still can't see why your clearance was revoked instead of just stopping your access to those files.'

Jo glared at Brooke again. 'As I said, though you didn't seem to accept it, it's a chance to make sure my report never sees the light of day. Not to mention my reputation and how this will affect my future work. This will impact my whole career. They must have intended that.'

Brooke put her pen down, pinned her hair back again, looked at Jo, and decided it was time to be frank about her prospects. 'I agree, Jo, that you can't just accept this decision. But the chances of winning through legal action…are not good. ASIO has regularly ruined people's careers for no better reason than having a Communist in the family. Your relationship with Mujo might be enough to explain ASIO's decision.'

'What did I say last night? Ordinary people can't rely on the legal system for justice.'

'Yes, well, in this case – an unusual one – you're right. And I can't see immediately how trying to negotiate something with ASIO would get us any further. Look, recent amendments to the ASIO Act give people the right to an independent review of adverse ASIO assessments. The Commonwealth Administrative Appeals Tribunal has a special division, Security Appeals, to deal with matters like this.'

'Good. We'll do it, then.'

'Well, hang on. You wouldn't want to go there if there's another way. The right to a review is a good thing, but, and it's a big but, the tribunal's processes for this division are governed by the ASIO Act, and that ties the tribunal's hands somewhat.'

'In what way?'

'As I half explained. For example, you have no right to be at the hearing to hear what accusations ASIO make. And, worse, nor have I. So we wouldn't necessarily know what they have on you.'

'But that's not fair. It's outrageous.'

'Even if you did win, or if ASIO caved in, it's a long and costly process, and you don't get your legal expenses reimbursed.'

'How could this happen here? In Australia? Why isn't there public outcry?'

'People don't know or don't care that much, Jo,' Brooke replied. 'They tend to have blind faith in things done in the name of national security. And mostly, one would hope, their faith is well-founded but, on the other hand, as we know, lack of accountability allows incompetence and corruption to thrive. ASIO has the freest of hands.'

'Well, if my appeal fails, the whole experience will give me something juicy to write about…'

'You have to understand that you're already in Kafka country, Jo, but once the hearing starts you'll see that the process is totally bizarre,' Brooke said. 'If you are admitted into the hearing room, you'll be sworn to secrecy. Anything you learn there has to stay there. Even the regulations made under the Act don't have to be tabled in parliament if ASIO claims that it would not be in the interests of national security. There can be no public discussion of any aspect of a hearing held in camera.'

'To hell with that, Brooke. We'll see. Meantime, you're the lawyer. What do you suggest?'

Brooke outlined her plan. It wasn't very hopeful but would do for the moment. There was no harm in taking the initial step of lodging the application to see how ASIO would respond. It might give some negotiating leverage. Sometimes their lawyers advised ASIO to cave in, Brooke explained. Immigration might be willing for Jo to work there, but with restricted access to documents.

'But you don't have to take my word about this.' Brooke remembered Jo's initial remark about coming to see Brooke because she was female. 'You're free to get other advice, and I could refer you to someone who has some experience in the area. Mind you, I have had other cases like this. I know how the tribunal works, and I'm competent to deal with it. On the other hand, while one of my matters was resolved happily outside the tribunal, I've had no success at any hearing.'

'No, Brooke, clearly you know what you're doing. And I have no choice, really. I have to proceed – even if we look to other avenues at the same time. There are people I can talk to who might help.'

When Jo rose to leave, she gave a resigned shrug.

In an effort to soothe, Brooke said, 'At least the security appeals division is headed by the president of the tribunal, a Federal Court judge, and that's a woman at the moment,' but the platitude did nothing to console Jo, who thanked her anyway.

Brooke picked up the used coffee cups and took them to the tea room. The cups wobbled in their saucers as Brooke wobbled in her too-high heels. She remembered one conversation she had had with a colleague who had presented security cases to the Administrative Appeals Tribunal. He had claimed a degree of success, playing within the limited framework allowed. He said that opposing ASIO was like a game of Chinese chess: 'You play with your back to the board and just have to guess what your opponent's last move was.'

Unfortunately she couldn't brief Brett Arnold to lead her in Jo's case. He was a judge now – upholding laws, rather than fighting bad ones. Brooke had sent him a congratulatory card when he was appointed to the ACT Supreme Court bench. In it she had inscribed a cheeky poem to remind him from whence he came.

> Congratulations, but remember:
> If you attack the system and do it well,
> They will make you a judge, so history will tell.
> And locked in the system you are out of harm's way,
> And the system survives yet another day.
> Don't succumb!

She would have welcomed Brett's advice now, on how to beat ASIO.

'Hello, Phil!' she muttered, when a colleague popped into the tiny tea room. The windowless cupboard-sized area was the place where twelfth-floor barristers often chatted. Phil was pleasant. That was the right word for him. Most of Brooke's colleagues were. To a man – they were all men – they didn't want to offend her. They sometimes referred to her as 'one of the guys', a clumsy way of acknowledging her equality. To reinforce this she was addressed by her family name, Talbot, in keeping with custom. Sometimes they tried to make flattering comments about her clothes.

Brooke was short; even in her stilettos she barely made five feet two. Women were used to 'looking up' to men, physically as well as metaphorically. Brooke knew that, over time, this had a psychological impact. Men's voices were deeper and louder. That was certainly an advantage in court, where an air of authority impressed clients and judges alike. Like Trevor, another of Brooke's colleagues. While pleasant enough socially, Trevor was a masterly bully. He was physically big, gross in fact, and loud-mouthed, and he used bullying as a negotiating tactic. 'Your client would be advised to take this offer,' he would say. 'I shouldn't be telling you this, but, well…I don't want you to look foolish in court…' and he'd mention something about the judge's prejudices that only he knew. 'If I were you, I'd tell your client to take it,' he'd say with a smug smile, turning his back on the barrister he was trying to persuade.

Phil was the one who always had time for a friendly chat. He was very conservative, teasingly calling her a feminist or a radical whenever she mentioned women's rights, or anything vaguely political. Perhaps he found her a little eccentric, but he'd never said so. Brooke thought it ironic that 'the boys' on her floor saw her as politically radical, while many of her friends thought her conservative. Jo Rowan would consider Brooke conservative, no doubt there.

Brooke told Phil about her difficult new case. 'It looks like I'll be doing another security review,' she said, and explained briefly. 'I've done them before. They're practically unwinnable – no one's allowed in to hear ASIO's evidence. They're meant to give details of the allegations, but usually say they can't because it's "secret".'

'That can't be right,' Phil said.

'Oh, yes, it is,' she said. 'Look at the ASIO Act.'

Phil was sceptical, so Brooke told him about the previous case of a public servant whose mother was a well-known Communist. He was two decades into his career when, without explanation, his security clearance was suddenly withdrawn. ASIO refused to give reasons. Brooke had concluded that the system simply wanted to sack him but, given the unfair dismissal laws, it was easier to ask ASIO to use his family's political connections to take away his security clearance.

'That's a bit far-fetched,' muttered Phil, as it probably was. He hovered behind Brooke who was rinsing cups at the sink. But he was interested.

'How can you prepare a case when you don't know the evidence against you?' he asked.

'You can't. We had to speculate and prepare submissions that might cover every possible angle.'

'Did you win?'

'Of course not. The tribunal upheld ASIO's assessment of him as a security risk – no reasons given. His career was ruined.'

'Well, I hope your client has plenty of money, Brooke.'

'Don't be a jerk, Phil!' Brooke had been too scared to raise the question of costs with Jo. She thought that Jo might expect her to act for nothing – in the feminist cause and all that. It would not be a new experience. She must talk to Jo about fees, some time. Then she admitted to Phil, 'Yep, I do tend to attract the difficult "free" jobs.'

'You do bring them on, Brooke. Don't forget why we studied law – to properly represent our clients and to make money!'

'I fear you're serious…'

'Of course not,' he laughed, 'but is this case worthy to take on pro bono, Brooke? Your Hawke–Keating left-wing government has made enough trouble with all that affirmative action crap, bending over backwards to give women a fair go. And it's not as if her livelihood depends upon it. She has her university job.'

'You would say that,' Brooke protested. 'Labor's reforms are a start, but real change won't happen until women get paid the same, have better bargaining power, and some economic strength.'

'Oh, oh!' he said. 'Just act for your whingeing feminist, don't become one.'

Brooke knew she had risked ridicule even talking to Phil whom she trusted more than most of her colleagues. As part of surviving, she had learned to be reticent about feminist issues. Absurd, since law was the one profession that boasted about its role in upholding equality before the law.

Another coffee in hand, Brooke returned to her room to finish an overdue advice to a solicitor who was acting for a computer company in a feud with a subcontractor. Then she would reward herself: Friday night drinks with friends.

7

Friday evening, 17 May 1991

There was a bar hidden at the back of the old Kingston Hotel where Brooke and her friends often came on Fridays after work. Its name, The Faceless Men's Bar, recalled former Prime Minister Robert Menzies' jibe that the Labor Party was run by a national executive of thirty-six faceless men, to the exclusion of the prime minister and his deputy. It was small and dark. You entered by a nondescript door that only those who knew about it could find. The bar was opened at the request of some United States Embassy staff looking for an exclusive place to drink. 'The Kingo' was convenient because from there they carried out the job of spying on the Soviet Embassy across the road!

Brooke had learned about this retreat from her schoolfriend Cath. At one level, Brooke regarded its elitism with distaste. Nevertheless, she enjoyed sitting by the fire in winter and listening in to the crowd wheeling and dealing in the background. More to the point, it served quality Chardonnay in overly large glasses and, because the men preferred to lean on the bar, the comfy couch by the fire was free for Brooke and her friends to sit and chat intimately.

The men communicated in a language of their own, emphasising points with expletives. There were bureaucrats, diplomats, a few politicians, journalists, one or two lobbyists, and businessmen who sat on boards; and all were networking. Deals and double deals were made, and agendas were rarely clear. Canberra was a small place and many men of influence wore more than one hat. Brooke liked to observe, try to identify the spooks – it amused her. It reminded her of the children's game of

Murder in the Dark; at least one player could not be trusted, but who? All were treated as mates and all were suspect.

The Friday after her interview with Jo, Brooke and her friends Deidre and Cath were there. One of Cath's friends, Russell Redmond, known as Rusty, joined them by the fire, followed by a man who Rusty introduced as Donald Fenchurch. Rusty was a freelance investigative journalist and knew everyone. He presented as a friendly gnome-like figure, slightly balding, always smiling. His trademark cigar gripped between his teeth bounced up and down as he spoke, and he had a large stomach bespeaking the quantity of beer that had been poured into it over the years. Donald seemed reserved and struck Brooke as a sincere person, not quite at home with the political predators around him. But then, who knew what lay behind his liquid brown eyes and unassuming manner? He engaged her with his smile. He was dressed casually and she noticed that his clothes were of good quality, worn carelessly – shirt not quite tucked in, fawn cord trousers short of a belt. Perhaps he's an academic, thought Brooke; but his interest in everyone and his obvious enjoyment of the buzzing atmosphere belied an inwardly focused intellectual.

Cath greeted Rusty with a warm embrace and then taunted him about some recent antic, now lost to memory, or so he said, 'thanks to Al' (as in alcohol), his constant friend and companion.

As they chatted, Gideon approached and asked, 'Can I get you ladies another drink?' Gideon was not very tall, but held his body erect, chest puffed out, and dressed immaculately. His white collar, starched and gleaming, suggested a diligent wife or a good launderer. His chatter was punctuated with humorous asides or frivolous analogies – generally irreverent and largely irrelevant, but with an eye for maximum impact. He had worked as a political analyst in Australia's peak foreign intelligence agency, the Office of National Assessments, usually referred to as ONA, until retiring from the public service, and now had a raft of business interests and, thanks to his connections, sat on several government boards. He left to get more drinks and, naturally enough, the subject of spooks came up.

'I shouldn't like him,' said Brooke, 'but I do. He does dominate the conversation, but his cynical view of pollies and government is very funny. And he gets away with murder, chairing this board and that. But he has been a spook, I'm sure, before or while he was with ONA, and I don't approve of people prepared to extract information from trusting friends.'

'Oh, it's just a job.' It was Donald who spoke up. 'Spies can be small L liberals. They're not all unprincipled.'

'Are you one of them?' she probed.

Donald laughed. 'If I was, I wouldn't say.'

Brooke came back. 'If you weren't, you would say.'

'Well, I'm not,' he grinned.

'I knew that,' she tossed back, biting her bottom lip, realising she might have offended him.

Rusty butted in. 'It's your left-wing upbringing, Brooke. It blinkers you. Remember, it was your Labor Party that established ASIO. Anyway, it's better to have decent people spying for us, isn't it? People who are nationalistic and open-minded, rather than ideologues who are selective about what information they feed back into the system. Ask Gideon.'

'What rubbish you talk,' Brooke retaliated, laughing. 'ASIO picks its agents carefully. It wouldn't let anyone work with them who had the slightest concern for human rights. It recruits reactionaries.'

Gideon arrived with the drinks, and Cath said, 'Just in time, Gideon, to defend yourself. Brooke thinks you're a spook, because you worked for ONA.'

'Ah,' said Gideon, 'what would we do without sceptics like Brooke? All I want to know is when are you going to invite me to that magnificent country cottage of yours, Brooke? I have my .22 ready and loaded so I can look at the beautiful view and shoot any native animal standing in the way.'

He was teasing her, but she hit back. 'I don't keep a rifle. Good thing too, because if I did, I'd probably use it on the first city slicker – you, Gideon – who came on to my land to shoot kangaroos. Then I'd be the one who'd end up in gaol.'

'I can always get her going,' he boasted to the group and gave Brooke a hug.

Deidre had been listening quietly to the banter, and turned to Donald and asked him, 'You don't look like one of this brutal crowd. How do you know Rusty?'

'We've been friends for years,' Donald replied. 'I was at ONA, too, before I joined the diplomatic corps. I still travel a lot and mostly live in Sydney when I'm home. So I'm not a regular here.'

Rusty offered another round of drinks. The girls said no, they were driving, and rose to leave. The men were into their third or fourth drinks by now. It was certainly time for the girls to go – that was the way things were.

During her half-hour drive home, Brooke thought more about Jo. She felt she had a better understanding of her now. Her approach to Brooke at the feminist dinner had been confrontational. They needed to get on if they were to work together. How to best handle her problem? That's what she had to think about. But right now there were practical things to consider – like juggling the demands of her household when she arrived home. No matter what time that might be, she always made a tour of inspection of the chooks and geese, and attended to and placated her two dogs and two cats, all of whom were visibly peeved when she was late. And it was late already.

She lived alone, having mislaid, somewhat carelessly, her last partner almost a year ago. She had given him too little time, and her work and animals too much. He had moved on quickly to someone who was happy to play the role of wife.

Brooke pulled into the carport and opened the door to be greeted first by Rex, his long tail wagging. He sniffed her with his wet nose and his body language said 'Where ya been? Why ya late and who've you been with?' The sort of interrogation she expected from her ex. But her dogs accepted any explanation, and did not answer back or slam doors; and if they sulked, they did it quietly.

Rocky, a brindle-coloured and bulky dog, nosed his way through the front door with her while Rex, a caramel-coloured short-haired terrier, barged past the two cats. The goal was to trip Brooke up!

The house was warm and welcoming. She dropped her gear, put a split of wood in the combustion heater and opened its vent, lifted the solar torch from its hook facing the window and, remembering not to ruin her shoes, she kicked them off and pulled on the gumboots waiting at the back door. The dogs followed her up to the chook pen. The chickens were safely perched and accounted for. The cats sat by the fridge waiting for Brooke and the dogs to return.

On opening the back door, Brooke saw that a flame had flared in the combustion heater as the wood had caught. She scooped off the layer of fat that had formed over the now cool bacon bone stock she had simmered on the heater the night before, and started to cut pumpkin, potatoes, eggplants, cauliflower, leeks, carrots and spinach. When done, she tipped them into the stock and returned the pot to the heater. She added two generous dessert spoons of moderately hot spiced black bean sauce and some chopped parsley. Soon the aroma of thick peasant soup was everywhere. She skinned the four large tomatoes she had dropped in boiling water, and popped them in. The soup would simmer overnight.

Only then did the distant beeping of her answering machine register. The message was simple: 'If you're considering taking on Dr Rowan's case, don't. It will do neither you nor her any good. Take this friendly advice.' Shaken, Brooke dialled *10# for the caller's number and received Telecom's recorded message: 'Your last unanswered call was from a private number. This cannot be returned.'

'How dare you – whoever you are!' She slumped down in a cane chair, but rose quickly to pour a large drink. Though not convinced by Jo Rowan's feminist conspiracy theory, Brooke was more convinced than ever that her client needed all the help she could get.

8

Friday afternoon, 17 May 1991

Jo tried to absorb what the breathless woman sitting opposite her was telling her, or, more accurately, showing her. Having returned to her office at Immigration after her consultation with Brooke, she felt bloody. Her problem was clearly more serious than she had realised. She didn't know if she could keep her office while finishing her report. She had been packing her papers to go home when Annette Armstrong had burst into her room after a token knock. It was serendipitous. Annette was the very person Jo wanted to talk to.

'Wait till you see this,' Annette gushed. 'I've found something; amazingly nasty. Can I sit down?' Annette was short, plump, with shiny straight black hair in a bob and a neat fringe. Her face was made up to perfection, heavy lip liner accentuating her blood plum painted lips. She was wearing a tightly buttoned dark red jacket over black trousers; power dressing it was called, designed to persuade male bosses that women were tough enough to do tough jobs. She thrust a sheet of paper at Jo plucked from the manila folder she was clutching.

Jo looked at the document. It was a memo of some kind, but it had no departmental logo, just a heading: 'Re: Operation F'. She read out loud, 'Jack, keep the girlie applicant out of your area. She would never understand the work and would stuff up our operation. Make sure that the panel has reason to doubt her, or discredit her referees. Maybe you could suggest that her boss only gave her a good reference to get rid of a bitch from his section, something like that.'

'How shitty is that?' Annette exclaimed. 'It's not signed, of course. And I don't know of any Jacks in the section.'

Jo guessed it was the sort of thing that went on behind the scenes in the public service to undermine women; always hard to prove, though. This was hard evidence, but she might be powerless to use it.

'How did you get it?'

'I found it last night, folded in half and tucked under papers on my desk. Obviously deliberately left for me to see.'

'Any idea who?'

Annette shook her head.

'Are there any Johns in the section, or anyone on the interview panel, who might be known as Jack?' Jo asked.

'No. And I can hardly approach the panel now they've made their decision. They'd go ballistic if I suggested they might have been influenced by something like that.'

Still looking at the paper, Jo said, 'But the words "your area" and "our operation" suggest the author's an outsider.'

'Perhaps from another agency involved in one of our operations? I don't know what F stands for either. We're not told the names of all of our operations.'

Jo turned the page over. There was nothing on the back.

'You can do something about this, can't you, Dr Rowan? Now you're investigating my case?' Annette asked, raising her thin eyebrows.

'Call me Jo, Annette. Look, I wanted to talk to you about that. My work here is on hold. This note could explain why. If the job selection process has been corrupted, no one would want me discovering that.'

'What's happened?' Annette looked alarmed.

'I asked to look at your interview report, and the other applicants' and the criteria for the position and so on, but I struck a brick wall. Next, I had to front up for an ASIO interview, and my security clearance has been withdrawn. I'm not sure I can even keep my room here, until this mess is sorted out.'

'Seriously? What's going on, Jo?'

'Hoped you'd know, Annette. Any clue?'

'Apart from being a woman giving directions to men, you mean? I don't know. I figured that the section head and his team wanted someone younger and greener, someone already under their direction and easier to manipulate than me. It would let them run their operations with less red tape.'

'You mean a woman in the section might be fussier about process?'

'Yes, and they'd know that I wouldn't be prepared to fudge press releases or pull the wool over the minister's eyes.'

'Could there be something bigger, more embarrassing, they didn't want you knowing?' Jo asked.

'That's what I don't know,' Annette replied. 'I only know that this memo was designed to stop me getting the job. It's offensive, and so terribly unfair. Though perhaps your being here motivated someone to leak it to me.'

'Why?'

'Because I'd show it to you, and you have the power to investigate – or did.'

Jo considered the possibility. 'We can't let these bastards beat us. They're wrecking both our careers. Can you tell me more about your work and the job you applied for?'

Annette spoke quickly, grabbing breaths mid-sentence. 'The public relations section where I work now prepares information leaflets, books and other material, and we liaise with other departments, handle press enquiries and issue press releases, you know…that sort of stuff. The position I applied for is a liaison position to deal specifically with sensitive issues that arise in special projects.'

'And one project at the moment is to stop asylum seekers coming by boat?' Jo asked.

'Yes. If boat arrivals are to be stopped, they need to hunt down not just the boat owners but the agents who drum up business, and the organisers – the guys who do it for profit especially, but those smuggling family members in too. I thought I was a strong candidate for the job. I have a good background in the politics behind it, better qualifications in media and communications than the guy who got the job, and because of my years here, more experience in liaising with other agencies, like defence and customs, the federal police, ASIO, et cetera.'

'What would be the most sensitive part of their operation, do you think?'

'I wouldn't know. But it's possible they use informants, here or overseas, you know, people on the ground, keeping their ears open and probably getting well rewarded for their information.'

'Undercover agents?'

'Possibly, yes. That's not unusual. Undercover agents are usually members of the federal police, or a civilian with a handler in the AFP. But, hey, you probably watch *The Bill*: the person paid for information is usually crooked, someone caught doing something illegal, and given a no-prosecution guarantee in exchange for information about bigger fish. They'd keep that one secret, even from the minister, because it's illegal, though it's sometimes done. End justifies the means, they say.'

'The fellow who got the liaison job would know if anything like that was going on?'

'Who knows? I don't know what his role in the section was, but yes, it will now be his job to deal with media enquiries, vet press releases, and advise the minister on how to handle questions in language that avoids being politically embarrassing. So why wouldn't they trust me? What didn't they want me to know, or see?'

The phone rang. Jo jumped and picked up. 'Yes. Okay. That would be good. Can I call you back? No? Okay. Call me later, ten or fifteen minutes.' She put the phone down and apologised to Annette. 'Sorry, don't mean to rush this conversation. And I do want to ask you a few more things…'

'Sure.'

'Have you shown the memo to Furzer?'

'I did. And he seemed taken aback. Then he said that he was confident that the selection panel, even if one of them had been approached, would have told the person where to get off. That is, it shows that someone didn't want me getting the job, but not that I lost it unfairly. He suggested I appeal it.'

'And will you?'

'It would be futile. They'll say that the panel took my seniority and experience into account, but required someone within the section familiar with the current project. That is, someone already privy to the sensitivity of a project, rather than having to brief an outsider. That's what they'd do – argue that they needed someone inside the section to safeguard the integrity of an operation. No one is going to own up that they just didn't want to work with a woman. And now they don't want you poking about to report on their gender bias.'

'Can I take a copy of this, Annette?'

Annette left the office and returned briefly with a copy of the memo for Jo.

Jo was ready to call it a day. She looked at the phone, though she didn't expect that Mujo would ring back. He operated on impulse. If he wanted to see Jo, he'd ring her. If she were busy, he would find one of his consulate mates to go with him somewhere for a whisky.

She picked up the small framed photograph sitting on her desk, the only photo she had brought from her university office. She returned the smile her daughter gave her from the black and white image. Five years old. Is she as happy now, twelve years on, Jo wondered. I must write to her, perhaps when I feel a bit brighter; no, it's probably okay that she sees her mum's vulnerabilities. Jo started to think through what she would tell her daughter about what was going on, as she packed up as many papers as she could fit into one cardboard box. She then headed home for a hot bath.

It wasn't cold in Jo's house but her teeth were chattering as she undressed. Shock, she thought, delayed shock. The reality of what Brooke had told her was beginning to sink in. She felt like she had been kicked in the guts. It had been an effort to concentrate on what Annette had said, but it helped to explain a lot.

The warm water calmed her. Her teeth were still. She remembered how she had felt when she met Brooke and told her that she might need a lawyer. At the time she thought it was probably a silly blunder on ASIO's part. When the revocation notice arrived, well, she hoped Brooke might laugh and say, 'No problem, I'll get a letter off and we'll get it fixed up.' But no, her lawyer told her that her chances were Buckley's or none. Next, she was packing up to leave the department. This was a nightmare.

Wrapped in a warm dressing gown, Jo went to the kitchen to make a fresh herb omelette. Then she made a phone call.

'It's Jo, Donald. I need to talk to you when you get in, please. Could you ring me at home? Thanks.'

It was close to eleven when Donald Fenchurch called back from his room at University House. He'd been drinking with his mates at the Faceless Men's Bar, he told her. She was in bed, reading Patrick Süsskind's *The Pigeon*, not a happy book but one that did not require much concentration. She felt envious not to have been with him, drinking with a crowd, talking about normal things, having fun like normal people. Trying hard to keep her voice steady, she told him briefly about her troubles. They arranged to meet the following night for dinner.

9

Monday 20 May 1991

It was mid-afternoon and quiet in the Canberra Hyatt's foyer, except for the tinkling of a piano sonata being played by a young man in a dinner suit at the far end of the room. Waiters hovered with silver trays, nodding to patrons as they discreetly emptied and cleaned ashtrays. Jo, in a pencil-slim grey skirt with a bottle-green three-quarter length jacket, weaved her way around the leather sofas through to a small lounge bar. Mujo was sitting in an armchair by the log fire, his long legs stretched out. He had a cigarette and whisky glass in one hand, leaving the other free to wave her into a comfy chair beside him. Two glasses of Chardonnay sat on the side table.

'Great coffee.' She feigned a smile and picked up a glass of wine.

He picked up the other glass and clinked with hers. 'Živjeli!'

'Sorry I couldn't talk last Friday. It was a bad day.'

He looked at her quizzically and returned to his whisky.

'I'm in serious trouble at work. I'd just seen a lawyer.'

'You kill someone?'

'Not quite.' She tried to smile. Not something she was used to. 'I'd like to, though. I've just had my security clearance removed. ASIO interviewed me, and well, basically it brings my work at Immigration to a halt. Goodness knows, potentially, my career. They asked about my relationships, including you.'

'This is not good.' He threw the rest of his whisky down his throat and put the empty glass on the tray of a waiter who was collecting used glasses. 'I was worried this might happen.'

'But they've seen us together. They know we have no secrets.' Jo was alarmed.

'But things are changing between our governments now, because of Milošević. Your government might yet support the Croatian independence movement. It's on the cards. Maybe they don't trust you with me?'

'Or they're just using our relationship to stop the work I'm doing at Immigration. You have no interest in our country's immigration policies.'

'Why would they want you out of there?' Mujo asked.

'Old school culture? I'm sure some men feel threatened by my gender equity work. I was investigating why a senior woman missed out on a promotion. That would annoy them. Everything was sort of all right, until I asked to see a file about the job she didn't get. It was in a sensitive section of Immigration. It's possible that the men there didn't want a woman working with them, or my investigating why she didn't get the job.'

Mujo picked up his wine. 'There are always secrets that bureaucrats want to keep to themselves.'

'But I'm sworn to secrecy. No risk there.'

'I mean secrets they have, cheating, breaking the law. And there you are, Jo, with your honest eyes.'

'Oh, I can't imagine there's any criminal racket going on. ASIO wouldn't get involved to protect them from that. Unless it's something bigger they're involved in.' Her voice faded as she fell into thought.

'What can I do to help? Not see you?'

'Don't joke. They can't tell me who I should see and not see.'

'You wouldn't have any friends left,' he grinned. 'Most of your friends are more dangerous than me...'

'ASIO doesn't seem to think so.' Jo told him how one ASIO interviewer had referred to Yugoslavia as part of the Communist bloc. 'He made it sound like I could be sleeping with the devil or, worse, a Russian spy.'

'They might be stupid. Or it is tactic, to annoy you.' Mujo stood up and, as was his way of terminating their public time together, he held his hand out to Jo, hauling her to her feet. 'I must cheer you up. We can think more about this later, implications. For now, we relax, talk about music and poetry, much more beautiful. I follow you home?'

They walked down the back stairs to the car park, and Mujo followed Jo's car around the lake to Yarralumla and her home.

Jo switched on a lamp on the coffee table, and her CD player. Rachmaninoff's Piano Concerto 3 filled the living room. They moved to the couch with glasses and a cold bottle of wine.

Mujo produced a piece of paper from the inside pocket of his jacket. 'I wrote you a poem,' he whispered.

She rose and took it to the light at the window to read it. She felt a well of emotions rise as she absorbed its beautiful words. Like Rachmaninoff's melody, Mujo's prose, albeit in a language foreign to him, was both complex and romantic. She stared through the window thinking, not about what to say, only about making love to him. She saw an occupied car parked across the street, and drew the curtains to stop rude reality from intruding. But reality won.

'There's a black car parked outside. Someone is sitting in it. Are you always tailed, or is it now me?' she turned to ask, clasping the poem tightly against her chest in both hands.

He looked puzzled. 'I'm a foreign diplomat. They always keep tabs on me, but not so crudely. Are they trying to intimidate you?'

'Oh, God. The nightmare gets worse.'

'Come,' he beckoned. 'Where no eyes but ours can see.'

He led her to the bedroom and through to the en suite. He turned on the shower taps and they dropped their clothing to the floor as they stripped down.

He kissed her all over her face, and she on his neck and down his chest, their hands sliding over each other's wet bodies as they crumpled to the warm and wet tiled floor, water pouring over their heads. He put his arms around her waist, protecting her back from the hardness of the tiled wall and brought her toward him until their bodies were where they most wanted them to be. She arched her back and threw her head up to let a restrained cry of pleasure escape her lips, his arm reaching to stop the back of her head hitting the wall. They slid sideways together onto the floor again, and he cried a little, telling her he was happy that she was no longer angry and despairing but floating with him, careless in a cloud of sensual bliss. They stayed in tight embrace, torrents of water washing away the pain of her day, and the days before.

They sat up facing each other, he cross-legged and she with her legs outside him, arms stretched, hands clutched. He slowed the flow of the water, enough to keep them warm.

'They want me to think it's about us,' she said. 'That's mostly what they questioned me about – you.'

'Something else is going on. There is nothing I can learn from you. You must be right. They are using me to discredit you, for some other reason.'

'And I might never find out what that reason is.'

He turned off the tap and as he reached for a towel he said, 'Jo, I am truly sorry. I give my word that I am not briefed to get information from you. Of course I rang you for a reason, other than because I was attracted to you. I'm told to meet people like you, journalists and politicians too, help us understand language, culture, politics – how Canberra works.'

'I know. You've been honest about that.'

'And now I am with you because I love you.'

Jo looked at him. It was true. He had been frank about his reason for meeting up with her when he arrived in Australia. He had asked her to correct his grammar and pronunciation when she could, and they talked a lot about politics and who was who, the conservatives and radicals. No harm in any of that.

'But on the other hand,' he teased, 'you could learn much from me. All those secrets I learned from my counterparts at Langley. That would make you dangerous,' he laughed.

Jo sat back. 'Langley?' she asked.

'CIA headquarters, in Virginia, in the States. I'm teasing. Many foreign countries send diplomats and intelligence officers there. I did attend CIA training school once. Not to learn secrets, though. We had two weeks training in counter-terrorism operations, because of Croatian terrorist movement. We met other trainees and military and intelligence officers and exchanged gossip. No more than that, just gossip. I learned about importance of your Pine Gap. Americans brag about its monitoring capacity, they like to display their power.' He spun her around to towel her back.

'It's weird,' Jo said. She turned to face him, took the towel and started to wipe the water droplets off the thick black hairs on his chest. Looking up at him she said, 'You know more about Pine Gap than the Australian public. No wonder ASIO's suspicious of me.'

'Hush,' he said, wiping drops off her face with a corner of the towel. 'Pine Gap's capacity to intercept foreign government communications is no secret. My government knows Pine Gap technology can intercept Milošević's communications, or any other leader's, friend or foe. It is common talk,' he said.

'Not here, it isn't.' Jo felt unnerved. 'Just mentioning Pine Gap at a party would be enough for ASIO to open files on everyone there. Since ASIO moved its headquarters here from Melbourne, Canberra has been infested with spies. Mind you, it has stimulated the local economy.'

'Ah, a smile at last,' he said, responding to Jo's rare moment of humour.

'No, I'm serious. But for you, I would never have met real spooks like your friends Larry and what's his name, in the flesh. I'm not sure I like Canberra being such a shadowy town. Spy city, that's what it's become.'

'Well, I can't believe that so far as your work problem is concerned, it is because of me. There must be another agenda. You will fight it?'

'Yes, my lawyer's filing an appeal. Donald Fenchurch has agreed to give me a character reference.'

'Donald? Good. Give him my regards, if he will receive them. I think he doesn't like that I have taken you away from him.'

'Oh, he's fine. Honestly. Donald doesn't do jealousy.'

10

Mid-June 1991

'A special tribunal will have to be convened to hear this,' the tribunal clerk had said, grumping, when Brooke had lodged Jo's application. The clerk clearly thought that the exercise was a waste of time. And from where Brooke sat, it probably was.

Two days in mid-July had been reserved for Jo's hearing. Brooke had a month to prepare. She placed the notice of hearing in the documents folder in Jo's file. The case was on her mind. It was difficult to concentrate on her other clients' problems. She picked up the one-page statement of grounds for ASIO's decision to revoke Jo's clearance that accompanied the hearing notice. It read,

Dr Josephine Rowan, born 1 November 1943, was granted clearance at 'top secret' level by the Director-General of Security in January 1991. She has had clearances in the past to undertake Government consultancies. A review of her level of clearance was initiated after certain information came to ASIO's attention.

Dr Rowan was interviewed by ASIO officers at the Department of Immigration where she is currently based. Dr Rowan displayed a rather casual attitude to her access to sensitive material, stating that the documents she read were benign and mostly over-classified. She could not remember details of various documents and material that she has handled in the course of her work and was vague about details of the sexual affairs she had had over the last twelve years.

It is the Director General's opinion that Dr Rowan should not continue to have access to classified information, notwithstanding that it is her Department Head's view that she is a valuable contract officer and her PM & C referee states that she has performed in an exemplary manner for Federal

Government departments over the past ten years. Her value as a consultant must be weighed against the risk to national security she poses given her foreign connections, radical political attitudes, and her apparent recent interest in a security protected government project.

That was all. The last sentence swept across all three areas she and Jo had considered as possible sources of concern to ASIO: her relationship with Mujo Zukić; her radical feminism; and calling for access to Annette Armstrong's file. But no detail was given as to how any of these interests implicated her as a national security risk.

How could she prepare a case with this scant information? Frustrated, Brooke telephoned the tribunal and requested a copy of all documents lodged by ASIO.

'You'll have to sign an undertaking to not show the documents to anyone or discuss their contents with anyone,' the clerk told her. 'And you'll keep them in a locked box and not remove them from your office.' The clerk had clearly given that spiel before.

Brooke buttoned up her leopard-print coat and wrapped a knitted scarf around her neck to brave the chilly autumn weather. At first, she made little progress as she battled against the wind the short distance from her office across Hobart Place's concrete square to Canberra House, where the tribunal's registry was located. Scraps of paper sailed by and swirls of gritty dust stung her ankles and her hair covered her eyes.

The atmosphere in the registry was as chilly as the weather outside. Brooke signed the undertaking, wondering how she could possibly comply, given that she did most of her reading work at home. But then again, her home was her office too, wasn't it? She wondered if the old seaman's trunk in the spare bedroom would pass as a 'locked box'. With the documents in a large sealed envelope tucked under her arm, she hurried back to the office, the wind in her sails this time.

Brooke tore open the envelope. She had already seen most of the documents: the revocation of Jo's security clearance; her request for a review; and the one-pager setting out ASIO's grounds for revoking Jo's clearance. Brooke continued, hoping to find something more helpful.

There was some correspondence between Immigration and ASIO, marked 'Confidential'. These letters might be important if Brooke could make sense of them, but the authors' names were blacked out.

Feeling desperate, she flicked over to the Immigration Department's response. She hoped it would back Jo's case. Her spirits sank when she saw that anything of any significance had been blacked out. Brooke read it again to see if she could guess what Furzer's attitude was.

Certain officers in my department have alerted ASIO to the possibility that Dr Rowan's unfettered access to classified material poses a risk to national security. However, her interest is limited to EEO concerns and I have no reason to assume that her request to see [blacked out] was other than a legitimate request.

I note that you do not believe this to be the case, and that it shows that [blacked out]

On the other hand [blacked out]

We have already agreed that [blacked out]

It has now been shown that [blacked out]

To my mind this has an impact on the weight which can be given to [blacked out]

It was apparent from our last discussion that [blacked out]

The above comments are based on the material you have provided so far and [blacked out]

The second sentence referred to Jo's request to see something, presumably Annette Armstrong's file, and seemed to be supportive of Dr Rowan. The rest suggested that there had been a subsequent discussion between Furzer and ASIO officers in Jo's absence. But what was the outcome? Had Furzer been persuaded to come around to ASIO's view? If so, what leverage had they used? His and Jo's affair?

As Brooke sorted through the rest of the documents, she saw that everything of any relevance had been redacted. Whether the tribunal members would be given the same copies, or unredacted originals, she didn't know. Brooke still had no idea whether Jo was suspected of disclosing secret material to someone, or whether someone thought there was a risk that she might.

Then Brooke came across what looked to be a transcript of the interview Jo had had with the ASIO officers. Just as Jo had said, they had put many questions to her about her sexual encounters going back ten years. Perhaps the questions had been designed to help persuade the tribunal that Jo's radical and unconventional lifestyle made her more likely to be a security risk. No matter how weak a case ASIO put up, the tribunal would need to have good reason to override ASIO's assertion that Jo posed a risk to national security. The outcome of a case like this would inevitably favour ASIO so long as politicians continued to convince the public that it was acceptable to take away people's civil liberties in order to protect 'democratic freedoms'. Brooke sighed, and decided she would take the material home to study it more closely.

She dumped her briefcase on the back seat of the car, feeling a pang of momentary guilt. Stuff them, she thought. Of course the documents will be safe at home. She unzipped her leather boots and threw them on to the back seat too, and pulled out a pair of soft elasticised slippers from the door pocket, and slipped them on over her fishnet stockings. More comfortable and it would save scuffing the heels of her suede boots on the car floor. She shook her head hoping to resettle her windswept hair. A good shake worked for the dogs when they were ruffled. It might work for her.

It started to pour. The two-lane highway wasn't a problem, but then came the narrow road where vehicles could barely pass. And the oncoming headlights belonged to a large vehicle. Brooke's mind was a jumble. She didn't know if she felt sorrier for Jo, who had the problem, or for herself, having the terrible job of trying to resolve it. Jo seemed to have faith in her, but could she help her?

Her mantra for winning cases crept into her head. 'Focus on your object, stay on track,' the earworm told her in rhythm with the windscreen wipers. Let them come from any direction but stick to your path and they will run themselves into a wall. 'You hope,' she said out loud, suddenly aware that this was what she must do right now. The rapidly approaching headlights were encroaching onto her side of the road.

Brooke flicked her lights to high but the beams couldn't penetrate the sheets of rain. She lowered them and squinted to make out the centre line.

She swerved to the verge, skidding, as the truck roared past, depositing a wall of muck on her windscreen.

'You bastard!' she exclaimed, and manoeuvred the car back onto the road. Her thoughts slipped back to Jo and the memo she'd phoned Brooke about which had come into Annette Armstrong's hands. If Annette's eyes weren't welcome in Special Projects, Jo's wouldn't be either. But how could she argue that ASIO was using false allegations to stop Jo seeing something, goodness knows what? Surely her access to the section's files could have been restricted, not taken away altogether.

The curtains of water parted, and Brooke heard the wipers squeal as they met resistance from the drying glass. A beam of moonlight crept through the shifting clouds. As she turned into her driveway, she glimpsed a nearly full moon. A large hare bounded in front of the car and disappeared just as Rex and Rocky came tearing down the drive to greet her.

'Am I glad to come home to you,' exclaimed Brooke, 'even though you haven't got dinner on the table.'

Rex wagged his tail, taking full credit for making Brooke happy. But there was something wrong. Rocky wagged his tail too, but his head was lowered, as if he'd let her down.

'What's wrong, Rocky? Has something upset you?' she asked and ruffled his head. He looked up at her and wagged his tail harder as if everything was now okay.

As soon as she opened the front door, she saw it. A large envelope was sitting on the kitchen bench. Someone had been inside. She tried not to panic. There was no one here now. The dogs would have told her. She ripped the envelope open and read.

Dear Ms Talbot

There is more at stake than you know in relation to the case you are running for Dr Rowan. Since you rejected my advice to drop the case, I am offering my help. I am holding some classified documents which, while you cannot admit to seeing them, might assist you prepare Dr Rowan's case.

Just leave a note in your RMB saying, 'Roger, I would like to meet you ASAP' and I will reply with meeting place details.

A Friend

'Oh, shit, what have I got myself into?' She was addressing the cats now, who were weaving in and out of her legs to remind her they wanted their dinner. 'Chooks first. Then you, pussy cats. That will give me time to think. Come on dogs.'

Brooke chugged up to the chook pen, going through the options in her head. There were three. Do nothing; contact the federal police and give them the chance of catching a letter writer willing to show Brooke secret documents; or play along and see what the documents said. The letter was designed to scare her, she was sure of it. Coming into her house to leave the documents, rather than in her letter box, spoke loudly of 'Look what I can do. I know where you live.' Then again, her friend and neighbour Greg might have brought up the mail from her roadside box. Anyway, why would someone mention documents that might help Jo's case if the object was to scare her off the case? Brooke smelt a rat. It could be a set-up, someone trying to get her to break the law by tempting her to see secret papers rather than reporting a security breach. She could be charged under the Crimes Act and that would take her off the case – a simple ploy to leave Jo without representation, and delay the proceedings.

By the time Brooke was back in the house, she'd sorted it. Definitely do nothing. Produce the letter at the tribunal if necessary, in the hope that would spark questions about ASIO's real agenda. She switched on the kitchen light and with it came a bright idea. She'd phone Greg. He was a kindly, fatherly figure, given their age difference – a thinker, a philosopher, and a good listener. He had been an academic geographer, but retired in his mid-fifties to look after his ill wife. She had died a decade ago from breast cancer and he had since lived quietly in the country, showing no desire to re-partner. Brooke enjoyed his company and he seemed to like being there for her.

Half an hour later, dressed in overalls covered by a red checked lumber jacket, Greg was tugging at his boots at Brooke's back door. He pulled off his beanie and Brooke sat him down by the fire. Sipping red wine and staring into the yellow-blue mesmerising flames as they flickered, Brooke established that Greg had not been near her house all day – as if he would enter it without telling her, he said. Brooke explained the lead-up to the moral dilemma that faced her. Greg listened, got the picture and waited for her request.

'Big big favour, if you're not doing much tomorrow morning,' she appealed. 'Could you sit at that window where you birdwatch and check any cars that stop at my mail box? Type of car, number plate, if you can?'

'Better still,' Greg said, 'I'll get my bike out, and do some birdwatching in the bushes near your driveway – close enough to see a rego plate.'

'You're a darling. I'll make you a meal at the weekend and we can hunt up another bottle of red.'

11

Brooke rose early to beat the peak-hour traffic. She padded up to the chook pen, Rex and Rocky at heel, and freed the birds from their fox-proof pens. A chicken, which she wanted to be a hen, greeted her with a tentative 'cock-a-doodle-do', to which she exclaimed, 'Oh, not you too!' But he tried again, telling her she had another male to look after.

She scrambled out of her tracksuit and into the shower, then wriggled into thick woollen tights over which she pulled a long-sleeved stretch-knit dress. As she readied herself for work, she decided to add a touch to her plan. She collected her briefcase and a folded piece of blank white paper and jumped into her car. Anyone watching would see her stop at the letter box at the bottom of the drive. She put the paper in – up against the back wall, wedged behind a warped piece of timber frame. Retrieving it would now take a few extra seconds, and give Greg more time to observe a car. She drove on to work.

Half an hour later when Brooke stepped out of the lift, Jo was sitting waiting for her. She had just lit a cigarette.

Brooke nodded hello and said, 'I'll be with you in a minute.'

By the time she had cleared her briefcase, opened the venetian blind to let in the day and returned to the waiting room, Jo was stubbing out her cigarette with a firm twisting motion. Stubbing a cigarette was one thing, but Jo's problem was not going to be as easily stubbed out.

After settling into their familiar positions across the desk, Brooke told Jo about last night's letter. 'A bit weird for someone to come all that way out of town and creep into my house.'

'I am sorry, Brooke.' Jo seemed genuinely concerned. 'What will you do?'

'It's a dilemma. It'd be great to find out what is really going on. Just why are the spooks concerned about your being at Immigration? But I'm old and wise enough to know that the best way of beating corrupt systems is to face them head on. You, Jo, will appreciate that. Being female, I have to keep my nose that much cleaner. Following up this tempting offer could backfire. I'm not convinced we'd learn anything that would help your case. But I'll do my best to find out who's behind this, and why, but that's it.'

Jo seemed to understand. In turn, she told Brooke about her own efforts to find out more, through Donald. 'He's a former boyfriend, and he knows a little about ASIO and intelligence methods generally, and he's agreed to be a character witness.'

Brooke picked up on the name. 'Donald? Where does he fit into this picture?' She was not surprised at what followed. Certainly there was more than one Donald in Canberra, but if there was a Donald who knew about Canberra's intelligence world and whom Jo had known previously, Brooke thought it likely that he was the man whom she had met last month mixing with well-connected people at the Faceless Men's Bar.

'Donald Fenchurch,' Jo replied. 'He introduced me to Mujo in 1987 when he was trade commissioner with our Belgrade embassy.'

So it is the same Donald, Brooke thought. What sort of man was he, she wondered. An image of soft eyes and appealing smile came into her mind. 'Tell me more about him. Your relationship with him, how often you see him, and how he has reacted to your affair with Mujo.'

'Christ. You're interrogating me like those ASIO guys!'

'Sorry, well, it maybe none of my business, and none of ASIO's, but I must know at least as much about you as ASIO. What they know they'll use against you. What I know I'll use to help you. I have to anticipate every possible snippet they could turn up. So bear with me. What does Donald do now?'

'He's retired from the public service, but has fingers in a lot of pies, including some commercial interests, drawing on business connections he made during his time as trade commissioner. He writes opinion pieces for newspapers, often critical of government policy. He's a bit of a loose cannon, some think. He wasn't always so outspoken. He graduated from Duntroon Military College, here in Canberra, and his military career led to the Office of National Assessments, hence his intelligence contacts.'

'What does he know about you?'

'He knows about my work, my family, and…' Jo grinned, 'my body of course.'

Brooke was taking notes and didn't react.

Jo cancelled her smile and spoke on. 'When we were an item, he came and went as it suited us both. We shared ideas, talked about our writing and we're still good friends. He's his own person, enjoying life and its adventures. I trust him.'

'Could he have told anyone anything adverse about you and Mujo that might have caused your problem?'

'Absolutely not!'

'I had to ask. Would ASIO trust him? Perhaps it's him they think you'll blab to, not Mujo?'

'I haven't come across confidential material that could interest anyone. Security has gone mad in this country. Anyway, I rarely take classified documents out of the office. It's verboten but sometimes it's convenient if I'm working at the university or at home.'

Brooke wondered if she was blushing, knowing that she had done just that the previous night. 'Does Donald know that you do that sometimes?' she asked.

'Of course. He'd stay with me when he was in Canberra, when we were together. I was doing a consultancy for Defence at the time, and I'd work at home at night.'

'I'm happy to use his affidavit, Jo. There's a risk he'll be questioned, and might be asked if he knew of any occasion when you took confidential material home.'

'Everyone does it, and if that's the worst they have on me…'

'It allows them to suggest that you might have left material lying around for one of your boyfriends to see, or at your office where students or staff might wander in.'

'They can suggest it. I'll deny it.'

'Look, after my experience last night, I wouldn't put it past ASIO to set you up. They could arrange for confidential documents to be found in your house to strengthen their case. They know you think stuff is over-classified.'

'Are you suggesting that they might fabricate evidence to suggest that Mujo had opportunities to access classified material?'

'I don't know. It wouldn't be hard to finger you,' Brooke said. 'There are plenty of ASIO stringers collecting information in pubs and universities, moles infiltrating political and other activist groups.

'"Sparrows" they were called, hopping around the universities in the sixties,' Jo laughed. 'They were part of the landscape and so you never noticed them. But the problem then was the Vietnam War. Surely it's not so bad now?'

'More so now, I'd expect. ASIO has money to burn,' Brooke said more forcefully than she had intended. 'They pay well for trivia about campus activities and I bet there are still students thanking ASIO for subsidising their university fees and trips overseas. Anybody could be telling tales about you.'

Jo was visibly taken aback. The dynamics of their relationship were changing. Brooke, still capable of being overawed by her, was seeing a Jo who could not disguise how vulnerable she was feeling. Her career was her life, and it was under threat.

Gently, Brooke spoke, 'So I have to ask: could any of your friends or university colleagues, even unwittingly, have talked about your political views, or relationships in places that might have reached ASIO?'

Jo shifted in her chair, and muttered, 'I'd be astonished if Donald, or any of my friends, had compromised my work, even by accident.'

'Don't raise it with him. I'm just playing devil's advocate. And neither Donald nor Mujo would like it if you started to distrust them. Remember, ASIO uses "divide and rule" to get information, so we wouldn't want to play into their hands. For the moment, let us assume your boyfriends have been solid supporters.'

Jo reached for her cigarettes.

Brooke hadn't finished. 'And you're not to admit to anyone that you might have been slack with documents you've taken out of the office. ASIO might know nothing about such things.'

'We don't know what they think they've got on me. Difficult, when I've done nothing wrong.'

'That's the injustice of it. Not telling you what you're accused of.'

Jo started to open her cigarette packet.

Brooke too needed a break. 'I'll get us some coffee. Then we'll go through the transcript of your ASIO interview.' she said.

'But this is not a literal transcript!' Jo exclaimed, putting her cup down heavily and slopping coffee on the desk. 'Oops, sorry.'

'It's okay. What do you mean?' asked Brooke, reaching for a Kleenex to mop up drops that had landed on nearby papers.

'For example, here.' Jo tapped her finger on the page. 'I sort of joked here about the quality of the red wine they serve in the departmental café. You know – remember the fuss about the department selling wine during work hours? That conversation isn't recorded. It's not important, but what else is omitted? I don't even know if he taped the interview. Probably just made it up later.' She bent over the transcript again. 'And here, we were talking about my time in Belgrade. This conversation went on for a while. A lot more than these few sentences. It's a bad summary.'

'Do you recall what else you said?'

'Yes. That I had met a Yugoslav diplomat in Belgrade, and that I met him again in Australia and started an affair with him. That's recorded. Then there was that bit of idiocy I mentioned where the ASIO guy asked me if I'd had any other affairs with a Soviet bloc national. I laughed, and said that I hardly regarded Yugoslavia as part of the Soviet bloc. It's a non-aligned country. He was embarrassed. That interchange isn't here.'

'I'm not surprised,' said Brooke. 'He wouldn't want his ignorance on the record. What else?'

'No mention of my affair with Furzer, thank goodness. I had to mention it to be consistent with my earlier application, or ASIO would have jumped on it.'

'They've held that back because they want a hold over him. Not good for you. We don't know if he's still backing you.'

'Shit, of course. He's pretty weak, and he'll want to protect his marriage.' Jo kept reading. 'There are words here I never use. The gist is there, but this looks like a summary, converted into a question-and-answer transcript.'

'Good, I'll call for the original tapes. If there aren't any, ASIO might be scared into trying to settle the case.'

'There's nothing here either, about my asking for Annette's file.'

Mention of Annette reminded Brooke to ask, 'Can I take a copy of that extraordinary memo?'

Returning from photocopying it, she said, 'Jo, you mentioned that you're writing a book?'

'Yes. It's giving me something to work on. It's about feminist theory. I use actual case studies from my various public sector consultancies – not using names or classified material, of course. I'm identifying the sort of cultures that encourage gender bias and gender inequity. I'll also be compiling a comparative report card on the performance of various departments, and I will enjoy embarrassing Immigration.'

The first thing Brooke did on arriving home was telephone Greg. Loyal Greg had done a good job. A black Ford Fairlane with a tinted windscreen had stopped at Brooke's mail box mid-morning, and a man in a black overcoat had poked around in her letter box for a while and taken the folded piece of paper back to his car. Greg had the number plate.

'I think I'll employ you,' Brooke told him. 'Should have been a detective.'

Brooke asked her friend Deidre, a 'crash and bash' lawyer, to enquire about the black Fairlane at the motor registry office.

Deidre telephoned her a few days later with a dismal answer. 'Nothing, Brooke. No such number,' she reported.

Brooke was not surprised. ASIO's car registrations wouldn't be on the public record. Goodness knows what happened when they were involved in an accident. The real number plate would be produced, no doubt; and the other party compensated, no questions asked.

'Well, that confirms it,' she told Greg the following night as she ran cold water through steaming hot pasta while he waited for her to serve the well-deserved dinner she had promised him. She stirred in pesto made from healthy home-grown basil and added large pieces of char-grilled pumpkin, eggplant and zucchini, and tipped it into a large ceramic bowl.

'It was no whistle blower offering me information,' she said, picking up the pasta dish and handing him two empty bowls.

They sat by the fire, a bottle of Shiraz open and breathing on the hearth.

Despite his deep grief, Greg was self-sufficient and seemingly comfortable living alone. Brook found his strong open face and clear blue eyes attractive and happily confided in him; used him as a sounding board when she had difficult cases, or ethical dilemmas to discuss.

'It had to be an attempt to get me to break the law. Someone wants me off this case, which I would be if I were found with secret documents.'

'What a compliment!' Greg said.

Brooke considered that and shook her head. 'No, I'm the only barrister stupid enough to take on a case like this. So it's my stupidity that's put a spanner in the spooks' system. I'll show them, though,' she vowed.

'I have no doubt you will,' Greg said supportively. 'You'll win the case somehow.'

Yes, but how, and at what cost? Brooke wondered.

12

Mid-July 1991

A silver shimmer of moonlight caressed the lake and reflected eerily through Brooke's bedroom window. She sank into the pillow eyes wide open in the half light, contemplating the events – or non-events – of the last three days. She had spent them waiting for the tribunal to call her into the hearing room. She and Jo had been excluded while ASIO put its case. In a regular hearing, the applicant would present their case first in the presence of the other party. But there was nothing 'regular' in security appeal processes. Still, she'd hoped to be given an outline of the case against Jo by now.

Brooke had worked tirelessly for a fortnight, reading, memorising, flagging and organising material. Preparing for Jo's case was like studying for an exam where you didn't know the syllabus. She didn't know what she might be asked and had to consider every scenario she could think of that might have triggered ASIO's concern about Jo. The possibilities were endless.

Then, this afternoon, the tribunal's clerk had rung her to say that she wouldn't be 'required' today. The hearing had been adjourned to a 'date to be notified'. Still in the dark. Pushing her hair back from her face, Brooke had tried to hold in tears of anger and frustration. She was powerless and felt like a suspect, a victim herself, rather than a lawyer looking after a client. But, not to be defeated, she requested that the tribunal president permit her to put some questions to the tribunal to circumscribe the case Jo had to address. The Act did not provide for such a procedure, but neither was it prohibited. Another call from the tribunal confirmed a win. She'd submit her questions within a week.

Her challenge now was to ask questions about ASIO's case without suggesting new matters for ASIO to use against Jo. For all she knew, ASIO might not have fully disclosed its reasons for its decision to the tribunal; too secret for even the tribunal to know. How would she explain this to Jo? How would Jo fare before the tribunal?

Drifting into sleep, her subconscious rifled her thoughts and soon she was engulfed in a dream in which she was like an outsider, watching voices and images play out before her.

A person appeared. He wore a grey hood which half concealed his grey featureless face. He was reading a charge while other grey and faceless hoodies stood listening. There a doll-sized Jo-like woman stood before them on a stool.

The reader spoke. 'You are charged with having breached security. How do you plead?'

Jo answered, 'Not guilty.'

'What do you have to say?'

'May I ask some questions?'

'You may.'

'What did I do?'

'You disclosed secret information.'

'What information, and to whom?'

'It is not in the interests of security to say.'

'But I must know the case against me.'

'No, you cannot, it is a secret.'

At that point Jo spun on her heels, and hit back with Wonderland logic: 'If I disclosed secret material, it is secret no more. And if I didn't do that, then I've broken no law.'

The grey wraiths continued, 'If you disclosed and we say that is so, we don't have to tell you what you already know. Our role is not to recognise doubt, it's simply to catch you out.'

Jo was flicking through a Hoyle's handbook to check the rules. She asked, 'Then tell me please how you define what is secret.'

'It's secret if we say so.'

'Who is "we"?'

'That is secret. You are not to know.'

'Is there a law that allows you to treat me this way?'

'Yes, the Security Act allows us that call.'

'And is there provision for an appeal?'

'None whatsoever, none at all.'

The head hood gave an evil laugh and turned towards a barman pouring drinks for the others. They were conversing in grunts. Jo's large cat's eyes glared at their grey backs. She was rising above them as her stool grew and grew. The grunting stopped and they turned to face her.

She looked down and addressed the head hood, 'Then I will run a case of my own.'

'What nonsense are you proposing?' was the reply.

'I will go to the highest court in the land to have your procedurally unfair rules overturned, you security-obsessed fools.'

The hoods howled and meowed. One of Brooke's cats jumped from bed to floor. Brooke moaned and turned in her sleep. Jo jumped from her stool with a thud.

Brooke woke abruptly. Had Jo defeated the faceless people? She closed her eyes to see with clear vision. But the hoods had gone. The cat meowed again, and went outside through the bathroom cat flap. It flapped noisily back and forth until it lost momentum.

Brooke often woke with solutions to difficult problems but none came to her this time. The bizarre dream unsettled her. It reflected her fear that she would not be allowed to play a role at the hearing; and she would have to leave Jo to her fate.

13

August 1991

Jo parked her Holden Barina next to Mujo's BMW with its DC plates. She could see him waving from the veranda of the yacht club. He walked down the stairs to greet her. They strolled on the shore of the lake and down to the boat ramp, saying little, before returning to cushioned wicker chairs and a carafe of wine on the deck. But Mujo looked distracted. Jo felt he had been drinking more of late. New frown lines had burrowed into his forehead, marring his easy-going facade.

It was warm for August. She looked out on the golden wattles in full flower and, on the bushes below, some blush pink Azalea buds – a taste of Canberra's spring to come. Within weeks, families would be bringing picnic baskets with rugs for sitting on around the nearby barbecues.

She put her hand on his. Yugoslavia was disintegrating. The independence movements in Croatia and Slovenia had changed Australia's relations with the Milošević-led government. It wasn't going to stop there. Hostilities were likely to break out in Bosnia and Herzegovina as well. She knew the situation was troubling him.

Both had watched a bombshell being dropped on last night's ABC's *Four Corners* program. Reporter Chris Masters had tracked down a key witness against six Croatian men who had been convicted in 1985 of bombing several Sydney buildings in 1979. They were serving fifteen-year gaol sentences. According to *Four Corners*, the witness had admitted he was a Serb who had infiltrated the Croatian community to report on its activities to the consulate. It was suggested that Yugoslavia's intelligence agency UDBA had entrapped the six Croatian-Australian activists in a fake plot to plant the bombs at busy Sydney venues. With the help of Australian intelligence and police, this agent provocateur had succeeded in blackening the Croatian-Australian community as extremists. While this frame-up had been scuttlebutt for years, it was now being suggested that an Australian in a top-level national security committee had suppressed knowledge of UDBA involvement at the activists' trial and that the Crown's witness used a script written by the police. The six were unlikely to have been guilty.

'Is it true, Mujo?' Jo asked.

'Could be. We use undercover agents. And if suit us, we work with other countries' intelligence agencies. We share intelligence with your country tracking Croatian extremists to find picnic camps. My government determined to stop young Croatians training here from returning home to fight for independence from Yugoslav state. One time, USA and Australia support "one Yugoslavia" idea and suppression of extremists. So, we think Yugoslavia and Australia have common enemy in Croatian Ustashi.'

Jo was aware that before the easing of the cold war, ASIO had changed focus from monitoring communists to squashing fascist extremism – at least until Attorney-General Murphy's heavy action to bring ASIO to heel.

'ASIO's done a few about-turns, haven't they? I guess they don't mind who they're supporting as long as their budget keeps growing,' she said.

'And they might switch again. Violence has broken out in my country with some states chasing independence, and my government is not popular with United States. Australia will be pressured to follow US line that Serbia is aggressor to be controlled.'

Mujo puffed smoke rings into the air. Jo waited. There was something on his mind. Something he was finding difficult to tell her.

'It's hard for me. My wife she is Serb, her family live in Croatia, and her father is already subject of persecution. My sister is Muslim, like me, and lives in Bosnia Herzegovina. She fears Serbs, hates my parents-in-law and their politics. Me, public servant in Serb government, meant to be without politics. I must play along to protect my mother in Belgrade, and my sister and her family. The generals cause our troubles. They start wars by playing on historic religious fears.'

Jo braced herself. Had he decided to return to his family?

She relaxed when he said, 'What can I do but have a drink and a smoke and consider futility of it all?'

Jo asked about domestic politics in Yugoslavia, trying to absorb the historic complexities that had divided its peoples. While racial and religious differences were ever present, mixed marriages were common. It was disgusting that groups could be set against each other by power-hungry soldiers. Then again, Serbia was led by a ruthless dictator – enough to unsettle any country.

These political developments could only make it more difficult for her to regain her security clearance. She was now convinced that her association with Mujo was being used to cease her gender equity work in Immigration. She wanted to ask Mujo if he agreed, but this wasn't the time. Instead, she probed for his thoughts about his wife.

'Politics do not come between Andjela and me. Other things about me make her unhappy, but I don't think it fair to uplift whole family to come here. I could be called back home before time.'

'Is that likely?'

'Maybe. I don't know if Milošević trust me not to defect.'

'But you wouldn't defect, because of your mother…'

Mujo nodded, and appeared to be following his thoughts to some distant place. 'I might go back for short time, and see what wife thinks; about me, about best for children. Spend Christmas with them.'

She knew then what he was trying to tell her. He needed to have his family back. It went unsaid, but both knew they would not be going back to Jo's place tonight. Mujo was with his wife and family and Jo had no intention of competing with them.

Beyond being preoccupied with her pending hearing, another level of misery was descending on her. Her job and reputation were in tatters, her boyfriend was not really hers, and she had an estranged daughter. What was her life about? She went home and buried herself in book writing.

14

Early September 1991

The dogs woke first. It was Saturday and Brooke needed their help to get up. They nosed and pawed at her doona until she rubbed her eyes open. She loved her farm at this time of year. Lake George glistened in the sun.

So did something else. A blob of white, maybe feathers, outside her window. Wearing just a T-shirt, she ran to the front door to investigate and trod on a plastic bag on the doormat. She bent and picked it up. Rocky and Rex were keen to help. Meat, that's what it was, raw meat tightly wrapped in thin plastic.

'What the hell…?' She turned the package over. It was partly frozen. Her first thought was that it was baited. She shuddered. At least she'd found it before the dogs. Who would do this? Had a fox stolen it from a neighbour and dropped it on his run home? She hadn't heard the dogs bark in the night.

'Sit, stay!' she commanded the dogs and crept along the veranda to inspect the white blob.

Just outside her bedroom window, horribly, was a headless hen. Stifling a scream, she peered at it. The chook's neck didn't look chewed; more likely it had been broken and screwed off. And it wasn't one of hers as it was a white leghorn. Brooke's chooks were mostly bantam crosses and none were white.

There was more to come. At the end of the veranda lay the severed head of a young kangaroo.

Her head pounded and she felt sick. Not so the dogs, ready to tear the corpses. She took the dogs back into the house and returned with an orange bin liner big enough to take the dead remains and meat. She placed the full bag on the roof of her car, out of the sun and away from the dogs.

Brooke went indoors and sat down. She bent over and hugged her knees, rocking with horror. The dogs came to sit at her feet and she wrapped her arms around them, dropping tears into their fur.

No good. Get dressed, do the chores, she directed herself and obeyed her sensible voice. She released the chooks, fed them and the animals, and at nine o'clock began phoning. The neighbour who kept frozen meat in a large freezer outside his house for baiting foxes checked to see if an animal had raided it, but the lid was firmly closed.

The next-door neighbour came to see for himself. A feral cat, he suggested. Kids playing a game? But surely not in the middle of the night? He'd ask around.

Then Brooke rang Greg. He came up with a surveillance plan he thought she should try for a few nights. She should sprinkle flour along the veranda and around the house. If things happened again, there would be animal or human footprints, 'Unless of course,' he fantasised, 'an eagle dropped the three items from the sky.'

'Smart eagle to fly low under my veranda roof,' Brooke said.

After an unproductive day, Brooke went to bed with her charged car phone under her pillow. She had spread the flour and closed the dog door to keep the animals inside. Greg had offered to stay the night, and the neighbour next door offered her a rifle. She said 'No, thank you' politely to both. Having Greg stay would make for complications. She was unnerved, but not scared. As for the rifle, she would be nervous having one in the house.

Come morning, the flour revealed nothing – no tracks, no paw marks, no unwanted items on the veranda. Brooke set the trap again on Sunday night, but Monday morning still brought nothing. She dressed for work complete with light pink lipstick and a pink clip to hold back her hair. She hoped her horrible experience would fade away like a child's memory of a nightmare. But she did want the mystery explained.

Was it, she'd kept thinking, just another ploy to scare her off Jo's case? A possibility was that ASIO might have recruited a local 'to put the fear of God' in her. Then she'd start suspecting everyone, or at least neighbours she didn't know.

The following day, Jo and Brooke worked on a letter to ASIO's lawyers. Brooke told Jo that she did not want to be scared into settling Jo's case by any 'dead meat' warnings, if that is what they were. But nor did she want to overreact and stubbornly resist a settlement opportunity.

'If ASIO is behind this juvenile act, it suggests they're worried about what you might say, or what the tribunal might do,' she reasoned. 'So let's explore whether ASIO would accept a downgrade of your clearance level or reduced access to Immigration files, unpalatable as that might be.'

Jo agreed. After all, if the letter wrinkled out an offer, she didn't have to accept it.

Their letter suggested that in the absence of any allegation that Dr Rowan had breached, or was likely to breach, her security obligations, the tribunal was likely to reinstate her clearance. It made veiled reference to ASIO's doctoring of the transcript of interview. So, while Brooke did not know what else the tribunal had been told, the letter was worth a try. Brooke faxed it direct to the Australian Government Solicitor's office.

It was a waste of time. The reply faxed a week later read in part,

> The Director-General is not prepared to consider your proposal unless your client first withdraws her review application. In that event we are open to discuss the terms and conditions of any qualified assessment, should one be deemed appropriate.

'So, if you give up your appeal, ASIO might consider…blah, blah. Quite unacceptable, but not unexpected,' Brooke said to Jo after reading the letter to her. 'If you withdraw your appeal, the hearing will be abandoned and you'll have nothing to bargain with.'

How could they trust ASIO to be fair now? Delay was what ASIO was offering and delay was not in Jo's interest. Jo agreed. She had no choice but to proceed with the hearing.

Yet another week later Brooke received answers to the questions she had lodged with the tribunal. Eight weeks to send answers, and here they were, reeking of arbitrary power:

Q1: Has the Tribunal been informed of the Director-General's reasons for the decision to revoke the applicant's security clearance?

A1: Yes.

Q2: If so, will the Tribunal inform the applicant of those reasons?

A2: No, the Tribunal accepts the Director-General's advice that it is not in the interests of national security to do so.

Q3: If so, please specify the reasons.

A3: NA

Q4: If the reasons are not to be specified please advise whether or not
(a) it is alleged that some work related act or omission of the applicant's has endangered national security?
(b) it is alleged some non-work related act or omission has endangered national security?
(c) it is alleged that any matter relating to the applicant's moral, or sexual behaviour might potentially endanger national security?
(d) it is alleged that the applicant's relationship with any particular person might potentially endanger national security?

A4: It is alleged that the applicant, by her own admission as well as choice of personal associates, has a casual regard for issues of security.

Q5: Is it alleged the applicant disclosed classified material to an unauthorised person, and if so, what material and to whom?

A5: It is not in the interests of national security to provide an answer to this question.

Brooke was back in her dream of faceless grey power that could not be understood or controlled. The answer to question five had been left open, possibly because ASIO was being duplicitous and did not want to reveal its real concerns.

At least a resumption date had been set for the hearing; Thursday 3 October. The pressure was on. Jo could be asked to give evidence then but it didn't follow that Brooke could represent her. On the day, she would have to seek leave to appear. The tribunal was putty in ASIO's hands.

Greg's detective work paid off. He had asked around to see if anyone had lost a fowl, or seen a decapitated kangaroo, or been harassed like Brooke. No, but three people complained of recent burglaries. A travelling clock, a watch, jewellery, loose change – that sort of thing. No one locked their homes. What was the use of it? If someone wanted to rob you while you were away, they could smash a window; no one would hear.

All three victims suspected the teenager down the road, but none wanted to upset his parents with an accusation. Greg thought otherwise. Most parents would want to know if their child was causing trouble, or else prove that they weren't.

He was tactful when he approached the boy's mother. 'I'm making enquiries of everyone, not just you,' he assured her, hitching up his baggy trousers, 'because we all want to come home in the evening without fearing that we may have been robbed.'

The mother's face said it all. She invited him in, and said, 'Wait, my son's here. He has something to say to you, and to a lot of other people he's stolen from. I don't know how many, or who they are, and maybe you can help,' she said.

Greg told her about Brooke's experience, and the woman looked mortified. 'Oh, no, my son wouldn't have done that,' she said. 'But I don't blame you for suspecting him, given what he's been up to. Let's clear this up now.' She called the boy.

A skinny, pale lad skulked in and slumped into an armchair. Greg was sure he had found the delinquent teenager who had caused Brooke's grief. Prodded by his mother, the boy admitted he had taken some loose change on an occasion from Brooke's bedside table. He had seen it through the window and the house was unlocked. He took nothing else, he said. The mother explained that he'd been caught, because he showed off 'loot' at school. The headmistress had telephoned her and asked her to take the boy around to personally apologise to his victims and promise to never do it again. 'We never got round to Brooke, as she works until quite late.'

Prompted by Greg's firm but calm interrogation, the boy confessed that it was also he who had intimidated Brooke. His mother listened in disbelief when he explained why.

He'd accepted two fifties from a man in a black Fairlane to 'frighten but not harm' the lady who lived on the hill. 'Do something to scare her, make it look like someone's targeting her. A carcass on her veranda might do the trick,' he had said.

'Why would someone ask you to do that?' his mother asked.

'He pulled up beside me when he saw me coming out of someone's driveway tucking a clock in my pocket. He knew what I'd been up to, so I said I'd do it for him. I'd been there before and I knew I could.'

His mother looked at Greg, who tried not to react.

'Go on,' Greg urged.

'I knew I had to do a good job, or he'd come back.' The boy saw his mother's expression and protested, his voice a pitch higher, 'Mum, the man was official. He showed me a card, and said I'd be helping my country.'

His mother lowered her head, shaking it in despair.

A few more questions established that the boy knew that Brooke's neighbour kept a freezer full of dog meat – easier than finding a dead animal. Then a fox had dug its way into the family's chook pen. It took one bird and left another for dead. The boy had offered to put the chook out of its misery and get rid of the carcass for his mum.

'Oh, I'm so sorry,' the boy's mother said to Greg. 'Yes, it was our hen, a leghorn.'

The boy said he completed the job by severing the head from a road kill kangaroo. His mother was sobbing now.

'I didn't hurt her, Mum,' the boy pleaded.

Greg comforted the woman and told her that he and Brooke thought it was a disgruntled client who'd paid her son to frighten Brooke, pretending he was some sort of government spy. 'He knew a lad with imagination would buy that one,' Greg said. 'Probably someone who was angry with Brooke over some court outcome.'

He said nothing about ASIO. Who would believe or understand anyway?

15

3 October 1991

The hearing was held, not in Canberra House as usual, but in a 'borrowed' room in an office block on the south side of University Avenue. It belonged to the Federal Industrial Court, and it was fitted out with sombre timber furnishings.

Morris Prendergast QC, counsel for the director-general of security, boomed a jovial 'Good morning, Tribunal.' He had a commanding presence. His several spare chins hung low, but not as far as his bulbous stomach.

There was no court reporter present, only the tribunal's clerk. The three tribunal members sat expressionless on the bench, papers spread in front of them.

Jo looked at Brooke sitting beside her at the bar table; Brooke had made no attempt to compete with Prendergast's bravado. She's letting him dominate, like a dog marking its territory, Jo thought. She'd sought advice from Brooke because she thought a woman might be a little brighter and probably a lot more conscientious than a man. She acknowledged she was displaying what she accused men of having – 'unconscious bias' about women's capabilities. Now, watching Brooke, she wondered if she had made a mistake. She wondered if a man might better represent her; a stronger presence, more authority. Brooke cared, no doubt about that. She had taken on Jo's problem, worked hard and resisted intimidation. But did she have enough fight in her to combat a ruthless adversary?

Brooke rose, gave her name and 'respectfully' sought the tribunal's leave to appear. Jo thought it a strange word. Whenever lawyers were about to disagree with a judge, they started with 'I respectfully submit, your honour,' or 'With respect, your honour,' when they weren't feeling respectful at all.

The three tribunal members were already taking notes. The president granted Brooke her leave, but only for the 'duration of your client's evidence'.

Jo realised Brooke was nudging her towards the witness box at the far side of the room. Two steps led to a raised square platform with wooden sides, just big enough for a chair.

Jo walked slowly. Her blazer couldn't hide how much weight she'd lost in recent weeks. She sat down, glanced at the faces on the bench and then looked across the room at Prendergast QC. The light from the windows behind him blurred his features while he had a clear view of her.

Feeling like a rabbit in a shooter's spotlight, she turned towards Brooke. 'Is your name Josephine Rowan?'

'It is.'

'Please state your residential address.'

Jo tried to steady her voice as she answered the first few predictable questions.

'Are you a professorial fellow in the Department of Sociology at the Australian National University? Are you also currently engaged in a consultancy to review the equality of employment opportunities in the Department of Immigration?'

Jo kept her voice low to project a calm she didn't feel and, as Brooke had instructed, she faced the tribunal members when speaking. 'Look at them, not me, when you answer. Keep their attention.'

Formalities completed, Brooke turned and addressed the president. 'Madam President, you are aware that neither I nor Dr Rowan are aware of the allegations against her. It would be helpful if Mr Prendergast could provide an outline of the director-general's reasons for his decision before leaving, or perhaps the tribunal might direct me to particular topics on which to examine my client. I don't want to waste the tribunal's time.' She had no joy.

'There is nothing more we can convey to you and your client, Ms

Talbot. If your client is now ready to give evidence, Mr Prendergast will leave the hearing room, as required by the Act.'

'With respect, Madam President, the provision that requires Mr Prendergast to absent himself while my client gives evidence does not redress the injustice my client is suffering by not being permitted to hear ASIO's allegations against her, or that evidence.'

At last, Jo said to herself, she's showing some spirit.

'How fair is it to ask my client to rebut allegations she has no knowledge of? The requirement that each party give evidence in the absence of the other masquerades as fairness, but that is nonsense. Justice would be better served if Mr Prendergast stayed in the hearing room and questioned my client. That would give her an inkling of what she is supposed to have done to precipitate an adverse security assessment.'

'Now, Ms Talbot, you know the tribunal has no discretion on that matter.'

Mr Prendergast made a suggestion. 'If it would assist Ms Talbot, I have a list of questions the tribunal might put to Dr Rowan.'

'It seems, Madam President, that ASIO's representative continues to be both prosecutor and defender, despite the superficial "equality" provision in the Act. A more unjust procedure can hardly be imagined. Why on earth could we not have been provided with these questions before the hearing?'

'Sarcasm and emotion do not assist your client, Ms Talbot. Mr Prendergast has no obligation to furnish you with questions in advance, or now. However, since they have been offered, we will consider them. Thank you, Mr Prendergast. You and your instructing solicitors may leave the court now.'

While Prendergast and his team bundled up their papers and filed out, the president looked at the list of questions and passed it to the other tribunal members. Turning to Brooke, the president said, 'Ms Talbot, the tribunal will ask some questions of Dr Rowan, after which you will be free to put some questions in reply.'

Brooke opened her mouth as if about to protest but then sat down. Jo's spirits dropped. The procedural rules were being turned on their head.

Images of Alice and the Queen of Hearts came to mind. They might as well have said 'Off with her head'. Brooke looked despondent.

The president then said to Jo, 'I will put the questions posed by ASIO's representative to you. You don't have to answer all or any of them. It is up to you. Ms Talbot, as your counsel, can guide you there. And she may have questions of her own to ask.'

Jo nodded, and without preliminaries, the president asked, 'On Monday 20 May last, did you meet Mujo Zukić at Hyatt Hotel Canberra?'

Jo was not prepared for the question. 'What? May 20? Possibly, I often did, but I can't remember that date.'

The president picked up another piece of paper and said, 'I'll refresh your memory. It was the Monday after your interview with ASIO officers at the Department of Immigration.' She turned back to Prendergast's list and added, 'Zukić followed you home.'

'We were tailed?' Jo tried to keep her voice steady.

'Dr Rowan, please answer the question, or state your wish to decline.'

Jo turned to Brooke for support. Brooke gave a small nod.

'Yes, yes, I met him at the Hyatt.'

'He handed you a piece of paper when you were at home. What was written on it?'

'This is outrageous!' Her calm had left her.

The president said more gently, 'You might be shocked, but you must either answer the question or indicate that you decline.'

Jo remembered the car she saw outside when she had stood up to read Mujo's poem. She knew now that they were being spied upon. 'It was a poem.'

'Do you have it?'

'Somewhere, probably. It's personal.'

'What did you talk about that evening?'

'A lot of things, nothing, nothing of any consequence. I don't recall specifically what, on that occasion. We generally talk about ideas, people, we read poetry, make love – the things lovers do.'

'Well, Dr Rowan, what about the conversation you had in the shower, with the water running...deliberately, do we take it?'

Jo reeled and had difficulty controlling her anger. 'Are you telling me my home is bugged? That is illegal. I am an Australian citizen!'

The president ignored her. 'Do you recall your conversation?'

Silence was punctuated by the clicking of the ceiling fan for four or five revolutions as it cut through the stale air in the small hearing room. It would have been easy to open a door, but both were tightly shut, pinned with notices declaring 'Closed hearing in session'.

'He wanted a shower,' Jo said quietly. 'I followed him. We made love, for heaven's sake.'

'And then you stayed in the shower to talk to him?'

'Yes. No, not just that. We were sitting on the floor of the shower, and, um, talking.'

'The water was still running?'

'Yes,' Jo said firmly, and loudly, almost shouting, 'a trickle of warm water to keep us warm!'

'What did you talk about?'

'Well, I initiated the conversation, not him. I had already told him at the Hyatt that I had seen a lawyer because my security clearance had been revoked. After the shower, I asked him if he thought our relationship could be the reason.'

'Why did you think it might be? Had you any reason to think that?'

'Because, of course, I had to declare all my affairs with foreigners in my clearance application, and he was the main one. What other reason – you please tell me.'

The president ignored her question, and asked another. 'What else did you tell him?'

'Nothing, for heaven's sake. This was after ASIO's decision to revoke my clearance, not the cause of it. They'd already told me they were withdrawing it. Are these questions designed to find something to justify ASIO's unreasonable action?'

Brooke got to her feet. 'I object, with respect to the tribunal, to this line of questioning, if they are questions Mr Prendergast posed. It does appear to be a fishing expedition.'

The president hesitated. 'We note the objection, but for the moment, Dr Rowan, it is in your interest to answer them, if you can. We will consider their relevance and other objections put by your counsel after your evidence is completed. Now, what did he tell you about his work?'

'About his work? Nothing. We're both professionals. I know that he carries out normal consular activities,' Jo replied.

'But some six months earlier he had introduced you to some intelligence agents as his friends. You must have known who they were.'

Jo looked to Brooke pleadingly. Brooke raised one eyebrow and inclined her head, meaning 'You'd better answer', so she did. Jo explained that Mujo saw it as important for their relationship to be in the open. He didn't want either of them to be vulnerable to blackmail or some such, given that he was a married man having an affair.

'And how did he explain knowing these agents?'

'That his and our government have a common interest in tracking down extremist Yugoslavs in Australia. They share intelligence.'

'Croatians?'

'Yes, Croatians.'

'Did he tell you anything more about tracking down these supposedly extremist Croatians?'

'No, of course not.'

'Did he tell you anything about "infiltration" of groups of extremists to gain information?'

The question puzzled Jo. 'He told me nothing about his country's intelligence activities. Though we did talk about a recent ABC TV program that accused a Serb intelligence agent of infiltrating a Croatian group, to provoke them into violent action, or to cause Croatians to be arrested for crimes they might or might not have committed. I asked him if it could be true, though it happened a decade before he arrived.'

Brooke rose to object. 'Your honour, I fail to see how anything Dr Rowan has learned from a foreign diplomat could constitute her breaching security...'

Before she'd finished, the president anticipated her. 'Yes, yes. We will consider whether this is relevant. For the moment, Ms Talbot, there is no suggestion that Dr Rowan was somehow trading information.'

Brooke sat down. Jo felt as relieved as Brooke looked.

'We will move on. The book you're writing, Dr Rowan. What is it about?'

'It's about barriers to women rising through the ranks of the public service. I use case studies based on work I have done in various government departments – de-identifying individuals, of course. My work has to pass a rigorous ethics clearance process, and other screenings.'

'Why did you ask to see files relating to Operation Fishnet?'

'Operation what? I've never heard of it.'

'Did you not ask for a file concerning it?'

'No. I asked for the files relating to the job description and selection process for a position in the Special Projects Section of the Department of Immigration. I didn't get them and it was only later I learned that one of the special projects was known as Operation F. I did not know till this minute what the "F" stood for. Now I do.'

The president looked disconcerted. 'You know that anything that occurs or is said in these proceedings is subject to strict confidentiality, and it would be a serious security breach for you to disclose anything said here outside this tribunal?'

'I learned about Operation F from a memo left lying around, not marked secret, no classification at all.'

'I repeat, you are not at liberty to disclose anything that arises in the tribunal,' the president said.

'I understand. But to finish my answer to your question, the reason I asked for those files was to assess whether or not it was reasonable for the selection panel to have deemed it a position unsuitable for a woman.'

'Did your friend Mujo Zukić ever mention the name of that operation to you?' the president asked.

'What? Why should he? How would he know about it? No, No. I told you, I'd never heard of it.'

'Did you mention Operation F to Zukić after you saw that memo?'

'Certainly not. I had no reason to, and I wouldn't.'

Suddenly Jo found herself answering questions about Donald.

'How did you come to meet Zukić, Dr Rowan?'

'I was introduced to him in Belgrade in about, um, 1986 or '87, by a friend.'

'By Donald Fenchurch, wasn't it? One of your character referees?'

'Yes.'

'Where did this introduction take place?'

'At the Australian Embassy in Belgrade. Some cocktail party Donald was hosting – I was visiting and staying with Donald. It was my suggestion that Mujo get in touch with me when he came to Canberra on his posting…'

'And at the time, Fenchurch was your lover?'

'Yes. Well, we were long-time friends, and we had been going out together. But not now.' Jo bit her lip. She realised that Donald sometimes wished he hadn't introduced her to Mujo. He and Jo had been an item before his posting to Belgrade. By the time he returned to Australia, Jo and Mujo were lovers and Donald had to accept being just good friends with Jo.

'You don't go out together now?'

'No.'

'Except for Saturday evening, 18 May last, perhaps?'

'What?' Jo was astounded at what was known about her.

'The Saturday night after your interview with ASIO?'

'Yes. Donald and I had a meal together at University House, where he was staying. But no, we don't go out together as a couple. We're still very good friends. We meet up for meals sometimes, yes,' Jo stuttered. Jo and Donald had often eaten at University House's bistro, enjoying its quiet ambience and excellent cellar.

'You were particularly keen to see him that night, weren't you? It was not a coincidence that you wanted to talk with him just after your security clearance was withdrawn?'

'No. Well, yes, I wanted to ask him to be my character referee.'

'Did you need to wine and dine with him, and hold hands afterwards, to secure that? To have him help look after you?'

'This is so unfair… ASIO spying on us… Who authorised that?'

'Just answer the question, Dr Rowan,' the president directed.

Jo cast her mind back. After eating at the bistro, she and Donald had walked on the veranda beside the goldfish pool, laughing at the urban myth that Bob Hawke, before becoming prime minister, had stripped and swum its forty metres, a bit hard in a pool that was barely eighteen inches deep. Donald affectionately took Jo's hand, swung it, and asked her about Mujo. Their conversation came back.

'You seem pretty attached to him,' Donald had suggested.

'Yes, he has a calming effect,' Jo had said.

'Wine, whisky and smokes will do that to anyone,' Donald jibed.

'We both drink too much, and smoke too much. That's why I can relax with him, guilt free. But I know, he knows, we can't be soulmates in that forever sense.'

'You should have settled for me, Jo. We could have had a good forever.'

'Our moment passed, Donald! You had a woman in every port… I'd rather be unattached with lots of lovers, than committed to a man I had to share with other women.'

'Your loss, Josephine!'

'Arrogant pig!' She had laughed and, unhappy as she was, squeezed his hand.

The president's raised voice brought her back to the present.

'Fenchurch is a pretty useful contact for you: a former diplomat and intelligence expert in the ONA. He knows how intelligence agencies work, tells you how to handle your problem with, uh, ASIO?'

Jo hesitated. It was true she knew Donald still had connections to various intelligence agencies in Australia and overseas and yes, she thought he might be able to throw some light on what was happening to her. She tried to explain, but was cut short.

'And over dinner, you asked him whether your relationship with Mujo Zukić could be the source of ASIO's concern, didn't you?'

Jo felt herself flushing. Had someone overheard them, followed them? Or had they interrogated Donald? What had he told them? She tried to picture whether anyone had been sitting near their table. But she only recalled Donald swivelling Shiraz in a glass while she told him about her relationship with Mujo. 'We – well, he – has a gentle understanding of me that I don't get from many people,' she had said. 'We enjoy things together – listening to music, sharing books, exchanging ideas.'

'Ah, please, spare me the details,' Donald had said evenly but lowering his eyes.

Jo had laughed. 'Sorry, just trying to explain that, well, we don't know that much about each other and never discuss our work in any detail. And I wouldn't discuss this in any detail with him.'

'No, I'd be careful there.' Donald had said. 'He'll be tailed, as a matter of course, and therefore you too.'

She glared at the President. 'I did ask Donald Fenchurch, yes, if my relationship with Mujo Zukić might be behind ASIO's revoking of my clearance,' she admitted, 'or whether it was more likely to do with my investigation of Annette Armstrong's failed promotion bid. I told him about the leaked memo Armstrong had received, suggesting someone was trying to rig the promotion process.'

'And what was Mr Fenchurch's opinion?' the president asked.

'He couldn't see why Mujo or his consulate would have any interest in anything I was doing at Immigration. Anyway, Mujo and I don't talk about our work…'

'So you have already said. But now, Dr Rowan, did you ask Fenchurch to find out what he could?'

'No, I certainly did not,' Jo protested. 'He said something like "I'll see what I can find out, but I'm not an intelligence insider these days," which I took to mean, he'd try to find out if Mujo Zukić might be of interest to ASIO. After all,' she rushed on, 'if there is reason for me to distrust Mujo, I would want to know. Just as you people should tell me, if you think Mujo is a problem. No one has suggested that my seeing him poses a security risk.'

'Did you consider it proper that Fenchurch might probe around to help you?'

'I didn't ask him to. I told Donald that I was not asking him to do anything he shouldn't. The only favour I asked for was a reference. And he provided that.'

The president put down the piece of paper she had been reading from and thanked Jo for her patience. She handed over to Brooke.

Brooke stood up. She simply asked, 'Dr Rowan, have you ever disclosed any sensitive or classified information to any person unauthorised to receive such information?'

'No, I have not.'

'Have you ever passed on any classified documents to any person without permission?'

'No, I have not.'

'Tribunal, despite the intense and personal questions you have put to Dr Rowan, albeit at Mr Prendergast's instigation, no allegations have been made that she has breached security in any way. That is, none that have been revealed to me or Dr Rowan in today's proceedings. Therefore, there is nothing more that I can elicit from Dr Rowan that would assist the tribunal. Unless the tribunal has questions of its own for Dr Rowan, of course.'

It was close to four o'clock. The tribunal started to pack their papers, and the president announced that submissions would have to wait for a new hearing at a date to be fixed.

Brooke raised her overriding concern again. 'Without knowing any specific details of the security risk allegedly posed by Dr Rowan, it is difficult for me to formulate a submission. And of course, under the Act, I am not permitted in the hearing room during submissions from the director-general of security.'

Brooke's statement was ignored. The president said the tribunal would consult Mr Prendergast and that the registrar would notify the parties in due course of a resumed hearing date. In the meantime, she reminded Jo and Brooke they were not to discuss any aspect of the proceedings with any person. 'Do you understand?'

They both replied, 'Yes.'

The tribunal members rose, turned and marched out of the room. Jo stepped out of the witness box. The clerk packed up and the fan continued to click on every revolution.

Brooke looked at Jo. 'Let's go. Let's get out of here. Grab some of those books for me please, Jo. Thanks.'

'I need a smoke,' gasped Jo, picking up a pile of books.

'Good, I need a drink and we both need some fresh air and some daylight. We haven't had much of those today,' Brooke replied.

16

Thursday evening, 3 October 1991

It was a bar that allowed smoking. Young men and women in tight black unisex trousers and floral shirts with starched clerical collars were shepherding trays of glasses through tables. Some wore sleeveless black waistcoats. All were run off their feet, appearing out of the smoke haze to replace dirty ashtrays and collect used glasses before melting back into the fog. The walls sported old advertising posters – 'Time for a Capstan', 'Craven A: They never vary' – with avant garde women out of the 20s in sleek-fitting skirts flared below mid-thigh, smoking cigarillos in long black holders, intent on praising bourbon and goodness knows what. Smoke streamed up to extractor fans in the ceiling.

Brooke scraped her stool across the wooden floor to where she could see Jo without craning around the pole in the centre of their small round table. The available chairs were occupied and Brooke regretted not only having to perch on a stool where her tight skirt wriggled its way to the top of her thighs, but the noise: noise of an echo chamber full of screeching chimpanzees. Chimps were chimps, but there was nothing endearing about this barn full of loud people. She was tired as well as intolerant.

Jo inhaled and lifted her chin to puff smoke slowly into the air. 'I feel as if I've been raped,' she stated matter-of-factly.

Brooke leant forward, not quite catching her words.

'I feel I've been raped,' Jo almost shouted.

'Oh, gosh, Jo. No.' Brooke was horrified. 'What can I say? Only that I'm outraged for you. The intrusion into your life, cameras and tape recorders, it's disgusting. But you handled yourself so well, and I'm in awe of you.'

'I'm angry. Can't you see? You didn't say much! Just left me to it.'

Brooke jolted upright, realising only then that Jo was angry with her. 'It was out of my hands, Jo. The best I could hope for was that ASIO had blotted its copy book. Prendergast's questions were about events after you lost your clearance. The tribunal isn't stupid. They'll ask why you received an adverse assessment in the first place. That's what you appealed against. And they twigged that the questions were more about what Mujo might have told you when it's what you might have told him that's relevant.'

'Ever optimistic Brooke,' Jo muttered.

'I'm not exactly optimistic, but there is still a glimmer of hope. You answered everything thrown at you and that impressed them.'

'Oh, God, you lawyers. You love it, don't you? It's a game. But what about the pawns, like me? What justice do I get?' Jo exhaled again, looking up to the ceiling. 'The only secret I've learnt is that our so-called "intelligence" agency spies on innocent people, takes cameras into their bedrooms and records conversations. My memoirs will make good reading.'

Brooke, unusually, was at a loss for words. Fortunately the drinks tray arrived and Brooke passed Jo a glass of wine. Jo muttered a thank you and swigged as if it were medicine.

'What I'm trying to say, Jo, is that it seemed clear from the questions that, while you've been seeing Mujo for some time, ASIO has only recently shown an interest in you.'

Jo just looked at her. 'We know that. It's like I told you. Alarm bells rang when I began investigating Annette's grievance and I asked to see files relating to Operation Fishnet, as we can now call it. They hashed that one, didn't they?'

Brooke giggled. 'Prendergast is a prick. In a rush, must have left the full word in his question for the president to read. That is funny.'

'Nothing's funny,' Jo said. 'Did you notice that they didn't ask about taking material home?'

'Yes, their focus seemed to be on Operation Fishnet – whether you mentioned it to Mujo or vice versa.' Brooke took a sip of wine, and holding her glass with both hands stared at it as if it held some answers.

'Thinking aloud, it looks like ASIO might be frightened that if you had access to those files, you and Mujo might twig to some important secret.'

'Ironic, isn't it?' Jo replied. 'I couldn't have asked him about something I didn't know. Now, I know what to ask.'

'Don't be tempted. Seriously, Jo, you must not mention that operation's name to him. You've given an undertaking, and ASIO will be watching you both like hawks.'

Jo stubbed out her cigarette and said nothing. Brooke let it go. Switching to something lighter, she chatted about her dogs, and how it was probably time to go home and feed them.

Jo listened. Then, staring at Brooke, she said, 'You needn't worry. I can look after myself. Anyway, these voyeurs are going to be disappointed because from now on I won't be seeing much of Mujo, not in the bedroom anyway.'

Brooke raised her eyebrows.

'He's going home at Christmas to spend time with his children and try and reconcile with his wife.'

Brooke winced. 'Oh, I'm sorry.'

'He thinks his days here are numbered anyway. Yugoslavia is disintegrating and tensions with Australia are building up. He could be recalled at any time. So, either way, it's goodbye.'

They stood up, their conversation destroyed by the rowdy groups greeting each other.

'No regrets, though. Great sex,' Jo smiled, without convincing Brooke she was happy.

'Shocked, Brooke? You're frowning.'

'No, envious!' Brooke was indeed envious of Jo's love life: a sexy foreigner and, before him, Donald. Why did Jo give Donald up? He would not have brought her the trouble that came with Mujo. But it wasn't those thoughts that had caused Brooke's frown. It was seeing Jo so deeply troubled. A tall poppy whose petals had been plucked one by one. Unhappy Jo.

'You need a fella, Brooke. One you can call up and dismiss as you please. One who won't interfere with your work,' Jo said.

'Easier said than done, Jo, particularly when you live out of town with a menagerie. I can attract a man for a while, but when they see my priorities, they lose interest.'

'Well, I envy your stability, Brooke. You seem to be on an even keel at work and home.'

'Is that code for boring?'

'Not at all,' Jo replied, looking at Brooke with her penetrating green eyes. 'Stability matters when the chips are down.'

17

November 1991

The house seemed too quiet to be hosting a party. Jo parked behind just two other cars. The Red Hill residence of the Yugoslav ambassador was more modest than those of embassy residences around the corner in Mugga Way, Canberra's most prestigious street.

The last thing she felt like was being social. She had accepted Mujo's invitation to the soirée because she wanted to let him know about the hearing. She was greeted at the door by the ambassador's wife, a pleasant woman in her late forties, who spoke clearly enunciated English.

'Pleased to meet you, Dr Rowan. Mujo speaks often of you and your work.'

'Thank you for inviting me, Mrs Nikolić.' Jo carefully pronounced the last letter as a 'ch', and held a hand towards her gracious host. 'It's good to meet you at last.'

'Come. I'll introduce you to my husband, Mirko. He's probably chewing Mujo's ear off.'

The living room was large and functionally furnished with a few imported rugs on the polished wooden floor. Only a handful of guests had arrived and they were standing in small groups, punch glasses in their hands. The several non-Slavic faces stood out including Larry, the ASIO spook she had met some months ago through Mujo. His dress was neat casual this time; white polo-neck skivvy under a brown suede jacket, at least not looking like a spy who was trying not to look like a spy. He smiled at her as though relieved to see someone he knew. Mujo and Mirko Nikolić were carrying on a discussion in Serbian. Mujo turned to welcome Jo and introduce her to his boss. After a civil exchange, they resumed their conversation, this time, as a courtesy to Jo, in English. She excused herself when she could and moved to greet Larry.

'How's the export business?' she asked with a sarcastic smile.

He responded, eyes amused. 'I've retired from business, keep myself out of mischief playing golf.'

Jo took that to mean that he was no longer working for ASIO. In any event, she wondered why he was here.

'And you?' he asked. 'I think you were starting a government consultancy when we met? How's it going?'

'No good, as I'm sure you know…' she said, slightly bitter. Then she saw surprise on his face. He was taken aback and she backed off. 'Oh, of course, sorry, there's no reason why Mujo would have mentioned my difficulties. I, er, ran into trouble accessing some information I needed.' Jo felt terrible, wishing she were somewhere else.

At that moment, Mujo joined them. 'Jo, you remember Larry?'

'Yes, of course. We're reacquainting.'

'Good to see you, Larry. Been quite a while.'

'Jo was telling me that her new job isn't working out as she'd hoped.'

'Umm, maybe comes from seeing too much of me? Perhaps some crazy person at Immigration suspects me of people smuggling and fears she'll tell me how they plan to stop the boats?'

Larry looked at Mujo and then turned to Jo.

Jo tried to read the subtext. Larry would have reported on her link with Mujo after their encounter at the café in Griffith last year. He seemed genuinely surprised to hear that her relationship with Mujo had been problematic. But his reaction convinced her that his report on her and Mujo would have confirmed their relationship as innocent. Now she realised that Mujo was renewing contact with Larry for her sake, hoping to discover something that could help her.

'Mujo and I have been out of touch. Our business interests diverged. Do you know who's behind your problem at work?'

'It's a mystery to me.' Jo was wary of saying too much.

'Trouble is, we live in complex times,' Larry continued. 'The past sends messages to the future and every event has downstream consequences.

The system's left hand never seems to know what the right hand is doing. That's my take on the public service.'

Jo wondered if Larry was conveying a message to Mujo. Was he suggesting that a specific event from the past was causing Jo's problem?

Mujo leant over to tap a long ash from his cigarette and looked up at Larry. When their eyes met, Mujo gave a barely discernible nod and changed the subject. 'What have you been up to, Larry? Seen anything of Eugene?' he asked.

'Golf, and no, to answer both questions,' said Larry. 'Happy to embrace the simple life, pottering and hitting a ball when I want some fresh air. Don't know about Eugene. He's retired too.'

A plate of canapés appeared. Jo didn't feel like eating. Larry helped himself. Mujo preferred a whisky from the tray that followed. Perfume wafted in with a voluptuous woman who pushed herself into the circle.

She put an arm around Mujo and said, 'You must please introduce me to your friends.' Her teeth gleamed under red painted lips and her thick dark hair was piled and secured by a single clip.

After Jo mentally removed the clip, she saw a temptress willing to put her long black curls to seductive use. Indeed, still holding Mujo, she was already seducing Larry with her deep blue eyes.

'Watching over me, are you, Marika? My friends, Jo and Larry. This is my associate, Marika Babić, whose job is to keep her eyes on me!'

Marika jangled with silver and gold bracelets. She kissed Larry's left cheek, right cheek, left cheek and held her hand out to Jo. High cheekbones and a tanned skin made for a strong face. A large colourful brooch and a tight black cocktail dress drew the eye to an ample bosom. It wasn't Jo's style to gush about a brooch any more than it was to tell or laugh at jokes. She said hello to Marika, politely but without being drawn into her aura.

Larry was still goggling. It was his turn to say something. In typical Australian style, he addressed Mujo for Marika's benefit. 'Where have you been hiding her, Mujo?' He turned to Marika and looked her up and down. 'You can watch over me, any time.'

Jo rolled her eyes.

Mujo caught her reaction and, standing close enough to squeeze her hand, he whispered, 'Game. It's always a game.'

Marika, Serbian with possible Greek or Turkish ancestry, was happy to flirt with Larry even though he was old enough to be her father, and they chatted intimately.

Mujo led Jo away, whispering, 'She's looking for a meal ticket. She'll want to talk with you too, anyone who might be able to help her start a new life. She thinks you work with Immigration.'

Jo nearly smiled. 'She's got that one wrong. Surely your ambassador knows what she's up to?'

'He doesn't care. No more than I do. We can't help her, but good luck to her if she can wangle a defection.'

'Who else is here?' Jo asked, watching more people being greeted by Madam Ambassador.

'The people who've stayed our friends, not swinging with the politics of the day. We want to thank people now while we can. But I don't have to stay tonight. I'll excuse myself – to take you for a drive, or home?'

Oh, God, Jo thought, perhaps we'll wind up in bed again.

Someone claimed Mujo's attention and Jo hovered until, as predicted, Marika swept towards her and asked about her work in Immigration.

'Mujo said you worked there. He's fond of you, you know.'

Jo nodded, listened and answered politely. Marika soon realised Jo wasn't able to provide the help she needed and floated off to pounce on a new arrival, winking at Larry as she passed.

'Come, let's go.' It was Mujo beside her again.

Polite thank yous and goodbyes to the hosts and they were into the still air and falling dusk.

At the summit of Red Hill, a scenic landmark, Mujo parked where they could see the panorama of the city's lights. A brightly lit glass-walled hexagon of the restaurant flashed a welcome festive feel. Doors slammed as the evening's diners arrived.

Mujo and Jo looked over the safety fence, watching car lights toing and froing along the avenues that fanned out from Parliament House to the suburbs.

'Nice,' Jo murmured.

Mujo turned to face her. 'Yes, but now we can talk. Tell me about you and the hearing.'

Jo told him that she was cobbling up a second best report using the material she had already collected, and that she was losing hope of ever clearing her name.

'They asked a lot about you at the tribunal. What you've told me about your work and what I might have told you about Immigration.' She was willing to say that much. 'And tonight, Larry seemed to hint that you might know something from the past that could be the problem.'

'He did. I think he wants to help.'

'Whatever it is, no one cared till I went to Immigration. Not then, either, until I asked to see the files about that messy promotion process I mentioned.'

Mujo reached for his cigarettes and offered one to Jo. Eventually he asked, 'What job was she trying for?'

'It was in a section dealing with refugees, how to stop people arriving by boat, supposedly illegally. You picked it with your joke tonight.'

'Plenty written about it in the papers.'

'Yes, but they try to keep everything secret.'

'Our only interest is in what the Croatians are up to. Are they still recruiting people here to fight in my homeland? Where do their weapons come from, that sort of thing.'

'Why would Larry be concerned? Is he your friend?'

'Not friend, but good man. Asking me to look back on what I have learned. Something that might help you or something someone doesn't want me to tell you?'

'My lawyer and I have focused on what ASIO thinks I might have leaked to you. Could it be the opposite? That is, something I might learn from you? Something that embarrasses Immigration or ASIO? That would explain a lot.'

Mujo seemed lost in thought. 'Remember my joke that it might be what I could tell you, not you telling me,' he said.

'Yes, you joked about Pine Gap…'

'Hmm, I don't think Pine Gap is a problem. But remember, I told you that one of our men was shot by one of yours?'

'Yes. You didn't explain how, or why.'

'An Aussie cop shot him thinking he was Croatian gunrunner. Listen carefully, Jo. This is complicated. Bozin was his name and he was engaged by us to infiltrate Croatian Ustashi. His job was to collect rifles from the wharf in Darwin and take them to several picnic camps. He'd give my people names and places and we shared that with ASIO.'

'Yes. Go on.'

'Well, your people were running similar operation. It seems the man importing rifles became their informant. There was a stuff-up because when Bozin turned up to collect the rifles, this cop, informant's handler, was there. It's never been explained why he was there. Australia's plan was to let buyer go but follow him to picnic camps, and make arrests there. Quite unnecessary, as Bozin would have told us who and where and we'd have passed that on. The cop didn't know that. He said Bozin pulled a gun and that he shot him in self-defence.'

'Well, that would be embarrassing if it came out – but I can't see why it would trouble Immigration if I knew.'

'Embarrassing for both sides. We certainly kept it quite. It became my job to negotiate compensation for Bozin's family because it's doubtful it was self-defence. Bozin was shot from behind, not in front. The importer provided witness statement supporting of cop. But he would support his police handler, wouldn't he?'

'If not in self-defence, why would the cop kill Bozin?'

'Might have thought he'd tell Croatians it was a set-up and that'd make him useless. Everyone was vague about the shooting and where it took place. It wasn't at the cargo dock. I didn't pursue it. When compensation for the widow was agreed, my job was done.'

Jo swung to face Mujo and grabbed his lapels. 'So the rifles could have been smuggled in with refugees on a fishing boat? That would fit.'

'Could be. Tracking Croatian terrorists is not Immigration's business, but…'

'Illegal boats carrying rifles is.' Jo finished the sentence for him, and released her grip. 'Immigration would be livid if a people smuggler was bringing in rifles to help ASIO identify Croatian terrorists.'

'If Immigration were told.'

'That's the complication,' Jo said. 'ASIO wouldn't want those dots joined up, particularly as the operation was a botch and a Serb agent was shot. It would come out that ASIO was working with Serbs against Croatians – more than embarrassing.'

'And if I'd told you all this earlier, you might have questioned whole thing as consultant to the Immigration, telling them something they knew nothing about.'

'And that would account for ASIO wanting me out of the department, while Immigration only wanted me out of their files.' She stopped and shivered. 'Hey, it's chilly. Let's go back to the car.'

'This is lot of ifs,' Mujo said as they slid into the car.

Joe was still puzzling out a possible scenario. 'But what does the importer get out of lying for the cop? His role finished when Bozin was shot.'

'It would give him a hold over his handler.'

'What, blackmail the cop to turn a blind eye to his regular smuggling?'

Mujo nodded. 'That's possible. There must be some waterfront corruption, for rifles to ever get in. Bozin had connections there. That's why we engage him.'

'What if the importer's still smuggling other stuff on refugee boats.'

Mujo raised his eyebrows. 'Perhaps we're beginning to make connections.' He started the car. 'Come, we go. I take you home. I stay, and we get your car tomorrow.'

Jo didn't argue, knowing their evenings together were numbered.

She kept thinking aloud as the car wound down the steep narrow road. 'When did this happen? I'd like to check whether the shooting incident coincided with a boat load of refugees. That's the connection to Immigration.'

Mujo answered quietly, 'I can get hold of copies of statements we were given, and my report. It will have dates and names of the importer and policeman. It's the least I can do.'

'It's not your fault. It's amoral spooks and faceless grey suits who are ruining my life. Best not give me any papers…not until my case is over. Just the date of that shooting incident. I'll match it against refugee boat arrivals.' She had a plan.

18

Jo felt invigorated. She wasn't sure how Mujo's revelations might help her fight ASIO. But if the bungled killing of Bozin could be linked to a boat being tracked by Immigration, Brooke might be able to convince the tribunal that ASIO was targeting Jo to protect itself. Jo wasn't a document leaker; but her work might require her to tell an embarrassing story about an intelligence stuff-up and cover-up.

She was still being paid to finish her Immigration consultancy, though without access to all the material she needed. She continued to talk with departmental staff, Annette Anderson in particular. Annette had access to an archive of newspaper cuttings and, if she was willing, might save Jo a lot of time wading through newspapers at the National Library.

'I'm interested in any dates when boat people arrived in Darwin during November 1989, particularly arrivals around Saturday 18 November. I'll explain later.'

Annette was happy to help, and soon confirmed that Saturday 18 November 1989 saw the first of a new wave of boats arriving in Darwin. 'Twenty-six Indochinese passengers, plus Indonesian crew, disembarked,' she reported. 'Two more boats soon followed, both caught on camera.'

They arranged to meet privately, as Jo thought Annette might know more than she felt able to talk about on the phone. And so it was.

'That first boat was burned,' she said when Jo asked if any contraband had been found on board. 'That was reported in one of the local papers. Here.' Annette fished around in her soft leather grip, big enough to double as a briefcase. She pulled out a wad of photocopied press reports and handed one to Jo.

'So it was the federal police who had the people smuggler's boat burned?'

'Yes, that's normal. It's a precaution against officials or civilians scavenging any money, gold or jewellery that asylum seekers are forced to leave behind. Some Chinese asylum seekers, trying to avoid the one-child policy, or disillusioned by Tiananmen Square, try to bring in portable assets. A Senior Detective Mitch Ormandy gave the order to burn this boat.'

'Whoever he may be.'

'Must get back to work, Jo.' Annette made to go.

'One more favour, Annette, if you don't mind. Can you check for reports of other incidents in Darwin that day? I'm looking for anything about a man being shot.'

'I wish I knew what this is all about, Jo. Something Special Projects wanted hidden from you and me?'

'I promise I'll fill you in, if I can piece an explanation together. But I have to be sure. Just confine your search to newspaper reports. Wouldn't want you dumped too.'

Annette stood up, buttoned her too-tight jacket, said goodbye, and left.

'I've got something for you Jo.' It was an excited Annette on the phone. 'A man was shot in the marina on the 18th. The initial report said he couldn't be named until "overseas relatives" had been informed. Can't have been an asylum seeker, though. Everyone on the boat was accounted for.'

Jo sat up. 'Any follow-up?'

'Yes, two days later, a very small report that a suspected smuggler had been killed by a federal policeman in self-defence. Allegedly, the police officer tried to arrest him and the man shot at him. The officer returned fire, killing the man. The policeman wasn't injured.'

Jo was about to speak but Annette had more.

'But here's the thing. Guess who the policeman was?'

'The policeman who gave the order to destroy the fishing boat?'

'Yep. Senior Detective Ormandy. Sounds like the shooting might have been over some contraband on the asylum seekers' boat.'

'Did the papers eventually give the dead man a name?'

'Yes, Miroslav Bozin, for what it's worth, a Serb.'

'It's everything I need to know. Thank you, Annette. I owe you an explanation and a big lunch. Soon. First, I want to see if Brooke can use any of this in my hearing.'

'Good luck, Jo.'

Jo decided it was time to let Furzer know about her discovery. She wanted him to know that ASIO had tried to stop her work in the department because, potentially, she might learn too much. And now she would enjoy seeing Furzer fuming that his department had been kept in the dark about ASIO using a boat that Immigration was trying to stop. Informing Furzer was not breaching security; on the contrary, it was her duty to tell him. That'll screw them, she thought.

Furzer listened without revealing whether the news had surprised him. He thanked her and warned her to keep it to herself.

'Tell me you didn't know about this,' Jo insisted. 'I would never forgive you if you'd stood by and watched them treat me like this.'

'If it's true, Jo, I certainly didn't know. I'll make enquiries. And I must direct you to keep out of Immigration's affairs now. I hope the tribunal returns your clearance so that you can write a useful report.'

'You're pissed off, aren't you, Mike?' Jo sensed it. They had once enjoyed an intimate relationship, and now he was doing his best to keep his head of department hat firmly on his head.

'We'll talk later, when your hearing's over,' he said.

Jo took her leave. She felt good; or at least better than a week ago. She hoped she had set the cat amongst the pigeons. Furzer would be questioning people in the Special Projects Section. If they had no knowledge of the overlapping operation, he would seek explanations up the line.

But any elation she had felt at stirring up the department was short-lived. Fingering their failure wouldn't reverse the damage being done to her. She needed to update Brooke before the tribunal resumed.

Brooke jumped when the car phone rang. It was just before six and she was driving home. She leaned to press the answer button, skidding slightly on the gravel as she pulled off the road. It was Jane, her clerk.

'The tribunal registrar rang to say your security case is being listed for further hearing next week.'

Excitement and alarm swept over Brooke as she braked. 'For submissions, or more evidence, did she say?'

Smart Jane had thought to ask that question. 'Oral submissions.'

Brooke had been trying to put Jo's case out of her mind for weeks, tackling the backlog of chamber work to be done between court commitments. But Jo's case kept resurfacing. She believed that the tribunal had been annoyed by ASIO's questions about what Mujo might have told Jo, rather than the reverse. Now, Jo's discoveries might help her demonstrate that ASIO was using the tribunal to camouflage its own agenda. Could she convince the tribunal?

Jo appeared flat when Brooke met her the next day. Brooke wanted her instructions on the conditions she would accept if the tribunal gave her a qualified security clearance.

'For example, they might award you clearance at a lower level, or access to files pre-approved by Furzer.'

'Do I care any more?' Jo said, head bowed, eyes down.

'Yes, you do. Or if you don't, I do,' Brooke said.

'Whatever you think,' was Jo's response. All fight was gone. She was accepting whatever this problematic legal system might dispense.

Brooke was unsurprised that Jo was depressed. Her life was on hold and her reputation clouded. She was under contract to complete a report, but without access to the material she needed. And even though the hearing would finish in a week, there was no guarantee of a quick decision.

Brooke did her best when she presented at the tribunal the following week. She was aware that her anxiety reflected in her strained voice. It was the tribunal's task to review the reasons for ASIO's decision to revoke Jo's security clearance and yet, she submitted, neither she nor Jo had been provided with those reasons. While Jo had been observed, tracked, filmed and followed, no evidence was offered to suggest that Jo had breached security in any way. As she spoke, she heard the echo of the hollowness of her words. She paused. She knew she had to tackle ASIO head on.

'It is my submission that ASIO has not acted in good faith. To demonstrate this, I ask the tribunal to compare the edited transcript of Jo's ASIO's interview with the full interview as recorded. The transcript provided to you is not a true record of what took place. Secondly, ASIO seems more concerned with events that took place after my client's clearance was revoked, suggesting that there was no basis for its adverse assessment of her. For these reasons, I suggest that ASIO has no concern about Dr's Rowan's access to Immigration files, but that it acted to prevent her having a presence in the department altogether.'

'What are you saying, Ms Talbot?' the president asked.

'I am suggesting that ASIO has abused its power, and that it has no real fear of Dr Rowan misusing information from Immigration files. Rather, it fears that Dr Rowan might possess information that ASIO wants to keep from Immigration.'

'Do we have evidence of this extraordinary assertion, Ms Talbot?'

'It is circumstantial, but plausible, and there is some supporting evidence on the public record.'

'If this is new evidence, Ms Talbot,' the president said, 'you realise it will have to be put to the director-general's counsel for a response.'

Brooke expected this, but had nothing to lose. 'Yes, Madam President. Let me start by saying that Dr Rowan's relationship with the foreign diplomat, Mujo Zukić, about which we have heard so much, is relevant, under my suggested scenario. Remember, his country is not hostile to Australia. On the contrary, Yugoslavia's intelligence agency and ASIO have worked on several projects of mutual interest. It is what he might have told Dr Rowan, but did not as it happens, that has alarmed ASIO.'

Brooke outlined the evidence that suggested that Immigration was never told about the use of a refugee boat for an ASIO operation. She detailed the news reports revealing Ormandy's dual role in the waterfront incidents and how Rowan, with her links to Zukić and access to Immigration files, might learn about two conflicting intelligence operations. 'Somewhat embarrassing to ASIO, one might surmise, Tribunal.'

'It's speculation, Ms Talbot,' the president said.

'Deprived of reasons for ASIO's decision, I can only speculate why ASIO might have taken this extraordinary action against my client. No one has suggested Dr Rowan poses a security risk. I am offering a reason why ASIO wanted it to appear so.'

'Do you have anything further, to add, Ms Talbot?'

'Only this, Tribunal. My submission is that, in the absence of evidence that my client might or has engaged in subversive conduct, an adverse security assessment is not warranted. However, if there is legitimate concern about my client having access to certain files, then, I submit that a qualified assessment should apply. That is, Dr Rowan's access to any sensitive files be restricted or subject to supervision by the head of the Department of Immigration.'

'Are you putting a proposal to us, Ms Talbot?'

'My submission is that Dr Rowan should have her high level clearance restored. If not, I am instructed that my client is prepared to accept appropriate but limited restrictions on access to sensitive files for the duration of her current contract.'

The tribunal adjourned to consider its decision.

One week, two weeks, nothing. Christmas came and went.

19

February 1992

Jo entered the Hyatt from the back stairs and made her way through the open lounge to the northern terrace, where a slight breeze fanned the hot February day.

Mujo stood up and greeted her warmly.

'How was Belgrade, and your family?' she asked.

'Belgrade grey and cold in politics and weather but my little frogs are my sunshine.'

'And Andjela?'

'She is well, too. We talk more about that later. First you?'

They sat down and talked. Jo didn't want to dampen things by beginning with an ASIO saga that was still going nowhere.

When an opening came, she returned to Andjela. 'Will you get back together, do you think?'

'We want to. Not just for children, but for us, for family life. Does this upset you?'

'You were always on loan, I knew that,' Jo replied graciously. 'And I want you to be happy. We can never be the family you want.'

'I told her about you. It is better she knows. She has affair too, I am sure. I didn't ask and she didn't say.'

'You suggested I meet her, so we can stay friends. Is she comfortable with that?'

'She would be okay. But we are not sure should she come here or not. My country is a mess. She wants to come, and bring her parents too, and stay. But then there's my mother. What they'd do to her if we defected.'

'But how can you keep working for Milošević?'

'What choice do I have? I ask for post somewhere else. My ethnicity helps me in a peculiar way. I demonstrate his racial tolerance, help him deny that he has a policy of ethnic cleansing.'

'It won't be comfortable wherever you are, representing a Serb-dominated government, will it?' Jo asked.

'No.'

Yugoslavia's consulate purported to represent the whole of the country even as more states were shouting for independence and Milošević was resisting them with force. Gareth Evans, the Foreign Minister, had already announced Australia's support for the now-independent states of Croatia and Slovenia, and Prime Minister Keating had just affirmed that stance.

Mujo blew smoke at the ceiling. 'It's possible our consulate here will be closed. Things are changing rapidly, including your government's attitude to mine. But enough of my prospects, what about yours? The case?'

'No decision yet,' Jo explained. 'I tracked down the 1989 shooting incident, and we were right. It happened the day boat people arrived, and importantly, the same federal police officer was involved in both incidents. That's the link.'

Mujo looked pleased. 'Could your lawyer use it?'

'Yes. She submitted to the tribunal that my adverse assessment had nothing to do with my integrity, and everything to do with ASIO protecting itself from embarrassment.'

'Did they buy it?'

'Don't know yet, but she's hoping that, whatever they do, they'll agree that there was no case for an adverse assessment.'

Mujo raised his glass.

Jo didn't. 'Nothing to celebrate,' she said. 'My name might, hopefully, be cleared, but my lawyer, Brooke, thinks that the tribunal will still restrict my access to files. Whatever stuff-ups ASIO has made, the tribunal is likely to agree that the situation not be worsened by my learning the extent of it.'

The noise level was rising and Mujo looked around. Friday's workers were tumbling in for happy hour, and the terrace was becoming crowded with public servants and business people talking loudly about the week that was. No one appeared to be watching them.

He whispered, 'I have those papers about the shooting. I bring next time we meet. Best we not talk here.'

The phone call that night was startling and chilling.

'Dr Rowan?'

'Who is this?'

'Alec Brown. You don't know me and I apologise for intruding, but it is important I talk with you in private, before your tribunal gives its decision.'

Jo said nothing. Was she being hoaxed? Should she hang up?

As if reading her thoughts, the voice said, 'It is in your interest to listen. I have a proposal which would let you continue your consultancy work unhindered.'

'And who the hell are you?'

'I work with Australian Intelligence, and I'm on the team in your case.'

After absorbing the shock that she might be speaking to one of the very spooks who had turned her life upside down, people she could only picture as shadowy fluid blobs with mean faces, she managed to say, 'If this is an offer of some kind to settle my case, you should ask your lawyers to put it to mine.'

'Quite right. But I need to discuss it with you first, in private. If you agree, and I think you will, the lawyers can finalise formal terms of settlement.'

If Jo hadn't known what she now did about ASIO's embarrassing secrets, she would have hung up. But then, the thought raced through her mind, this man wouldn't be ringing unless he was worried about the tribunal's pending decision. Of course he'd know what she knew, because Brooke's submission had been sent to ASIO for a response. Why shouldn't she find out what he had to say?

'I need to be sure you are who you say you are,' she said.

He suggested she meet him at ASIO headquarters in the Russell Offices the following Monday. She would be signed in and escorted to his office. She was satisfied by that.

Jo put down the phone and thought of ringing Brooke, or Donald. She wanted someone's advice. The man hadn't told her not to. Then she realised that her phone would be bugged and it was clear from his tone that she was expected to keep quiet and come alone. It was better anyway that she appeared strong; not in need of support. If ASIO was on the back foot, it couldn't hurt for her to go, hear what he had to say, and decide from there.

Jo spent a restless weekend alone, as she often did, scribbling notes about everything that had happened; working out what she might get away with in her book.

The fountain, a forty-metre water spout, was sucking up the calm waters of Lake Burley Griffin and spray drifted across Commonwealth Bridge. Jo turned on the wipers and told herself to be calm, to listen to what Brown had to say but not feel compelled to respond. But what would he say?

Russell, a suburb of government offices, full of car parks and free of shops and crowds, was probably a safe place for a clandestine meeting with the spook, Brown. Thinking rationally did nothing to allay her anxiety.

Now facing the man across a paperless desk in an interview room with a 'Private' sign on the closed door, she fixed him with a steady gaze and waited. Something shiny held his hair down, she noticed.

Brown opened. 'It's come to our attention that you are still seeing that foreign friend of yours. He must trust you, mustn't he, offering you still more information?'

She tried not to flinch. How much of her conversation with Mujo had been heard? Brown's eyes were unreadable, probably in permanent shadow they were so deep-set. The fluorescent ceiling light cast its own shadow. His wiry eyebrows were a degree more expressive, one arched in anticipation of her response. But she was at a loss for words.

'You might do yourself a favour and, as the loyal national you claim you are, help us along the way. Accept our proposition, and your life can go on. If not, you probably won't work again.'

Like a lamb to the slaughter, she had come here to be crudely threatened. What had she expected? That he'd be reasonable? She had her back to the wall and a mugger's knife to her throat. Accept or else. Would Brooke have told her not to come? Probably. Perhaps that's why she hadn't asked. Curiosity had won and now she had to handle Brown as best she could.

Jo rolled her hand, inviting him to spell out his proposition. She knew that if she spoke, her voice would crack. All she could do was sit and listen.

20

Early March 1992

Sitting by the window of Red Belly Black, the café on the ground floor of Brooke's building, Jo watched Brooke trip through the door in strappy high heels and a short tight skirt. Brooke looked as pleased as she had sounded when she had called to tell Jo of the tribunal's decision.

'They accepted my submission. Thanks to your investigative work. It's not a complete win, but your high reputation is no longer in doubt,' she had said to Jo on the phone.

'Am I meant to cheer?' Jo had replied.

Jo felt depressed and barely looked up when Brooke sat down opposite her and apologised for being a few minutes late.

'The phone rang, as it does, just as I was leaving.'

Jo didn't respond.

'I know you're disappointed we couldn't get your full clearance back, but you have access to material to "secret" level. That will allow you to finish your work, won't it?' The upward intonation reflected her diminishing hope that Jo might express the tiniest bit of pleasure over Brooke's win.

Jo didn't lift her head.

Brooke tried again. 'Your access to sensitive files will be supervised, but you can live with that, I hope.'

A waitress approached. They ordered coffee, and Brooke scrabbled around in her bag for a copy of the tribunal's decision.

'Sorry, Brooke,' Jo said, taking the paper, 'Yes, thank you for everything you've done. It's just, well…it's a qualified clearance, and too late, really.'

'I know. It's unfair. At least the tribunal recognised that none of what happened was your fault, and your being in the wrong place at the wrong time did not warrant an adverse assessment. You turned up at Immigration with the background to join the dots and jeopardise one of their stupid operations.'

Jo turned the paper over but it offered no reasons for the tribunal's decision. 'And I had no information to give, until this kangaroo court forced Mujo and me to look for it. Incompetent idiots.'

'You can always reapply for a higher clearance level if the need arises.'

'Huh, as if I would ever be offered another consultancy.'

'You don't think so?'

Jo spat, 'My integrity was trashed by people without any. Everyone will remember that I caused trouble, not that the tribunal secretly cleared my name. Anyway, there are new reasons now for doubting my future. If I didn't have valuable information before, I do now. I'd like to tell you more, but I can't.'

Coffee was set down on the table in front of the two women.

Brooke looked puzzled. 'Oh, okay. Are you sure you can't tell me?'

'You've done your job, Brooke. Sorry, no. It's me that's got to sort out where I go from here.'

Brooke nodded. 'It's an evil world when people can hide their criminality by smearing others. You couldn't have known that your relationship with Mujo would bring collateral damage with it. And I do understand your wanting to protect his interests.'

Jo didn't contradict Brooke's assumption that her reluctance to tell Brooke more was because of Mujo. Brown was 'persuasive' in demanding that she should not reveal what he had asked of her in that room. And she had no intention of compromising Brooke's integrity by telling her; Brooke would only want to take up her cause, and Jo had her own plan of action, and not one that Brooke would approve of. Not that Jo had agreed to Brown's proposed deal. Had she done so, she could have quietly resumed her career – just wouldn't have been able to live with herself.

She had told Brown that she'd rather risk an adverse tribunal decision than breach Mujo's trust. She had known that Brooke's submission wasn't going to deliver the result she wanted but, hopefully, some of the cockroaches associated with ASIO's dirty little operations had been hurt.

Brown had not been fazed by Jo's refusal to cooperate. 'Let me know if you change your mind,' he had said. 'I'm not asking you to spy on your boyfriend, just ask him some questions. He'll come to no harm, and you'll get your security clearance and peace of mind back.'

Now facing the trusty Brooke, she said nothing about the extraordinary proposition Brown put to her several weeks ago, or why she was depressed. Thinking about it, she hardly heard Brooke's commiserations. She was beyond caring. She knew that however it was sold, the security review process was a sham. The tribunal didn't care that she needed particular files to complete her work; to confirm the lack of a merit promotion process for senior women. It had kowtowed to ASIO, accepting its assessment that, even if she was not a security risk, her work at Immigration might generate one. She had nearly finished her book. The intense writing process had been a welcome distraction during the upheavals of the last year. There was a bit more she wanted to add now, though, and she was too tired to risk having Brooke censoring her.

'Jo? Are you okay?' Brooke asked, noticing that Jo was not listening.

'I was thinking about my book.' Jo tried to smile and said, 'I'm moving on. It's what I should do, isn't it?'

Brooke pushed her empty cup away. 'And Mujo?' she enquired, 'How is he coping with the difficult political situation?' It was clear that Australia intended to continue its recognition of various former Yugoslavian states as they asserted independence from the Serb-run Yugoslav government. 'Mujo must be feeling uncomfortable.'

'I'm not seeing him any more. He's likely to be sent home in the next few months. He'll reunite with his family,' Jo said with a smile of acceptance. 'Others in the consulate will go too, now that relations between Yugoslavia and our government have deteriorated. Mujo has no choice. His Muslim mother's in Belgrade, too old to travel, and he's reconciled with his wife. She's Serbian, which complicates things further.

I asked him not to contact me, except to let me know when he's about to leave.'

'Oh, I'm so sorry. It's terribly sad for you. The end of a fairy tale romance,' Brooke said softly, 'though I know you sort of expected it. '

Jo came back. 'Fairy tale? Passion, sex, romance, yes. But look at the fall-out — total destruction of my work and career and ruination of my gender-equity findings that potentially might have helped women in the public service. It's nothing short of bizarre.' Jo slumped back into vacancy.

Brooke leaned over and lightly touched her hand.

21

Wednesday 17 June 1992

'I'm calling to say goodbye. My consulate is packed up. I leave tomorrow,' Mujo came straight to the point when she picked up the phone.

Jo's heart sank. 'Will I see you before you go?' she asked.

'Tonight?' he suggested.

In May the Australian government had recognised the Republic of Bosnia-Herzegovina, adding it to the list of Yugoslav states it recognised which had already declared their independence. On 1 June, Prime Minister Paul Keating had announced Australia's support for the United Nations Security Council resolution to impose sanctions against Serbia and Montenegro, including 'a reduction in Belgrade's diplomatic representation'. Code for expelling us, Mujo explained. Australia had already downgraded its consular presence in Belgrade. The Yugoslav consulate was no longer welcome in Australia, purporting as it did to represent the whole of Yugoslavia. Mujo, though not a Serb, was a career public servant in the Milošević administration, and had to go.

'Where are you?' Jo asked him.

'I'm staying at the Hyatt and leaving early in morning. I'm packed, and car will be collected tomorrow.'

Jo had already eaten. She was at home finishing a publicity flyer for Jamisons, the publishers of her book. 'I'll be there in twenty minutes.'

Jo parked behind the Hyatt and entered the building from the rear. She climbed the stairs and walked to the lounge, where Mujo was sitting back on one of the long leather lounges. As always, he rose to greet her, and she saw shadows under his eyes.

They sat side by side, and he took her hand.

'It's time we say goodbye.'

'Are you all going, the ambassador and Marika too?'

'The consul-general, yes, in a day or two. Marika, as you know, sent here to keep eye on me, a trusted Serb with university degree and a future. Well, she managed to defect. She obtained visa permit and made application for residence. Larry helped her. The world is a strange place. I am rebuked for not informing on her.'

'You suspected, but did you know?'

'I didn't enquire. She do what I would like to do and can't. So I turn my head.' He looked at Jo, as if to take an imprint in his mind of every detail of her face, her features, her hair. 'I'd like to spend night with you…'

Before he could add 'but', Jo interrupted, 'I know. Me too, but we mustn't. We don't belong to each other, and we must move on… You, happily I hope, with Andjela and the children you love so much.'

'At least we kiss goodbye, but not here. I have some things I want to give to you before I go. We take a walk?'

Whispering as they walked, Jo said, 'Mujo, there's something I want to tell you. I couldn't tell you before, why I said I didn't want to see you again. I'm only telling you now because you're leaving tomorrow and there's no harm in it.'

Mujo stopped and looked at her.

'I gave an undertaking which I'm now going to break. I now know we were overheard when we were last here. Someone must have had a very sensitive tape recorder in their pocket.'

'It's always possible. But what could be made of it?'

They linked arms and strolled along the corridor and down the back stairs. She told him about her meeting with Brown. He shook his head in disbelief.

When she had finished her story, he squeezed her hand and said, 'I am so sorry for harm I have brought upon you. Thank you, brave Jo, for stand you take.'

'Now you understand, I couldn't afford to see you, or talk about anything.'

He stopped, let her hand go, and fished into his jacket pocket. 'Here are papers you might be interested in,' he said. 'The report of the shooting might help you fill in the jigsaw. Some explosive stuff for your book?'

She took the folded sheets and quickly slid them into her shoulder bag. 'Thanks, but, uh, it's too late for that. The book's with the publisher. But at least I don't have to hand over anything you give me to that bastard Brown. My case is over, and you'll be gone tomorrow. He's lost control over us.'

'The book is finished? Congratulations, Jo. Good work. You must send me a copy.'

As they approached the glass doors, a group entered, bringing a gust of wind.

'My car's just outside. It's warmer there and dry,' Jo suggested, feeling the drizzle on her hair as they left the portico.

She took the keys out of her shoulder bag and unlocked the driver's door. Mujo opened it for her and went around to the passenger seat.

They sat quietly staring through the spray on the windscreen at the footpath and windows in the brick wall of the hotel. They managed a few words about their joyous time together, but could not dispel their unsettled and sad feelings.

'I'll tell you something more. The man, Bozin, who was killed. We engaged him, not just to infiltrate Croatians, but to deliver them a supply of rifles.'

'Your government supplied Croatians with rifles?'

'To set them up, yes. Nasty business. Bozin used a list of names of customs officers who could be bribed. The list was sold to him by a former ASIO officer. He and the importer used corrupt officers to get rifles through customs. Our knowledge about this ASIO leak is embarrassing for them.'

Jo was astounded. This was a dangerous story, one that a foreign service could spill about ASIO. Although she hadn't known it, she potentially had access to it. And it was surely this that had cost her her job.

'Why are you telling me only now?'

'I didn't know. Only when packing up at the office, I find historic material, messages between our office and Bozin. I sent it home in diplomatic bag. Knowledge might help you if Brown tries to bully you again.'

They sat silently. Jo thought of Mujo's oft-used words: 'It's all a game.' Yes, a dangerous one.

He leaned over and handed Jo a neatly folded sheet of white A4 paper. 'For you to remember me.'

She held it up to the windscreen but there the dim light over the path outside the hotel was not enough and she flicked the cabin light on. She started to read.

'No,' he said, and snapped the light off. He covered her hand and brought her arm down. 'Not now. Read it later.' He took the paper from her, folded it and propped it up against the dashboard behind the gear stick. He had tears in his eyes.

She placed the palm of her hand against his cheek. Mujo turned to kiss her and she twisted to reach him. Their lips parted as they slowly and tenderly touched and allowed their tongues to savour the taste of the other. He took her hands in his and held them tightly against his chest. The surge in their bellies was like a drug rush, lips and tongues firmed against each other, craving for more. It was goodbye.

'I keep your spirit nestled inside me,' he said as he opened the door to leave.

Their last goodbye.

She watched him walk back to the hotel before she turned on the light to read the paper he had given her. She read it, and read it again. Only then did a tear come. It turned into a sob. She bowed her head into her hands. It had been a long time since she had cried, certainly not over a man, but despair and emotion had opened the flood gates. She tried to reason with herself through the tears. Where had her fragility come from? Was it grief for Mujo, for her loss of career? Was it regret? She had abandoned her daughter for a career, for this? She wiped the tears with the back of her hand, folded the paper and replaced it behind the gearstick. She switched the roof light off, turned the ignition key, and pushed the gear stick into reverse.

22

Five days later, 22 June 1992

Wild and wintry weather had arrived, sweeping away the autumn colours and pushing chilly air into and around the office buildings and their concrete surrounds. The city rugged up and fireplaces were stoked with half-seasoned wood that crackled and spat sparks. Potted geraniums and veranda ferns were shifted under cover to thwart Canberra's frosts, killers of all but the hardiest plants. The community knuckled down to the serious business of getting through winter and waiting for spring.

It was frosty on Monday 22 June, and Brooke shivered in the cold coming into chambers. The landlord's meanness in not turning on the heating until seven on Mondays allowed winter to spend the weekend inside turning the building into a freezer. Without removing her coat, she collected her mail and went to the tea room to make a coffee.

'Hello, Talbot,' greeted Phil.

'Hi, Phil,' replied Brooke, visibly shivering.

'I see you lost your client.'

'Which one?'

'Your feminist high-flyer.'

'My what? What do you mean?'

'Haven't you seen the papers this morning?'

'No, I pick mine up in the evening. What are you talking about?'

'Shot dead. Found Saturday. In her car. In bushes behind the Canberra Yacht Club.'

'What?' His words hit her like a punch to her stomach. She was rooted to the spot. Images of Jo came and went. She spun to face Phil and, feeling dizzy, overbalanced and caused hot water from the urn to splash on to her. 'Jo Rowan? When? How? An accident?'

'Suicide, it seems. Nothing suspicious. I'm sorry. I thought you'd have heard.'

'No, it's not possible. I know her.'

The memory of their last meeting surfaced. Jo's distraught face had caused Brooke to reach for her hand.

'She would not have done that,' she said to Phil emphatically. 'It must have been an accident… I must see the paper.'

Brooke ran to the waiting room and picked up the *Canberra Times*. She shook so much that she found it difficult to turn the page. The headline jumped out at her: 'Feminists mourn academic's death'. She read on. The body was discovered on Saturday evening by a couple whose curiosity had been aroused by seeing the same car partly hidden on successive days in undergrowth behind the Canberra Yacht Club, in Mariner Place, Yarralumla. Walking late on Friday evening, they had surmised that young lovers were using the cover of the bushes for privacy. But by Saturday evening they decided to peer through the back window and were confronted by a gruesome sight.

Brooke's mind was spinning, her pulse racing. She would need to be convinced there was no foul play before accepting that Jo had killed herself. She couldn't forget Jo's conviction that corruption of some kind was behind ASIO's efforts to stop Jo using Mujo's information to embarrass them. 'I know I'm right,' Jo had said and, mysteriously, that she was not at liberty to tell even her lawyer, more. But Brooke also remembered Jo speaking despairingly about her work, her career, her lost lover. Could she have become despondent enough to take her own life?

Picking up the *Times* and her coffee, she returned to her room. She knew little about Jo's family but wanted to contact them. She found no useful contact details on Jo's file. Of course, you idiot – the phone book. Didn't her mother live in Lyons? Yes, there was a Rowan: Unit 9 Lemonthyme Court, 29 Burnie Circuit.

She picked up her bag and keys and hurried to the lift, saying an unhelpful 'I'm out,' to her clerk, who was emerging as she jumped through the closing door.

Brooke reverse parked into a gap at the kerb and surveyed a wall of letterboxes fronting the footpath of a quiet street. She opened the car door and was slapped in the face by a gust of dried leaves. The sky was overcast. Taking a deep breath, she walked slowly towards the block of flats. Number 9 was ground level. She was self-conscious, feeling too colourful for the occasion, in a bright yellow swing coat over a navy woollen tight fitting dress. Her patent leather high-heel boots covered some of her fishnet stockings. She was intruding. She had no real reason for being here.

The curtains parted when she knocked on the door. A tall woman with grey hair opened it and peered out. Her fine-featured face was strained and her green eyes were bloodshot. There was a familiarity in her penetrating gaze.

Brooke explained, 'I'm sorry, ah, so sorry to intrude. I'm Brooke Talbot, Jo's lawyer. Are you her mother?'

The nod was imperceptible but the woman opened the door for Brooke to enter.

'I'm sorry, it's terrible, terrible…a shock…' Brooke wanted to embrace the woman but restrained herself.

'Come in, dear,' said the other, her eyes fixed on Brooke as if she was seeing through her. 'Edith Rowan,' she said, holding out a limp hand.

Brooke took it and, no longer able to contain herself, gave the woman a hug and sobbed, 'I'm so sorry. Is there anything I can do?'

'Thank you, no. My son will be here soon. Sit down, please.' She plumped up some cushions on the settee, and looked nervously around the room, 'Sorry, sorry for the mess…'

'No, don't – I'm sorry for intruding unannounced.' Brooke sat awkwardly on a floral couch and waited for Mrs Rowan to sit in the chair opposite.

'Why would my Jo do this?' She was crying, and Brooke could see just how red her eyes were. 'They say she did. She wouldn't, though. She would have told us if she was that unhappy. It's not her. But they're trying to tell us that depression does that.'

'I'm sorry. I'm so sorry,' Brooke repeated. 'Are the police investigating?'

'I suppose so,' Mrs Rowan sniffled, and wiped her nose with the back of her hand, 'But they say it looks like suicide. Anyway, if she didn't kill herself, the alternative is even more horrible. She didn't have enemies, did she?'

'Not that she told me. Only the trouble she was having at work. It was worrying her. But she was a fighter. She wanted to fight it. Do you mind my asking, ah, when they think she died?'

Edith pulled a folded white handkerchief out from her cardigan sleeve and blew her nose. She sobbed, 'Probably Wednesday or Thursday night. She wasn't found until Saturday evening. It's terrible, her being there so long. No one knew.' Edith wiped her eyes with the crumpled handkerchief.

'Oh, no,' exclaimed Brooke feeling the horror of a lonely death undiscovered for two or three days. 'Anything I can do…?' Brooke offered again.

'Thank you dear. Jeremy, my son, will be in touch with our solicitor, Deidre. I don't know the procedure. A coroner's inquiry, I hope. Deidre will handle the estate matters, of course. But then, should someone represent us at the inquiry?'

'Deidre will advise you about that. I'll ring her, and I'd be happy to help in any way if there are legal complications.'

'Thank you, Ms Talbot. Jo trusted you. It was kind of you to call by.'

Brooke turned to go. What else could she do? Calling on Jo's mother only brought home the reality of what had happened. She knew it was for herself, not Mrs Rowan that she had come.

Back in chambers, she called Deidre. Deidre suggested they meet for coffee at Red Belly Black café.

'Be there in five minutes,' Brooke said.

Deidre had already had several hours to adjust to the morning's tragic news. She had known Jo for longer than Brooke, but had not become as close.

Sitting opposite, Brooke spoke remorsefully. 'I feel powerless,' she said, staring at the table. 'Jo came to me with a problem. I failed her. She was treated so badly: squeezed out, isolated, destroyed professionally, let down by the legal system. I let her down. I'm part of the system that killed her.'

'Don't be melodramatic,' said Deidre. 'That's indulgent crap. Don't go on a guilt trip, or look for people to say "There, there, it wasn't your fault" – of course it wasn't. People don't kill themselves because they lose a court case, or a job, unless they're suffering from full-blown depression.'

'I know, sorry. But if she did kill herself, why? Could the break-up with her boyfriend have had anything to do with it? Speaking of which, does he know? He might have gone home already, but perhaps not.'

Brooke saw from Deidre's puzzled looked that she needed to explain that the Yugoslav consulate was to be closed down and Mujo was returning to his wife.

'Gosh,' Deidre responded, 'on top of everything else…losing him too. She had reason to be depressed.'

The funeral held a week later was simple. The small chapel at the Mitchell Crematorium on the north-west outskirts of Canberra was nearly full, though not overflowing as Brooke would have expected for someone as prominent as Jo. Deidre had rung Brooke to tell her that Jo's body had been released by the coroner for cremation even though the family was calling for an inquiry into her death.

Brooke scanned the room for Deidre. It was designed to feel like a modern chapel: light-coloured oak benches rather than the traditional dark wood of older churches. Large windows welcomed the light. A tall young man in jeans and a navy blazer sat in the front pew beside Edith Rowan. Jo's brother, Jeremy, no doubt. A little girl, about five with short sandy hair, was holding his hand. He shuffled sideways to let the child squeeze in. Others looked very much like public servants. Jo's work colleagues perhaps? There was a large contingent of women, including Wilma in jeans and a shirt unbuttoned carelessly exposing a large amount of bosom, and several others from the feminist network dinner she had attended. What an attention-seeker, Brooke thought, watching Wilma greeting friends as she stepped over legs to reach a vacant spot.

She spotted Deidre in a woollen suit near the front and trekked towards her.

Deidre whispered that she had been instructed by Jo's family to act for the estate and that in Jo's papers she found a publisher's contract for her book. 'I don't know where it's up to, though.'

Brooke whispered back that it would be good to know, and Deidre said she would contact the publisher.

A hush fell.

An awareness of suicide hung over the mourners. Brooke felt the crematorium would have been overflowing if Jo had died from cancer or in a car accident. Faith stretched so far, Brooke thought. If Jo had taken her own life – something she didn't want to believe – Brooke still wanted Jo to be honoured. ASIO had hounded her and must be held responsible.

Jo's family and friends apparently weren't up to composing a eulogy and left it to a professional. Tactfully, and with dignity, he gave a potted history of Jo's work. He talked of the stresses of life – of hope and despair, and loving memories. It made Brooke sad. What should have been a celebration of a champion's life had become just another funeral.

Jeremy said a few words on behalf of the family, and mentioned Jo's daughter, Kitty, and her sadness at not being at the funeral. That Jo had a daughter surprised Brooke. Jo had never mentioned her. She was in London but with her mother in spirit, Jeremy said. He then called on Wilma, who fumbled with the top button of her shirt as she approached the lectern, and then spoke proudly about Jo's glittering record on women's rights. She finished by urging feminists to take the baton from Jo; in her memory and for the sake of women everywhere.

Just before the service finished, Brooke turned round. She had felt his presence. Intuition, she later supposed. Donald Fenchurch was standing at the back of the chapel, unobtrusively. He was wearing the cord trousers and jacket he had worn at the Faceless Men's Bar. His face showed no emotion. He turned and walked off quietly before the crowd milled out. His being there unnerved Brooke. Apparently he did not want to be acknowledged or even seen, perhaps wanting to farewell Jo without having to support others.

23

Early July 1992

Donald Fenchurch's room at University House was dark. He sat in a chair by the window, not bothering to turn the light on or take his jacket off after returning from the funeral. He pulled out a white envelope tucked between pages of his diary. He received the note a year ago, just days after he had agreed to provide Jo with a character reference for the tribunal hearing. He turned the pages over in his hand as he had done many times since Jo's death. Dated 28 June 1991, its single typewritten line read, 'Does this answer some of your questions?' It was unsigned. A second page was attached. He had not told Jo that he had used his extensive networks to enquire what might have made the Special Projects Section nervous about recruiting a woman like Annette, or about Jo's checking of the recruitment process.

Donald had not seen Jo since they dined together at University House. He might have been called to give evidence and wanted to be seen as objective, no emotional involvement.

She had telephoned him, though, soon after the hearing had been completed. 'I'm getting somewhere,' she had said. 'Mujo has helped put the pieces together. I'm sure there's more, but we've learned some secrets which ASIO mightn't want to reach Immigration.'

She had rung again in March, after the tribunal's decision, to thank him, and told him that the tribunal seemed to accept that she wasn't a security risk but that her access to Immigration documents was still to be restricted. 'There's something going on at Immigration that they're scared I might find out, something which, combined with Mujo's knowledge of some previous operation, could be explosive,' she had said.

She was cagey about saying more. He suggested they talk over a meal, but she was reluctant and he hadn't pressed her.

He read the typewritten attached sheet again.

I heard you have been asking questions about Dr Rowan. We never asked ASIO to halt her work, only that she not be given access to our special project files. I am ashamed of how she is being treated, and prepared to blow the whistle about things going on here. Just put a notice in the *Canberra Times* on any Monday, saying 'I miss you, Sally, please call me,' and I'll contact you. Please don't talk to anyone about this.

He'd done nothing, of course. It seemed genuine enough but it was all too clandestine, and might have been a set-up to discredit him before Jo's tribunal hearing. Now Jo was dead. How he wished he'd acted. It might not have resolved her work situation; it was unlikely that any leak from an anonymous whistle-blower would have changed things. Nevertheless, had Jo known more about what was going on she might have avoided agonising about what, if anything, she had done to attract ASIO's attention; or whether her relationship with Mujo was the problem.

Two days after Jo's death was discovered, another unsolicited letter arrived, thicker than the last and in a manila envelope. It contained the sort of information he thought Rusty Redmond, his intrepid journalist friend, could make into a story that would expose at least those responsible. It would be ironic to reveal, after Jo's death, what spooks feared she might reveal when alive. He smiled. Had they let her be, their secrets would probably have remained secret.

He read the recent letter again. It was about a project that Immigration's Special Projects Section was running in collaboration with the Australian Federal Police. An informant, a boat owner who had been recruited to flag boat people arriving in Indonesian fishing boats, had proved untrustworthy, as they usually are. In this case, members of the informant's family were passengers on one such boat. Yet he was retained as an informant. The letter explained that the informant's handler 'convinced us that using a boat owner's services allayed suspicion and would provide us with enough evidence to convict the big-time crooks behind the boat owners'. But there had been no convictions and refugees continued to pay enormous sums for a boat passage from Indonesia to Australia, only to be detained for months on arrival, or sent home to Cambodia, Vietnam or southern China. Incompetent public servants had painted themselves into an embarrassing corner.

What made him sit up, though, was the whistle-blower's assertion that 'every boat crew arrested has pointed to just one person as organising and profiting from people smuggling – our informant'. How embarrassing that a master people smuggler had been engaged to assist ASIO and the federal police to arrest people smugglers.

The whistle-blower went on to explain that 'the informant can't be prosecuted because he has been given immunity, in exchange for information. Why, though, is he still working with the police?'

Donald's research confirmed a rise from one or two boats a year in the late 80s, to six boats in 1991; and still coming at the same rate. If the whistle-blower was correct, it explained why Immigration did not want Annette's or Jo's eyes on its files. This was a stuff-up that had to be covered up.

He wondered what Mujo knew that had made Jo unwelcome at Immigration. What knowledge could he have about a previous Australian intelligence operation? There must be a link with Immigration's Operation F because their friendship only became a problem after she started working there. Despite the request not to, Donald rang his well-connected friend, Gideon. Did the Office of National Assessments see any risk to Australia in the current Yugoslavian domestic unrest? And Gideon, who worked at ONA, was the one to know if any current intelligence operation was going pear-shaped. Donald wanted some background before contacting whistle-blower 'Sally'.

'The place leaks like a sieve. Shouldn't be difficult,' was Gideon's response.

Donald was at a table that looked over the rose garden outside the Lobby restaurant when Gideon's erect silhouette appeared across the room. Donald rose and shook his hand.

'My commiserations on Jo's death,' Gideon said. 'I know how close you were.'

It was the Lobby's proprietor who greeted them with menus, and while Gideon charmed her with bonhomie, Donald wriggled impatiently in his chair. She recommended the fresh asparagus soup with crusty bread, and Gideon ordered a bottle of wine.

Donald went straight to the issue as soon as he regained his friend's attention. He told Gideon that this whistle-blower, Sally, probably worked in the section handling Operation F, the one in the leaked memo. 'He – and I assume *he*, given the dearth of senior women in the department – suggests that Jo's interest in one recruitment file alarmed the Special Projects team as much as the prospect of Annette Armstrong joining the section. The same guy offered to talk after Jo lost her clearance but I stupidly ignored him. Now he's sent information which I'd love to pass on to Rusty Redmond. This is a big story if it can be verified.'

'I couldn't find much about Operation Fishnet for you, apart from it being a bit of a joke around the intelligence traps. I don't know the details but, as your Sally suggests, it seems they recruited a field informant who has run amok and is now handling his handlers.'

'Operation Fishnet, is it? Jo didn't even know that. Okay. Yes, you've got the gist, although Sally suggests the informant is an even bigger fish.'

'Does Sally mention any names?'

'No. Neither the informant's nor the handler. He only refers to "officers" of the federal police, ASIO, et cetera.'

'You know, we had two rules at ONA.' Gideon leaned back and grinned. 'First, if you have to choose between a conspiracy and a stuff-up, assume a stuff-up. Second, if it is a conspiracy, it's to cover up a stuff-up!'

'Pretty big stuff-up. The federal police engage an informant to help get people smugglers arrested, and allows him to dabble in a bit of people smuggling himself, including his relatives.'

'Is that what Sally says?' Gideon asked, gesturing to the waiter to pour wine into both glasses.

'More or less. The informant has business connections in Indonesia and is married to an Indonesian. Once his wife got residency, he did a deal to allow her relatives in – a sister and her husband and children – on a fishing boat. It was towed into Darwin, and after other asylum seekers on board were processed, the captain was allowed to return to the fishing zone. The informant got away with it by arguing that he'd get information about further boat departures if he gained the trust of their owners.'

'And did he?'

'Yes. He alerted authorities to a couple of boats heading for Darwin and Broome. Trouble was, it seems he was the one to find the passengers. The boat owners protested they were only small players and fingered the informant as the organiser. They were paid a pittance, while large sums were extracted from the refugees packed on their boats.'

'I can guess the rest. The informant promises that he's close to getting the big fish but he needs some latitude?'

'That's about it. But why keep him on when the evidence points to him being the big fish? What hold has he got over his handlers?'

'Embarrassment? If the so-called informant is really the big fish behind it all, the federal police, ASIO and Immigration would all want the story kept quiet.'

'Especially as Operation Fishnet hasn't achieved a single conviction and the informant can't be convicted. He'd have written guarantees and immunities in place. '

'Not the first time a big crime figure has been recruited as an informant.'

'Question is, is it intelligence incompetence or official corruption?'

'Both. There have to be people getting kickbacks,' Gideon surmised. 'Customs officials must have been co-opted or bribed. The police handler must have known what his informant was up to. Canberra agency bosses might not know why it went so wrong.'

The soup arrived, and the two pulled in their chairs to attack it.

Between slurps, Donald said he thought that the whistle-blower was also the recipient and leaker of the memo Annette had found. 'In his note to me, Sally mentioned pressure on the promotion panel to stop women joining the Special Projects Section and so he could well be the Jack who was sent the memo. Annette doesn't know any Jack, but she did mention that a James Pratt, who works in the section, expressed sympathy about Jo's work being stopped short.'

'James Pratt?' Gideon seemed lost in thought for a moment, and then repeated the name. 'Could be Jack – James Pratt, Jack Spratt – drop a few letters and you have J…sprat – Jack Sprat. The sort of nickname those operation guys give each other.'

'Ah. Good thinking. Pratt might be worth talking to. Save me contacting Sally through the *Canberra Times*. So when this informant was found to be a master crook, why wasn't the operation wound up?'

'That'll be the bigger story. The one the journalists might be interested in pursuing, particularly if corruption is involved. Rusty will do a good job if he investigates it. Though you probably have enough already to interest ABC current affairs presenters like Kerry O'Brien for *Lateline* or Quentin Dempster for the *7.30 Report*, or perhaps Richard Carlton for *60 Minutes*.'

'It'll be a load off my shoulders once it goes public. Be nice to see a few ministers squirm and made accountable.' Donald was still troubled. 'None of this explains why ASIO acted as it did against Jo. Apparently her boyfriend, Mujo Zukić, knew something about an earlier operation that might be linked to this, and ASIO panicked at the possibility of the two combining their knowledge. Wish I could have extracted more from her after her case had finished.'

'Why didn't you?' Gideon asked.

'She seemed nervous about meeting me. How stupid of ASIO to put her through that. All they had to do was restrict her access to sensitive files at the outset, and let her get on with her work, which is what the tribunal did anyway in the end,' Donald puzzled.

'You need Rusty to get the whole story. From what you say, the explanation goes back to an operation involving Yugoslav intelligence. We've had joint intel operations when it suited, like over the Croatian menace.'

'What's Australia's attitude to Yugoslavia now?'

'We wouldn't be working with the Yugoslavs now. Rusty's best bet is to find out how long this out-of-control informant has had something on his handlers. Was he involved in an operation that Jo's Yugoslav boyfriend knew about? If he was crooked then, he shouldn't have been used again. Generally, the hold crooks have over their handlers isn't just because they know too much about operational irregularities, but because the spoils from the "authorised" illegal activities are often shared between the informant and corrupt handlers and others in the know.'

'You're not suggesting that Jo's death wasn't suicide?' Donald asked.

'No. It was found to be suicide, wasn't it?'

'We know she was depressed and for good reason. I didn't think breaking up with Zukić would affect her that badly, but her professional integrity was challenged and maybe her reputation as Australia's top expert on gender equity. But I wouldn't have picked her as someone who'd let despondency overwhelm her. She was a fighter. Nevertheless, we never really know people, do we?'

'I was only suggesting that there might be people out there with corruption to conceal who might have welcomed it when she topped herself.'

'Shot herself,' Donald corrected, and went on, 'I owe it to Jo to help retrieve her reputation.'

24

Mid-July 1992

'Yes,' snapped Brooke.

'It's Deidre,' came a tentative response.

'Oh, sorry, Deidre. I thought it was my clerk.'

The suggestion that it was all right to be rude to a clerk hung awkwardly before Deidre said, 'Well, I don't want to disturb you, Brooke, but I need to let you know that the family will ask for a coroner's inquest. It's four weeks since Jo's death and police enquiries are not concluded, but I have the autopsy report, and, well, Jo's mother has some concerns. Would you be prepared to represent the family?'

'Of course, Deidre. I'm keen to help if I can. Does Edith Rowan still have doubts about how she died?'

'Well, yes. She wants it further investigated.'

'Well, she has to be satisfied that it's properly investigated. How strong is the autopsy conclusion? What does it say?'

'What you might expect. It's gruesome reading, and while it would appear she shot herself, it's not conclusive. The police examination of the scene supports suicide. There's no forensic evidence of anyone else having been there, but how hard they looked, who knows? Once suicide is assumed, it's easy to find support for the idea. No prints, other than Jo's, were found on the gun, and none, surprisingly, on the passenger side of the car inside or out, where you'd expect to find some, at least Jo's. But there were unidentified prints on the driver's door. There were no visible footprints around the car, apart from the people who found her. The coroner visited the scene and certified that she died of a gunshot wound to the head, leaving open the possibility of suspicious circumstances.'

'And Edith's concerns?'

'Well, one thing she said was that Jo had never handled a gun in her life and, moreover, she loathed them. Jo used to argue that carrying a gun around was never justified even for self-defence. Also, she was right-handed, though sitting in the driver's seat she could have taken the gun from the glovebox and shot herself using her left hand. But why would she have a gun? Easy enough to obtain without a licence, but why? Had she planned to kill herself? Did she drive to the lake from home, or from somewhere else? There are a lot of unanswered questions. I've asked for an independent forensic pathologist to look at the autopsy report and police photos, and we'll get more when the police conclude their investigation.'

'Can you fax me the autopsy report please, Deidre – I know you'll get me a brief later, but I'd like to see the report.'

'I'll do it now.'

The body was that of a female, possibly late forties, 173cm tall, 65 kg. There was some reddening of the skin and linear red markings on the feet and ankles and on the hands, particularly towards the fingertips. The abdomen had a greenish tinge with greenish blue demarcation of superficial veins, which became more intense towards the upper chest above the breast, and towards the neck. The left index finger was extended.

As if holding a gun perhaps, Brooke noted, reading on the way back from the fax machine.

Through the skin of the neck just posterior to the point of the jaw, approximately 15mm, was an oval-shaped skin wound approximately 30 x 15mm, with blackening of the surrounding skin to approximately 4mm, with hyperaemia of the skin further out. There were multiple fractures to the maxilla, with displacement of much of the bone, including the hard palate, particularly on the left side of the face, and blackening of the exposed tissue. The mandible was also fractured in numerous places, and the lower lip was charred and partly blown away. Much of the tissue on the left side of the face was blown away. The brain was displaced from the cranial cavity, with blackening of the bones forward.

The right eye and right ear were intact. The hair was black. There were numerous blowfly larvae in the wound.

'Ugh,' Brooke exclaimed out loud. Not the company one would want after dying alone. The pathologist noted death occurred on the evening of Wednesday 17 June. There was a lot more, about the state of the heart and lungs. Having dealt with the thoracic cavity, the report moved on to the abdominal cavity. Brooke skimmed through to the conclusion:

Cause of Death: Bullet wound to head. Consistent with having been self-inflicted.

She turned over the other papers. There was a list of items found in the car: the gun, a Glock .22 pistol, on the floor of the passenger's seat; her shoulder bag with wallet intact (nothing stolen); and a screwed-up piece of paper that had been found on the driver's side floor, not a suicide note but related to her despair perhaps. It was a handwritten poem, not in Jo's hand.

Brooke called Deidre but she wasn't there. She waited, fingers tapping, to be put through to Deidre's secretary, who proved helpful.

'It's about Jo Rowan,' Brooke explained. 'Deidre just faxed me a copy of her autopsy report and some other material. Do you have a report containing the words of the poem found on the floor of the car? Maybe in one of the police witness statements. If so, could you fax it to me, please?'

Brooke was transfixed by what she read:

> Of words and poetry
> Undercurrents of Life Energy transfer
>> radiant auras gently overlapping
> Life forces lock
> Thoughts block
> As with a teenager's wide opened eyes
>> experiencing life's passions
> Framed not in the poem to be told
>>> but in the magic of life
>>> which divinely frightens us
>>> pushed and sucked back into life-giving embrace

Savouring the clarity of her green eyes
    a softness of presence
    the never-broken hope of her voice
    ecstasy struggling gently within a brisk mind
    now urging to fly
    and forgetting to cry
While being gently nestled in spirit of mine.

She lowered her head into her hands and wept. She wept for the gentle love Jo and Mujo had enjoyed; she wept from sadness; she wept from emotional exhaustion. These words spoke of ongoing love, not of a farewell. When was it written, she wondered. Could Jo have taken it to read, to reflect on what might have been, before killing herself?

Must be coming down with flu, Brooke decided. Why else would she be feeling so frail? That was it. Explaining her meltdown made her feel better. And it was a good reason to go home. But before she did, she phoned Deidre's secretary again and asked her to make a note for Deidre. Could she ask the police to provide a photocopy of the original crumpled piece of paper on which the poem was written, plus any forensic report on it? If not done already, have it examined.

'Tell Deidre,' Brooke emphasised, 'that if the police won't cooperate, to request an order from the coroner that this be done. It might be important.'

Brooke filed the papers and the poem and made for her car, driving first to the supermarket. Making her dazed way through the aisles, she picked out some essentials for the evening. Granny Smith apples filled a large fruit bin. She did not intend to work tonight. Her briefcase sat lonely in her office, and the other half of her brain, her laptop, lay idle with it. She noticed how she referred to 'the office' when talking to herself, and not 'chambers' – Jo's influence. She rejected an apple with a bruise mark on it and then felt sorry for it. She picked it up again. Nothing, no one, should be discarded out of hand. Stop it. Stop projecting your all-too-human feelings onto an apple.

Brooke shifted into neutral, as she often did on the downhill part of her drive home. She knew it was dangerous. The car had fuel, but

Brooke was running on near-empty and her driving reflected a need to keep something in reserve.

Why had everyone been so quick to assume Jo had suicided? How important was a crumpled tender love poem to that conclusion? Was it because people couldn't imagine any other explanation for its presence? Just what was the evidence? A gun, a handbag still with money, a poem, pathology reports and photographs of a body now cremated. On the other hand, only Jo's prints were on the gun. But why no fingerprints on the passenger side of the car? Had she wiped the seat and the dash down for some reason? Or had someone else wiped them? Deidre was right. Questions had to be answered about Jo's movements and demeanour in the days and hours before she died, and, for Brooke, much more.

She refocused as she pulled into the car port at the top of the winding gravel drive. She was greeted by two eager wagging tails. Inside, she unpacked the groceries pausing to slice the bruise from the apple into the scrap bucket for the chooks. She took a bite from the rest. It was sweet and crisp. Does every bad thing in life have a sweeter side?

That evening, with the combustion stove glowing, Brooke lay on the couch, sharing it with the cats and Rex, to watch television. Rocky was sleeping with his eyes open on the floor beside her. A glass of white wine was within reach. She was watching the *7.30 Report* when she heard the word 'whistle-blower'.

A person identified only as 'Donald' was being interviewed. Brooke sat up. The cats rolled off her stomach as one. The ABC's current affairs presenter and ferocious truth-seeker, Quentin Dempster, was introducing the story. Backdropping him across Lake Burley Griffin was Parliament House sitting under its eighty-one-metre flagpole supported by four 'extraterrestrial' splayed metal legs. The scene switched to a living room. Dempster was talking to a silhouette with an electronically distorted voice. As the silhouette came into the light, Brooke thought he looked familiar. He was casually dressed, open-neck shirt, jeans and a cord jacket which, for Brooke, despite his face being deliberately blurred, was a giveaway. The man had information from an unidentified whistle-blower about the

Immigration Department's irregular and unlawful methods of tracking so-called 'illegal immigrants' arriving in Australia by boat. He refused to identify his source.

The ABC's research team had done their homework. The department, on legal advice, had refused to comment. 'Operations of this kind are sensitive and cannot be discussed.' However, a spokesman for the attorney-general had been questioned, and ruthlessly, about prosecutions and numbers given immunity from prosecution in exchange for information.

Brooke studied the semi-disguised figure closely. She was sure it was Jo's friend Donald Fenchurch, the one she'd met at the Faceless Men's Bar and seen briefly at Jo's funeral. The camera shifted and Brooke stood up to look more closely. The papers he received, he was telling Dempster, described an operation which he believed was known as Operation Fishnet, part of a larger attempt to identify and monitor people who owned smuggling boats. Details of its highly irregular intelligence-collecting methods were supposedly known only to a tight circle of senior public servants and key people in the intelligence agencies involved. It was alleged that an Australian boat owner had been 'authorised' to operate illegally, bringing in would-be refugees. His federal police handlers promised him immunity from prosecution in exchange for information about other boat operators and refugees. They turned a blind eye to his continuing activities, waiting for useful information. There had been no prosecutions, no convictions, no outing of corrupt officials to date.

The interviewee paused and ran his finger down the side of his nose. Brooke recalled Donald doing just that when they met at the Faceless Men's Bar. Her first thought was that Jo must have breached her undertaking to the tribunal and given Donald the name of the operation. But no, Jo knew none of the extra information 'Donald' seemed to have acquired. It was clear now why the Special Projects Section dared not risk a principled woman being promoted into their project team, nor having it investigated by a gender equity expert like Jo Rowan.

Neither Jo nor ASIO were implicated, but this was definitely Donald Fenchurch. What was the connection? Had Jo's death triggered the whistle-blower and Donald to go public? If so, did Donald believe that Jo had been driven to suicide? Or was it not suicide? Brooke wanted to talk to him.

She rose and phoned her friend Rusty Redmond, to get Donald's number. He was watching the ABC too and, surprised by her call, confessed that, at Donald's request, he had done a 'bit of poking around' to check the whistle-blower's claim. The program was pre-recorded, he told her, and Donald wouldn't be happy to have been recognised. She rang him anyway. An answering machine talked to her. She slowly lowered the receiver into its cradle.

The next morning, the papers were full of 'no comments' from relevant ministers, and opinion pieces about the rule of law. When and in what circumstances was it legitimate for an arm of government to disobey its own laws, and where did accountability feature in such activities? There were editorials predicting government inquiries into the federal police and Immigration's intelligence-gathering methods. Suspending the law for the security of the nation was one thing, but allowing civilian informants to profit from it was another.

25

Monday 20 July 1992

Brooke yawned, arched and stretched. Monday again. Why were there so many Monday mornings in a year? They were forever turning up when a Thursday or Friday would be better. She forced herself out of bed and added to the country's seven o'clock power surge as she turned on the radio, plugged in the kettle and headed for the shower. She washed and dressed in time with the rest of the nation – a society comfortable with conformity.

Listening to a program of familiar golden oldies as she drove to town reminded her that she was one of the lucky country's baby boomers, pandered to in every way by market forces from the 50s when they were young teens till the 90s, and now they were monopolising the plum jobs. Pity about the pre-boomers who were older and fewer, and the post-boomers, younger and frequently unemployed. Yep, there was a lot to be thankful for, even if the price was playing by the rules. She was alive, unlike poor Jo, who hadn't been told what rules she had to play by. Intelligence agencies were meant to protect people like her, not hound her to death. It didn't make sense.

She parked under Canberra House and walked swiftly to work, thinking about the inquiry into Jo's death. Brooke had already been briefed by Deidre to appear at the inquest. No date had been set. The slim volume of police material supported a cold and compelling suicide story. There were graphic photos, depicting Jo's ripped and bloodied face pressing against the steering wheel; gun on the floor just under her dangling left hand; car tucked into the bushes; a screwed-up ball of paper beside her feet in blood-spattered flat leather shoes. A numbered list itemised her clothes and everything in her handbag and the glovebox. The couple who had found her had both provided statements.

Deidre reported that the police were interviewing family and neighbours about Jo's movements and her demeanour before her death – looking for evidence to support suicide, Deidre thought. Nothing suggested a second person at the scene. Brooke would get a supplementary brief when more material became available.

When Deidre did receive more material from the coroner's office, it included Jo's bank statements and telephone records. Jo had received a call on Wednesday 17 June from Mujo Zukić's room at the Hyatt. The room had been cleaned and occupied since and no prints were found to match those on the driver's door of Jo's car. There was a match, however, with prints in Jo's house, and, eventually, more in the now abandoned Yugoslav consulate. The Hyatt's CCTV footage for Wednesday 17 and Thursday 18 June was requisitioned.

A picture of Jo's last hours was coming together. Within twenty minutes of being phoned, Jo was on CCTV, entering the back door of the Hyatt at 7.58 p.m. At 8.16 she left with a dark-haired man slightly taller than herself. They turned right towards the row of parked cars. At 8.32 the man returned the same way. He was next recorded catching a taxi at the front of the hotel early on Thursday 18 June. Taxi records confirmed that a Mr Zukić had been taken directly to the airport and airline records had him leaving for Sydney mid-morning and on to Frankfurt and Belgrade.

Police attention turned to Zukić. Experiments showed that he could not have driven with Jo to the death site and returned on foot by 8.32 p.m. While he had time to follow her and return by car after killing her, the CCTV did not capture him exiting the hotel again that night. Anyway, he had left his car keys at reception in a sealed envelope ready for collection the next day. While there were no footprints around Jo's car unaccounted for, they would have been expunged from the short grass by several days of wind, drizzle and sunshine.

Zukić's prints were collected from the consulate and the police material also included a statement taken from the defector Marika Babić. She confirmed that the poem was written in her colleague's recognisable scrawl. She described Zukić's separation from his family, his recent trip to Serbia and his decision to return to his wife and children in Belgrade. She knew about Jo, describing it as a relationship with no future because Zukić would never defect without the mother of his children. Nor would he leave his aged mother, who was too ill to travel, to the mercy of the authorities.

While the police would have to treat Zukić as a suspect if it eventuated that Jo had been murdered, they clearly felt she had suicided. This was the premise when they interviewed officers from Immigration and the Department of Prime Minister and Cabinet about Jo's reaction to losing access to departmental documents.

Deidre kept Brooke abreast of these developments. The police material showed that the Glock handgun was unregistered. Registration requirements were slack and cash sales were common, Deidre explained. Glocks were used by the New South Wales police force and were readily available from gun shops. Perhaps Jo had purchased one after learning at the tribunal that her home and privacy had been invaded; or more recently for the specific purpose of shooting herself. Police were checking local gun shops, particularly in Queanbeyan, the NSW town across the Australian Capital Territory border, where Jo would have been less likely to be recognised.

A search of Jo's home found no suicide note. Counsel assisting the coroner sent the police material including the witness statements to two forensic psychiatrists together with a briefing note stating that Jo had been outraged by ASIO's surveillance activities, and that she and her boyfriend had broken up when he returned to Yugoslavia. It asked for their opinions on whether Jo's work and personal situation might have triggered enough despair for her to have killed herself. If so, might the suicide have been premeditated, as evidenced by her bringing a gun, or spontaneous, using a gun already in her glovebox? Their opinions were not yet available.

Although nothing concrete suggested foul play, both Deidre and

Brooke felt it was still possible that someone had shot Jo and put a gun in her hand. For example, had Jo's hand been swabbed for gunshot residue? It was a chilling thought. Who would kill her and why? Obviously it would have something to do with Operation Fishnet, even though Jo had known nothing about it. Deidre had also asked a forensic pathologist for alternative scenarios around Jo's death. Would it help, Brooke wondered as she walked to her office. Clearly it would be difficult to prove Jo was killed, but Jo's family needed to have murder ruled out.

Preoccupied as she was, Brooke nearly missed the shop window full of books. She stopped and turned back. All were the same: *The Unfair Sex*, by Dr Josephine Rowan. Stunned, Brooke stood and looked. So the publishers had gone ahead despite Jo's death. Perhaps Jo had waited till it was in press before killing herself – if indeed she had.

Brooke bought a copy. On opening it, she noticed a dedication to 'KRM'. Who was KRM, she wondered. A lover perhaps? Leafing the pages, it didn't look like a light read, but she was eager to get her day's work finished so that she could get into the book that evening.

Once home, Brooke toasted some cheese on rye bread and smothered it with home-made fig chutney: thick, sweet, sour and heavenly. A friendly neighbour had left thirteen ripe figs in her roadside mail box some months before. She had boiled balsamic and red wine vinegar, brown sugar, lemon zest and juice, mixed spice with ginger and some slightly caramelised red onions. When the mixture had been reduced to syrup, she added the figs and cooked them and bottled it.

She turned on the ABC television news and opened Jo's book. She listened, read and ate all at once. The book was heavy in parts. Jo outlined the enormous improvements in the position of working women between 1975 and 1986, singling out the contribution of Labor Senator Susan Ryan. She had been Minister assisting Prime Minister Hawke on the Status of Women between 1983 and 1988 and Minister for Education from 1984 for three years. The Labor government's *Sex Discrimination Act 1984* and *Affirmative Action (Equal Opportunities in Employment) Act 1986* were giant leaps towards equality for working women. But, the book asked, what progress since then? Women were being appointed to government and industry boards and tribunals and for some that was enough. The policy aspiration was that by the year 2000 half the people in parliament and in senior public service and business leadership positions would be women. Yet in the last decade the percentage of middle management positions occupied by women hadn't improved. Why?

Brooke moved to the sink and rinsed the plate and her sticky chutney fingers. She wiped the sink and picked out a shiny red apple to take along with the book to the couch. She chomped and browsed until arrested by Jo's take on recent gender politics. It was bold and plausible.

Jo postulated a secret and powerful force working behind the scenes to prevent women emerging in any significant way as government and industry decision-makers. She went further: there was an organised network of influential men whose quiet agenda was to keep women out of decision-making roles. And like Freemasons they could identify each other. When all the applicants for senior positions were male, merit principles were ignored. When a woman was an applicant, unscrupulous men would craft 'legitimate' reasons to reject her on merit.

In an all-male field of applicants for a top job, merit lost out to a clubby 'who-you-know' process, particularly if the selection panel itself could be 'selected' or its members influenced to ensure a particular outcome. A flow of 'right' men into positions of influence ensured continuity of the establishment. Once in power, those who were willing to would rejig job criteria, provide ambiguous references to discredit effective female bureaucrats, turn up adverse performance assessments when required, and bully women into becoming victims who lacked confidence in themselves.

Jo supported her thesis with carefully documented evidence, unpicking cases where the 'club' system had worked well. They resonated with Brooke, who had encountered chauvinist policies at both the Commonwealth Club at Yarralumla and the Canberra Club in the city. Huge protests had been mounted to get the male membership rule ditched. Deidre had often complained that the men in her office could take a lunchtime dip in the Canberra Club's pool while she had to content herself with a walk around the block for a bit of exercise. The Commonwealth Club had been a popular venue for business meetings except that business women weren't allowed in. Seeing the need to placate the wives of top public servants, judges and politicians, that club introduced 'associate membership' for wives, a move which undercut the feminist protesters. Associates could access club facilities unescorted by their husbands, and husbands could quietly do business in the corners of the private lounge. Associates had no vote in club affairs, but no matter now they were being treated as 'equals'. It took longer for the Canberra Club to understand that men bringing female colleagues or friends to lunch were embarrassed at being deliberately served their meal before any woman present.

The book was indeed about the 'unfair sex'. But not all men were unfair in the moral sense of that phrase; far from it, as Jo was happy to point out. The conspiracy worked equally against men who genuinely supported equality in employment. Moreover, when fair-minded men were denied promotion, they couldn't ask for a gender equity investigation as women could.

Jo's case studies described other demoralising experiences of de-identified female public servants, the last being the blatant discrimination Annette Armstrong had recently suffered. She referred to the revelatory leaked memo to show the lengths a person or organisation was prepared to go to keep a woman's nose out of a secret intelligence operation. The case provided a segue into the power of an organisation, such as ASIO, to manipulate government appointments. Jo postulated that women were harder to control than most men. Men usually had enough skeletons in the cupboard to give in to pressure, or recognise the wisdom of seeing things ASIO's way, whereas women, on the other hand, had to battle to achieve positions of influence and were too busy to collect skeletons. Anyway, women who had successfully climbed corporate or bureaucratic trees were unusual by definition and generally unmoved by threats to reveal clandestine affairs or sexual preferences. They were less vulnerable to pressure. Jo's thesis was that ASIO regarded feminists as 'one of the great threats to Australian security'.

Brooke was in awe of what Jo had pieced together to heighten awareness of the barriers to women in employment. But what made her sit up was the postscript. It was written as a personal note and described the consequences she suffered from investigating Annette's case. She wrote,

> A case was fabricated that I was a national security risk and my authority to inspect relevant files was withdrawn. I challenged ASIO's rigged assessment but the appeal hearing was itself so secret that I could not be told the grounds on which the decision had been made. So I was powerless to defend myself.
>
> Because I was not able to complete my investigation into how a senior female executive had been discriminated against, the report I was contracted to write was compromised.

Jo detailed the Kafkaesque process she had to endure to have her security clearance restored and that, in preparing her case, all her lawyer and she had to go on was that it probably had something to do with her request to see recruitment files from the Special Projects area which was working on a secret project, Operation F. She told of ASIO spying on her and her boyfriend, and that her home was bugged. She gave as much detail as she could without mentioning what actually took place in the hearing room.

But what came as a shock to Brooke was Jo's revelation that ASIO had attempted to recruit her. She figured that Jo had kept this from her, knowing that she would have advised against its inclusion in the book.

Brooke reread the last few paragraphs.

> Just weeks before the tribunal handed down its decision, I was approached by a senior intelligence officer, an ASIO spook. I met him at ASIO headquarters. He had a proposal. It was simple, he explained. All I had to do was to have a small hidden tape recorder with me – as he spoke, he tapped a little case on his desk – whenever I met a friend of mine, a Yugoslav diplomat. No, that was not quite all. He suggested a few key words I should drop into our intimate conversations. The aim was to prod my friend into telling me what he and his government might know about aspects of Australian intelligence operations.
>
> If it weren't so serious, it would be laughable. ASIO gave me an adverse security assessment and at the same time were recruiting me to gather

intelligence. If I refused, or told anyone about this proposition, my career would suffer. I declined, of course, and my career has suffered. So, having nothing to lose, I am telling my story in the hope that someday people will have to account for their clandestine activities, whether to keep women out of senior positions, or to fulfil some other political agenda.

Where does good end and evil begin? There is more to my story and it is with regret that people cannot publish freely until death. Vive les memoirs for truth in history.

Brooke stiffened on reading the word 'death'. Had she written these words in contemplation of her death?

Sinking back on the lounge, Brook momentarily closed her eyes. Jo had avoided any speculation that an intelligence cover-up was behind the treatment she received, probably for legal reasons and not wanting to hold up publication of the book. But Donald's recent revelations about the underhand work of the Special Projects Section of the Immigration Department now allowed readers to join many of the dots.

26

Tuesday 21 July 1992

'Brooke, it's Deidre.'

'What's up, Deidre?' Brooke asked, noting the urgency in her friend's voice.

'Jo's publisher has just been served with an urgent injunction to stop further sales of the book. The director-general of security, ASIO's head, wants the book recalled. Can you be at court at two this afternoon?'

'Goodness, yes. Representing the publisher?'

Brooke could expect a call from Jamisons Publishing, Deidre explained, and a brief was on its way.

Brooke asked several questions, relieved that she had browsed through the book last night. 'I bet it's because of the postscript. It'll be interesting hearing their argument for grounding an injunction,' she exclaimed.'

When Brooke put the phone down, it rang again.

'Brooke Talbot.'

'Brooke, my name is Alison James. I'm a director of Jamisons Publishing. We've just published *The Unfair Sex*.' Alison was a leading publisher of feminist works and Jamisons, a play on her name, was well-regarded in several other fields as well. 'Deidre will have told you that the Commonwealth Attorney-General is seeking an injunction on ASIO's behalf. We have alerted our lawyers in Sydney, but senior counsel can't be here in time. The Supreme Court has granted an *ex parte* hearing this afternoon, but we want to be there. Will you accept an informal and hurried briefing?'

Brooke listened – and started to work on the arguments in her head. 'Any evidence of loss if book sales are put on hold?'

'We have Professor David Alexander. He wants to put it on his students' reading list. Other university reading lists are being prepared now, and hold-ups with the Rowan book, even a week, will leave us with a large and calculable loss.'

'Good, good. Sure, Alison, get me whatever paperwork you have, and a copy of the book – mine's at home – and can you send Professor Alexander to Deidre Dawson, who will draft his affidavit, and I'll have her file an appearance immediately so that the proceedings don't start without us.'

There was no time to waste. Urgent injunction hearings demand fast work. In extreme cases, a judge can order an interim injunction based on an application by telephone or in person in the judge's chambers, even in the absence of the party against whom the order is sought – *ex parte* as it is called. If there is time to notify the respondent, the applicant is obliged to do so.

Alison James had arrived at work early enough to collect the notifying facsimile as it came through. While the immediate issue for the court would be to weigh up the damages each party might suffer from the publication of the book on one hand, and temporarily stopping sales on the other, it would also assess the applicant's ultimate chances of success. In this case, the competing issues were the right to freedom of speech and the possible risk to the nation's security. A long shot on ASIO's part, Brooke thought, but not unexpected from an agency indifferent to people's civil rights.

Brooke already had the broad thrust of her submission in mind: the essence of national security is to identify and eliminate threats to a democratic society where freedom of speech is held dear, not to curtail it. And, she wondered, how would ASIO overcome its problem of revealing in open court the reasons for its concern – no doubt secret by definition? Brooke felt her excitement rising at the prospect of a very public clash of values.

By two Brooke was in court. It was a chamber hearing, even though held in a courtroom and open to the public. She was dismayed to find that the ghastly Prendergast QC was again counsel for the director-general of security, instructed by the attorney-general. Conversely, she was delighted that the presiding judge was Brett Arnold, her old friend who had so often in the past appeared on the other side of the Bar table in the Security Appeals division of the Administrative Appeals Tribunal.

Each side put their client's position, briefly, to the judge. Prendergast urged that national security was at risk each day the book was on sale, and that it should be removed immediately. Brooke noted that he produced no evidence in support of his claim. Without evidence, she put to the judge, the application was premature, and was outweighed by the democratic right of freedom of speech, and the damages her client would suffer in the meantime. She referred to Professor Alexander's affidavit as evidence of potential loss of book sales. She asked that the interim hearing be deferred a few days to allow each party to prepare and serve the other with an outline of their arguments and alleged loss and damage. Importantly, Jamisons' barrister, Brian Thornton-Brown SC, would be available by then.

Prendergast protested, but the judge, scratching his head as if giving serious consideration to the matter, declared without hearing further argument that it would save time in the long run if both parties came prepared. The application was adjourned for an interim hearing three days later, Friday 24 July at 2 p.m.

Brooke pulled books and authorities off the library shelves, finding both blind alleys and leads for arguing the 'balance of competing interests'. As with the tribunal hearing, her preparation was hindered by not knowing the applicant's reasons for wanting an injunction. She talked with Thornton-Brown by phone, Brooke giving him what she knew about ASIO's attitudes, and he directing her to relevant law. A call came from a *Canberra Times* court reporter who, having received Friday's court list, wanted to know more about the case. Brooke was delighted to brief him. Airing ASIO's high-handed but risky action couldn't hurt.

The hearing came in a rush. There was much donning of robes and wigs and fastening of starched collars around an assortment of necks in the court's small barristers' robing room. Historically, wigs and robes gave them anonymity. But with flapping jabots over their shirt fronts, modern barristers looked like they were ready to stage a Gilbert and Sullivan opera. In the foyer, solicitors carrying large folders of documents talked in huddles with their clients. When the barristers emerged, their solicitors followed them into court to vie for positions at the bar table. Brooke, as junior counsel, carried documents required by her leader, Thornton-Brown SC, and noted that her colleague, Phil, had been briefed as Prendergast QC's junior.

'That's a turn-up,' Brooke thought. 'At least he'll have to read the ASIO Act now, and see what I was on about.'

The various representatives of ASIO and Jamisons Publishing competed for seats at the front of the court while interested onlookers packed into pews at the back.

'All rise,' cried the court attendant as the judge entered. 'The Director-General of Security and Jamisons Publishing Company,' announced the young bespectacled judge's associate.

Counsel identified themselves, and proceedings commenced.

Brooke was relieved to see that Justice Arnold had retained the case. She knew he would engage quickly with the issues and would again want more than assertions that Jo's book posed a threat to national security. And indeed he did.

He tackled Prendergast. 'Mr Prendergast, why is this book such a threat to national security that its publication and sale should cease?' Justice Arnold asked.

The air conditioning unit was noisy and it was difficult for anyone away from the bar table to hear.

Prendergast threw his shoulders back and pulled his robes around his stomach with his thumbs before answering. 'Your honour, the postscript to the book is the subject of our concern. We can't reveal more of our client's case in open court and respectfully request that you order the court to be closed to the public,' he said.

'You have a problem then, don't you, Mr Prendergast?' His Honour responded, smiling. 'You would need a very strong argument to exclude the public from a hearing, particularly in a case about freedom of speech, an important matter of public interest.'

'I am aware of that, your honour, and do not make the application lightly. I tender an affidavit by the Director-General of Security certifying that an open court hearing could prejudice national security.'

'What is your attitude, Mr Thornton-Brown?' the judge asked.

'We were not informed, your honour, that such an application would be made. Could we have a copy of the affidavit please, and I will take instructions.'

Brooke smiled to herself at the gamesmanship. Of course the judge knew Jamisons would have had no forewarning, and Thornton-Brown knew that the director-general would not put sensitive material in an affidavit that the opposition would read.

Prendergast slid a copy of the affidavit across the bar table and addressed the judge, 'I tender an affidavit of today's date sworn by the Director-General of Security, certifying that in his opinion the publication of the book poses a threat to national security, given current political and economic circumstances.'

'We oppose the application, your honour,' said Thornton-Brown, barely rising from his seat.

Brooke glanced at the affidavit over his shoulder and saw it contained no reason in support of the opinion.

'Exhibit A,' the judge noted. 'Anything else, Mr Prendergast?'

'I tender the book *The Unfair Sex* by the late Dr Josephine Rowan,' Prendergast replied.

'Exhibit B,' the judge noted as the associate received the book. 'I thank the respondent for providing me with an unmarked copy last night,' he added, 'and while at this stage I have only perused it, my attention had not been drawn to any particular part of the book.'

It had been Thornton-Brown's idea. He directed Brooke to contact Jamisons and arrange for copies to be delivered to opposing counsel and the judge. He knew that ASIO would not want the judge to have an advance opportunity of seeing how harmless the feminist treatise was.

'Yes, Mr Prendergast, and now I ask, can you indicate the offensive material in the postscript?'

'Not in open court, your honour.'

'I will adjourn the hearing for a short time, and I will see counsel in chambers,' the judge declared as he rose from his chair.

'All rise,' shouted the court attendant. 'The court is adjourned.'

The judge left and the bar table was abuzz.

'What is this about, Prendergast?' Thornton-Brown asked his adversary.

'Let's not keep His Honour waiting,' was Prendergast's gruff reply.

The four barristers left the court and marched upstairs to the judge's chambers, leaving solicitors and others in the courtroom, bewildered. News reporters milled about.

Wigs in hand, the four waited for the judge's associate to let them in through the security door. They followed the associate along the corridor and into Justice Arnold's large room.

'Coffee, gentlemen, Brooke?' offered the judge.

The associate took the orders and bustled around clinking cups and saucers.

'Come on, Morris,' urged Justice Arnold, 'what is the gist of this application? Nothing can be so secret that you cannot publicly outline in general terms the reason for wanting to have the proceedings heard in camera.'

'Judge, an explanation for seeking a closed court would in itself embarrass – that is, compromise – security.'

'So you say. But the court is not concerned about embarrassing your client. The issue is whether or not there is a genuine risk to national security from the release of a book, which for some forty-eight hours or so has been generally available to the public and the press, and the sky has not fallen in.'

'For a start, publication of some material in the postscript is in breach of the law,' Prendergast said.

'The postscript might be somewhat embarrassing, but it mentions no names, identifies no one. Where's the danger in that?'

'Rowan refers to her house being bugged,' Prendergast replied. 'That in itself is classified information.'

The judge looked to Thornton-Brown for a response.

'Judge, Rowan had an expert come to her home to search for and remove any bugs. It was a fact she was being spied on by ASIO which she could, and ultimately did, discover independently of what transpired at the hearing.'

The judge turned back to Prendergast and said, 'Not surprised your client wants to keep that quiet, Morris. Last I knew, it was unlawful for ASIO to spy on Australian citizens.'

'Not necessarily so, Judge. Cabinet's security committee has power to approve guidelines for ASIO and can decide not to table them.'

'Are you suggesting that there are new guidelines to allow ASIO to spy on Australians?'

Everyone in the room turned to Prendergast, waiting for his answer. He looked uncomfortable.

'I'm saying nothing either way,' he said. 'However, there are other matters of concern. The author mentions an approach to recruit her. That too, is a breach of the Act.'

'I'd need to hear argument on that,' said the judge. 'She was not recruited, and signed nothing. Anything else?'

'The book refers to a covert operation, Operation F, about which she was sworn to secrecy. And, it refers to an alleged memo to "Jack" which has potential to compromise a current intelligence operation,' Prendergast blurted.

'Hasn't the horse bolted, Morris, with the operation's full name having been broadcast nationally on ABC TV?'

'That was unfortunate,' Prendergast responded, 'and indeed, the ABC has agreed to suspend further coverage of the story pending the outcome of this hearing – otherwise its representatives would have been here today, too.'

So that's their agenda, Brooke thought. This is about muzzling the

ABC, stopping them pursuing the story. Until now, she and Thornton-Brown couldn't understand why ASIO would be so stupid as to draw attention to Jo's book. Either ASIO spied on Jo illegally or secret new guidelines had been approved by Cabinet allowing it to; either way the press would make a deal of it.

Prendergast continued, trying to sound confidently authoritative, 'However, the author's perception that the Special Projects Section of the department conspired to prevent women being employed and her mention of a name – even a nickname – is dangerous information in the hands of someone intent on thwarting an operation important to national security. The danger is greater, given the ABC broadcast, with its allusions to undercover agents involved in an operation.'

Brooke's mind was working fast. So 'Jack' was a nickname. That was a revelation in itself. And it seems that Jo's enquiry into Annette's grievance about promotion processes was indeed seen to threaten Operation Fishnet, whatever it was. And of course it would, if she found evidence of improper conduct.

Brooke whispered in Thornton-Brown's ear, 'Jo got the name Operation F and the name Jack from the leaked memo, not from anything revealed at the hearing.'

Thornton-Brown interjected to point out Prendergast's error. 'Dr Rowan heard the full name of the operation at the tribunal hearing and did not include it in her book. She was told nothing more at the hearing about the leaked memo and the name "Jack". No security breach there, Judge,' he said.

'Secondly,' Prendergast went on, ignoring his opponent's comment, 'there is a revelation in the book about ASIO's interest in her foreign boyfriend, and reference to bilateral relations.'

Justice Arnold jumped in and rhetorically asked, 'You mean the revelation that ASIO pried on their sex life? They didn't seem to get up to much else at Rowan's home.'

Brooke noted that Arnold had read the book more closely than he had implied.

'Unless, of course, you are suggesting that her lover was a double agent? Is his life at risk because he is mentioned in the book?' Arnold was enjoying himself now.

'No, of course not, Judge. His association with Rowan adds to a body of information that potentially provides leads to other information that when pieced together might compromise a current operation. It concerns matters about which I am not fully briefed. The evidence must come from others on the authority of the director-general.'

Brooke could not contain herself, and although she knew that Thornton-Brown saw no reason to enter the exchange, the judge doing their work for them, she butted in anyway. 'Judge, this is ridiculous. With due respect to Mr Prendergast, I know he has his instructions, but these vague assertions of an unspecified threat are more than fishy – excuse the pun. I suggest that this injunctive action is designed simply to hose down public pressure for an inquiry into the circumstances of Dr Rowan's death. There is no disclosure in the book of classified information that is not already in the public arena and nothing in it justifies a restriction on freedom of speech.'

Prendergast glared at her, and the judge rescued control. Thornton-Brown seemed not at all perturbed by Brooke's outburst, perhaps amused.

'One issue at a time. We must deal first with the application to have the court closed for the duration of today's proceedings,' Arnold directed. 'Morris, I am not presently disposed to grant the injunction – not without further evidence. If you have more, say so, and I'm prepared to consider it.'

'I rely on the director-general's certification. I'm not in a position to produce any other evidence, certainly not today,' Prendergast replied. 'Should you grant an interim injunction today, we would undertake to provide evidence to support the claim in camera at a substantive hearing.'

'So we just trust you and our intelligence agencies, do we?' Arnold asked provocatively. Grinning, he continued, 'Because there is nothing you can point to in the book which, on its face, could possibly pose a threat to national security. I need more than to be told that the linking of a nickname "Jack" to an intelligence operation, details of which are already in the public domain, to justify the extraordinary step of preventing distribution and sale of a seemingly harmless book.'

'There is no more I can say at this stage,' Prendergast conceded.

'I don't understand,' said the judge, scratching his thinning hair, made itchy from wig-wearing day in and day out, 'why you didn't just let this somewhat indulgent feminist treatise go through to the keeper, not attract attention to it. Sorry, Brooke, but there's nothing especially gripping or convincing about Rowan's conspiracy theories.'

Brooke's lips twitched as she tried to suppress a smile. She wasn't upset at the judge's derogatory view of Jo's feminist theories. Not in these circumstances.

The judge continued, 'If there's no more to be said, I suggest we return to court and I will formally deal with your application – in open court. I will refuse it. Then we can fix a date for a substantive hearing, if you want one.'

'It might then be too late,' Prendergast said, by way of an impotent warning.

'That might be so,' said the judge good-humouredly.

Back in court, the judge placed on record that he had heard counsel's submissions in chambers and that the hearing was now open to the public. Prendergast had no further evidence to offer. The judge turned to Brian Thornton-Brown and indicated that he did not need submissions from him. He formally found that no evidence had been presented to convince him of a prima facie case for an interim injunction and refused the application.

'What I propose to do, Mr Prendergast,' the judge offered, 'is to direct that an expedited hearing date be allocated if your client intends to pursue the application for a permanent injunction restraining the further publication and distribution of the book. Please let my associate know if you require me to determine a timetable for the filing of pleadings and service of affidavits.'

His Honour leaned over the bench and tapped his associate on the shoulder. They conferred and his associate flicked through the court diary.

'My associate tells me that two days are available from Monday 24 August, gentlemen and Ms Talbot. Four weeks. That should give all parties time to prepare. Is that suitable?'

'Suitable, your honour,' counsel murmured in unison from the bar table.

The court was adjourned and the press buzzed around. It was explained to Professor Alexander why his evidence was not required, and he congratulated and thanked Thornton-Brown and Brooke. Deidre was beaming.

Alison James looked worried and whispered to Deidre, 'I can't risk distributing the book to retailers. The cost of having to collect all unsold copies is too great.'

Brooke disagreed. 'Prendergast and his team were banking on that. They know they can't win the substantive proceedings, but they'll hold out because as long as the proceedings are on foot, neither the ABC nor the current affairs programs will follow this story. By touching on it, Jo's book provided leverage.'

Deidre supported her. 'Alison, that would make our victory hollow. The publicity around this case will help sell the book, and the wider its distribution, the weaker the case for an injunction. Be brave. Take the risk. Brooke's right. They're not likely to proceed.'

Brooke glanced over Alison's shoulder. The news reporter she had spoken to the evening before was standing just outside the courtroom with a cameraman who captured the group as they walked into the foyer.

'I think the press want to talk to you, Alison,' Brooke indicated.

Thornton-Brown took Alison by the arm and beckoned Professor Alexander towards him. 'We'll talk to them together. Publicity can only work in our favour.'

Soon the reporter was scribbling on a pad and more photographs were taken while Alison answered questions.

'Yes, Professor Alexander would be happy to write a review of the book for your paper... Is that okay, Professor?'

Thornton-Brown's contribution was to remind those listening that the book was not dry reading. 'You'll see that when you read about ASIO's cameras in the author's bedroom…'

'Good on him,' Brooke giggled to Deidre as they emerged from the courthouse. 'I think Alison has already changed her mind. Sales will soar.'

They wandered across the road towards Brooke's chambers, congratulating themselves.

'You know,' Brooke mused, 'I wonder whether ASIO is plain incompetent, or has real concerns that investigative journalists might stumble across something with the help of the book. The tragic irony is that if Jo has been killed because someone thought she knew too much, then her death was not only unnecessary, but has had the opposite effect.'

'It's even more important now,' Deidre replied, 'to ensure a thorough forensic review of how she died. The police were pretty slack at the outset. Do we assume police incompetence, or something more?'

'Probably incompetence, but let's consider possible corruption.'

'Then the family must be at the coroner's inquiry. It's not a case I would leave to counsel assisting,' Deidre said.

'In the meantime, let's hope that with the help of Donald and Rusty, we might discover what's at the heart of this Fishnet fiasco. Three things keep surfacing: Operation Fishnet's attempts to keep outsiders having knowledge of it, what Mujo might have told Jo about intelligence operations, and a shooting in Darwin that was somehow connected with a boatload of refugees. We have to find out how they're related.'

Deidre agreed. 'If an inquiry into Jo's death uncovers how ASIO tried to stop her work at Immigration, it would be a win for Jo.'

27

Early August 1992

'Something's come up, Brooke, and it's important,' said Deidre. 'Can you find time to talk to Kitty McGrath, Jo's daughter?'

'Jo's daughter? Kitty? Here, in Australia?' Brooke repositioned the phone trying to absorb the information.

'Yes, she's here with me now. She lives in London and came out to be with her nan and daughter. I'll come with her. Would tomorrow be okay?'

'Yes. Okay.'

Deidre outlined how a complication had emerged with respect to a life insurance policy Jo had taken out in favour of a granddaughter, Billie. 'Billie is Kitty's daughter. She's five now. The insurer has refused to pay out unless it's established that Jo did not suicide. There's a lot at stake, Brooke. Kitty was barely fifteen when she gave birth and, for reasons I won't go into now, went to live with her father in England. Billie was raised by Jo's mother with financial support from Jo. Kitty wants to resume her role as mother.'

Brooke recalled the man, she now presumed to be Kitty's uncle, Jeremy, holding a little girl's hand at the funeral. The family had been coping with grief for a week, and now they were going to have to sensitively introduce Kitty, an estranged mother, into her daughter's life.

Brooke put the phone down, thinking. She was anxious to see what proof the insurance policy required to establish that death was not self-inflicted. Would it be necessary to prove that foul play probably caused Jo's death, or just that it was a possibility? She would need evidence that shed serious doubt on suicide to win an argument with the insurer.

In the last two weeks, Jo's book had been widely reviewed and read. Although ASIO's injunction proceedings formally remained on foot, no further documents had been filed and the court vacated the allocated hearing date. Now, with Kitty's appearance, it seemed that Jo's spirit was destined to bounce around in and out of courts and inquiries for months to come.

The next day was dank and windy again, although spring was supposedly around the corner. Mother Nature would not submit to a man's calendar. Brooke entered the lift, unbuttoned her fake fur, shoved her faux leopard skin scarf in its pocket, and with perfect timing stepped out at the twelfth floor, computer in one hand, briefcase in the other.

There was an attractive young woman in the waiting room; dark curly hair peeped out from a snug woollen hat that covered her ears. Brooke had been shy about wearing sensible warm hats since outgrowing the striped knitted beanies with waggling pompoms that children wear. The woman's girlish dress made her appear younger than her nineteen years, but a weary sadness in her eyes marked her age.

Brooke passed through the glass door to her pigeonhole, to collect her newspaper and messages.

Her clerk whispered, 'That's Kitty McGrath. I don't know if you're expecting her.'

'It's okay,' mouthed Brooke. 'Dr Rowan's daughter,' she explained quietly.

Kitty was a younger, fresher, version of her mother. She was shorter and had a broader smile and was more gracious, but there was no mistaking Jo's green eyes. Brooke took her hand and gave it a warm squeeze, and placed her other hand on Kitty's shoulder – not a handshake, more a warm greeting.

'I'm so pleased to meet Jo's daughter. But I regret the sad circumstances. I'm Brooke Talbot.'

'Thank you for seeing me. I'm Kitty Rowan-McGrath. Deidre will be here soon. Yes, Jo spoke well of you. I hope you're willing to help me.'

Deidre exited the lift as they spoke.

Once settled in Brooke's room, Kitty did most of the talking, a nervous accounting of herself. 'As Deidre has told you, I have a child, Billie. I've been a bad mother. I went to live with Dad in London, and I stayed there to finish my studies. I'd never got on very well with Jo, and haven't had much to do with her really, or Billie, although we have been writing recently. Teenager and mother falling out stuff. You know. She was always busy, and angry about life, and knew more about it than me. I found it depressing. When I wanted to marvel at the world, she would "enlighten" me – tell me how dark everything was. I began to wonder why anyone bothered to live if everything and everyone was so bad.'

Kitty stopped short, and covered her mouth, horrified at hearing her own words. 'I didn't meant to suggest that Jo…you know, wouldn't have wanted to live…'

'It's all right, Kitty. We understand,' Brooke reassured her.

Deidre squeezed her hand.

'I know Dad couldn't cope with her. And now we're told she took her own life. It's hard to believe. In fact, I don't believe it. Jo lived to change things.'

Kitty paused and looked at Deidre, who smiled and nodded encouragement.

'Anyway, when I fell pregnant…fell? – that makes me sound like a fallen woman, which I wasn't. When I had Billie, it was decided I should go to London and live with my father. I didn't think I could give the baby what she deserved and agreed to her being cared for by Nan.'

Brooke dropped her head to scribble a note on her pad, 'Billie, with Nan,' anything to hide her pained expression from Kitty. It was Kitty she felt for, poor kid, but Kitty might think her anguish was for Billie, an abandoned baby. And perhaps it was, too, but it was not Brooke's responsibility to make moral judgements about her clients. Kitty forged on with her story and Brooke was able to look up again as she talked.

'I've always hoped to study and come back and be a responsible mother. Dad and I live in a two-bedroom flat in Canonbury, near Islington, north London. Jo sent me money for tuition fees, and helped Nan with Billie. She was good like that. Dad's great, but clueless. He never worries beyond tomorrow, but he was always there for me. Brooke…can I call you Brooke?'

Brooke nodded, without comment, hoping to preserve Kitty's flow and gain her picture of a different Jo. Deidre was still, quietly supporting her client. The light coming through the window behind burnishing her yellow coarse straight hair reminded Brooke of Deidre's story about her horse mistaking her thatch of hair for hay. Deidre was a short woman and was grooming her horse when it chewed at her head. She grabbed her head in pain and before the horse yanked out a large tuft, it seemed to realise its mistake, and let go.

'It was Dad who insisted I come to Australia to fight for Billie's insurance money when we learned that an inquest had been scheduled.'

Kitty's words brought Brooke back to the present. Fancy being distracted by a stray memory. But she knew why: it gave her a moment in emotionally safe territory.

'I couldn't face the funeral and wouldn't have made it in time anyway. Dad thought that if it was work stress that had caused Jo's suicide, then Billie, being financially dependent, might be entitled to compensation from the government. And if someone killed her, then, well, the insurer should cough up.'

Brooke was impressed. 'Yes, those are possible outcomes. The important thing for the insurance claim is, as you say, what the coroner concludes as to cause of death.'

Kitty fished around in her drawstring bag, and pulled out a bundle of letters secured by a thick rubber band. 'I don't know if these will help,' she said, handing them to Brooke. 'I'm so glad that Mum and I began writing recently. Those are her letters and Nan retrieved my letters from her town house. They're not in any order.'

As Brooke took the bundle, Kitty began weeping. Brooke plucked tissues from a nearby box and offered them. Deidre left to fetch a glass of water. She returned, handed it to Kitty, and pulled her chair in close. Kitty looked up and Brooke saw a frightened child. Her Jo-green eyes lacked the powerful 'you'd better agree with me' Jo-glare. Kitty's eyes allowed you in, whether she wanted you there or not. She tried to smile, but her thin lips quivered, and she started to sob again and reached for another tissue.

'Thank you both. You must think what an awful daughter and mother I've been. And I feel worse, being here, asking you for help, for money from Jo's death. She did everything for me, and I gave nothing back. But I promise myself, and Jo, if she can hear'– Kitty looked up to the ceiling – 'that I will complete my studies and support Billie and help look after Nan.'

She brightened up and went on. 'We didn't always see eye to eye, but I loved and respected Jo. Once I left Australia, she didn't lecture me, just supported my choices and provided money for my studies. It went unsaid but we both hoped I'd be able to return and take care of Billie. I didn't expect it to be in these circumstances, though.'

Kitty reached for more tissues and sobbed, 'As soon as I heard of Jo's death, I wanted Billie close to me, wrapped in my arms where no one could harm her. She's my family. My uncle has been good to Billie, too. She's never lacked a family.'

Why did Jo lose Kitty to her former husband, Brooke wanted to know. Instead she asked, 'What about your father, Kitty. What does he suggest you do?'

'He'll support me whatever I decide. I love him too. He's a really nice guy – sensitive, sweet and easy to live with, but ineffectual. He'd let anyone walk over him – not emotionally strong enough to face things. He doesn't talk about the world's problems and that suits me as I'd had a gut full of that growing up with Jo. But living in London I've found myself turning into a feminist. I'm not the radical my mother is – was – but I do want to see change. Maybe Mum's death will inspire me to do more.'

It was the second time she referred to Jo as 'Mum', Brooke noticed, perhaps slowly letting her guard down.

'If you return to Australia, what about your studies?'

'Well, subject to finances, I can finish here. I'm doing well at UCL

– University College London – and I'll get credits here so that I can still major in political science and economics. I am in debt, though. I used Dad's bankcard to buy my air ticket. He's pretty relaxed about it. But he expects me to pay him back. He's a rotten money manager – likely to telegram any day and ask for money, because he's forgotten to pay his phone bill.'

She gestured towards Deidre. 'Deidre thinks that I might be able to live in Jo's town house with Billie and Nan if I can pay my way. There is a mortgage on it, but Nan's pension must just cover that, and she wouldn't be paying rent.'

Deidre told them that Jo's estate was modest. Most of her income had gone to support Billie and Kitty, but the equity in the town house would come to Kitty. Clearly Jo had anticipated that if she died while Billie was a child, the substantial insurance payout would be placed in trust for Billie, and the interest used to keep up mortgage payments on the town house.

Reverting to the business at hand, Brooke briefed Kitty on the difficulties of using the existing evidence to throw doubt on the suicide theory the police favoured. Brooke asked Kitty whether Jo's recent letters suggested a depressed or despairing state of mind.

'I actually received a letter the day after her death, written a few days earlier.'

'That must have been distressing,' Brooke said.

'Hmm, it sort of was. She didn't mention seeing a doctor, or psychiatrist or anything like that, but as I recall, she often took sleeping tablets and sometimes Valium if she was stressed at work. And she had seen a psychiatrist in the past, for depression, sleep problems. Now she was distressed by happenings at work, and her boyfriend's return to Europe.'

Brooke supposed Kitty had lived with Jo, or Jo and Edith, as a child. But home life must have been difficult for a teenager with a sometimes depressed mother.

Kitty went on, 'Other letters were just newsy or responsive to things I told her. Several times she wrote about the ideas she was developing for her book.'

Here Brooke remembered KRM, and interrupted, 'She must have loved you very much, Kitty. She dedicated her book to you.'

'I know,' Kitty agreed. 'I truly appreciate that. But her last letter somehow warned me that one day she might not be around for me. Mind you, I was reading it hours after hearing about her death, so my head was buzzing.'

'I know the letters are personal and private,' said Brooke gently, 'and I thank you for entrusting them to me, but if I think we need a psychiatrist's opinion, then the insurance company will also want to see them, particularly if it comes to litigation. And it's more than likely they will be called for at the inquest. Are you prepared to have them scrutinised and answer questions about them?'

'Whatever you advise I'll go along with.'

When the pair had left, Brooke put the letters in her briefcase, keen to get home and read them. They were a wild card. Depending on their interpretation, they could make or break the claim against the insurer.

28

The flames of the fire jumped around excitedly behind the blackened glass door while Brooke spread the letters out on the floor to put them in date order. She soon had them replying to each other. They were disturbing. Jo's letters were measured and thoughtful, clearly trying to reach her daughter with supportive and wise words. By way of contrast, Kitty's were streams of consciousness, fluctuating between perceptive insights about life matters and indulgent outbursts about things that irritated her.

The letters read of a typical mother–daughter relationship. Jo's earlier letters were regular, with Kitty replying lengthily as the spirit moved her. Kitty's later letters were increasingly responsive to Jo's observations, demonstrating their growing bond and her own developing maturity perhaps. It was these that Brooke particularly wanted to study.

Dear Jo-Ro,

I'm scribbling this from my No 73 bus crawling up Oxford Street. I've just handed in my essay to Prof. George. My studies are going well. He likes my work. Hell – I hope I don't start enjoying it and become an academic like you!

We just passed a hoarding 'customer is King' – how sexist – see, your influence! I never understood what you were on about when I lived at home – but I get angry now when I come across sexist pigs, and some men just are.

I miss you, and Billie, and Nan. I think it's nearly time to come home and face my responsibilities. I don't want Billie to hate me for abandoning her. The UK is crumbling. Its people have lost respect for the government and are becoming demoralised. I wonder if individuals can suffer personality crises when their country has become unimportant on the world stage. It's horrid seeing people sheltering in cardboard boxes on London streets. Anyway, this is not a place for me or Billie in the long term. It's a good place for Dad, 'cause he doesn't see things. He just is, just being.

Now, how about you? Your last letter sounded down, disillusioned. What is happening to my ever-hopeful mother? The world needs energetic people like you. Keep up the good fight. You instil fight in others. One day I'd like to think I could take over from you – if I were as clever, and as dedicated as you. Oh, who is Brooke?

Oops, nearing my stop – must get paper and pen into my satchel.

Love you, and Nan and Billie heaps. Kisses.

Kitty.

P.S. (Written later) I enclose a photo of me outside our front door, with our teensy bit of garden. Where does my name 'Kitty' come from?'

Brooke picked up her yellow highlighter and marked the sentence beginning with 'Your last letter sounded down…' But why wouldn't she feel down given what she had been going through? Brooke shuffled through the bundle to find Jo's response. She was surprised to find how much Jo put into in replying to this hurried spiel from her teenage daughter.

Kitty dear,

It was lovely to receive your breezy and thoughtful letter. I am so proud of you. The photo helps me visualise you in your surroundings. At night time when I can't sleep I know it's day time in London. Winter here, but I can feel you warm enough in the not so hot London summer. You must enjoy the long days.

Who is Brooke, you ask? My lawyer, a different sort of lawyer from Deidre, who is a solicitor, and Brooke appears in court as an advocate for clients – same as in England. I need her to help me sort out the dreadful work situation that I'm facing here. I feel diminished by the way I've been treated. But, as to why, I'm in the dark. It's all about my security clearance, a matter clouded in secrecy. It's causing me a great deal of misery and concern about my future, and what I'm doing with my life. I'm not sure I'd encourage you to follow my path. I want you to follow your heart and, above all, be happy.

It's not my influence that's causing you to think about the things you see around you. You're bright and educated and, less commonly, you're compassionate. That means you can't help seeing the inequalities that exist in our society. Yet kings and the ruling class are part of the history that has shaped us. Without a sense of the past, we can't think sensibly about the future. We have to see where we've been to make the best choice about where to go.

Incidentally, talking of kings brings me to explaining your name, Kitty. Your father and I played many card games, mostly Five Hundred, by the light of campfires in our younger days. That wonderful surprise bundle of cards you receive when you win the bidding is 'kitty'. You were the bonus when I bid to join up with your father, at least for as long as we felt we wanted to stay together…

I'm fascinated with the origins of our playing cards, speaking as they do of our history and culture, tradition and religion. Think about it. They give greatest value to the royals – kings and queens and princes (the jacks) and put the commoner (number cards) in their place. The emotions are there too – love in the suit of hearts and the reality of aggression in the clubs. The object of card games is to win, just as in life. So we ask, what is winning? Do we win if we become rich or powerful? Or do we win if we find happiness and fulfilment? Winning has to be defined. What tools are required: luck, skill, aggression, cheating, fear, partnership, cooperation? This innocent stack of cardboard truly mirrors life.

Right now, I am not a winner. When you've got a really poor hand, you have to bid misère – that's how I feel right now. I can't win a trick.

Jo's letter chattered on for a while before telling Kitty about losing her latest love, Mujo. And she returned to how her security troubles were interrupting her work, and took a few swipes at the legal system.

Brooke shut her eyes, emotionally exhausted. She stretched and shivered. It was late and the fire was as tired as she was. Brooke braved the chilly air to collect a few sticks to feed the struggling embers, but they needed a bit of encouragement before springing to life. A prod with the poker helped.

She knew she should go to bed but, well, she wanted to read Kitty's response.

Dear Jo-Ro,

People have let you down – your boyfriend, your work bosses. And I've let you down too, leaving you and Nan to look after Billie. And I want to cry. You are wise. I think that everything you say is wise. You know so much, and you think so clearly that I feel inadequate, never able to meet your standards.

I love your card metaphors, and I loved us playing together as a family. I will never be as clever, or as strong as you. The more exceptional the parent, the less likely the child will meet the parent's standards. That's why I came to London, to Dad. He's so mild and he admires me – goodness knows why. I have confidence in his presence, like fat people feel good in the presence of the obese. I hate saying this, but as I lose respect for him, I gain confidence in myself. (Is that why businessmen marry their secretaries – because they see them as inferior, and can go home and feel good, after being made to feel inadequate by more successful business men?)

How would Jo respond, Brooke wondered. She was disappointed on readying Jo's reply. Her response verged on the emotionally manipulative, almost seeking sympathy:

Oh, Kitty dear, what have I done? You have cut me down to size. Whatever I touch seems to fragment. Your father, now you. We're all vulnerable, me too. I love you too much. That's why I cause you pain.

It's me who is inadequate. My mother helped me to bring you up, and she's raising Billie too. You're asking me to be what my mother is to me, a raft. I'm sorry, Kitty dear, but you can't afford to need me. You must find what you need in yourself. You'll understand that after I'm gone.'

Brooke shivered as she read the last sentence. Not helpful to Kitty's case. What would a forensic psychiatrist make of it, if asked for an opinion in court?

Jo's emotional outburst brought the response from Kitty that she was looking for. Kitty made everything all right again.

Dearest Jo,

I'm so sorry. I've hurt you. You come across so strong I think I can say anything to you. Mothers are the dumping ground for daughters' feelings, but you're right. I have to grow up sometime, and I can see you are really soft inside. This letter will be strictly newsy.'

Kitty went on then about her day, her studies and the latest movies she had seen.

Jo replied,

Thank you, dearest daughter. Don't get despondent about my depression. We all have feelings, and families indulge in trading them. We deflect our problems on to each other. I can see that my despair directed itself on to you. I am sorry, and I do want to be there for you. I just want to prepare you for the day when I'm not.

Keep heart, keep strong. Keep the good parts of me in a little parcel inside you. But see me for what I really am, and not what you want to see. Put your energies into your future, not me as mother who only represents the past.

All my love,

Jo Jo.

Brooke sat still, staring at the fire. This was the letter that Kitty had received after Jo's death. She shook her head to deny flow to the tears that had formed. Was this a 'goodbye' letter? She folded up the letters and told the fire that it need struggle no longer to stay alive. The flames subsided, as if relieved.

The next morning, Brooke sifted through the letters with professional deftness. She photocopied those she thought might be important to the forensic psychiatrist, and then circled the relevant paragraphs on the photocopies. She put the originals back in the order they had come to be returned eventually to Kitty. She collated the copies for the psychiatrist, a well respected man who would give a conditional opinion on limited information. Brooke drafted a covering letter, outlining the work and other problems Jo had, by way of background. She requested Jo's medical clinical records from her GP, hoping they would show no history of depressive illness, and no record of discussion of anxiety or depression. But she needed something more to challenge the preliminary finding of suicide. Everything hinged on the cause of Jo's death. She decided to try again to talk to Jo's friend, Donald Fenchurch.

29

She dialled his number hoping that this time an answering machine would not greet her. Her heart pounded. A male voice answered.

'Donald?'

'Yes.'

'You won't remember me. My name is Brooke Talbot. We met at the Faceless Men's Bar one evening, a year ago now – you were with Rusty Redmond. I'm a lawyer. I was Jo Rowan's lawyer, in fact.'

There was a silence. Brooke was just about to say 'Are you there?' when he replied.

'Yes, yes, I remember you. How could I forget – you practically accused me of being a spy! And Jo has spoken of you since.'

Brooke gulped, remembering her uninhibited jibes that evening. 'Jo mentioned you too. I'm now representing Kitty, Jo's daughter. It might seem pushy, but I'd like to meet you. There are several things you may be able to clarify.'

Donald's voice lifted. 'Is Kitty here – in Australia?'

'Yes, she is.'

There was another silence.

'I'll be in Canberra Thursday. When and where would you like to meet?' he asked.

'Oh, thank you, Donald. How about coffee Thursday morning, say, Gus's?'

Everyone knew Gus's. The café proprietor regularly broke the law by placing tables and chairs outdoors, but away from the footpath so as to not create a hazard. The bureaucrats wouldn't have it. Flies, they said, might land on the pastries or in coffee cups. Heaven forbid. It was a risk to the health of patrons. Gus was willing to go to gaol if that's what it took

182

to make Canberra cosmopolitan. He won. It was hard, but Canberrans could now risk their health in exchange for sun or cool breezes, as they read the papers and chatted.

They agreed to meet at ten and Brooke put the phone down, aware of an excited nervousness. What might she learn from Donald? What more had he learned from the whistle-blower? He was unlikely to be able to add anything to how Jo died. But, at the back of her mind, she thought he might be able to put her in touch with Mujo. He was the one person most likely to know about her state of mind before her death, and according to Jo, he held the key to explaining why ASIO might have been so troubled by Jo working at Immigration.

Brooke nursed a secret thought. She was due for an overseas holiday. She had space in her diary, having kept aside time to prepare for the injunction proceedings concerning Jo's book. It appeared unlikely that the government would pursue it. A new date would have to be obtained if they did proceed. The coroner's inquest was some months away. She had friends in London she wanted to visit, and why shouldn't she make a side trip to Europe. Perhaps she could get to Belgrade and meet Mujo? It was imperative, as Deidre kept saying, that every aspect of how and why Jo died be investigated before the inquest. Mujo might have some leads. No, she was being fanciful. Nevertheless, it was important to meet Donald. He knew things about Immigration that Jo had not uncovered. And he knew Jo well.

Donald was as charming as she remembered. But he looked older – and tired.

'It wasn't hard for me to recognise your silhouette on television,' Brooke said as she approached the table on the pavement.

'Others will have too,' Donald replied, as he pushed his chair out to stand up.

'You did well to provoke a government commission of inquiry. Will your whistle-blower give evidence?' Straight into it. She kicked herself.

'I doubt it. I treat the government's prompt response with scepticism. Here, have a seat and we'll order some coffees.'

Brooke shook his hand and she was drawn into his shiny brown eyes, like Rocky and Rex, heart-melting eyes. Donald's came with a warm smile. Pull yourself together, Brooke told herself as she felt her eyes sticking to his like a magnet. She thanked him for making time to see her. She pulled her trim flared skirt down under her as she sat, but it was too short to protect her thighs from the cold seat. They gave the dark-suited waiter their orders, and Donald resumed.

'Announcing an inquiry shuts everyone up for a time. Then people forget about the issue and their outrage. When terms of reference are drawn up, they're too vague to expose how any particular operation is run.'

'Yes, of course, it could be a whitewash exercise…' said Brooke.

'And, if the whistle-blower comes forward, he or she might be charged and convicted of security breaches. It has happened before.'

'Oh.' Brooke couldn't think of an adequate response. She pushed her strong-willed hair out of her face and found the courage to say, 'But it was brave of you to speak out and I judge that Jo's death was the reason. Do you blame Immigration for that?'

Donald wiped his brow with a paper serviette. He was sweating. Nervous, upset? Brooke couldn't tell.

'I feel responsible,' he said.

'Why?'

Donald told Brooke that after Jo had asked him to be a referee for the tribunal review he had talked to various people, including in the department, to background the threat to her security clearance; and help him focus his reference. He told Brooke why he didn't act on the anonymous note he received a year before her death.

'Now I feel terrible,' he said, shifting his chair back as the coffees arrived. 'If I had talked to the whistle-blower then, maybe things would be different now. She might have seen that it wasn't her integrity at issue, and that her life was worthwhile.' His eyes were watering. Was he fighting back tears?

'It's not your fault. I was suspicious too when I got an anonymous letter. Mine wasn't from Sally, though. It was signed "A Friend" and I'm pretty sure it was a set-up.'

Brooke told Donald about her letter and the ambiguous reference to 'Roger' that could have meant 'Yes' or been a name; and about the black Fairlane seen at her mail box. Donald was about to respond, but before he could, Brooke said, 'But you sound convinced that she did take her own life?'

'Oh, well, we have to accept that, don't we? Isn't that what the police found, and the autopsy?'

'Her family have doubts. That's why I wanted to talk to you. Did you keep in touch with her after the hearing?'

Donald looked at her with surprise before answering her question. 'Over the phone a couple of times. She was very down and she had been depressed on occasion.'

'Down because…? Her career in ruins, or losing her lover – broken heart?' Brooke fished for Donald's insights.

'Broken heart? Goodness no, not that. She was a realist, and knew what she was getting into with Mujo. No, her work was her life, and the only thing that drives single-minded people like Jo to suicide is having their integrity questioned. Being treated as untrustworthy, like a traitor, being so misunderstood would have ripped her apart.'

'That was cleared up at the tribunal, though,' Brooke interrupted.

'Yes, sort of, but then, as she reveals in her postscript, being asked to choose between her career and spying on Mujo was wrenchingly distressful. But…' Donald was looking across the road and Brooke followed his gaze to a parking attendant, a 'bomber', placing a sticker on an out-of-time vehicle. He continued, '…now that you've raised it, I do doubt that even that dilemma would trigger her to kill herself. She's a fighter who would be looking to retrieve her reputation, by writing the book, for example. She would have wanted to hang around and watch the hornets fly.'

Brooke nodded. 'But if so, it means someone killed her. Which is what I've come to believe, but who and why? A number of people, apart from Sally, could have blown the whistle on Immigration's operation. Something else is lurking here, something to do with Mujo.'

Brooke told Donald what she knew; that after the hearing Mujo had talked freely to Jo about the waterfront shooting incident, and speculation about Customs corruption. 'They thought that one of Immigration's current operations might link back to a much earlier Yugoslav–ASIO joint operation. There was cooperation to find Croatian military training camps, and he told Jo how his people used an undercover agent to help locate Croatian Ustashi. That has to be aligned with Jo saying in her book that ASIO wanted information from Mujo on what he might know about goodness knows what. There has to be a connection between the two projects.'

Donald was deep in thought. 'Yes, in a phone call she suggested something like that might be the case. I've already suggested to Rusty that he look into Operation Fishnet, why ASIO is interested, the crooked informant, to find the bigger story.'

'Is your whistle-blower Jack the one who got that memo?' Brooke saw that she had caught Donald off guard.

He looked at her balefully. 'It's important that you don't try and guess who the whistle-blower is. Honestly.'

'No, of course. But, it seems clear that the whistle-blower must be involved in Operation Fishnet, and it's unlikely there are two grasses. Point is, I'm interested to know what would prompt someone to dump on a project they're part of.'

'Becoming implicated in what was turning into a farce, perhaps? I can say this much. Now we know the department's informant is probably a people smuggler himself, everyone involved with the operation must be concerned, particularly with ASIO pulling out all stops to keep Jo in the dark.'

'So why would anyone want to kill Jo? We're no closer. It's Mujo we need to talk to.' She suddenly thought to ask Donald, 'Do you think he knows about Jo's death? Do you know where he is?'

'Goodness, I hadn't thought… He must know. Or had he already returned to Belgrade?'

'Strangely, the morning after it had happened,' Brooke said. 'But, remember, her body wasn't found until a few days later. The police seem pretty satisfied that he didn't kill her, given CCTV evidence of his movements at the Hyatt that night. He and Jo did meet that evening, and it doesn't rule out one of his own people being involved, maybe wanting to prevent Jo from broadcasting something Mujo told her.'

'But because they've concluded suicide, I take it that angle has not been investigated?' Donald asked.

'Seems like foul play was ruled out early.'

'No point, anyway, in the police fishing around the Yugoslav embassy. They have diplomatic immunity and, being already under an expulsion order, hardly likely to cooperate in a murder investigation.'

'Do you know how to get in touch with Mujo in Belgrade?'

'I do. I still have his home phone number. At least I should check that he knows what has happened, though I'll need to be careful not to cause an upset between him and his wife.'

'Can you ask if he might be willing to talk to me too, as the Rowan family's representative at the inquest? For Kitty's sake, as well as for Jo's reputation, my job is to cast doubt on the suicide theory. If ASIO has a bigger agenda than just keeping Immigration's intelligence secrets, then it's worth trying to find out who had a motive to kill Jo.'

'You have to be careful, Brooke. Yugoslavs could be involved and phones might be tapped.'

Brooke plunged in. 'I'd visit him!'

'You'd what?'

'Go over there, if he agrees to see me.' Brooke explained Kitty's claim against the insurance company, and the importance of learning more before the inquest. 'If the coroner's finding raises doubt on the suicide theory, we can fight the insurance company,' she explained. She paused and scooped the remaining froth in her coffee cup with a plastic spoon, and then, looking up so that her eyes met Donald's, she said quietly, 'I want to talk to Mujo. He's the key to this.'

They made to leave, Donald promising to do his best, and to let Brooke know as soon as he had made contact with Mujo.

'Oh, Donald, one more thing. Tell me, I've been worried about it, did Jo tell you the name of Operation Fishnet, or did you get it from the whistle-blower?'

'Neither. I talked to Annette Armstrong at Immigration and, after she showed me the memo that quoted Operation F, I mentioned it to a friend who knows things and he blurted out the full name.'

'Oh,' Brooke laughed, relieved that Jo had not breached her legal undertaking. 'That's how Jo and I found out too. One slip by ASIO's counsel at the tribunal, and we were immediately sworn to secrecy.'

30

Donald steeled himself as he waited on his long-distance call to Belgrade. He didn't want to be the one to tell Mujo Zukić that Jo had died. He hoped he already knew. Either way, with both having been her lover, the call wasn't going to be easy.

As he hung on, he reflected on his meeting with Brooke a few days before. She was a determined woman. She had pranced up to greet him, in a too-short skirt and loud high heels, a most unlikely-looking lawyer. He'd already encountered her frankness at the Kingo, and now he saw that, professionally, she wasn't to be messed with. He would like to have told her about his meeting with Immigration's James Pratt, but he couldn't break the whistle-blower's confidence. He had called on Pratt at the department after his conversation with Gideon. Pratt had offered his condolences and suggested they leave the building and talk over a coffee. In fact, they hadn't bothered with the coffee. Pratt started to speak as soon as they left the building and Donald had guided him across the road to a park where they would not be observed or overheard.

'Dr Rowan was working on the wrong topic at the wrong time and in the wrong place, meaning my department,' Pratt had said. 'She arrived when a woman's promotion was being stalled, deliberately, because we were worried that she might brief our minister about the abysmal results of our operation targeting refugee boats. And Dr Rowan, too, had to be prevented from learning what was going on. I was part of that move, I admit,' Pratt said uncomfortably. 'It was important that the details be kept secret until we found a way of handling our informant.'

If Donald had been unsure before meeting Pratt, he now knew he was talking to Sally, the whistle-blower, same person as Jack in the leaked memo.

'Our informant was people smuggling, and we couldn't prosecute him. Nor could we lay charges against the boat owners, because they were all fingering him!' Pratt had told Donald. 'But I drew the line at Dr Rowan having her project and career ruined from ASIO forcing her out of the department for unstated "secret" reasons. I'd already leaked the memo through Annette to Dr Rowan to show her that the selection process was rigged. I hoped she'd investigate it because my concerns about this informant were being ignored. Our informant was blatantly organising more boats. There aren't any he hasn't been involved in. It was time someone investigated.'

Pratt had turned back towards the Immigration building, as if checking for prying eyes as they walked towards a park bench under a tree. 'Then, before she'd properly started, Dr Rowan's work was stopped short, and now she's dead. How do you think I feel?'

Donald had hidden his expression, scraping dirt from his shoe.

Sitting on the bench, Pratt had continued, 'We ruined her career, took away her life.'

'You did, yes,' Donald had said. 'Not you personally, you collectively.'

They then talked at length about what Pratt was prepared to reveal on ABC's *7.30 Report*. It would have to be through Donald. Pratt wanted to keep his distance. Donald took notes as Pratt talked, starting points for Rusty's investigation.

He started as Zukić's wife came on the line.

'Let me get him,' Andjela said. 'He'll want to talk to you.'

Mujo Zukić's unmistakable voice came through. 'My friend, Donald, I'm glad to hear from you.'

Donald collected his thoughts, and breathed more easily as Mujo explained that his female colleague, Marika, who was now living in Australia, had told him everything. He was devastated and wanted to know more than what he read in the newspaper reports that Marika had faxed. His wife, he said, was sympathetic, but had not met Jo, and Mujo welcomed the chance to express his grief to someone who had known her.

The call was longer than Donald had planned, but he was pleased that Mujo had been so open. Donald told him about Immigration's scandalous operation, his role in arranging the whistle-blower's story, and the upcoming formal inquiry.

'You were their excuse to ease her out of the department, but it would have been much easier to simply stop her seeing sensitive files. We think there might be other reasons, things you know perhaps, that they didn't want her discussing.'

'Did your whistle-blower name the operation?' Mujo asked.

'It's public knowledge now. It's called Operation Fishnet,' Donald answered.

'Jo never told me that.'

Donald sensed that the name meant something, and asked him.

'No. I don't know anything about Operation Fishnet,' he said – too quickly, Donald thought. 'I don't like to talk here. I have secure line at the office,' Mujo said.

Donald gave Mujo his phone number and Mujo said he'd fax the secure number. They agreed to talk later in the week.

'Hello, Brooke?'

She recognised his voice and felt a flutter of excitement. He must have talked to Mujo; she hoped that was the reason for the flutter. 'Donald. Yes?'

'Can we mix a little business with pleasure? I've talked with Mujo and have something to report. Would you like a picnic lunch?'

The suggestion took her by surprise. This man was hard to read. Brooke had been preparing some advices at work. She looked at her watch. It was not yet 10 a.m. She had a client scheduled for 2.30. 'Today?'

'If you can. I'll pick up some bread and cheese and collect you at work.'

'Lovely idea. I'll wait below. Pull into the circular driveway, say 12.30?'

Donald arrived in an old pale blue Peugeot and leaned over to throw the passenger door open.

Brooke jumped in and grinned. 'I feel like a kid playing hooky,' she said.

They wound their way up the narrow road to the summit of Black Mountain. Not wanting to appear too eager to hear whether Mujo was willing to talk with her, Brooke began with chit-chat. She told Donald that the road was still the subject of an injunction lingering from the Black Mountain Tower case in the early 70s. The court's decision to stop work on the tower was over-ridden by an executive order-in-council and construction went ahead anyway. But other aspects of the court's injunction still stood, despite a government appeal to the High Court. For example, the road could not be widened once the Supreme Court accepted the evidence that widening would spread the soil-borne fungus *Phytophthora cinnamomi*, and cause root rot in Black Mountain's magnificent eucalypts.

'But you don't want to hear all that,' Brooke laughed. 'More important is what you learned from Mujo.'

'Indeed,' said Donald negotiating another sharp bend in the road. 'I think we'll stop before the top. There's a picnic table where…' he turned to Brooke and smiled, 'you get a grand view of Canberra and the lake but not the tower that the people tried to stop.'

He flashed his right indicator and returned to the subject of the phone call. 'He was very responsive, and we had two long talks.'

A black car which must have followed them up the hill continued on. Donald and Brooke looked around and turned towards each other and laughed.

'Funny how alert I've become to the possibility of being followed… If we are, you'd have to be the person of interest, not me,' she said to Donald.

'I don't think we're of interest to anyone, unless your chamber clerk is after you for wagging work!'

Donald pulled up and lifted a large brown grocery bag and an esky out of the boot. He took out fresh bread, a couple of cheeses, a large ripe tomato, a knife, and a misty bottle of Schweppes soda. A second parcel contained slices of Hungarian salami wrapped in flimsy paper.

'And something I made in Sydney,' he said proudly, producing a container of home-made ratatouille and a couple of forks and plates.

'You planned this before you rang me,' Brooke chuckled. 'I'm touched.'

They talked and ate. Scoops of ratatouille on crusty bread, cheese and slices of salami on more bread. Donald reported the gist of his conversations with Mujo and included the thought that the word Fishnet stirred something in Mujo's memory.

'One thing he's sure of is that Jo would not have killed herself.'

'Is he? Oh, good. That means he's not trying to protect anyone.'

'Here's the important bit. Just before he left, Jo told him something that worried her.'

'Being asked to spy on him, perhaps?'

'Yes. And it was clear from his conversation that he thought she died some days after he left. I didn't have the heart to tell him it was the night before he left, and that he was momentarily a suspect!'

'No need,' Brooke agreed.

Donald continued. 'One thing Jo told Mujo was that the Intelligence officer who contacted her went under the unlikely name of Brown and if the name of Operation Fishnet meant anything to him, he wasn't going to say so over the phone. I think we might have to communicate through another friend of mine in Belgrade.'

Brooke, mouth half full, managed to speak. 'But I told you. I'd like to visit him.'

Donald looked at her. 'What if she did kill herself? Jo was confronted by a deeply distressing choice. Spy on Mujo and regain her reputation, or refuse and blight her career. It's a real possibility that she took her life. I can understand why Mujo doesn't want to accept that. He probably feels responsible too, for leaving her.'

Brooke looked at him, and changed the subject. 'How did you make this delicious ratatouille?', making it clear that she didn't accept his interpretation.

Donald shrugged, looked quizzically at his offering and back to her, before answering. 'It's pretty easy,' he said. 'You take a large eggplant and cut it into smallish cubes, then do the same for one green and one red capsicum and one zucchini. Fry the eggplant in a little oil until yellowy-brown. I spiced it up a bit with some garlic. Transfer the eggplant to a large pot, or a slow cooker, and add the other vegetables. Add about half a bunch of chopped basil, some coriander and parsley and a can of tomatoes (or fresh tomatoes if they're juicy). Blend the tomatoes with a cup of tomato puree and some tomato paste, and Bob's your uncle. Salt and pepper to taste of course, and cook slowly for a couple of hours. Simple! Now, are you ready to be serious?'

'Hmm, nice,' Brooke responded. 'I wonder what Serbian food is like.'

Donald played along and returned to the ratatouille. 'You can have it as a pasta sauce, or add it to a meat dish, or serve it as a snack on toast, like bruschetta. I always keep some frozen for snacking. In this case, I thought of you, and a picnic.'

Brooke kept scooping, ignored his compliment and looked up at him. 'I'm due for a holiday. I'd have friends to see in London. Is there any reason I couldn't manage a short trip to Eastern Europe, and drop in on Belgrade?'

'You're not someone who lets go, are you?' was Donald's response. 'But it's hardly a place for tourists right now. Do you really want to go?'

'Yes, I do. Would you sound the idea out with Mujo for me?'

'It's not a trip I'd advertise,' Donald said, 'just in case.'

'Perhaps you're more doubtful about the suicide theory than you admit? By the way, I noticed that black car going back downhill a while ago,' she said looking at him. 'Didn't say anything in case you thought me totally paranoid.'

'I saw it too,' he said, 'and for safety's sake, it's probably best not to publicise any plans you have for further investigations.'

'I gotta go,' Brooke shrieked, checking her watch and remembering her 2.30 client.

They packed up and Donald said he'd get a message to Mujo and see how he reacted to the plan. He suggested she'd need to travel to Belgrade via Hungary, given the embargo.

'No telephone calls about this, Brooke. I'll just ring you and ask if I can see you onto your plane to London. That will be my confirmation that Mujo is happy to see you. If you give me your flight details, I'll meet you at the airport and give you his address and advice on how best to get to Belgrade from Budapest.'

Brooke leant over and kissed his cheek.

'Don't apply for any visas here. You can do all that at the consulate in London, a few days before you travel,' he said, and gave her a small smile.

'It's a bit cloak and dagger, isn't it?' Brooke said with a nervous laugh.

'Just insurance. But if Jo was killed because of her links to Mujo, then your scrabbling around to find out if Mujo told her things that he shouldn't have known could put you at risk.'

That stopped Brooke in her tracks. 'Oops. Well, yes, I suppose so. I'll certainly be careful about my travel plans, but I don't expect to run in to any trouble.'

'Rest assured, if Mujo knows anything that could make it unsafe for you to meet him, he will say.'

31

Late August 1992

He sauntered into the Qantas lounge. Brooke was sitting by a window checking her flight details. She was in jeans and a white shirt, and had a blazer draped over her carry-on bag. She had decided to dress more conservatively while overseas. She had packed a simple skirt for more formal occasions, and otherwise would make do with slacks and some colourful T-shirts, jumpers, and scarves for lifting her spirits.

She took a deep breath. It had been a crazy busy time preparing for the trip. She had to change appointments, hand a few briefs to one or other of her colleagues, organise her trusty farm-sitters to look after her animals while she was away, contact her friends in London, and plan her trip.

Donald had returned to Sydney after their picnic. His contact in Belgrade operated as a go-between, delivering messages to Mujo and faxing responses back to Donald. He had called to ask her how her 'holiday plans' were going.

'Great,' she had told him. 'I fly from Sydney to London on Qantas leaving at 2 p.m. Monday week.'

'I'd like to wave you off,' he offered – casually for the benefit of any listeners.

'That'd be nice,' she replied equally offhandedly. 'I'll be loitering in the Qantas domestic lounge soon after eleven.'

Relief had swept through her learning that Mujo was happy to see her and that she could stick to her carefully made plans. She had to admit that she was glad that her partner in this clandestine game was the intriguing Donald. 'Thank you, Jo, for introducing us,' she said in her head.

She accepted Donald's light kiss on the cheek knowing that while he was acting out the role of a close friend they were in fact becoming friends. She gave his hand a squeeze.

'You have to obtain your Serbian entry and exit visas in London. Book yourself a flight to Budapest. That's as far as you can go in these times of sanctions on flights and trains.'

She knew all that, but she listened and nodded.

'From there, you'll need to chance it on the haphazard minibuses between Budapest and Belgrade,' Donald explained. 'They're readily available, though there can be long delays at the border crossing. Passengers sometimes have to cough up cash for the border patrols to let them queue-jump. You'll also be delayed when your driver queues for fuel to avoid black market prices across the border.'

Donald told her how to go about finding a bus, what to expect to pay, and what currency to carry. 'It will be a long tiring journey, so make sure you take plenty of water and some food. Now, Mujo insists you stay with him and family. He and Andjela want the children to speak fluent English, so having you there chatting in an Aussie accent will be perfect. And you may as well have a holiday and be shown around. It's safer too, not to be alone.'

'How kind of them. It certainly simplifies things for me. Though I'm surprised that they'd welcome a stranger to their house, particularly someone associated with matters that both would want to put behind them.'

'You'll find them generous hosts.'

'Yes, but Mujo will be grieving about Jo, and Andjela is likely to be suppressing resentment and jealousy, and in I come trying to extract information from him.'

'If anyone can handle it, you can, Brooke. You exude warmth. They will like and trust you. Believe me, they'll enjoy having you around, bringing news from the outside world. They really are very isolated.'

Brooke felt her face flushing. Donald delivered his flattery in a matter of fact way.

'Don't buy them a gift,' he continued. 'Instead, leave your spare Deutschmarks and dollars. They'll go a long way. Likewise, don't be tempted to change any large sums into dinar.'

A couple of coffees later, Donald took his leave. He held Brooke's hands in his and wished her safe travel and very good luck. She saw sincerity in his eyes, and thanked him for his efforts to help her journey run smoothly. Brooke gathered up her hand luggage and made her way to the international terminal.

Back in his Sydney apartment, Donald placed an international call. Minutes later, the phone rang and he snapped it up. 'She's leaving for London today,' he told the man at the end of the line. 'In all likelihood, she'll arrive Budapest sometime Friday. Sorry I can't give you flight details. You'll just have to hang around for flights from London. She's easy to spot.' He listened to the other's response, and said, 'No, don't alarm her. She shouldn't see you. Just be sure to track her movements. Yes, I particularly want her watched on her way back, about three days later. I don't know how you'll do that. The agent will tell you the name of her bus driver. Most likely she'll arrange for the same driver to collect her for the return trip. Use our Belgrade contact. Be aware that she might be bringing papers back in either her hand luggage or main bag. We need those papers. Keep me informed and good luck.'

Come Tuesday evening, Brooke was sharing curry dishes at the local Indian restaurant in Belsize Park, in north-west London with her friend Jill, whom she had known since university days, and husband Peter. The weather was mild, much like the late winter she had just left. The three chattered away about life since their last meeting, and Brooke, relaxed, enjoyed this short lull in her mission.

She would stay with Jill and Peter for two nights. She had applied for Hungarian and Yugoslav visas on arriving that afternoon, a process likely to take a few days. Her plan was to find a cheap hotel in central London, if anything was cheap there, for her last night to avoid lots of questions about her movements in Europe. 'I'd like to visit Budapest, if I can get a visa, and take it from there,' she could say, vaguely. It was prudent not to publicise her itinerary.

The next day, Brooke found a friendly travel agent who sorted out her onward travel plans, leaving her to enjoy a bit of window shopping in Oxford Street and check out shoes in Selfridges. Might even pop into the Old Bailey and watch English justice being dispensed to petty criminals, she thought. So much to do, but Brooke the keen shopper and sightseer couldn't enthuse. She walked and thought. Her mind was preoccupied with what lay ahead in Eastern Europe.

She meandered up Threadneedle Street looking for a Lyons where she could buy a sandwich. She laughed at the futility of that when she discovered that the famous string of tea houses had closed more than a decade ago.

Later, she found time to sit quietly in the back of a magistrate's court watching solicitors scurrying in and out with papers and clients, bowing and nodding. It reminded her of home. There was a difference, though. The young female solicitors were dressed in conservative black suits, short skirts and white shirts under jackets. Female solicitors in Australia were much more colourful.

Brooke returned before Jill and Peter and seized the chance to again think through just what information she wanted from Mujo, and how she would phrase her questions. Her mind was not in London.

It was noon Friday when Brooke touched down in Budapest. She joined the long customs queue and was caught up in a team of volleyball players, young, noisy, female and French. Languages from everywhere flowed around her, none English.

A porter who saw her dismissing a plague of taxi drivers offering cheap fares to the city guessed what she wanted. 'Putnik?' he asked.

'Da,' she replied, 'Belgrade, Minibus?'

'Belgrade, da. Ne minibus.'

He picked up her bag and led Brooke through the crowds to a large bus set to depart for central Belgrade, possibly a ten to twelve hour drive. It was not what Donald had told her to expect. Minibuses were available, she had understood, that would drop their few passengers off at the door of their destination. She did not want to deal with Belgrade's phone and taxi services at close to or after midnight. She had no Serbian currency, only Deutschmarks and some Australian dollars.

She grabbed her bag back from the porter, and tried to explain with her hands that she wanted a minibus.

Then a well-dressed man approached her. She hoped he was one of the agents she had heard about who organised passengers into minibuses.

'Minibus Belgrade?' she attempted to ask again.

He had a 'fixed price' air about him. Brooke showed him Mujo's address, and he replied in perfect English, 'Eighty Deutschmarks'. She offered seventy Australian dollars. He accepted too cheerfully. If one of them didn't know the relative values of the currencies, his fine clothes suggested that it wasn't him. No matter. It was a reasonable price and she had the cash.

As she was paying him, she became aware of a man in a light blue suit and a black open shirt loitering behind the agent. He seemed to be watching her. Perhaps he was waiting to buy a ticket, but he turned away quickly when she looked at him. It was good that she would soon be seated safely on the bus.

The agent regained her attention to warn of border delays and the possibility of the driver having to take another route which would require some 'extra dollars'. Like Brooke telling Rex and Rocky to 'sit, stay,' he held his hand up and said something like 'Wait here, stay,' and hurried off. The Black-shirted man behind him melted into the crowd.

The agent soon returned with Prederik, the young man who would be Brooke's driver. Prederik received complex directions and picked up Brooke's suitcase. He led her to his minibus, a converted van in fact, which had been parked in the sun since early morning.

She sat by the window three rows behind the empty driver's seat. When she looked out the window, she saw the driver talking to the agent again, and the man in the black shirt, who was pointing at the van. The agent said something and the man nodded and walked away.

Prederik jumped in and opened windows before starting the engine and driving off. Brooke was the only passenger. Twenty minutes brought them to the domestic terminal, where, like a Cheshire cat, there was the agent again. He helped a young Serbian couple to board while Prederik packed their bags into the back of the van.

And there was Black-shirt too. He, like the agent, had beaten the bus between terminals. Brooke was relieved to see that he was not moving to accompany them to Belgrade. She caught him looking at her again, but as soon as Prederik pulled out he turned away. Brooke breathed in deeply, closed her eyes, waited and breathed out. It's a beautiful sunny day, everything is going to plan and there is no reason to be anxious, she thought.

It seemed to Brooke to be a remarkably casual start to a long demanding trip. She and the Serbian couple were the only passengers. Oops. What if they were just being driven into the city to be transferred to another bus, or to collect more passengers? She felt a rising panic. That would add more than an hour to the trip, detouring north, before turning south-east to Serbia. She pulled out her map of Budapest and surrounds and tried to get her bearings by matching it with passing road signs.

But it was soon clear they were travelling south, through a rural setting. Modest cottages on small plots of flat land were replacing suburbia. Corn cobs were strung over verandas to dry and harvests of hay bales were stored under rusty tin roofs held up by spindly wooden poles.

She felt relaxed enough to break the ice with her fellow travellers. She turned and smiled at the young couple, 'Hello, I'm Brooke. I'm Australian.'

They smiled back and, in halting English, explained they were returning from a holiday in Greece.

Smiles work. The Serbs engaged with the driver and translated for Brooke as best they could. Prederik, it seemed, was a trained civil engineer, working as a driver until he had enough money to move to Germany and put his qualifications to use. He made the return trip between Belgrade and Budapest every day, six to nine hours each way, depending on delays at the border. Brooke was appalled at his long hours, not to mention the risk of accident from driver fatigue. Bus owners and marshalling agents would be rich long before drivers like Prederik.

They had left the terminal after 3 p.m. local time, and Brooke was now peckish. Remembering Donald's advice, she had tried to buy sandwiches in London the previous evening, but searching Oxford Street near her hotel she found only Boots open and chemists don't sell sandwiches. But they did have 'healthy' snacks, and she had some smuggled fruit from the dingy breakfast room in her overly-expensive hotel where she had been given a room with a single bed and barely enough space to stand. She also had a packet of salty biscuits and a plastic-wrapped slice of cheese scavenged from the plane. Now she pleaded with her bladder to see her through the trip.

High summer had passed but it was still hot, and the minibus had no air-conditioning. Most of the windows were open and the wind, blowing her hair into her face, brought some relief. They travelled in fast dense traffic through Hungary's Great Plains between the Danube and Tisza rivers. Brooke marvelled at the colourful mosaic of farms, orchards and market gardens that appeared between large tracts of natural dry grasslands and forests.

The bus stopped at a gas station at Kecskemét about halfway between Budapest and the border town of Szeged. The young couple bought Brooke a bottle of spring water as she had no Hungarian currency. She thanked them and hurried to a unisex toilet to reward her bladder, which would have to hold up until they reached the border.

A kilometre from the border, Prederik became worried and conversed rapidly with the other two. Brooke didn't need to speak Serbo-Croatian to understand his concern. It was Friday evening and the traffic ahead was a log jam. An array of families all wanted to be somewhere for the weekend. Fields of stationary cars sat waiting for as long as it would take to get through.

Prederik parked and went to talk to a uniformed man at the guard house. He returned and spoke to the Serb couple who dug for some notes and handed them to Prederik.

'Four to five hours' wait,' the couple reported.

The couple had agreed with the driver to try the commercial crossing. The queue was shorter. Brooke guessed that this might mean a bus fare's worth of bribes. Prederik took the minibus out of the queue, past the rows of stuck cars and approached a different checkpoint. Here he passed a bundle of Deutschmarks to a Hungarian border patrol guard. No one had asked Brooke to contribute because, she surmised, they thought she would not understand. She opened her purse and handed some Deutschmarks to the young man who smiled and nodded his appreciation.

They waited patiently in the hot sun, part of the throng of cars, trucks, buses, dogs and people who had to be checked and searched. Some paraded along the road to the duty-free shop and some hung from their cars. Serbia observed daylight saving and at half past six it was still light.

Nearly an hour later, with the sun dipping, they were waved through to customs. They waited again. Apparently the Serbian border officials were taking their tea break. The line of stationary cars backed up beyond no-man's-land.

Brooke watched a guard offloading gas in large plastic containers from a truck. The containers were spread out on the ground among the milling people and cars with idling engines.

'One and a half litres from each car,' the young man told Brooke. He pointed to the fuel containers and added, 'The owners will get it back, but they have to pay.' Serbs were crossing the border to buy large quantities of fuel in Hungary to on-sell in Serbia. Hungarian officials were supposed to search vehicles and seize contraband fuel. Corrupt officials confiscated a litre or so from each vehicle, to satisfy United Nations observers, and let the rest through. The confiscated gas would find its way across the border by a back route where the Serbs from whom it was taken would buy it back from the Hungarian officer at a higher price. The market determined the price for the profiteers.

Finally they were moving again and soon reached the Serbian border. It amused the guards that Brooke's visa said 'tourist'. One asked her a few questions in broken English about the length of her stay, and how she intended to return.

'Same way,' she replied, 'via Hungary.'

'Entry papers?' The officer pointed to her Hungarian entry visa and now she saw the problem. It clearly said 'single entry'. He smiled in a way which said 'bad luck', and handed the papers back to her.

She had believed that her time-limited entry visas to both countries allowed multiple entries for the short time she was in Europe. So how would she get back into Hungary? She had no Romanian or Bulgarian visa for an alternative exit.

'Damn!' She shook her head in dismay and her new friends looked at her sympathetically. Never mind, it was a problem to be addressed later. Hopefully Mujo would come to the rescue. For now, she couldn't keep her travel companions waiting. Short of bussing back to Budapest, she had no choice.

Once in Serbia, Brooke noticed vehicles pulling off the road and opening their doors wide. Each had a large empty Coca Cola bottle on its roof – indicating gas for sale.

'See,' said the young man, 'Gas. It's being sold again. No shortage, just more expensive.'

Cars pulled over to fill up.

The two-lane highway to Belgrade was impossibly crowded. Those who once flew now travelled by road, wedged in a vast convoy of cars, buses and trucks. Rusty rattlers and shiny Mercedes vied for a place.

Brooke watched the car ahead pull out as if to overtake, but it didn't. It stayed in the wrong lane and was soon followed by others. Both lanes were being used by southbound traffic. Seeing an oncoming car, Brooke held her breath and waited. But the oncoming car simply slipped onto the verge, creating a third lane used by vehicles following it.

The southbound traffic continued using both lanes until a large oncoming truck of some kind flicked its lights. Its verge had run out.

There had to be an accident this time, Brook just knew. To her amazement the line of traffic in which she was travelling took to the verge on its side of the road, allowing outriders in the wrong lane back in. Using the verges on either side, the two-lane highway had been organised into four lanes.

As the road dance continued, the rules became clear. If an oncoming vehicle, a truck, a posh Mercedes, a police car approached with flashing lights, everyone zipped across to the kerb lane of the verge, or even the grass if necessary. Brooke thought about the new will she'd made before leaving home.

Sunflower plantations and verandas hung with drying red peppers sped past. The neat fields were spoiled by an occasional upended rusty car body, suggesting that the road dance was not always perfectly executed.

They stopped at several security checkpoints. The minibuses were known to the duty officers and since Prederik's three passengers didn't look like gunrunners they were not delayed. The roads carried Jugos and Ladas as well as Mercedes and Audis which signalled that at least some Serbs had learned to profit from the embargo.

Darkness fell as they passed the last villages and travelled through New Belgrade with its grey cement high-rise apartment blocks and on to the centre of the city. Come midnight, the minibus was weaving around back lanes looking for the street name that Brooke had written down for Prederik.

Then the young woman cried out and pointed. 'There!'

Waiting in the dark were a man and a woman. As she later learned, Mujo and Andjela had heard the bus's engine, and on seeing the wandering vehicle from their balcony had descended to flag it down. Brooke had arrived safely in Belgrade.

32

Belgrade, early September 1992

Mujo and Andjela greeted Brooke warmly, each kissing her cheek twice and then again. Brooke thanked Prederik and the young couple, and handed Prederik a few more Deutschmarks as he pulled her suitcase from the back of the bus. He gave her a card with the phone number for arranging her return trip.

Brooke followed her hosts through wrought-iron gates, up two flights of wide stone stairs. Paint was peeling off the relief sculptures that decorated the high stone walls of the once grand and beautiful, now dilapidated, building. They entered a spacious second-floor flat through a large carved wooden door. Through another doorway she glimpsed two small bodies sprawled out in the heat on a large double bed.

'It's been very hot,' Andjela explained. 'Last week's temperatures were in the high thirties, much hotter than normal.'

Mujo dropped Brooke's bag into the next room and said, 'The children will sleep with us and you have children's room. It's not a problem. The children come to our bed most nights anyway.'

The flat opened onto a balcony overlooking a pocket-sized garden. A large leafy tree overhung the balcony, giving it a sense of privacy. A jug of white wine laden with marinated peaches sat on a table beside three wine glasses.

Brooke's hosts seemed genuinely eager to get acquainted before retiring. She looked across at the man who had been Jo's lover and wondered how he felt about the role of their relationship in her death. And how did Brooke feel about him? Did he have blood on his hands? He had left Jo to slip back into quiet domesticity and now she was dead.

'Have you been to Yugoslavia before?' Andjela asked.

Brooke shook her head. 'No, regrettably,' she replied. 'The UK and western Europe, but not here.' She smiled at Andjela, trying to hide her racing mind. It seemed unreal to be sipping drinks on a warm September night in a strange country on a balcony with a couple of whom she knew so much and so little.

There were so many questions, and gentle conversation soon turned into a dynamic exchange. Her hosts talked in whispers about Serbian politics, the disintegration of their society under the current regime, of friends who had died violently and relatives who had fled the country. Few were unaffected by the brutal policies of the country's president, Slobodan Milošević.

Andjela's English was near perfect. Mujo was articulate but syntactically challenged. They talked till three. There was much that her new friends needed to tell someone, while Brooke was intent on learning about them and their country. The reason for Brooke's visit, to find out how and why Jo Rowan died, did not come up.

When Brooke eventually collapsed into a narrow children's bed, her head was buzzing with facts. The man in the black shirt flashed into her mind and she worried again what his interest in her might be. She relived her journey through orchards and farms, the border delays, and her warm welcome from Mujo and Andjela.

She had learned how intolerable the conditions were under which Serbian families lived. Inflation was rampant, driven by the government printing money to support a less than popular war. The authorities tried to distance themselves from the recent atrocities in Bosnia. The United Nations trade sanctions were hurting everyone, everywhere. Andjela had described how on receiving their weekly wage people ran fast to the market to buy meat and vegetables at prices which soared from minute to minute. If you waited until the end of the week, she said, the price of a fresh egg might have risen by a month's pay.

As the dinar lost value and banks were failing, long winding queues of people tried in vain to withdraw their money. Mujo and Andjela also lost their savings when their bank failed. Just before it collapsed, queues outside it were measured in days, not metres. State-run courts protected the banks from claims made against them. Cases would be adjourned on technicalities, creating opportunities to pass the frozen funds to the Serbian mafia, masters of the illegal currency dealing which propped up the government. The cash-strapped government started to sell housing it had long rented to the people. Mujo, having been born in the house he and Andjela now occupied, was lucky, as were any long-term tenants who had the modest sum needed to purchase their home. Smart business people were making fortunes by buying out tenant-owners cheaply and reselling at an inflated price. Property prices were soaring. Speculators quickly converted their profits into hard currency destined for German banks. Millionaires emerged.

The Zukićs' situation, like many others, was typical of a mixed-marriage family caught up in the turmoil of a generals' war. Andjela was Serbian, brought up Catholic in Croatia. Mujo was a Bosnian Muslim, educated in Belgrade. He was prohibited from visiting Croatia, the province where Andjela's parents lived until they fled to Canada to escape her father being persecuted by newly installed anti-communist rulers. It would have been suicide for Mujo to visit friends in Bosnia. Yet in Belgrade he was tormented by stone-throwing neighbours. Because of threatening calls, answering the phone had become a frightening ordeal. Having spent their lives in Yugoslavia, they now belonged nowhere.

It was clear to Brooke that, having separated and reconciled over personal issues, ethnic differences were bonding, rather than fracturing, this family. The country's political chaos taught them the value of what they had. Their personal agendas meant nothing compared with the cultural and political struggles of the old Yugoslavia's ethnic groups who were stupidly blind to the fact that war solves nothing.

If she slept at all, it was only a few hours. Brooke was woken around seven by a little noise from the toy cupboard. It was Fadil. She was the Australian who had taken over his bed, but not his toy cupboard.

'School is at ten,' Mara whispered, peering into the room. She was to start primary school on Monday but today was an introduction for families. It was a big event. Business talk would have to wait. Mara, nearly seven, wore a new pink floral dress, bought in Greece on a recent family holiday. She had a matching shoulder bag, blue shoes, and a wide-brimmed straw hat with a navy ribbon.

Brooke asked her how to say in Serbian, 'You look beautiful.'

Mara told her, and laughed at Brooke's attempt to repeat it. Her parents told Brooke later that it was important she be well dressed, not appear poor. She would have a hard enough time at school with her Muslim family name.

Fadil was not going to miss out on the admiration. He was wearing new trousers, a shirt with a matching belt, and a bow tie, all presents from his aunt, who had fled to America from Bosnia. She at least had escaped the consequences of having the wrong ancestry in the wrong country at the wrong time.

'How pretty I look,' said Fadil. His preschool English classes were supported by the cartoons he watched on TV. American telecasts, proscribed elsewhere in Serbia, could not be censored in sophisticated Belgrade.

'Mara, Fadil – idemo!' called their mother.

'Let's go!' echoed Fadil in English for Brooke's benefit.

They clattered down the stairs, through the large iron gates and piled into an old but serviceable Audi. Mujo had returned to his public service position in Serbia, despite his ethnicity. His Australian equivalent of $300 a month was supplemented by Andjela's cottage industry of handmade household items. This allowed her to look after the children at home and the family to live comfortably, including a recent holiday.

There was an air of excitement in the forecourt of the small school. The families filed in. Children and parents were in their best clothes. Cameras hung from the shoulders of the better-off. Children at the back peeked through the legs of the adults in front. Older children sang and danced a welcome. Metal chair legs scraped on the stone floor as parents negotiated viewing positions.

Mara started to cry. How would she hear her name in the hubbub? She would never learn what class she was in, and a whole year would be wasted, she sobbed.

Brooke looked around to see if she could help and caught a man staring at her. He seemed to be on his own. She was relieved that it wasn't the Black-shirted man. Probably someone curious to see a foreigner here. She heard Andjela reassuring Mara that it would be okay.

At last. 'Mara Zukić.'

Mara let Andjela's hand go, and wove through skirts and trouser legs to join her new classmates and their teacher. Brooke joined the parents when they followed the children upstairs. By the time they squeezed into the small classroom, the children were seated, Mara in the front row. She was the only one with a hat and she wore it with style. Her parents hoped she would wear her Muslim surname with the same panache.

The parents crowded down the sides of the room to hear what the teacher was saying.

'Saturday, did she say?'

Yes, lessons would take place on Saturday morning for some of the classes and Saturday afternoon for others. The school had to make use of limited facilities and resources. There would be no heating in winter, because of trade sanctions, and classes would have to be short, or cancelled if it was too cold, so while the weather was good, additional classes would be held. The children must not miss out on their education. No one seemed surprised or concerned. This community, accessible only by expensive road transport, was not going to disappear at weekends.

Fifteen minutes later, the children emerged with smiles, a pencil each and the school badge to be sewn onto their bags. Mara's tears and fears had vanished and she was excited. Mujo revelled in her pleasure, hugging her and swinging her around. Other children found their parents, took their hands and chatted happily.

Mujo drove the family and Brooke a short distance to an open-air café for kafa and Sedam-up (coffee and Seven-up). They sat looking over tennis courts, watching the children play on some nearby grass. If her parents worried about Mara being teased about her ethnicity, they would have to worry more about Fadil with his Muslim first name. One mother tried to change her daughter's name when she fled the country. She gave the child a sedative as they approached the border so that she would not wake and give her correct name.

'You are here about Jo Rowan,' Mujo opened. He sounded detached.

Brooke looked across questioningly to Andjela, who smiled and said 'It's okay, Brooke. You can speak without hurting me. What happened in the past is in the past, and Jo was not the cause of our troubles, just a result. What happened to her shouldn't happen to anyone. Mujo is upset, of course, and I am for him too.'

'Thank you, Andjela. Your understanding makes it easier for me to speak freely, because it's important I find out what I can, for the sake of Jo's daughter and grandchild.'

Mujo asked, 'Tell me what happened: when, how did she die?' There was emotion in his voice this time.

Brooke told him how Jo was found by a couple out walking near the yacht club. 'Shockingly, she had been dead for three days,' she said.

'That can't be,' Mujo was visibly shaken. 'News reports said her body was found on Saturday 20 June.'

'Yes.'

'I was with her Wednesday evening. The night she died? It would have been 17th. I left Thursday 18 in the morning.'

Brooke was relieved by what he was saying. She knew from Deidre that the Hyatt's CCTV had images of Mujo with Jo that evening. Silence would have been ambiguous. It could have meant fear of upsetting Andjela or a fear of making Brooke suspicious of him.

'You might have been the last to see her?' she prompted.

'Not if she was killed, and I never thought she took her own life.'

Andjela looked alarmed and took in Mujo's dismal face.

'Then I am suspect if it was not suicide…' he said, placing his hand on Andjela's.

'No, you're in the clear, I think,' said Brooke hastening to remove their anxiety. 'The CCTV shows you returning in too short a time for you to have followed her, killed her and come back to the hotel. Anyway, your prints are only on the driver's door, not the passenger door, nor inside the car.'

Mujo considered this, and again shook his head. 'But I was…in the car,' he owned, looking at Andjela sheepishly.

Now it was Brooke's turn to be shaken. Andjela looked up at Mujo, disappointment on her face. Their eyes met.

'Sorry,' he muttered. 'It was just to say goodbye.'

Andjela gripped her other hand over his, so as to encourage him to speak frankly.

'Why were your prints not found in the car?' Brooke asked, not expecting a reply.

'Somebody wipe them – and their own?' Mujo offered. 'Unless… unless Jo wipe them so not to implicate me. But I don't think she kill herself.'

'Mujo, this is important information.' It was and Brooke knew she needed to take it home in a sworn statement.

'Whoever did this might not be happy that you're talking to me. Did Donald think it risky for you to come here?'

'I think he believes Jo killed herself, particularly when he learnt about ASIO's miserable attempt to blackmail her. But just what you said now, about risk…' She trailed off as the memories of the Black-shirted man at the airport and the staring man at the school came back.

'What is it?' Andjela asked, seeing Brooke shifting uncomfortably.

The children raced up to them. 'Ice cream, can we, Mummy?'

'No, it's time we go,' said Mujo. 'We go home to eat.'

They drove back silently, the children fighting over who would sit next to Brooke. It was settled by Brooke squashing into the middle, feet on the console, knees high, and the children chatting and trying to punch each other across her. Worrying about being followed would have to wait.

At dusk the family drove to the Danube. Downstream from its junction with the Sava, it was wide and fast. They parked and picked their

way along the river bank to a large old wooden boat that had become
a club house, a meeting place with bar. They had to watch for missing
boards to the gangway. Once aboard, they sat on deck and drank Seven-
ups and wine with soda. All was calm.

The club house had once been exclusive. How lively the area must
have been on Saturdays past when cafés and restaurants were thriving. A
hydrofoil had carried tourists between Belgrade and the university town
of Novi Sad. A large empty structure on the water's edge had once been a
popular function centre. Now, although the streets were safe, most people
stayed home. There was nothing to visit, no money for such spending.

It was quite late when they returned home. Andjela organised the
children into a bath, and Mujo and Brooke talked quietly on the dark
balcony.

'Now, please, say what else was on your mind this morning.'

'At Budapest airport, there was a man. He seemed interested in my
minibus, and talked to the agent who sold me a ticket. As we pulled out,
I saw him point at the bus and ask the agent something. Then, when we
pulled up outside the domestic terminal, the agent was there with another
couple and I saw the same man. He looked directly at me this time, and
stayed until the bus pulled out. And, well, today I saw a man, in the crowd
of parents, a different man, staring at me. Perhaps I'm just edgy.'

Mujo turned to face Brooke. 'I am sorry about this. Perhaps best to
assume you are being watched. It might be my people. They are interested
in foreign friends who visit – in case I try to defect.' He looked thoughtful.
'But what you said about Jo, it's possible someone wants to know your
movements, like coming to see me. You gave the agent our address?'

'Yes. Oh, I am sorry... I don't want to put your family at risk.'

'No, no. We are okay. Anyone can find my address. But we must be
sure you are safe. Question is why someone is interested in you being
here?'

'How would they know my travel movements?'

'That's easy. Not many English speakers ask for bus to Belgrade. First
man must check with agent your destination address to be sure it was you,

and he must go to domestic to make sure you don't change your mind, or leave bus.'

'My goodness. Smells like an organisation, having someone here in Belgrade as well, to watch me?'

'More important to take care on your way home. I make other travel arrangements for you. I have trusted friend who drive another minibus.'

It was time for Brooke to mention her visa problem. She explained what had happened. 'Will it take many days to get a Hungarian re-entry visa?'

'Let me see what I can do. I will make phone call to friend at Hungarian embassy. He might do me favour and help us tomorrow, even though Sunday.'

Brooke thanked him as she rose to join Andjela in the kitchen. She was slicing zucchinis and about to attack some large ripe tomatoes when Brooke walked in.

'Are you hungry, Brooke'? she asked. 'I thought we might have a simple zucchini bake. It one of the children's favourite meals.'

Brooke could hear them playing in the bedroom. 'It sounds delicious,' she said. She picked up a knife, and offered to slice the tomatoes.

Andjela was steaming the zucchinis and, under direction, Brooke whisked some egg yolks and stirred in a small carton of sour cream.

'Hmm, what's sizzling? It smells good.'

It was garlic and parsley frying in a little oil. Andjela put alternative layers of zucchinis and tomatoes into a baking dish and topped it with the garlic and now-crisp parsley. 'Now for the sauce,' she said, pouring the egg and cream mix over before adding a topping of breadcrumbs, salt and pepper, and grated cheese. All done, the dish went into the oven and, by the time they had cleaned up and set the table, it was beautifully brown.

Andjela sat down with Brooke and Mujo on the balcony.

'It's strange,' Brooke said, looking into the dark sky. 'I came here to find out if you thought Jo was unhappy enough about her work, or your leaving, that she might kill herself. But now, unless the police were incompetent at taking fingerprints, that's all changed. It's still important to understand why Jo's knowing you triggered a security problem when she started work at Immigration. Being friends with you hadn't bothered ASIO up till then.'

'My theory is this. Jo and I swapped stories just before she die. What you are looking for might be in them. We exchange information after dinner, then we can chew this over.'

Brooke chuckled at the conjunction of metaphor and reality.

The children rushed in and sat at the table without being called; and everyone had a second slice of hot bake. Brooke offered to help clean up, but Andjela insisted she take the opportunity to talk with Mujo. Andjela shooed the children off to prepare for bed.

Mujo had helped himself to a large whisky, and offered her one. Brooke settled for a second glass of wine, and they returned to the cool quiet balcony.

'Now I tell you everything about the night I said goodbye to Jo.'

'Yes, please,' Brooke replied, 'and I hope you don't mind if I take notes.' She dived into the children's room and fetched notebook and a pen.

Andjela was telling the children a bedtime story in the bedroom next door. Seeing her copy of the poem from Jo's car, she picked that up too, thinking to ask Mujo about it while they were alone.

Mujo was hanging over the balcony staring into the night when she returned. He turned to face her. 'I walked Jo to her car at back of hotel. She unlock driver's door and I open it for her. My fingerprints should be there. I went around to passenger side and sat beside her. We talked. I gave her piece of paper on which I wrote poem for her. She took it and turned on the roof light to read it, but I switched off light, and said it was for her to read later.'

'The poem, is this it?' Brooke unfolded her copy and gave it to him.

He read the first few lines. His eyes watered. 'Yes,' he said unevenly. 'Where did you get it?'

'The original was found crumpled up on the floor on the driver's side.'

Mujo gasped. 'Jo would not screw poem up. No. If she angry, or upset, she tear in half, and half again. Not crumple. Deliberate, not histrionic.'

Brooke read his eyes. He knew Jo. Nothing in what he was saying was self-serving. He was certain that this was not Jo's doing. The implication was that someone else had crumpled the paper.

'Could anyone have been watching? Seen you both in the car?'

'Footpath in front of the car was well-lit. From window in Hyatt perhaps? Anyone walking behind car or sitting in car behind us might see us kiss, or see her holding piece of paper up to light.'

'How might that be interpreted? Could someone from the consulate have thought you were passing on information? Arranging a defection, or something?'

'No. They kill me, not her, if I cause a problem for my government. But I did give her a document when we walk to the car.'

'You what?' Brooke thought she'd misheard.

'A report on how an agent of ours was killed by one of your policemen in Darwin.'

'What did she do with it?'

'Slipped it into her bag.'

Brooke was gobsmacked by the revelation.

'You didn't know?' Mujo explained, 'The report was no longer important to my government but might help her find out why she was blocked in Immigration.'

'But Mujo, apart from the poem, no papers were found in her car.'

'Then someone took them. Two pages. Jo was interested in possible connection between the waterside killing of our man and a refugee boat. Report was police summary including date of shooting and name of victim's wife. I had to meet his wife – to explain. Very sad.'

Brooke told him she knew some of this, that Jo had discovered that the same policeman had been involved in burning a refugee boat that arrived in Darwin and was at the scene when a man was killed nearby. She explained that she had apprised the tribunal of a possible link between the Serbian and Immigration operations. 'I hoped it would help the tribunal understand that Jo's potential to embarrass ASIO didn't make her a subversive,' she said.

Mujo told Brooke about other documents he discovered when closing up the embassy. They told of the frequent use of corrupt customs officers to bring in contraband. 'Neither Jo nor I knew or cared about this, but ASIO probably feared we did.'

'Someone must have wanted to know what you gave her that night.'

Mujo looked horrified. Then he said, 'But that means someone was watching us. Maybe they already planned to kill her.'

'Well, if someone was intent on following her from the car park, what were they planning? Anyway, why would she pull up near the yacht club instead of driving home?'

'She and I just said goodbye, and she might have pulled up car to read poem, feel sad and reflect. She would do that. Then go home and start life without me.'

'If someone wanted to kill her, it was convenient that your poem was there to be crumpled up – evidence of a suicide triggered by a broken heart. And your fingerprints got wiped when they wiped their own. And whoever did that wiped them from the gun, too.'

'Hmm, the gun. What sort of gun? Jo didn't have a gun.'

Brooke told him it was a Glock, an Austrian pistol popular in Australia.

'Glocks are used by police and military everywhere. Not for shooting rabbits.'

'The police thought she might have had it to scare intruders, after she found her house had been bugged. Or that she bought it specifically to kill herself.'

But Mujo hadn't finished. 'Glock is popular with crime gangs too,' he said. 'Could be smuggled in and sold to criminals. Your gun laws not strong, I know.'

That night, trying to absorb everything she had learned, Brooke lay wide awake in Fadil's bed. She had to consider all possibilities. If, just if, Mujo had killed Jo, not withstanding her own intuition and the police view that it was impossible, she was in a very difficult position. But what if Jo had been killed by Mujo's people, someone from Yugoslav intelligence? If so, and Mujo knew, he was not going to tell her. Loyalty to his government or, more likely, concern for his family would prevent that.

Brooke turned over, and over again. No one but Donald knew where she was. Perhaps that was a mistake. Information she obtained from Mujo would be difficult to transmit home from Yugoslavia, at least not without Mujo's help. She had no choice. She had to trust him and she had to rely on him to protect her from lurking danger.

<h1 style="text-align:center">33</h1>

Sunday was market day. The challenge was to arrive early because prices kept rising as the day wore on. There were acres of fruit and vegetables, beans, cheeses and chickens from the surrounding countryside and clothes from across the border. Andjela carefully chose peppers, bread, yoghurt and vegetables, and Mujo found some inexpensive local white wine. The family proceeded through the market at quite a pace, watching prices inflating before their eyes. There were plenty of 'gas stations' too. Vehicles with doors open and a Coca Cola bottle on the roof dotted the car parks around the market. It seemed that half the population was in the business of selling gas to the other half.

Brooke lagged behind, trying to catch the atmosphere with her camera. She attracted attention. Tourists were a rare sight these days. The cheese vendor wanted her to photograph him tending his stall. His rival, selling goat cheese next door, wanted her picture taken too. Brooke captured her broad smile – lots of gum and two teeth. Then the woman moved around, took Brooke's camera from her and offered it to her rival vendor. He waited while the woman put her arm around Brooke and grinned her cheeky toothless grin. As the camera clicked, the man frowned and looked past Brooke. She turned and saw a man boring into the crowd, almost losing his distinctive straw hat trimmed with red and green braid as he pushed people aside. The photographer lifted the camera again, and when Brooke turned back to him he clicked and laughed, satisfied with the shot this time. He handed the camera back, still whirring as it rewound the finished film.

Brooke hurried to catch up with her friends. She hoped for some great photos, she said, apart from one spoiled by a loitering stranger in a straw hat.

'I can get film developed tomorrow if you like,' Mujo offered.

Brooke nodded her thanks and handed him the roll.

'See if he the same man you saw at school,' Mujo whispered.

Back in the car, the children dug deep into a loaf of still-warm bread, leaving a crusty shell to be politely offered to the adults. Once home, they helped haul bags of fruit and vegetables upstairs, before rushing out to play.

'Snack at twelve,' Andjela called after them, 'and then we go for an outing.'

Brooke helped Andjela unpack the shopping and together they chopped up vegetables for onion soup. Andjela fried five or six white onions with bacon till they were soft and golden. Mujo looked in as Andjela was scraping them into a pot of stock, and Brooke was adding chopped carrots, potatoes and leeks.

'My friend at Hungarian consulate will be at his office in half an hour. I take your passport, Brooke, and get re-entry visa stamp. I drop off film too. Will be back in time for afternoon outing.'

Andjela looked up from adding presoaked white beans and lentils to the stock pot and set the soup to simmer. 'OK. The soup will be ready in forty minutes or so. We'll wait for you.'

The children were already sitting around the stockpot and an unsullied loaf of fresh bread when Mujo entered and slapped Brooke's passport down, complete with transit visa that would allow her to travel back through Hungary.

Brooke looked at Mujo's triumphant smile. 'Thank you, so much,' she said.

The children chatted and, between mouthfuls, Mujo and Andjela questioned Brooke about her life in Australia. Business was taboo inside the house, in case of listening walls.

The afternoon outing was for Brooke's benefit, as a tourist. Novi Sad was an enlightened city, home to university intellectuals and flourishing artists, people who deeply resented what was happening in Serbia. Like

Belgrade, Novi Sad was exempt from the foreign television ban, because the government feared an outcry that might spread and spread. Rural people rarely watched television or read newspapers anyway, and accepted what Serbian radio presented. But Mujo had another reason for taking Brooke to Novi Sad. There was someone there who might be able to help Brooke.

They left Belgrade by the route Brooke had entered it, through ugly New Belgrade. Coming in she had not seen the unbalanced clock tower, tall and awkward, and symbolic of the city's turmoil.

'We need gas,' said Mujo.

'There,' shouted Fadil. He pointed to a red Lada by the roadside, doors open and a Coke bottle on the roof. Plastic containers with a dozen litres of fuel sat on the hood.

Mujo pulled in and after a quick negotiation fuel was funnelled into the Audi. Safety regulations meant little in a country where nothing got cheaper except the price of human life.

If Belgrade was about people, Novi Sad was about place. The small city was brimmed with history, charm and grace. The five walked in drizzling rain on clean quiet streets. Families in a nearby park were grabbing their picnic gear and seeking shelter under trees. The cobbled streets leading to the old city were closed to traffic. In the old city square Mujo recalled the history of its council chambers and impressive Catholic church. The family walked to Vlica Dunavska (Danube Street), an old street that had survived name-changing. Here, at an outdoor café, they sat under a large colourful awning and drank short sweet black coffees.

In times past, Novi Sad had been a haven for outspoken intellectuals, a place where political dissent was more tolerated than in Belgrade. A new theatre, first welcomed for its cultural promise, still caused controversy. Its architecture was an uncouth challenge to the immaculately kept historic buildings around it. Ironically, a more tasteful McDonalds nearby strove for harmony with its historical surrounds. Fadil saw it and tried to pull his mother towards it.

'We can't,' his father said. 'It's empty.'

McDonalds had brought private enterprise to the centre of Novi Sad, but were still waiting to open. Demand had evaporated in an economy devastated by the United Nations' economic sanctions, ironically, ones engineered by the United States, home of the Big Mac.

'We went to McDonald's in Belgrade,' Fadil argued.

'That was before the trade sanctions,' his father explained.

The distinction was too fine for a four-year-old to grasp. But then, who did understand what was going on in the country where Fadil was growing up?

'There are things to see across the river,' said Mujo, trying to distract the child. 'Let's fetch the car and go over.'

Thanks to the cessation of shipping, the Danube was enjoying a reprieve from pollution. The water was fresh and fish had repopulated the river. As they approached the crossing, they could see people swimming from a sandy beach at the river's elbow, not mindful of the rain.

Mujo pulled over before the bridge and spoke rapidly to Andjela. She would take the children down to the river to play while Mujo escorted Brooke across a road to an austere block of flats. He pressed a buzzer on the wall, after consulting a piece of paper from his jacket pocket. They waited. After two more persistent rings, they heard someone shuffling downstairs.

An elderly and tired-looking woman opened the door. Brooke listened to the exchange, understanding nothing but absorbing the sharp changes of expression on the woman's face. She was shaking her head but Mujo kept talking. The woman shrugged, then turned to climb slowly back upstairs.

Mujo looked relieved that the woman had relented. He turned to Brooke. 'Her daughter is Bozin's wife, the man shot dead in Darwin. I hoped daughter lived here. She said daughter now live with Bozin's family near Svetozarevo. She's getting address. Mother is not happy daughter and grandchildren live with in-laws.'

'You're thinking we should talk with Bozin's wife? Why?'

'Who knows? Bozin might have told wife things he didn't tell us — letters perhaps? Would you enjoy a trip through the countryside?'

The woman returned, slopping downstairs, her worn-out slippers offering little support for her feet. Mujo looked at the paper she gave him. He smiled and handed her a bundle of notes. She made a gesture of rejection. He closed her hand over the money and she thanked him with her own small smile. It was a gift, not a payment.

The children ran back to the car when they saw Brooke and Mujo returning. They wanted to share stories about ducks on the river, and fish you could see swimming through its clear waters.

Mujo drove them across the bridge to an old castle where they could wander through many small artists' studios, alcoves really, in the castle wall. Art works were displayed on studio walls and, rain permitting, outside. The government allowed student artists to live there provided they permitted public access to their work areas. Loss of privacy was considered a small price to pay, at least when tourists with money to buy artworks had been around. The family were greeted warmly, even when they were interrupting late lunches, which looked more like very late breakfasts, of bread and jam and coffee.

It started to pour and the family decided it was time to go home. But Mujo had a last curiosity to show Brooke on the outskirts of Novi Sad: the small old church of Snezna Maria.

'Snow Mary,' Mujo said. 'The story is that on 2 August 1512 in high summer, as now, while the Muslims and Christians were at war, it snowed. On both sides, the snowfall was seen as a sign from God that there be no more war. And it was so.' He pointed at the spires and explained that Muslims and Orthodox Christians came together to build a church with two spires at the front and one at the back, all three displaying the symbols of both faiths. 'This is the last church in the world decorated with the Orthodox cross and the Islamic crescent moon. We don't listen but it reminds us that peace and goodwill are possible.'

Indeed, the church was decrepit and abandoned. The grass was high and indifferent traffic ran by. If it symbolised anything now, it was social breakdown.

The children were tired and slept most of the way home, giving Brooke the chance to ask Mujo whether it was possible for her to travel to Svetozarevo and find Mrs Bozin.

'Let me see what I can do. I need to make a few phone calls.'

In the evening while Andjela was preparing a supper of baked red capsicums and salad, Mujo was on the phone. Brooke's passing thought was that a few days of eating Andjela's light and tasty food might make her as slim and healthy as her hosts. While bacon and meat stock lifted Andjela's vegetable dishes, she served very few meat dishes. Andjela told Brooke that she usually slow-grilled the capsicums, but when she had time she baked them, so the skin burnt and bubbled and peeled easily. The peeled capsicums went into a glass dish where they were salted and sprinkled with chopped garlic. She finished by mixing vinegar, olive oil and capsicum juice, and pouring that over too. The capsicum dish went well with a tomato and cucumber salad cut small, and again dressed with vinaigrette, and topped with small pieces of feta cheese.

After supper the children, ready for bed, went to play in Brooke's room, while the three adults, wine in hand, sat in the privacy of the overhanging trees on the tiny balcony. Here, Brooke was to be briefed on her trip.

'We must assume that what happened to Bozin is linked to something going on at Immigration at the time Jo was there. Before I speculate, tell me about Operation Fishnet, the one Donald mentioned on the phone,' Mujo said.

Brooke told him about the memo Annette had received and the anonymous messages to Donald from a whistle-blower. 'Donald said you had never heard the name Fishnet,' she said.

'No,' Mujo said, 'but there was a man called Fish involved in an ASIO operation, Operation Picnic, in mid to late 80s. Our man Bozin, the one who was shot, had dealings with Fish after he'd infiltrated gang of Croatian militants. Fish was also informing your people. Both ASIO and the federal police wanted to arrest these Croatians. We were all on the same side, but there was a mix-up.'

'And your man was shot by one of ours. And it had something to do with the refugee boat that reached Darwin?'

'Yes, it would seem.'

'So the name Fish is unlikely to be a coincidence. He's probably Immigration's man inside Fishnet. So, as Jo thought, we have a connection, tenuous no doubt, between a joint Yugoslav–Australian operation that you knew about and an operation carried out by Immigration where Jo was working.' Brooke whistled, 'Amazing. Mujo, we have to piece this together.'

Mujo noted the similarities between the two Australian operations. 'The man, Fish, smuggled rifles through Darwin. Operation Fishnet's concern is with smuggling people into Darwin.'

Brooke added, excited now, 'And we know that the boat owner and people smuggler used in Fishnet was an Indonesian-born Australian, but not his name.'

'In file I gave Jo, the statement taken from Fish after the shooting show his real name is Rexi Pike.'

'A name? That's great. But not one that rings bells, though it accounts for his nickname.'

'Well, here's what I know about our operation to identify Ustashi. Pike, call him Fish, imported .22 calibre rifles for Croatian Ustashi. In mid-80s, before my time, we send undercover man Miroslav Bozin to infiltrate Ustashi groups. He collect rifles from Fish in Darwin relying on a group of customs officers who could be bribed. They falsify papers to show that containers with weapons had been searched. Bozin report to us when a delivery was to be made, and to which Ustashi picnic camp where our countrymen are trained to return home to fight for independence. Our intelligence told yours and federal police made arrests at training camps in Victoria. Then, without telling us, they arrested Fish and released him after recruiting him for their Operation Picnic, helping to track NSW camps. We didn't tell them about our methods, or Bozin. So Fish continue to import guns without being prosecuted if he give details of time and place of sale.'

'So when Bozin showed up on the wharf in 1989, he found Fish with a police officer and pulled a gun, and the policeman shot him, not knowing he was working for you? He got shot for being in the wrong place at the wrong time?' Brooke asked.

Mujo nodded, 'Yes. Fish would never have planned to meet him there, not with police around. I told Jo what I knew about this stuff-up, and that my job was to negotiate compensation for his family from your government.'

'So now we have to wonder if Jo's theory that Fish brought in rifles on that refugee boat is true?'

'That would be stupid. Far as our people knew, Bozin was picking up rifles coming in regular cargo boats.'

'It would explain why the policeman was at the wharf when Bozin appeared. Federal police have line control over all refugee boats.'

Mujo nodded. 'I brought copy of report for you from my office. The one I gave Jo.' He lit a cigarette and took time to draw. He turned to Brooke and said, 'Bozin's family think he was murdered.'

'So that's why the woman was so agitated this morning?'

'She and her daughter, Nevena, believe that is why the Australian government agreed to pay compensation.'

'She's got a point. Why would our government pay compensation if Bozin tried to kill a policeman, no matter who he was working for?'

'Ah, you underestimate my negotiating skills.' Mujo gave a sly smile. 'Do you think our two governments, now enemies, want these activities to come to light? That we were working with Australia against Croatians? Of course they would pay compensation, on condition it is end to the matter.'

'To buy silence?'

'Yes, but, when you read the papers I give you, you will agree that it looks like Bozin was shot from behind. So of course the family want the truth.'

'Hmm, so do I,' said Brooke, 'for Jo's sake too. Who the hell is this Fish, a crook walking both sides of the street? He's permitted by Australian authorities to smuggle in guns in exchange for information, and after all that, engaged as an informant for Immigration. If he has smuggled people too, and he's still an informant for Immigration, it's a damn good story. Somewhere there are important people who figured that, with your help, Jo might reconstruct it. I hope Bozin's wife can tell me more.'

Mujo looked at Brooke, thoughtfully, as she fidgeted with a napkin, using it to wipe a wet ring from her glass.

'I hope you don't mind my not coming with you. I don't think she would talk to me or any Belgrade official. It's working for us that got her husband killed. But she might talk to you, once she knows that you want the truth too, to help someone else.'

Brooke took a deep breath. 'Why not? It's why I'm here, to find out what happened to Jo. And see a bit of the country too? Yes, why not?

34

Svetozarevo, September 1992

Svetozarevo was more than two hours from Belgrade by bus; almost three by train. Mujo knew the manager of the state-run tourist hotel, Hotel Jagodina, in the heart of the city. In the golden 80s it had been a stopover for German and Swedish tourists en route to Greece for their holidays. It now doubled as a local function centre, which helped it to survive troubled economic times. Mujo had rung through to make arrangements for Brooke.

Mujo drove Brooke to the railway station, queued for her ticket, negotiated a window seat and took her to the right platform. He suggested she board without her bag so she could better push through the crowd to reach her seat. The corridors were filling up with people not having reserved seats, waiting for the train to pull out before grabbing those still unclaimed. Mujo tracked Brooke from outside the train and when she had settled into her seat he pushed her bag through the window.

The countryside Brooke had hoped to soak up proved to be flashes of fields and forests through grimy yellow windows but, mercifully, the trip was uneventful.

On arriving, Brooke walked over to two taxis parked outside the station and confidently, as if she were familiar with the town, asked one of the drivers for 'Hotel Jagodina'. The driver stubbed out his cigarette in the gutter with his shoe and chuckled. He ceremoniously opened the door for Brooke and off they drove – one block – to the five-storey tourist hotel that dominated the skyline of the rural town, its large sign clearly visible from the taxi rank.

Svetozarevo, before 1946, had been called Jagodina, and the talk was that it would soon revert. Fronting on the Belica River, and surrounded by woodlands, it was a beautiful place, especially popular with local tourists.

The man who greeted Brooke, Rus, looked more like a bouncer than a porter. He was tall and muscular and had dark-set eyes and a square jaw. What stood out, literally, was a moustache which expanded past his broad smile like cats' whiskers, she mused, to clear a pathway as he negotiated doors and weaved through groups of people in the foyer.

Sign language and a phrase book saw Brooke and Rus communicating. That is, Brooke pointed to a word, without attempting to pronounce it, and handed him the book so he could reply. The first word she tried was 'Money?'

Rus, who liked foreigners who tipped, immediately grasped the importance of her quest and escorted her through to the back of the hotel, to a bank across the street. In an attempt to strike up a 'conversation', Brooke pointed north and said 'Belgrade.' Rus muttered 'Milošević' and rolled his eyes as his index finger mimed the action of a knife slitting his throat.

News of Brooke's visit had travelled fast. Miroslav Bozin's cousin Llubla worked at the hotel and the manager told the staff that as Brooke was here to help Bozin's family, she would be a guest of the state.

Rus organised a small meal for her before taking her to meet Rad, his 'English-speaking friend', and manager of the hotel. Rad was sitting in the bar chatting to the chef and his wife. His few words of English were more useful than Brooke's non-existent Serbo-Croatian.

Rad greeted Brooke warmly and then, looking serious, he pulled a scrap of paper from his pocket. It was a yellow message slip headed 'Mujo' – he had phoned the hotel immediately after her train had left. The only words from Rad's transcription that she could decipher were 'Straw-hat friend'. She guessed that Mujo must have seen him boarding the train at the last minute.

She turned to Rus, who grinned and pointed at himself as if offering to be her minder. Rad confirmed that Rus would be watching for anyone following her. He apologised that there was no official interpreter available to assist Brooke, but that he and Llubla would do their best during her stay. Brooke's anxiety about Straw-hat was allayed by the steady topping up of her wine glass. The hotel seemed to have no other guests.

Come dinner, Brooke was invited to eat with the staff, though meeting Llubla would have to wait until he was on duty. They occupied a large table in an otherwise empty dining hall. Even the chef sat with them and everyone talked and laughed loudly while they ate. Having Brooke join them meant that no one had to wait on her. The arrangement delighted Brook, and meals and drinks were on the house.

Rus enjoyed telling his colleagues that Brooke had come from Belgrade and they all laughed sympathetically. They wanted her to know that she'd have more fun here. Rad quietly asked Brooke what she knew about Bozin's death. News had reached Svetozarevo that Bozin had been murdered by an Australian policeman. It had to be so, as Bozin was no killer and had been working for his country. Why else would his family be receiving compensation?

Brooke too was beginning to have doubts about the self-defence theory, but was careful not to say so. Until she knew more, she had no intention of fuelling antagonism towards her own country's police.

After a long evening, her new best friend, the whiskered Rus, escorted her to her room. He used body and sign language to invite himself to stay the night. Brooke gave him a clear 'no', and he smiled with a shrug, which said, 'It was worth a try', and bowed, kissed her hand and disappeared into the night. Brooke was, if anything, amused. After all, it was the rascal's job to keep a watchful eye on her!

The following morning the hotel was abuzz. Two weddings were scheduled for early afternoon, and guests were already in the reception area carrying cakes, clothes on hangers and a medley of string instruments. As busy as the day promised to be for the hotel, Rad and Llubla were waiting for Brooke in the foyer.

Llubla shook Brooke's hand and offered to accompany her and Rad to nearby villages where Bozin's family lived. Llubla's English vocabulary was limited, but it was good enough, and he owned a car.

Among the small houses on the city's edge there were a few mansions surrounded by hedges. It was explained that Yugoslavs who worked in Germany and France grew rich under current exchange rates. US dollars had more than doubled in value the past year as the dinar inflated out of control.

They drove through open flat fields and wooded hills to Drazmirovak to first meet Bozin's elderly parents, who lived in a small cement cottage on a hectare of land. Here they were self-sufficient, growing and harvesting their own wheat and making their own bread. The old lady was dressed in black, including thick black stockings and a black scarf over her grey hair. She was small and shrivelled and her tired face was lined from pain. Brooke discovered later that the couple were only a few years her senior; and she was not yet forty.

When Llubla translated Brooke's words of condolence, it brought on extensive tears and wailing. Bozin's mother threw her arms around Brooke and cried for her son. Still weeping, she shuffled to the kitchen to make Turkish coffee. Her husband beckoned Brooke to the well, and invited her to help him draw up a bucket of water. It was hard work, but she was rewarded with a glass of cool and delicious water, better than she had ever tasted.

Over coffee, the couple poured a little corn and wheat into Brooke's hands, trying to explain they usually managed a small surplus to barter for goods or food. When Miroslav was alive, he had sent thirty Australian dollars a month. Since then, the father had worked as a farm labourer to make ends meet. Life was tough. Their daughter, Verica, lived in the next village and could help a little because her husband earned a regular wage. But they had children of their own, as well as helping Miroslav's wife and children.

The mother continued to weep until the visitors left. She farewelled Brooke with an embrace and wailed some more. How and why had her son died? 'Why do Australian police murder people?' and 'What will become of our family now?' There was so much they wanted to know.

The three drove downhill to Doboka, a somewhat larger village, where Bozin's sister, Verica, and his wife, Nevena, and their families lived. It was another emotional meeting but Verica and family were much more sophisticated than her parents up the hill. The conversation flowed after Rad and Verica's husband, Stevan, discovered they had been at school together. Brooke left them reminiscing and wandered out into the 'backyard' to admire some piglets ('little porks' was Rad's translation), and lambs ('little sheeps'). Even inside the village they could grow wheat and corn. There were beehives and a large plum tree whose fruit would be distilled into slivovitz, the local plum brandy.

During lunch it came home to Brooke that this family had a quality of life that many middle-class Australians looking for 'the simple life' would envy. Hot dumpling soup followed by cabbage salad, pieces of chicken and pork (could I eat my own animals, Broke wondered) and plenty of tomatoes and chillies were part of the spread. A cake appeared, made with home-milled flour, and topped with home-churned butter and backyard honey. Each course was washed down with slivovitz. Their marvellous meal finished with Turkish coffee.

With her interpreters gabbling away in Serbo-Croatian, it was impossible for Brooke to receive or give information. She and Nevena smiled politely across the table. The children had disappeared to play when Nevena leaned across and touched Brooke's hand lightly. There was a break in the conversation and everyone was looking at her.

Rad announced, 'Nevena and Verica tell me they trust you to help find what happened to Miroslav.'

Whooh! Brooke was touched, but wondered if she was out of her depth. She spread her hands and said, 'Rad, I want to help, but I don't know very much. Is there anything Nevena can tell me that might help?'

Rad interpreted, and Llubla seemed to want to add something.

Nevena then looked at Brooke and spoke in a very quiet voice, in English. 'We can talk. I have paper Miroslav gave me to safe keep.'

At which, Verica shooed them into the garden. Rad called out that he was on hand to interpret if needed.

Miroslav had written many letters home. Nevena knew that he had been helping the Yugoslav government locate Croatian training camps in Australia. He told her that he had become increasingly uncomfortable with his role of infiltration, and then informing. And it was dangerous. Nevena sobbed as she told Brooke that the trip to Darwin where he was killed was to have been his last. Nevena wiped her eyes and told Brooke that he had lined up a job as a bricklayer – good money – and she and their children would be able to join him in Australia.

Brooke moved to sit beside her, putting an arm around Nevena's shoulders.

Nevena looked at her. 'You want to see the paper he said was secret? I should keep safe, in case he one day needed it.'

Brooke nodded. Nevena went inside and returned a few minutes later with a folded piece of paper in a plastic sleeve. She handed it to Brooke. It was headed 'Darwin' and it was a list of names and phone numbers. Beside each name was a notation, in English, such as: sick son; medical costs; compromised; previous bribe; affair with B's wife. This, surely, was a list of the corruptible customs officers Fish and Bozin had needed to help them bring in illegal weapons.

'Names,' Brooke muttered.

'Yes.'

'How did he get this?'

Nevena struggled to explain. She left the garden to find Rad. On her return she said, 'Black market', the words she had been looking for.

'The list could be bought? Who did he get it from?' Brooke asked.

'Man called Max, Mad Max, my husband say in letter. He sell list to man Miroslav deal with in Darwin. Nasty man, used to work with your secret police.'

'Secret police?' It didn't take long for Brooke to understand. 'ASIO, that's our name for them. So this Max used to work for ASIO.'

Llubla dropped Brooke and Rad back at the hotel late evening. To clear her mind, Brooke swam lap after lap alone in the fifty-metre waveless pool in the basement. It served the local schools, as well as hotel patrons. Her Australian crawl amused Rus, and he called Rad down to watch this woman swim like nothing he had seen.

She had just returned to her room and was drying her frizzy hair, when she heard a loud knock. Hoping it was not Rus trying again, she tightened her wrap and opened the door a little.

A pasty-faced man, speaking urgently and unintelligibly, put his foot in the doorway and pointed to the window. As Brooke turned to look, he pushed the door open and squeezed past. He grabbed her handbag and pushed Brooke roughly aside.

Brook raced in pursuit, waving a high-heeled shoe above her head. She threw it well, hitting him in the head, but to no effect. Then, behold, there was Rus coming out of the lift, a tray in his hands.

'Stop him,' she yelled.

Rus put his foot out and tripped the man. Brooke's bag and the papers it contained went flying along with bread rolls and bowls of soup. Rus dropped his tray and headed for the stairs when he saw the man entering the lift. Brooke picked up her bag, collected her scattered papers and her shoe, and unsteadily returned to her room.

It had to be Straw-hat. Thank goodness Mujo had warned Rad. Rus soon returned to clean up the mess and to check on Brooke. She assured him she was OK. He shrugged apologetically, indicating that he had tried, but the man had escaped.

35

Belgrade, September 1992

Brooke returned to Belgrade by a crowded bus. She shuffled up the aisle manoeuvring her bag awkwardly in front of her. A lean young man jumped up and offered his seat because, he said in English, he was 'younger'. He pulled his bag down from the rack above and sat on it in the aisle. Brooke accepted graciously. If Pasty-face were around, he'd have trouble getting past the solid body blocking the aisle. She pressed her shoulder bag and its papers to her lap.

The young man wanted to practise his English. He told Brooke that he was visiting his girlfriend in Belgrade. 'Buy her a drink,' Brooke said as they arrived, handing him a note. He laughed and pushed it back to her. Like all denominations it was full of zeros, and a second look showed that she had offered him the equivalent of fifty, not five, dollars. She put her hand over her mouth, and dived for her purse. But he'd gone.

Brooke had much to tell her Belgrade family that evening. Mujo listened, and went over all the information they had accumulated.

'So what have we? First, we have Immigration's Fishnet operation. That sounds like they use some of same people involved in Operation Picnic. Perhaps Fish, the gun smuggler, now provides intelligence on people smugglers,' he suggested, 'taking opportunity to smuggle more guns.'

'Why would Immigration want to use him? It would be madness.'

'Federal police convinced Immigration that he was a well-connected boat owner, useful to them?'

'Why would they do that?'

'Perhaps when Croatian Picnic operation closed down it was

convenient to let him continue smuggling guns to keep him quiet. Who knows? They recruit him into Fishnet, then new intelligence operation – for catching people smugglers?'

'Utterly corrupt.'

'Maybe they have no choice. Fish saw how Bozin was killed. Also, we know that Fish and Bozin had list of crooked Customs officers. Maybe ASIO is embarrassed that this man, Max, is into black market.'

'What would that have to do with ASIO?'

'Names must have come from ASIO files.'

'You can't be serious?' Brooke couldn't believe what she was hearing. 'Why would ASIO have that information?'

'ASIO vet all officers who work with Customs to check if open to bribery – financial problems, sick child expenses, closet homosexuality – on Nevena's list.'

'Would ASIO give out such information?'

'Maybe given to Max to help Fish keep rifles coming to assist Operation Picnic? Maybe Max then still with ASIO. Need to find out who he is.'

Brooke was flabbergasted.

'Somehow Bozin obtained the list. That helped us. His wife told you he kept it safe, insurance for trouble later, so he must have known who Max was.'

'But it didn't help him.'

'No. We, he, didn't know Fish was engaged in an ASIO operation.'

'If Fish was also used in Operation Fishnet, it's understandable ASIO might fear that you and Jo might make the connection, and find out that Immigration had stuffed up, engaging a gun and people smuggler as an informant.'

'And reveal how we cooperated with Australian government. That would hurt the US alliance.'

Brooke stopped to think it through. 'It would explain why both of you were being watched. Paranoid that you would exchange information, and so when Jo asked to see the Fishnet files, they were convinced she'd made the connection.'

'She told me nothing until her trouble at work. The fools brought it on themselves, made worse for them after she was killed. Secrets might come out now because you and I are working out what they did to her.'

Brooke found Mujo's scenario plausible. 'What we don't know is who, out of all the crooks, spooks and corrupt officials in this web of deceit and betrayal, had sufficient reason to kill Jo?'

When Mujo left to find a whisky, Andjela poured two glasses of their newly purchased local wine and began questioning Brooke – about Jo's book, the evidence for her conspiracy theory about women being held back in the public service, and the reasons given for the book's injunction attempt. Andjela had a sharp mind, and suggested that a detailed chronology of events around her work and her book might reveal a motive for Jo's murder.

'If Jo's enquiries at Immigration and her book were causing ASIO such concern, Fish's operations would have been shut down, at least temporarily,' she guessed.

Mujo returned and chipped in, 'And if he is big fish making big money, he's not likely to give up easily…'

'And he can't be closed down because…' Andjela said, and Mujo broke in to finish her sentence, 'because he knows too much.'

'And because he shares profits with his handlers?' Andjela suggested.

'Possible. Maybe he told the truth about Bozin being killed in self-defence. But either way, he'd support the cop to keep his smuggling racket going.'

Brooke plunged in further. 'Suppose he still smuggles guns, in people-smuggler boats and, because so many people have been compromised, or have shared in his profits, he not only can't be prosecuted, but he can't be stopped. But then why wasn't he killed, not Jo?'

Mujo replied, 'Fish must have way of protecting himself, like documents, names with lawyer somewhere?'

'And why was Jo killed the night you left? Why not before?'

'We only guess. But until my consulate expelled it's a safe bet we'd reveal no secrets. After? By then we have no love for your government.

United Nations, with Australia's support, start war against us. You know why Pine Gap is so important?'

'Probably not as much as you!' Brooke laughed, already amazed by Mujo's knowledge. Here was a foreigner, telling an Australian more about her own country's intelligence operations than she could have ever uncovered.

'Honour among spies,' was Mujo's explanation. 'You'd be surprised how much information we find reason to share with our foreign counterparts.'

Brooke egged him on. 'Well, tell me about Pine Gap.'

'Prime Minister, Bob Hawke, lived up to his name following USA line when in 1988 joint USA–Australia Pine Gap initiative commence. He announced that Pine Gap is satellite ground station used to collect intelligence data "in interest of the national security of Australia and United States". We know Pine Gap technology is capable of breaking into any government's communications. My government thinks it will be used to intercept Serb communications about recent Bosnia atrocities. Milošević fears USA agents will try to assassinate him. For this and its role in United Nations embargo, my government has no love for USA. Your government supports the embargo and is our enemy now too. But then, Milošević did this to us, and many Serbs, including me, are very unhappy with him. Perhaps ASIO thought I would tell Jo just before I left details of how we Serbs worked closely with them.'

Brooke could see the fix ASIO had got itself into, helping Milošević's regime to resist Croatia's independence, and ASIO would be particularly embarrassed if it got out that it allowed Serbs to learn the names of corruptible Customs officers.

'The Mad Max who supplied Fish with lists of corruptible customs staff might have sold the same list to other sorts of smugglers.'

'Possibly. Fish would not be the only smuggler around.'

'I need to get all these thoughts down, and work out what information I need to take home – or better, send before I leave. Can you help me fax material home? I'll feel safer, then.'

'It's good idea. We can do that from my office.'

'The Customs list could be useful, all potential witnesses. And your

ASIO pals, would they testify? Are they clean, do you know, or were they in on it too?'

'First names, Eugene and Larry. I find their full names, also at office. I not know much about them. Not really my pals, though Larry was quite friendly.'

'Whoever killed Jo, my job is to prove she didn't kill herself. Telling me about waterside corruption is helpful because it shows there were people who might have wanted to silence Jo. It gives us leads to follow back home.'

She recalled something that had been nagging her. 'Back to Pine Gap. Did you mention its intercept capabilities to Jo?'

'I don't recall. Oh, yes, I told her about foreign diplomats' collegiality when we were training at Langley in the US. In our country, all diplomats have intelligence training. I mentioned gossip I pick up about Pine Gap. Nothing secret, though.'

'Do you recall when you talked about it, or where – that is, at her home where she was bugged, or over a drink when you were out?' Brooke asked.

Mujo thought carefully. 'It was after her interview with ASIO and we were trying to think what was concerning them. I made a joke, and said something like "It is not as if I am giving you secrets I learned at Langley, or something."'

'Perhaps ASIO wanted Jo to find out what secrets you knew about Pine Gap. They would love to tell US intelligence that someone at Langley was leaking information. Particularly so if there was a plan to use Pine Gap to intercept Serbian communications.'

Mujo looked downcast. 'She didn't say what they wanted. If it was to find out what I knew about Pine Gap, she could have safely accepted that offer and we could have laughed about it together. But she was too principled to play their game.'

'How tragic if Jo died because someone thought that you and she might have made some politically embarrassing connections. How ironic that it's only because of her death that you and I are looking for those connections. It's another case of the corrupt and incompetent precipitating the very things they're trying to avoid.'

36

The next day was grey; everything – the sky, the buildings, the people. News was circulating that the United Nations was about to pass a resolution that 'the state known as the Socialist Federal Republic of Yugoslavia' no longer existed. Anger and resentment spilled over. Hard-working honest families were frustrated by trade sanctions that squeezed them but not the powerful and corrupt who managed to live well by exploiting the weak.

Brooke and Mujo sat on a stone bench in the centre of the city studying Brooke's photos. The market shots pleased her; they captured the colourful produce and equally colourful stallholders. She passed each photo to Mujo in silence until she came to the picture of the happy toothless woman and the watching man in a straw hat.

'See?' she tapped it, and Mujo looked over her shoulder at a round pale face staring from under a hat with a red and green band.

'The same man,' she declared, and looked at him anxiously.

'Yes, this is the man I saw at the station. Same hat.'

'But not the man I saw at Budapest airport. That one was better-looking. This man here, though, could be the one who stared at me at the school.'

A shadow crossed Mujo's face; then he smiled and said cheerily, 'I can make some checks from my people,' he said. 'Let me have the photo. I drop you home now, and make arrangements about your travel later. If this man is not local, he will have applied for a visa to come here too.'

Mara was at school and Fadil at preschool. Brooke was packed ready to go, even though she might have to wait until the following morning. And she'd have to change her flight to London somehow. She collated the material she wanted to fax home, including Mujo's recollections and the names of the two ASIO officers who had talked to him about Operation

Picnic. She would send Nevena's document too. It was important back-up to despatch her material before leaving Belgrade. The safest destination was Deidre's office, not hers, and not Donald's home.

Mujo arrived home for lunch with news for Brooke. Mr Straw-hat was Hungarian. He had crossed the border at Szeged three hours after Brooke's minibus. Mujo thought he'd probably taken the earlier but slower bus, which Brooke had declined. 'He must know that you are here to collect information from me. He missed grabbing your bag in Svetozarevo. You must be vigilant on your way home,' Mujo warned Brooke. 'He might get back ahead of you, so watch your bags, particularly at checkpoints and airport.'

Late that afternoon, Brooke went with Mujo to his office, carrying the papers to be faxed. In a covering note to Deidre, she outlined Mujo's story, including the fact that he had given Jo papers that were not listed on the police inventory of items found in her car, and that he had been in the car the night Jo died. She wrote, 'His prints should have been there, he says. If the police say they weren't, then someone has wiped them…unlikely he would have owned up to being there if he wiped them himself.' She also asked Deidre to engage an expert to study the Hyatt's CCTV and an investigator to ask Jo's neighbours if they had noticed any vehicle movements that night.

Mujo made phone calls while Brooke fed the fax machine. He called out that he had secured a seat on a minibus leaving Belgrade that night. 'I know the driver. He will take good care of you. He'll pick you up around 9.20.'

The timing meant that, with luck, she'd make her 7.30 a.m. Budapest–London flight. The catch was that having to sleep through the night on the bus was no preparation for the long haul back to Australia.

Brooke had spent only three of her five days in Serbia with Mujo and family, enough to make her sorry she was leaving them. The children stayed up to see her into the minibus, and gave her long, warm hugs and asked her to please come back.

Mujo boarded the bus and ran his eye across each of the passengers before having a word with the driver. He stepped out of the bus and told Brooke that she would be the last passenger to be picked up.

They exchanged goodbyes and thank yous. Brooke told them where she had left her spare Deutschmarks. Andjela handed her a bag containing bread and cheese, a slice of spinach quiche, and some plums and an apple. She watched Mujo and the driver stow her bag carefully in the back of the bus. As for the hold-all containing her notebook and documents, she intended to keep it by her at all times.

The bus was nearly full but the bench seat at the back was empty. While it didn't offer the comfort of a chair with arms, it was a place where she could stretch out and hopefully sleep. She introduced herself to the passengers in front of her, happy that they spoke a little English. One man had business in Budapest and intended to return to Belgrade by minibus the following night, a punishing schedule. An elderly couple were visiting relatives close to the border and would leave the bus at Szeged.

They crossed the border at 1 a.m. There was little traffic and no delay at passport control where the officials were standing around joking and smoking. The next stop was a short wait at a garage near Szeged which Brooke filled in by talking with another passenger, a Portuguese United Nations official. Everyone queued for the toilets. Brooke hugged her hold-all and checked that the bus driver was standing close to his bus while it was being refuelled.

Well ahead of schedule, the bus pulled into Budapest airport at 4.30 a.m. Brooke had only dozed during the trip and was tired and in need of coffee. No eatery appeared to be open. She saw a bus pull in heading for Budapest itself, and approached the driver to ask where she might find food and coffee. He looked at his watch and said something she didn't understand, and he pointed.

She walked in the direction he had indicated, heaving her bag in one hand, hold-all in the other. The airport was starting to wake up. She had just decided to head to the check-in before looking again for a coffee when it all happened. She heard feet pounding the pavement behind her and, turning to look, she was viciously knocked to the ground. Her hold-all was grabbed by – she couldn't miss it – the man in the straw hat. He stumbled, righted himself and ran towards the road.

Still prostrate, she shouted after him, furious she had released her grip on the bag. Then she saw him, a man in a black suit, chasing the thief. A couple came to lift Brooke up, but she had eyes only for the scene ahead. As they steadied her, the man in the black suit grabbed the thief, holding him tightly by the shoulder and spun him around. They stood for a moment, belly to belly, exchanging venom. Without any struggle, Black-suit took the bag from Straw-hat, and let him scurry away.

Black-suit came back to Brooke, who was standing between her good Samaritans.

She thanked the couple, who nodded and spoke in Hungarian. Assuming they were asking her if she was all right, she confirmed, 'Okay, yes, thank you, I'm fine.'

She fumbled for her purse and pulled out some American dollars, but the woman made a gesture that meant 'Absolutely not.' She and her husband linked arms and walked off.

Brooke turned and took the bag from the waiting man and thanked him, assuming him to be a security guard.

He appeared embarrassed, or was he nervous? 'It was nothing,' he murmured. He turned away quickly.

But Brooke knew. Black-suit was Black-shirt, the man in a light blue suit she had seen on her first arrival. Of that she had no doubt.

Landing in Sydney was a relief. Her knees were grazed but no longer sore. Her swollen elbow was stiff, but an ice pack provided by the flight attendant had eased the pain. She was shaking between Budapest and London, but started to relax on the long flight to Sydney, sleeping as she could in the cramped and noisy cabin.

As the customs hall doors flapped shut behind her, she saw Donald amongst the crowd waiting for relatives and friends.

'Goodness, what are you doing here? I didn't give you my return flight details.'

'Meeting you. I heard of your bad experience in Budapest, and I was worried.'

'You heard? How?'

'Let's get over to domestic and I'll explain before you board for Canberra. Let me take your bag.'

Brooke continued to grip her hold-all. Her instinct was to distrust even Donald. She covered up by pretending to be flustered, handing him her large suitcase. 'Thank you.'

They checked her suitcase through to Canberra, before catching the bus to the domestic terminal. Saying little, they collected coffees and found comfortable seats by a window in the Qantas guest lounge.

'Now,' she said, 'I must know. Please explain how you heard about my incident, and how you knew my flights.'

'The man who retrieved your bag is a Hungarian friend of mine, Brock Mészáros. I confess that I arranged for him to watch over you.'

Brooke spluttered. 'You! You did that without telling me? You caused me all sorts of worries. Your man, he was hanging around when I arrived. He frightened me, and then the man who knocked me down, wearing a straw hat, apparently followed me to Serbia and then back to Budapest. For all I knew, they were partners. I changed my minibus booking in case I was being followed, but I was mugged anyway.'

'Brooke, Brooke, I am really sorry for alarming you. And I didn't have you followed to Belgrade. Brock's job was to see you safely onto a minibus at Budapest airport. If he'd seen anyone following you, he would have been close behind. But he was satisfied that you were in safe hands on the minibus. I knew Mujo would look after you in Belgrade. Good thing Brock was at the airport when you got back to Budapest.'

'Why didn't you tell me, let him introduce himself to me?'

'Couldn't afford you being seen with him. That might have made it more dangerous.'

'Yes. Sorry. It's just, well…I don't know what's going on any more. But for Brock, I would have lost my hold-all and my notes.'

'Were you injured?' Donald asked.

'I'm okay now, thanks. The man got away, though. Brock had him covered, but let him go.' Brooke looked to Donald to explain.

'Brock found out a good deal. He had him covered, as they say, literally, with his gun pressed hard against the man's stomach. He called me immediately afterwards and told me that he gave the man three seconds to spit out what he was after. The man said he was acting for a foreigner, supposedly an official, who paid a sum into a bank account, with more to come if he succeeded stealing any documents from your luggage. He was just a bit player, paid to track your movements. He obviously decided he would have to pull your hold-all away from you. With a gun to his belly, reckon he told the truth when he said that he was acting on instructions...'

'Whose?'

'An Australian...you might have guessed. From a man he knew only as Alec. Not hard to track. Using a public phone, I left a message at ASIO's Canberra headquarters for "Alec, with news from Belgrade", and I waited. The phone rang. It was a local call, and I hung up. I then contacted the whistle-blower, Pratt – I can tell you that now – who told me that agent Alec Brown was the ASIO officer handling Jo's security clearance – presumably the same Brown from ASIO who tried to persuade Jo to report on Mujo. More about that later.'

It was a lot for Brooke to take in. 'Is this Alec Brown Jo's killer?' she asked.

'I doubt it. ASIO might be interested in what you've found out about her death, but kill Jo? A bit far-fetched, I think. There's more of this Fishnet to be unpicked before we find out where Jo fits in, and how she died. Hopefully you have some information from Mujo that might help.'

'I certainly have,' Brooke said patting her hold-all, but saying nothing about having faxed stuff to Deidre. 'I, uh, I'm sorry I was a bit over-protective of it,' she said, blushing because she had refused to let Donald to carry it.

'No offence, Brooke. You have to suspect even Donald in this treacherous world.'

'I didn't mean…'

'Don't worry,' he said and squeezed her hand with both of his.

'I'm shaken by all this. You know, Straw-hat actually made an earlier attempt to grab my bag in Svetozarevo. I had help there too, and got my papers back, but he escaped.'

'What were you doing there?'

'I'll tell you about it later. More important, I do know from something Mujo said that someone else was in Jo's car the night she was killed. She was murdered. I know that now.'

'Yes, I agree. I've got new information too. I'll visit you in Canberra soon.'

Brooke used the one-hour flight to Canberra to mull over what Donald had told her. He excited her. Could something develop between them? She let her fantasies run until brought back to earth by first, self-doubt, and then doubts about Donald. His actions might have been motivated not so much by wanting to protect her as by wanting to protect any information she acquired. What if his agenda was to feed some agency, ASIO or Immigration, with Mujo's information? She shivered. But no, it couldn't be. After all, it was Donald who spoke for the whistle-blower on the *7.30 Report*. Then again, if he hadn't, the whistle-blower would surely have found someone else who would, and Donald wouldn't have been privy to all of Pratt's information.

It calmed her to realise that the very worst an unfriendly Donald could do was to control the flow of information into the public arena. Either way, the sooner her new evidence became public, either in court or in the media, the safer she would feel. She resolved to contact Rusty, whom she did trust, when she got home. He would help her piece together the information she had accumulated. He might even be able to connect her information about Customs corruption in the 80s to current players in Operation Fishnet. He'd already done some sniffing around for Donald, so yes, just to be safe she'd approach him before talking to Donald again.

37

Canberra, mid-September 1992

'I have some great news, Brooke!' was Deidre's telephone greeting when Brooke returned to chambers.

'You got my faxes?' Brooke asked.

'Yes, yes, thanks. And I have forensics on the poem. We have to meet.'

Steady, reliable Deidre sounded positively excited. Brooke moved quickly to find out why and to share her own adventures and discoveries.

Over a sandwich and coffee in the arcade below Canberra House, Deidre summarised the scientific findings on Mujo's original sheet of poetry. The only signs of blood were some wiped-over faded smears on one-quarter of the back of the sheet.

'The paper must have had been folded, in fact, not scrunched-up, Brooke, at the time of the gunshot,' Deidre exclaimed.

'My goodness,' was all Brooke could manage considering the implications of what Deidre was saying.

'It's a bit hard for someone who has shot themselves in the head to wipe blood off a piece of paper, screw it up and throw it down without spattering it with more blood,' Deidre spluttered through a mouthful of over-filled salad sandwich.

Brooke took the forensic report Deidre held and started to read it while Deidre kept talking.

'It's conclusive, isn't it?' Deidre said.

'Certainly hope so. And along with Mujo's statement that he was in the car that evening without apparently leaving any prints, it puts an end to "no suspicious circumstances". Even if we don't know who did it, we do know Jo didn't shoot herself.' Brooke felt a surge of relief, terrible as it was to think of Jo being murdered.

'Sure. And there's more. We have our own pathologist's report now. Dr Bates thinks it unlikely she pulled the trigger. It would be awkward for her to hold the pistol in her left hand and angle it towards her neck. More important, the bullet fragments recovered at the autopsy could not have come from a Glock .22 handgun, which is chambered for a 40 S&W cartridge.'

'Well, well! ' It was Brooke's turn to talk with her mouth full.

'A different make of gun was used,' said Deidre. 'Work that out.'

'Curiouser and curioser,' Brooke mused. Jo is shot at close range; the murderer replaces the weapon with a decoy gun, then clears up and screws up the poem to make it look like suicide? Or does someone else arrive to set up a suicide scenario to protect the murderer?

Deidre's other piece of good news was that a solicitor from Attorney-General's had rung to say that the director-general of security had withdrawn the injunction application. The court ordered ASIO to pay the publisher's costs, so Brooke would be paid too. They both would have time now to prepare for the inquest.

Brooke told Deidre all about Belgrade. She was pleased to hear of Mujo and Andjela's hospitality but gaped when Brooke told about being followed, and kept gaping as the story moved on to Straw-hat's failed mugging. Then Brooke segued, somewhat bashfully, into Donald's part in facilitating her trip and his efforts to protect her.

Deidre was immediately concerned. 'How come Donald is so well-connected that he can call in a gun-toting professional who, at short notice, could spend days checking arrivals and departures of various sorts until he finds you? Brock would have been expensive. Who was paying?'

Deidre had gone straight to Brooke's worries. For the sake of her warming heart, she needed Donald to come up with a convincing explanation for his magic.

'I don't know the answers there,' Brooke replied. 'It's always a possibility that ASIO has asked him to get close to me to find out about and report on my discoveries. Perhaps he's been persuaded that it's not in the public interest that ASIO stuff-ups are exposed. But I don't believe for a minute that he would do that.'

'Listen to yourself, Brooke! You're smitten. Be careful.'

'I will. If Donald has a second agenda, I will find out.'

'Rusty, it's Brooke Talbot. Sorry to bother you again. Have you got a moment at this ungodly hour?'

She had caught him at 7 a.m. and he was barely awake. She told him she was just back from Yugoslavia and had information that might interest him.

'Uh, Brooke, sure. Hang on while I fire up the kettle. Sounds like I'm going to need coffee.'

She described her discussions with Donald and Mujo; and the failed attempts to steal her notes. Winding up, she said, 'I have no doubt that Jo Rowan was murdered and I want this crime exposed by a reliable agency or an investigative reporter.'

Rusty was on side at once. 'I knew you were over there, Brooke. I've been working with Donald on a follow-up story. You know he's tracked down the whistle-blower from Immigration?'

'Yes,' said Brooke, 'but we haven't had time to discuss the details yet. My primary task is to win an insurance case for Jo's granddaughter by proving that she was murdered. But I'm so involved now that I want to understand the big picture.'

'It's a good story,' Rusty replied. 'Donald and I have been talking to the current affairs people at ABC and the Nine Network, trying to get them interested. I'd like to go to Darwin with a camera crew and talk with people on the waterfront.'

Brooke was relieved to hear that Donald had been working with Rusty with a view to further publicising the story. 'Ah, I'm so glad. I didn't know whether to offer you all my material or just deposit it with the commission of inquiry?'

'We should definitely talk, Brooke.'

'I can give you some names to follow up but I won't say more over the phone.'

'Tell you what,' Rusty said, 'Donald will be here next weekend. Why don't you come over to my place Sunday week, and we'll go through everything together.'

Donald visiting was news to Brooke. She hadn't heard from him since Sydney, but she agreed to Rusty's suggestion.

'Rusty tells me you've been in touch.'

It was Friday afternoon and her heart pounded and her mind raced as she reviewed her evening's commitments in case he was in Canberra.

'I'm planning to come to Canberra at the weekend.'

'Oh, good,' Brooke replied. 'Rusty suggested we might all meet Sunday morning.'

'I told him to make it around 11. I'm driving down Sunday morning. I'll leave here at 7 and go straight to his place at Kingston. How are you, by the way?'

'I'm good. Really. Preparing for the inquest, though. Its findings are crucial to the insurance claim. It starts Monday.'

'Well, I'll leave you to it. Look forward to seeing you.'

'Yes, that'll be good. How long will you be here, Donald? Are you staying at University House?'

As soon as she asked, she kicked herself. Why did you do that, stupid? He was in a hurry, and you should have just said, Me too, and hung up.

'Ah, not sure. I haven't booked in yet. I usually bunk down on Rusty's couch if I'm only here overnight.'

'I've always got a spare bed,' she couldn't help herself, and quickly qualified her offer, 'though I'm not good company when I'm immersed in a case,' so as not to appear too keen.

'Thanks, Brooke. I'll let you know if I'm staying longer. And I can always cook for you, you know, if you're flat out working.'

'Okay, play it by ear. See you Sunday.'

He mentioned cooking for her. Was he just being nice? Not that she had time to play host, or get involved with Donald. When she was preparing an important case, she avoided people. Her thoughts were interrupted by a sharp knock on the door and in walked the bully, Trevor Christian.

Brooke braced herself. Trevor would only come to her room to make an offer to settle the insurance claim. She decided to play her cards close to her chest and not mention that she and Deidre had new information. Insurance companies were diligent in their investigations, and it was quite likely Trevor knew something she didn't.

He came straight to the point. 'If you wait for the inquest, Brooke, you'll lose. If there's a finding of suicide, your client gets nothing. Cut your losses and take what we're offering – twenty-five thousand inclusive of legal costs.'

'You're priceless, Trevor!' Brooke replied. 'That's under 25 per cent of the insured sum. Try eighty thousand, plus legal costs, that's a 20 per cent discount, and I'd be prepared to ask Deidre to seek instructions. Jo's daughter might accept that on Billie's behalf, just to avoid delay, the legal costs and angst of litigation. We don't have to prove who killed her, Trevor, only that she didn't kill herself. And we think we can throw enough doubt on the suicide theory to satisfy a judge.'

'We have witnesses to show how despairing and depressed Dr Rowan was. Our psychiatrist has studied the statements and believes that a contribution of workplace stress and a crumbling love life could have triggered suicidal depression.'

'Then why are you here, making an offer, Trevor? Not your style. You'd normally go to a hearing like this confident of winning and making your costs.'

'My client insurer is responsible, not unreasonable.'

'What else did your investigator find out? Come on, out with it.'

'Some circumstantial evidence. Nothing to shake our case.'

'Such as? I'll be calling for the investigator's report anyway. Have you accessed the police files yet? Do we know Jo's movements that night? You must have interviewed the neighbours by now.'

Trevor heaved and, prepared to talk, sat down on Brooke's small couch. 'A neighbour did see her drive out on the night she died, and noticed that a car parked outside her house followed her. She thought at the time that it might be a boyfriend or friend leaving with her, and then worried when she heard Rowan was dead.'

Well, well, well. The reason for Trevor's settlement overtures was emerging. He was worried as to what further investigation of this second vehicle might bring.

'Really? Did she describe the car or driver?' Brooke tried to be nonchalant.

'A man in a white Commodore. She's given a statement to the police. Your solicitor will get it. The neighbour had the impression Jo left in a hurry, as if to an emergency – a sick relative or an accident perhaps.'

'Hmm.' Brooke pondered how much she needed to reveal to have Trevor increase his settlement offer. 'We know she went to see her boyfriend at the Canberra Hyatt. We want to see a copy of the hotel CCTV footage, in case it shows someone following her inside, or out when she left. We reckon we have enough to suggest foul play. Our pathologist is doubtful that it was suicide, or even that the gun found in the car killed her.'

At that, Trevor broke into a guffaw. 'Well, you'll have a problem explaining that one, Brooke. There is the gun – almost smoking – and you say it didn't kill her! I'll suggest that your pathologist isn't qualified to comment on the niceties of weaponry and gunpowder residue. You'll need other experts to do that.'

Brooke, fully aware of the difficulties surrounding her case, battled on. 'As I said, if you want to settle the insurance claim now, make a more generous offer.'

'No. I can't do that. My offer of twenty-five thousand remains open until the end of the day. Remember, you must put all offers to your client.'

'You're exploiting my young client's vulnerability. That's unconscionable, Trevor. You know she's fearful of going to court. The insurance is for her child, and you're playing on her fears to get her to accept an inadequate amount. Anyhow, I'll relay your offer to my instructing solicitor and I'll suggest she advise her client in the strongest terms to reject it.'

'You're making a mistake, Brooke. Don't say I didn't warn you.'

He left. There was no ill-feeling. Socially, Trevor was jovial and friendly. Professionally, his style left a lot to be desired. Then again, he got results. His rough tactics often paid off. Brooke and Deidre could only hope that the coroner would accept Dr Bates's opinion, and that he would be persuaded that the pattern of blood spatters on the piece of paper proved that it had been screwed up after, not before, the gunshot. It would be helpful too if there were stronger evidence to support the gun switch theory. Mujo's statement that his prints should have been inside the car might not be accepted because he was unavailable for cross-examination. On balance, while there was no certainty that the coroner would make a finding of murder, the odds were better than the one in four that Trevor was offering. Without proof, truth often fell by the wayside in courtrooms.

38

Late September 1992

Rusty greeted Brooke warmly through a cloud of cigar smoke as he opened the door and beckoned her in. His old brick house in Currie Crescent, Kingston, though in need of some loving care, was prime real estate.

The hallway was dark and the living room not much brighter. A mishmash of old furniture sat on a patterned wool carpet from the forties. Brooke surmised that the couch and sagging armchairs were cast-offs from previous wives, just like Rusty himself. The floor was scattered with books and papers and on two wobbly laminated side tables smelly ashtrays and dried-out coffee cups jostled for space. He was pointing to the couch when there was a knock on the half-open door and Donald pushed in.

Removing his cigar, Rusty held out a hand to Donald, who clasped it warmly.

'Hello, Brooke,' Donald said. He placed his hands her shoulders and leant down to kiss her on the cheek, lightly brushing her lips as he lifted his face. 'Good to see you both. Coffee would be good too. I didn't stop on the road.'

They followed Rusty into the kitchen and watched him plug in an old kettle and put bread in the toaster. He opened painted yellow cupboards and pulled out jam and honey. Donald found milk and butter in the fridge, and a couple of cracked plates in a cupboard. It was a 50s kitchen scene that took Brooke back to her childhood.

They sat down in the living room, Rusty in an armchair and Brooke and Donald on the couch opposite.

'So, you two, a bit of a couple, eh?'

'No, we're not,' Brooke got in first.

'I'm a betting man,' Rusty stated. 'I'll give it a week.'

'What you are is a cheeky man,' Donald retorted, and smiled at Brooke.

'I'll just get the rest of the toast,' Rusty said, responding to a popping noise from the kitchen, 'then we'll talk. Donald, you brief Brooke on what we've turned up so far.'

Donald started to tell Brooke about his meeting with James Pratt, the Jack referred to in the memo leaked to Annette, he confirmed. Pratt was an officer in Special Projects at Immigration. Pratt sent Donald a second note because of a rising concern about Jo's death. He couldn't prove it but, given ASIO's concern over Jo's working at Immigration, he believed her death must be linked to Operation Fishnet. Pratt's preference was to remain anonymous and let Donald explore whether the ABC might be interested in investigating that link. 'According to Pratt, Fishnet's top informant, Rexi Pike, or Fish, as they call him, has threatened his handler that he will take 'matters into his own hands' if he is not allowed to continue his activities.'

Brooke's delighted squeal interrupted him. 'Ah, so Pike is Fish and is up to his neck in it all. Just as Mujo supposed.'

'Okay, let's come back to Mujo later.'

'Sure, go on.'

'According to Pratt, Fish said it wasn't his problem if the department couldn't get rid of some sticky-beak woman. Fish accused ASIO of stuffing up and demanded that "something must be done to make sure she doesn't talk", meaning Jo. He threatened to come to Canberra, bang on doors and reveal intelligence secrets if things weren't "fixed up". Pratt conveyed all this to Alec Brown, his ASIO contact.'

'Is that his real name?' Brooke asked.

'It seems so. Pratt confirmed that his full name is Alec Brown. Pratt also warned Brown that Fish needed to be watched while Fish's police handler argued that Jo's presence in the department threatened Fish's cover. Pratt said he worried about what Fish might do next.' Donald stopped, and lowered his head, shaking it from side to side.

'Poor Jo,' Brooke sighed. 'Could be Fish, then, who did the deed?'

Rusty returned with more toast, on the black side this time.

'Seems there's more than one suspect,' Donald said, and continued his tale. 'While Brown took Fish's threats seriously, he didn't seem surprised hearing about Fish's tantrum. His response to Pratt was "Leave it to me." After Jo died, Pratt got frightened, and sent me a second note. "Something was not right", he said. From the moment he told Brown he was nervous about Jo asking to see certain of the section's files, he thought Brown's reaction signalled something more than preventing exposure of Fishnet's dubious methods of catching people smugglers.'

'This is where Mujo's theory might help,' Brooke broke in. 'Mujo thinks he knows what ASIO's real concern was,' she said. She told them about Operation Picnic – the Croatian terrorist operation – including the role played by Rexi Pike, known to Mujo as Fish. 'What he knew amazed me. Talk about camaraderie amongst spies. In the 80s he was sharing intelligence with two Australian counterparts about Croatian extremists. I have their names if we need them. What's important is that Fish played a key role in an Australian intelligence operation to track down training camps run by Croatian extremists. Fish was a well-connected boat operator and a known gun smuggler. He was importing and selling rifles to the Ustashi groups who were running the camps. Yugoslav intelligence informed Australian intelligence and demanded that the Croatians be arrested.'

Rusty looked at her. 'With that leverage, Fish has the potential to reveal an even nastier story about our God-fearing intelligence organisations.'

'Including the stuff-ups,' Brooke continued. 'A Serb undercover agent had infiltrated the Ustashi by posing as an Ustashi sympathiser. His brief was to collect rifles imported by Fish and transport them to the camps. It was through him that Yugoslav intelligence learned enough to demand Australian authorities take action against Croatian extremists. Unfortunately, the Yugoslavs didn't tell ASIO how they collected their information. Had they done so, their undercover man might not have been shot. Anyway, the federal police had apparently approached Fish with a promise that he would not be prosecuted for gun-smuggling if he turned informant. He was permitted to continue importing rifles as long as he reported details of all shipments and sales. It was this plan that became Operation Picnic. The Serb plant continued to deal with Fish while the federal police watched, followed the rifles, and eventually made a few arrests.' Brooke paused. She wanted to get the story in logical order.

'What I glean from the widow of the Serb undercover agent is that he was ready to pull out, knowing it wouldn't be long before the Croats fingered him as their weak link. Unfortunately, he found Fish with a cop, not knowing Fish had turned informant. That's when the shoot-out occurred.'

The men had listened carefully without comment as Brooke spoke. When she had finished, they were silent for a moment.

'Shit, Brooke,' exclaimed Rusty, 'you did have a productive trip!'

After a thousand questions, Brooke completed the story by telling Donald and Rusty about Mad Max, the ex-ASIO man who apparently provided Fish with names of customs staff who might be corruptible, or vulnerable to blackmail.

Donald interrupted. 'I bet I know who Mad Max is. I used to work with a spook, Max Peacock. We called him MP because he was a law unto himself, but Mad Max suits him better. I wonder if it is him. He can't still be with ASIO after Operation Picnic was wound up. I wonder what happened to him.'

'That makes sense. He's important to the story,' Brooke said. 'According to Mujo, Fish's success relied on bribing or blackmailing various Customs officers. Fish assumed that the names on Max's list were people whom ASIO had checked when they applied to be Customs officers. Max probably sold his names to all sorts of crooks besides Fish – a one-man waterfront corruption machine.'

Brooke had one more piece of exciting news. 'There's another way forward,' she said. 'I have the list of crooked Customs officers the Serb agent used to help him clear Fish's rifles.' Brooke looked and sounded smug. 'Even though the list is out of date, it could be useful evidence for the commission of inquiry into the immigration racket. If the *7.30 Report* exposes the role of Customs corruption in ASIO's operation, the commission will be forced to investigate.'

Where, they asked, did you get this gem?

Brooke told them about her trip to Svetosarevo, meeting the Serb agent's family and that they believed he was murdered, not shot in self-defence, by an Australian policeman. 'And there's evidence to support this,' she said. 'Fish was a witness. For his own protection, he wrote a second statement that would suggest that the Serb agent was shot from behind. Mujo discovered it and gave Jo a copy the night she died. It disappeared.'

'Jesus,' Donald gulped. 'Now I see why Fish was kept on, to keep him quiet. Notwithstanding his history, he was palmed off to Immigration as an informant for Operation Fishnet. If Pratt's right, Immigration had no idea.'

'Seems that Fish is something of a puppeteer,' Rusty grinned.

'Well, he scored again when Immigration turned a blind eye to the arrival of his wife's Indonesian family on an Indonesian fishing boat that was towed into Darwin for an inspection of their gear and catch,' Donald added. 'That alerted Pratt. What if their informant was himself a people smuggler?'

'Surely,' Brooke was almost yelping with excitement, 'it's more than coincidence that the last consignment of rifles and a boat load of refugees from Indonesia arrived on the same day, the day the Serb agent was shot. The same federal policeman, Ormandy, investigated both. London to a brick they came in on the same boat.'

As Brooke spoke, she warmed to her own story. But as the bigger picture became clearer, the identity of Jo's murderer became more open. There were a lot of suspects: Fish, his police handler Ormandy, Mad Max, ASIO would all have an interest in silencing Jo via a fake suicide.

Donald was leaning forward looking thoughtfully at Brooke, and as if confirming her thoughts said, 'This gives several people a motive to shut Jo up.'

'The sad reality, Donald, is that Mujo and Jo were never going to join the dots,' Brooke said. 'Mujo only made the connection when you told him over the phone about Operation Fishnet. It led him to surmise that the Fish involved in Operation Picnic might also be involved in Fishnet: one man, two operations. Fish's motive is to protect a lucrative business arrangement, ASIO's motive is to hide the knowledge that it collaborated with the Serbs, even if they weren't baddies at the time. Let alone the stench of corruption around these operations.'

Rusty said, 'Well, we have plenty of leads to follow.'

'Leaving motive aside,' Brooke said, 'we now have evidence that she was murdered. We may not know who killed her, but there's a good chance the coroner will find that she was killed by a third party.'

Brooke told them about Deidre's persuasive forensic tests and reports, and the blood spatter pattern on the piece of paper in the car, in particular.

'More good news,' Rusty said, fiddling with his pipe and stroking his chin. 'Presumably someone was following Jo and Mujo that night. Maybe Fish wanted to send a message to his handlers not to mess around with him.'

'No,' Brooke responded. 'If he was sending a message, he wouldn't go to the trouble of making it look like suicide, would he? Maybe wipe for prints, but why risk leaving a gun just to make it look like suicide?'

The three brainstormed for a while but, finding more questions than answers, decided it was time for a plan.

'Wonder if any retirees on the corruptible customs officers list might be willing to talk,' was Rusty's thought. He wanted to suss out Fish's and Mad Max's recent doings and their whereabouts, if he could. Donald undertook to track down Mujo's ASIO mates, Larry and Eugene. They might have an idea of how Fish was able to stay in the game as an official informant.

Brooke still wondered why ASIO waited so long to approach Jo to inform on Mujo. 'Was their offer another attempt to shut her up? It can't have been part of their original plan,' Brooke said. 'Or did they really think Mujo might know too much about Pine Gap, and they decided to appeal to Jo's patriotism? Even so, it's unlikely that a failed attempt to lure Jo into ASIO's web would be sufficient reason to kill her.'

'We don't have enough information to make sense of this, yet,' Donald said. 'We have to go carefully. Rusty, can we leave it to you to get a broadcaster journalist interested in pursuing the waterfront story? And I'll use the prospect of a television exposé of the material we have to shake some truths out of this Alec Brown. He can't wriggle out of the admitted fact that he hired the thug who accosted you, Brooke,' Donald said. 'And because you are a person of interest now, the sooner this goes to air the safer you'll be.'

Brooke couldn't have agreed more.

'I'm on to it,' Rusty said, grinning, announcing he needed to go for a leak.

'Meantime, I have to convince the coroner tomorrow of the significance of what we've learned,' Brooke said as Rusty left the room.

Brooke still hadn't had an opportunity to ask the one question of Donald which was on her mind; now was the time. 'Donald,' she asked nervously, 'why did you engage that man, Brock, in Budapest to watch me? Were you acting alone? Someone had to pay for him.'

'I'm really sorry, Brooke. I meant to explain. No. It was my initiative. I was worried for you. Brock owed me a favour, something I did for him and his family when I was posted in Eastern Europe, and I knew he was trustworthy and a good operator. I briefed him and I put two hundred dollars into his German savings account, very useful to him.'

'But the gun?'

'Yes, I knew he owned one, and he promised not to use it within miles of you – under any circumstances. In fact, he told me it wasn't loaded, but made a convincing clicking noise when he cocked it against that buffoon's stomach.'

Rusty returned, and started to take things out to the kitchen, clearly wanting to get on with his investigation.

'Do you want a couch to kip on?' he turned to ask Donald.

'Rusty, thanks, that would be great. Just for one night. I have people I must see this afternoon,' said Donald.

Brooke was busily sorting her papers and pretended to ignore the exchange. 'Here, Rusty,' she said, holding out a plastic sleeve with a few pages in it. 'A copy of my notes, and the names you want. Thanks for the tea and toast. I'll be off too.'

Outside, Donald caught up. 'Brooke, could I take up your offer of a bed and company tomorrow night? I know you'll be very busy for the next couple of days with the inquest, but I can work quietly on my own. Maybe cook for you, feed the chooks?'

Brooke felt embarrassed that she had probably been unable to hide her disappointment at hearing Donald accept Rusty's offer of a bed. Now, minutes later, she was trying to hide her joy. She had worked hard the day before, not just preparing for the inquest, but cleaning up the house and making sure the spare bed was made up with crisp white sheets, and preparing a meal in a crock pot that would be tasty no matter when it was served. Just in case.

'Sure, Donald. It'd be my pleasure. I have some food we can use up,' (which will be the case, she thought, after I've dipped into the casserole tonight). 'I won't be home until after six, though.'

'That's fine. Why don't I ring you at work and perhaps we can drive out in convoy, so I won't get lost.'

'Good idea. Ring me at chambers, about five tomorrow.' She could barely contain her excitement.

39

True to his name, he had a beaming round face. Benny Moone was an experienced local magistrate and Brooke was relieved to hear that he would be the coroner for the Rowan inquest. He granted Brooke leave to represent Jo's family and Trevor Christian QC leave to represent the insurance company, both having explained their clients' interests in the proceedings. Counsel assisting was Marcus Chessman, from the ACT Government Solicitor's office. It was his task to elicit evidence from the witnesses. Coronial proceedings are inquisitorial in nature and the coroner, too, can ask questions of witnesses.

Chessman, a short, rotund and confident young man with small round tortoiseshell glasses, tendered a folder containing a bundle of material neatly indexed. He handed duplicate folders to Brooke and Trevor. In them were copies of the autopsy report, police statements, a list of items found in the car including the handwritten poem, forensic and psychiatric reports and statements taken from employees of the departments of Immigration and Prime Minister and Cabinet, and other people who knew or had worked with Jo Rowan. He tendered the CCTV tape from the Hyatt.

Brooke informed the coroner at the outset that the family did not accept that the deceased took her own life, and that she had questions for the investigating police officers and the police pathologist about their evidence and findings.

'You're not suggesting the death was accidental, are you?' Moone asked.

'No, your worship. We have evidence to suggest that foul play was the cause of Dr Rowan's death – that is, that she was murdered, and that the killer, or killers, took steps to make the murder look like suicide.'

'Oh, ho hum,' Christian murmured, giving a bored yawn and twiddling his pen from side to side.

Moone shot him a scolding look and then flicked through papers on the bench. He turned to Brooke. 'I wasn't expecting this. No one seems to have suggested anything other than that Dr Rowan killed herself.'

'Material that throws doubt on that, your worship, has recently come into our hands, and I will be tendering it.'

Chessman told the coroner that Superintendent de Fraga, the officer in charge of the police investigation, was in court and available for questioning. The coroner thanked him and at the completion of formalities, the policeman was called into the witness box.

De Fraga gave evidence of the emergency call made to the police station on the evening of Saturday 20 June that a woman was found dead in a car near the yacht club. Drawing on statements taken from police who attended the scene, de Fraga stated that the deceased woman's left arm had dropped down between the two front seats, with a gun, still hooked onto her trigger finger, dangling almost to the floor. He confirmed that the evidence collected at the scene, including a dearth of footprints and fingerprints, gave a picture of what appeared to be a clear-cut case of suicide.

Brooke asked him if efforts had been made to preserve the footprints of the couple who had found the body or any other prints. The officer looked through the various statements he had to hand and, finding nothing relevant, turned to the coroner to explain that it was standard practice for the first officers on the scene to look for footprints before walking around the area. 'There had been rain in the preceding twenty four hours,' he explained, 'and indentations in the grass were not likely to be visible after the rain.'

Brooke asked if swabs to be tested for gunshot residue were taken from the left palm of the deceased.

De Fraga gave a polite smile and said, 'No, ma'am, not then, not by us. The gun in her hand spoke for itself.'

Moone addressed the officer. 'I take it that from your perspective the scene was so clearly one of suicide that you decided that forensic assistance was not required?'

'Yes, sir. That is correct.'

A second police witness described the Glock pistol, its firing mechanism and its ready availability in Australia and stated that Rowan was not a licensed gun owner.

Brooke had questions for him too. He was shown the police pathologist's report that described the bullet remnants found in the deceased's head and the flecks of gunshot residue found in the car. She asked him whether the bullet remnants and residue were consistent with an Austrian 9mm Glock .22 pistol having been used.

'I assume so, since that was the gun found in the car,' said the witness, conceding after Brooke's next question that he was not an arms expert.

'And it would be true, wouldn't it, given your lack of ballistics expertise, that you are unable to say if the shrapnel remnants could also have come from a shot from an Italian Beretta 92FS?'

Moone looked up at Brooke, surprise on his round face, and the courtroom stirred.

'That's true, I wouldn't know. Only that it was a Glock, not a Beretta, found in the hand of the deceased,' the policeman said, addressing the coroner.

'What's this about, Ms Talbot?' Moone asked.

'Your worship, it might be convenient if at this point I tender a copy of the report of independent pathologist Dr John Bates. It is his view that the bullet remnants were not from a Glock .22 pistol. We have a statement from an armourer, too, your worship, saying that, on the available evidence, the bullet was more likely to have been fired from a Beretta.'

The coroner looked sceptical, so Brooke elaborated.

'If the deceased were murdered, your worship, it would not be surprising for the murder weapon to be removed from the site. We have evidence that supports this possibility.'

'Perhaps we should first hear the rest of the police evidence and other material which counsel assisting wishes to present, and then consider your fresh material, Ms Talbot,' Moone directed.

Chessman called other members of the police investigating team, all of the view that there were no suspicious circumstances. A statement by Jo's mother was tendered in which she said that her daughter had an aversion to guns and had never possessed or used a gun to her knowledge.

The coroner wanted to know why there was no evidence as to when Jo had been last seen and by whom. Chessman explained that, given the case for suicide, most effort had gone into interviewing family members, friends and colleagues in search of indicators of depression.

Rowan's use of her left hand to fire the gun was easily explained. Right-handed people commonly pick up a telephone or a cup with their left hand, while they use their right hand to dial a number or stir their tea. It might have been convenient for her to access the gun with her left hand from the glovebox or her shoulder bag, and it was not heavy enough to require the use of her stronger hand. Glocks can be used by either left or right-handers.

Counsel assisting indicated that the deceased's daughter, Kitty Rowan-McGrath, was present to give evidence. She had received letters from her mother in the weeks before her death. 'Her interpretation of those letters might assist your worship in deciding whether or not suicide was the most probable cause of death.'

Brooke had explained to Kitty that the coroner had the power to call witnesses, and that it was important that she answer honestly. Strict rules of evidence did not apply in an inquisitorial proceeding, as they do in adversarial litigation – or in theory anyway – Brooke remembered to add, anticipating that Trevor might interrogate Kitty about those letters as one might cross-examine a witness in a court trial.

She was right. Trevor Christian interjected ruthlessly, even before it was his turn to ask questions.

Brooke questioned her first, as gently as possible, about Jo's last letter. 'And when did you receive it?'

Kitty sobbed, 'About two days after her death.'

A loud voice boomed from the end of the bar table, 'I didn't hear the answer, your worship.'

The coroner had heard and said, 'She said, "About two days after her death", Mr Christian.'

'Thank you, your worship,' Christian replied, not caring that everyone in the room knew too well that he had heard every word.

'And when did you hear of her death?' Brooke continued.

'The day before.'

'I didn't hear that, your worship,' boomed Trevor.

The coroner repeated the evidence word for word, without asking Kitty to speak up.

Brooke continued, 'How did you feel then?'

'I froze. I felt numb. Then I dropped the phone and screamed. Nan said that the police thought it was suicide. She wouldn't do that. The police are wrong.'

'She's not an expert, your worship,' Christian interjected.

Kitty was weeping helplessly now. It pained Brooke to watch. Nothing could have prepared Kitty for her ordeal or her deep and involuntary emotional response.

Christian continued to interrupt the flow of Kitty's account. When it was his turn to question Kitty, he was loud and brash. 'You were upset, but not surprised, weren't you, to hear of her death, given the letters you had recently received?'

'What do you mean? What did her letters have to do with it?' Kitty bravely batted back.

'You knew your mother was emotionally unstable and very unhappy. You assumed she had taken her own life, didn't you?'

The coroner had had enough. 'You have already pointed out, Mr Christian, that Ms McGrath has no expertise in this area. Her opinion is not relevant.'

'That is so, your worship, but what she knew and observed about her mother is relevant,' Christian argued.

The coroner had read the police brief. He replied, 'As a fifteen-year-old, she had already moved away from her mother, Mr Christian, geographically speaking anyway. The question is of no help to me.'

Kitty cried out belligerently, 'If you can give me any evidence that Mum killed herself, please tell me. I want to know who did this to her, and have them go to gaol.'

'Just be quiet and answer the questions,' Christian shouted back.

'It's my hearing,' said Moone, coming in hard. 'Let me direct the witnesses, please.'

Kitty was weeping uncontrollably. Brooke rose and asked for a short adjournment.

The coroner agreed to take an early morning tea break. 'We'll resume at 11.15,' he declared.

Brooke and Kitty found a quiet outside table at the café behind the courthouse.

'I can't go on, Brooke,' wept Kitty. 'I want to accept the insurance company's offer. I want the court to find Mum didn't kill herself, and I want Billie to get the insurance money mum planned for her. But I dread the result, whichever it is. Suicide? Murder? Not nice either way. Can't we accept their offer? Billie's money will let me finish my studies in twelve months, and I won't need to find full-time work.'

Christian was on track for his goal of getting the insurance case settled before the coroner brought in an open verdict on cause of death. Brooke had to do something.

'I'll try and get your evidence delayed till tomorrow, and we can discuss things tonight. Okay?' Brooke put to Kitty.

Back in the hearing room Brooke asked the coroner to defer Kitty's evidence until the next day, on the grounds that Brooke had further evidence which might make Kitty's views on her mother's mental state irrelevant.

Moone agreed. Trevor started to say something but it turned into a resigned loud grunt as he slumped back into his chair.

Before the afternoon adjournment, Brooke asked for overnight access to the Hyatt Hotel's CCTV footage.

Donald followed Brooke north along the Federal Highway in his old Peugeot as far as the Eaglehawk service station on the ACT border.

Brooke needed fuel and Donald decided to leave his car there. He seemed comfortable sitting beside her while she drove. She told him of the day's events; particularly about Kitty's ordeal.

'Poor kid,' Donald said. 'I'd like to see her sometime. I knew her as a youngster, before she left to live with her father.'

'I'm sure she'd like that,' Brooke replied. But her mind was still on the case. 'I have the CCTV footage which we'd better look at tonight,' she added. 'I need to weave our material into a story for the coroner, to shift his presumption of suicide. Even an open verdict would be better than suicide. Wish we could prove that Jo was murdered.'

As they reached her front gate, Brooke wound down the windows. The scent of peppermint gums wafted in. Birds flew from tree to tree searching for overnight perches before dusk. Donald was saying something as they drove by the reed-edged dam, but his words wore lost in the deafening chorus of froggy evensong. To Brooke's delight, her mournful mopoke made his presence known, as he often did, at the point where the drive curved to take them up the last steep slope to her home on the hill.

The dogs gave Brooke only a cursory greeting as she opened the door, intent on interrogating her passenger. Would they approve, she wondered, and out loud warned Donald that if they didn't like him, he'd be going home – car or no car! He laughed, giving each dog an affectionate rub on the head, while protecting his face from exuberant slobbery kisses. He was a hit. First hurdle over: Brooke made a tick on an imaginary list.

Donald stopped on the veranda to take in the distant expanse of Lake George and its backdrop of blue hills. Brooke went ahead to turn on two hot plates on the stove. Her casserole was sitting on one in an earthenware pot, and a bamboo vegetable steamer atop a cast iron pan of water on the other.

She tugged Donald in with 'I'll show you a better view', and led him through the back door and pointed at a row of gumboots. He pulled on the largest pair and followed Brooke up the rocky steps to the chook pen. At the top he turned to take in the extraordinary view of the lake glistening pink in the setting sun.

Brooke bustled around coaxing the ducks to bed and locking the chooks in their pen. She joined Donald, now gazing up at the night's first stars, so brilliant away from city lights. He reached to squeeze her hand, but she jumped back sharply.

'Oh, oops, you'll crack the eggs,' she said, trying to swap the two eggs she was carrying into her other hand, but the moment of intimacy had gone.

They laughed and joined hands anyway swinging their way as old friends might, back to the kitchen.

Brooke invited Donald to turn on the lights and look around the house, while she fed the dogs and her meowing cats. He returned with a comment on the farm's remoteness from neighbours and roads. Brooke pointed at two glasses and a bottle of red wine on the bench.

Donald opened and poured. 'Here, cook,' he said, handing her a glass.

She took it and, looking him in the eye, held her glass out to his. 'Cheers, Donald. It's lovely to have you here!'

He moved towards her so that their glasses clinked. He put his arm around her waist and said, 'Thank you. I feel at home.' Without being asked, he opened cupboard doors and pulled out two plates. 'Are these okay?'

'Sure, and forks are in that drawer,' pointing to the end of the bench.

Brooke lifted the lid of the casserole and invited Donald to sniff in its richness. She removed rosemary sprigs from the brew of tender lamb pieces, slow cooked with whole tomatoes, leeks and lots of ground pepper. She tipped small steamed potatoes into a dish together with barely steamed green beans. As if they were a team, Donald dropped a knob of butter on top and ground pepper over everything, and Brooke gave him the dish to carry to the table.

They chattered away until Brooke asked Donald if he minded their watching the CCTV footage while they were eating.

They sat watching, side by side, plates on laps. Grey and white figures entered and left through the Hyatt's back door. Then, eerily, the tall and graceful figure of Jo appeared, her bag over her shoulder, her hands in the pockets of her winter coat, drawing it tightly around her. Donald lowered his head.

Brooke felt his pain at seeing an image of a woman he knew and loved, just minutes before she died. 'I'm sorry,' she whispered and rested her hand on his thigh for a moment.

'It's okay,' he choked. 'I wanted to see it, and I'm glad I'm not alone.'

Rocky jumped up at that moment and licked Donald on the cheek. Another mark of approval for Brooke to tick off.

After Jo disappeared, groups, couples and singles came and went. Cars were visibly parked in front of a hedgerow, along with blurred images of moving vehicles cruising for a parking spot.

Little happened until, after twenty minutes, Jo and Mujo left the hotel. They turned right and walked through the patio arch. Brooke ignored the people who continued to shuffle through the doors and kept scanning the screen for signs of movement in the car park.

'There!' she exclaimed, pausing the video. 'I'm going to go back and come forward in little jumps. Can you look at the cars in the back row in front of the hedge? I think I can see someone standing next to one of them.' She rewound and replayed, both focusing intently on the three cars visible in the back row.

'The middle car,' Donald said, 'it's a light-coloured Commodore, I think. Go forward a bit again. There he is.' Donald leaned forward to watch a man walking towards the parked cars. 'Keep going…yes, he's walked behind the light car, and…he's stopped. Pause again, Brooke.'

She had already frozen the picture and they could see a blurry figure, a man in a suit, standing with his back to the bushes, behind and beside the light car.

'He could easily be watching a car in the front row up where Mujo and Jo just walked,' Brooke said.

They decided to rerun the tape and would watch for anyone entering the hotel behind Jo, or exiting behind Jo and Mujo. There was a possible match. A man in a suit had come into the hotel only a minute after Jo had entered, and left again just seconds after Jo and Mujo. He was the same height as their Commodore suspect and he was walking towards the same car.

Then Brooke saw someone else and paused the video. 'Look there, another man, just seconds behind, keeping an eye on Mujo and Jo perhaps. Where's he going?' The man turned left and disappeared. 'Keep going until we see Mujo come back,' Brooke suggested.

The video showed 8.32 when Mujo re-entered the hotel. The man standing behind the car hesitated and then walked across the road and out of view. About thirty seconds later, they caught a few frames of Jo's car leaving the park, passing in front of the Commodore.

'So Jo was being watched,' Donald sighed. 'I'm relieved, in a way, to know that she didn't do this terrible thing to herself. Her killer must have followed her.' He put his arm around Brooke's shoulders and gave her a squeeze.

'I guess the police who viewed this tape were focusing their attention on Jo and Mujo, not on anyone who might have been following them,' Brooke said. 'But if Mujo or Jo were under ASIO surveillance, the spook following them would surely have seen anyone following Jo. What are they hiding?'

'ASIO's got to be implicated in some way. But it's a complex story, and we might never get it sorted,' Donald replied.

'We will,' Brooke said emphatically.

They tried to understand what they had seen and, along the way, finished the bottle of red.

'Meantime, tomorrow I'll ask the coroner to look carefully at the video. We don't know who's tailing Jo but it is strong evidence that she was followed. Particularly given the neighbour's statement that a white Commodore pulled out of the street after Jo left home that evening. It supports our murder theory.'

'It was Donald's idea.

'A massage?' Brooke looked at him trying to assess his intentions. It didn't matter. She'd had enough wine to say yes to whatever he was offering.

'I'm a good masseur,' he assured her while he took the plates to the sink. Brooke laughed. She was busy fast-forwarding and pausing the tape, jotting down the times she would ask the tape to be stopped when it was played in court.

Donald was true to his word and went about the task conscientiously
– at least at first. The double bed served as a massage table. Brooke
accepted the indulgence and stretched out on her tummy clad in T-shirt
and knickers. He straddled her body to work his strong hands on her
shoulders and up her neck to the back of her head, so her whole scalp
tingled, and then he spent time undoing the knots in her shoulders.

'You need this at least once a week,' he said.

Brooke gave a blissful sigh of agreement.

It was a good twenty minutes before he moved to the small of her back,
and as she felt his palms press into the top of her left thigh her feeling of
sinking into the bed gave way to an awareness of exploring hands. She fought
an impulse to roll over and face him. He must have felt her body twitch.

'Whooh, I'm not finished yet,' he teased, and leaned over her to work
on the insides of her thighs.

She giggled into the pillow, 'It's wonderful, but I can't keep…'

Sitting across her legs, he gave her buttock a light slap before
abandoning the massage. He leaned forward and inched up her body
to kiss her gently on the back of her neck. She rolled over to meet his
kisses with her lips and the massage seamlessly turned into something
very different – less passive on Brooke's part – roaming hands over the
other's body, until they were one. Then rolling and moving in sync, tender
at first, accelerated to the point where Rocky barked and tried to jump
on the bed. Brooke ignored the intrusion, though she suspected that
Donald's right leg might have had something to do with Rocky giving
up. But the dog had succeeded in distracting them anyway. They laughed
and laughed, uncoupling and rolling onto their backs, hands entwined.

'Do you encourage your dog to be a voyeur?' Donald asked.

'It's okay,' Brooke replied. 'He won't tell, I promise. His question is
whether you always abandon your ethics when your clients aren't paying!'

'Tell him that I admit to being a fraud, on the path to being a failed
masseur.'

'But not as a lover…' she said, and they dropped into a hazy happy
sleep.

40

Brooke shook her tangled red hair, tried to smooth her big smile, and backed out of the car port. She swapped a grin with Donald and tried again to be serious. By the bottom of the drive, Brooke had assumed a lawyer-like persona, ready to show the coroner where the evidence lay.

The evening with Donald left Brooke relaxed and happy. There had been a moment when Donald cried for Jo, and Brooke had comforted him. And they had also laughed together.

'You know, I feel refreshed,' she told him, placing a hand on his thigh without taking her eyes off the road, 'despite our broken sleep.'

He squeezed her hand. They were silent for most of the drive. Brooke knew that Donald was a free spirit, and she would let him be. She pulled up beside his car at the service station. He leant over and kissed her cheek. Neither asked, 'When will I see you next?'

Once in court, Brooke pre-empted the order of proceedings by rising to address the coroner as soon as he was seated at the bench. She held out the video and requested that it be shown before Kitty was asked to return to the witness box. The clerk took it from her, together with the list of times at which she would ask the video to be paused. She called on Trevor to produce the statement from Jo's neighbour taken by the insurance company's investigator, explaining its significance to the coroner.

'The CCTV will show a similar vehicle parked close to Dr Rowan's car at the Hyatt that same evening, and a person, possibly its driver, following her in and out of the hotel, your worship,' she told the coroner. 'A careful study of the CCTV will allow your worship to decide for yourself whether Dr Rowan was, in all probability, followed just before she died.'

Brooke then tendered a bundle of documents, briefly describing each. She referred to Dr Bates's report again, emphasising that he had more than one reason for doubting that Dr Rowan had handled the gun in her vehicle.

'The suggestion that there was a gun swap sounds incredible, your worship, but not, of course, if the deceased was murdered and the scene rearranged to look as though she had killed herself. As I said yesterday, a killer is unlikely to leave his gun behind,' she submitted. 'But there's more,' she said, producing the report of the forensic analysis of the paper on which the poem was written. She explained that signs of blood smatterings were neatly evident on only one discrete portion of the paper.

'This makes it highly unlikely that Dr Rowan screwed up the paper before she was shot. That is, your worship, someone else did it after she was shot.'

The coroner leaned forward resting his chin on a cupped hand. He looked at Chessman, who had his head down burrowing into a pile of papers.

'I will be asking your worship to look past the images of the deceased and her boyfriend on the CCTV and focus on the images of a man who might well have been the last person to see Dr Rowan alive. The times displayed on the CCTV images are important,' Brooke continued, 'because, included in the bundle of documents, is an affidavit by Dr Rowan's boyfriend, Mujo Zukić, in which he states that he was in Rowan's car that evening; and yet we know that his fingerprints were not found inside her vehicle. Assuming he is not implicated in Dr Rowan's death – and the police had good reason to conclude that would be almost impossible – then who wiped his fingerprints from the inside of the car? Was that done after Dr Rowan was killed?'

Everyone in the room was listening.

'Would Dr Rowan wipe her boyfriend's prints off the inside of the car before killing herself?' Brooke asked rhetorically. 'The pattern of blood spatters on the paper found beside her, and the fact it was lightly wiped over, would suggest not. Your worship, these are the matters I raise in support of my request that the CCTV footage be studied and considered at this stage of the proceedings. Thank you.' Brooke sat down.

'Indeed, Ms Talbot, unless counsel assisting has anything to say, I suggest that we run the CCTV footage before proceeding further.'

The video was run, paused and rerun on Brooke's direction and she was satisfied that the coroner had seen everything she wanted him to see – Jo and Mujo's movements, the two men who might have been following them, and a view of someone standing behind a light-coloured car, agreed by everyone to be a Commodore, possibly within sight of Jo's car.

The coroner asked for the tape to be rewound and played again up to the blurred image of Jo's car leaving.

'Ms Talbot, I see that the Commodore beside which a man had been standing has remained in the car park. This counters your suggestion that Dr Rowan was followed, does it not?'

It was then that Brooke realised how stupid she had been. She should have let the tape run to see when, if at all that evening, the Commodore left the car park.

'Your worship, not necessarily. But I do apologise. I should have kept the tape running to check the vehicle's ultimate movements. Would your worship indulge me again? Could the tape be fast-forwarded, say twenty minutes, to see when the vehicle in question leaves the car park?'

'I'll leave the bench while you and Mr Chessman satisfy yourselves that everything I need to see has been seen. Let my associate know when you're ready.'

The lawyers clustered around the video. The tape was fast-forwarded to the point where the male figure had left his position beside the Commodore and crossed the road. He might have been walking towards Jo's car, but they did not know where she had parked. Half a minute later, Jo's car was glimpsed leaving. They let the tape run.

Twenty minutes on, Brooke saw movement. 'Wait, freeze that,' she asked the clerk holding the remote.

'The car's still there,' Christian scoffed.

'Yes, but look.'

There was a figure walking into the car park entrance around the hedge and it approached the Commodore.

'He's returned to his car on foot – from somewhere. Bloody hell!' It dawned on Brooke then, that Jo might not have been followed by someone in another car; rather someone might have been in Jo's car before she left. 'This might be the killer.'

'Oh, please,' Christian retorted. 'What an imagination you have, Brooke.'

'Still,' said Chessman, 'we must show this to the coroner.'

The coroner was called back to court. He watched the relevant footage and wanted to question the officers in charge of forensics at the scene of Dr Rowan's death.

'There is a strong possibility that someone cleaned up after the deceased was killed, whether she killed herself or was killed,' the coroner said, directing his comments to Chessman. 'On the material before me, the latter seems more likely.' He requested that the court adjourn until after lunch so that he might consider the import of Brooke's material. But first he directed counsel to arrange for the first officers on the scene to be available for questioning.

Senior Constable Kaczmarek entered the witness box. His evidence matched that given in summary form by Superintendent de Fraga.

In response to questions from Chessman, Kaczmarek was refreshing his memory from his notes when Moone interrupted to ask, 'Was there anything that struck you as unusual, Senior Constable, in the course of your team collecting material, taking photographs and so forth... anything at all you had reason to question?'

'No, other than the subject herself,' Kaczmarek answered.

'What do you mean "subject"? I assume you're referring to the deceased? What was unusual about her?'

'Yes, sir, um, sorry – the deceased. We were informed by the AFP that she was the subject of surveillance...um...under surveillance,' Kaczmarek said apologetically.

'When were you told this and by whom?' Moone asked.

'Soon after arriving on the scene. Detective Constable Beam radioed base with the number plate of the vehicle to ascertain the registered owner. The deceased's face was mutilated but in terms of gender and age she matched the registered owner. We took fingerprints from the driver's door and we were looking for prints inside the car, when we received a radio message that the owner of the vehicle was under surveillance in connection with a national security operation.'

'Why haven't we been told this before?' Moone asked Chessman.

'Your worship, I, um, understand it was one of ASIO's operations. I, ah, only became aware of this matter on talking with Senior Constable Kaczmarek during the lunch break. Ah, whatever interest ASIO might have wouldn't impact on police forensics at the scene, well, at least not when the death appeared to be a suicide.'

'Surely, whether or not there has been any impact and whether or not it is a suicide is for me to decide. I am entitled to be assisted by you, as counsel assisting, not to be kept in the dark.'

'I understand, sir.'

'Do I take it that another investigating team took over? Can this witness enlighten me about the process? And are there other investigating officers who should be called?' Moone asked.

Kaczmarek, still in the witness box, looked perplexed. He answered, 'No, your worship. Officers of the ACT police are federal police officers, recruited by the AFP but contracted to the ACT. The same team continued the investigation. Our reporting line changed, that's all. That is, the AFP headed the investigation.'

The coroner went on, 'Assuming the deceased was under surveillance or followed before she died, those involved might well have seen or observed something that would assist this inquiry as to the manner of her death. It is incumbent on counsel assisting to ensure production of all information, records, reports, photographs and evidence of any sightings of the deceased in the hours before her death, whether in police hands or another agency.'

Kaczmarek appeared embarrassed, his revelations having been responsible for the coroner's outburst, and turned to the coroner to explain. 'I was informed that Senior Detective Mitch Ormandy, team leader of the national operation, would lead my investigation, and I reported to him. It seemed to be a clear case of suicide but we nevertheless looked for footprints, dusted for fingerprints and took the usual photographs, following normal procedure for any murder or suicide.'

Brooke drew in a big breath. Here he is again, Ormandy, appearing at every turn.

The coroner thanked the witness, and then addressed Chessman. 'Do I assume that the person in the Commodore was engaged by a federal agency to follow the deceased, and if so, should we not have that person here? He or she might have been the last person to see the deceased.'

'Your worship, anticipating your question, I made enquiries during the lunch adjournment, and I was informed that the deceased herself was not under surveillance by any federal agency or officer that night. The Commodore is not a government vehicle. But Mujo Zukić, the deceased's boyfriend, was being watched.'

'Go on,' urged the coroner.

'The CCTV footage contains an image of an intelligence officer leaving the Hyatt Hotel close behind Zukić and Rowan, someone other than the man seen beside the Commodore. I am assured that once Zukić returned to the hotel, that officer left the scene. There is no more information I can offer the inquest.'

'This is most unsatisfactory,' the coroner muttered. 'That intelligence officer might well be able to describe the other man who appears to have followed Zukić and Dr Rowan out of the hotel. I am not impressed, therefore, with the assurances you have been asked to convey to this inquiry. I am going to leave the bench for a few minutes and consider where this inquiry should go from here.' With that, he departed, leaving an excited hum of voices behind him.

Brooke turned to Kitty and her grandmother who, sitting beside Deidre in the front row, were looking puzzled and anxious. 'Well, we've surely blocked the coroner from finding suicide,' Brooke said, 'but I'm not sure how much further he can take this inquiry given the gaps in the police investigation to date.'

'What will he do, then?' Deidre asked.

'My guess is that, unless there's any other useful evidence to come – and I don't think that means you, Kitty – he'll make what's called an open finding and recommend that further investigations be carried out.'

As she finished her sentence, the clerk announced that the coroner was returning.

'All rise,' she intoned.

Everyone returned to their seats and waited while the coroner made a few notes on the papers before him.

He looked up and said, 'I intend to find that the deceased's death was not suicide, there being considerable doubt as to whether the gun found in the car was used to kill the deceased. The forensic analysis of the blood spatters on the paper found in the deceased's car is compelling evidence that the scene had been interfered with between the time of the deceased's death and the time the police arrived.'

He started to read from notes, 'The evidence concerning fingerprints is unsatisfactory in the light of the information that Zukić had sat in the deceased's vehicle. His assertion that he went with Rowan to her car is supported to a degree by the CCTV tape. Yet no prints were found in the deceased's vehicle. I find it unlikely that he talked to Dr Rowan outside her car for the period he was absent from the hotel given the drizzling rain, or that he would fabricate this evidence. I make no findings as to his or any other person's role in the circumstances of the deceased's death.'

He went on, 'Since it's clear that the police did not identify or interview the various people who seem to have had an interest in Dr Rowan the evening she died, I do not intend to carry this inquiry further at this stage. Subject to submissions from counsel, I am inclined to find that the deceased was killed by a person or persons unknown. I also intend to make a strong recommendation that further and full investigation take place to ascertain who killed the deceased. If further information comes to light, I will entertain any application for the inquest to be reopened.'

Chessman indicated that in the circumstances he had no objection to the coroner's proposed course of action and offered no submissions to the contrary. Brooke and Trevor echoed their agreement. The coroner formalised his findings and the proceedings were over.

Trevor slapped his papers together and shoved them into his briefing folder making exasperated noises.

Brooke grabbed the opportunity to ask before he left, 'Can you let me know as soon as possible if your insurer will pay out fully on the policy?'

He glared at her, and said, 'I'll get instructions.'

Devastating as the day's proceedings had been for Kitty, she was thankful that her mother's reputation had been restored and with the insurance money she would be able to support herself and Billie. Nonetheless, Kitty and Edith were very upset that dismissing Jo's death as suicide circumvented a more thorough investigation. Finding the killer had been made that much more difficult.

On the steps of the court building, Brooke explained to Deidre, Kitty and Edith that a private investigation to unravel why Jo was killed was already underway. The media was interested in the story and she'd let them know if she heard any more. The police, too, would keep the family in touch with developments. Brooke embraced them both gently, by way of a farewell, collected her papers and left for chambers.

41

October 1992

Rusty was thoroughly enjoying himself in Darwin doing what he liked best, poking his nose into things. Nor had it been difficult to persuade Quentin Dempster to run a sequel to the ABC's initial story about irregular methods of collecting government intelligence. An ABC cameraman came to Darwin with Rusty.

Rusty found customs officers who slammed doors on him, unwilling to talk about corruption on the waterfront. But others, victims of bullying or blackmail fifteen years ago, opened up. Several on Bozin's list talked freely when they learned that the smuggler, Rexi Pike, had obtained their ASIO assessments from a former spook. Now they knew how they had been blackmailed into acting corruptly and why they had been retired out prematurely from the service.

One recalled that indiscretions revealed at his initial ASIO security clearance interview would remain secret from his wife if he missed inspecting crates containing concealed guns. Another gave Rusty permission to obtain his employment and ASIO files under freedom of information legislation.

Rusty was given chapter and verse on how easy it had been for Pike to import guns, starting with rifles and then Berettas, the Italian pistol used by the Indonesian navy. Although unlicensed, and not an accredited government supplier, he also imported Glocks for the customs service, the preferred pistol for front-line officers. Licensed gun dealers' protests fell on deaf bureaucratic ears. Pike, the Fish, was untouchable.

Mad Max proved to be a shadowy figure. No one to whom Rusty

spoke admitted to knowing anything about him. While most had heard of or met Rexi Pike, Max couldn't be found.

Rusty ambled around and talked with local fishermen and crew from Australian and Indonesian boats operating between Darwin and Ujung Pandang in Sulawesi. Yes, Pike had been around often enough in recent years. He was definitely in Darwin in mid '92, according to several people, but no one seemed to have seen him since.

Then, the evening before Rusty's departure, while he was enjoying a beer at Mindil Beach, Fannie Bay, a group of men approached looking for a cold beer after a hard day's work. They were wearing grimy moleskins and they smelled of fish. One had a badly scratched arm, still redolent with blood spots. Rusty raised his glass to them, in an invitation to share his table.

''Ow ya goin', mate? Great sunset, eh?' one addressed him.

And it was. Rusty had watched the sky go through the full palette. From yellow to orange to deep blood red, it mimicked the changing colours of a slowly ripening tomato until it fell inexorably below the horizon taking the orange sea to an inky blue.

Rusty exchanged pleasantries for a while until he thought a direct enquiry was worth a try. 'I've been looking for a fellow called Rexi Pike? Know him?' he asked.

'Huh, Pike?' one of the men said. 'He went down south to visit his family a way ago now, middle of the year. He shoulda been back in July as we 'ad some business to discuss, but we 'aven't seen 'im and I reckon he's gone back to Indonesia.'

'More's the pity,' the blood-streaked guy said. 'He owes me money. We bet on a dog at Winnellie Park, an' I won twenny quid off him.'

Rusty noted that Fish's trip south was around the time of Jo's death in June. Over another round of beers, Rusty chatted with the men, learning this and that, including a tip on which greyhound to back come the weekend. They did suggest, however, that Pike's wife in Canberra would know where he was.

'They come from Indonesia and got a nice govy house, Pike boasts about it,' one of the men said.

'Yeah, but ya'd have to live in Canbra for that!' another scoffed.

Rusty grinned. He would get the ABC's investigators on to it.

Back at his hotel, Rusty started to collate all his material into a story of long-standing customs fraud, corruption of customs officers and gun-smuggling, from the late 70s when Fish was part of Operation Picnic. He made two phone calls – one to Donald to tell him what he had learned and one to an ABC producer.

Donald was on a roll. With Gideon's help, he had located one of the two intelligence officers with whom Mujo had liaised in Canberra and arranged to meet him at the Royal Canberra golf course.

'Larry? Donald Fenchurch,' he said, approaching the first hole where a man in navy and white checked trousers was practising his swing. Donald offered to caddy for a few holes and the two men walked and talked.

Donald had already explained on the phone that he was trying to find out more about how Mujo Zukić's girlfriend, Jo, had died, and that Mujo had suggested talking with his former intelligence associate, making sure to mention the name Fish. It had been enough for Larry to agree to meet him. He told Donald that he remembered meeting Jo briefly on one occasion, and talking to her subsequently about her difficulties at Immigration. Her death had been upsetting, and he would help, if he could.

'But how could I possibly be of any help?' he asked, pulling out an eight iron for a mid-distance shot.

Donald chose his words and trod carefully. 'Mujo has told me a lot,' he explained, bypassing Brooke's role for simplicity. 'From what he knew he suspected a link between Operation Picnic and the Fishnet Operation which Jo stumbled into.'

The spook swung like a pro, Donald judged, watching the ball head for the green.

'Something about Jo working there definitely alarmed ASIO,' Donald continued, 'because her relationship with Mujo had been of no concern till then.'

'That, I can help you with,' volunteered Larry, as they made for the next tee, 'Off the record of course. The common link is likely to be the field agent that Zukić told you about. Rexi Pike was engaged by the federal police in Operation Picnic, to help us arrest Croatian mercenaries. It was wound up after a shoot-out on the waterfront. But there was some difficulty keeping Pike quiet. He continued to smuggle guns and he got away with it because we'd helped him corrupt a lot of customs officers to get rifles in for Operation Picnic.'

The two paused to talk. Donald was all ears. 'You said "we helped". That is, ASIO helped to corrupt customs officers?' Donald asked.

'Hmm, unwittingly. You don't want to know about that. The thing is that Pike knew too much and had to be kept happy. The story around the ASIO traps was that, stupidly, he was foisted on Immigration. They were assured that Pike would be a useful source of information about people smugglers. I wasn't surprised to hear he was one himself and that his handlers exploited the fact that other boat operators trusted him. The condition, of course, was that he provide Immigration with names, places, arrival dates et cetera of refugee boats. Immigration weren't told they had been handed a defective asset.'

The men started to walk again, Donald diligently pulling the bag of clubs.

'I knew he'd be trouble. But our operation had finished, and he wasn't our problem. Those running Operation Fishnet at Immigration ought to have known what they were getting into and what the political fallout would be if it went public.'

'Well, it has now.' Donald chipped in.

'Yes, I saw the ABC report,' Larry said. 'However, neither Pike's history with us nor the corruption around his people smuggling activities came out, did it? The Immigration whistle-blower wouldn't have known. If I'd known that Zukić's girl had started work in Immigration, I would probably have warned him that ASIO was likely to keep an eye on them both. He continued to share intelligence about Croatian militants with me and my colleague Eugene. That's what we were doing when Rowan joined us for a coffee one lunchtime. But we weren't involved in any operation at the time.'

'So Pike had three federal agencies eating out of his hand? What sort of bloke is he?'

'Unsavoury, greedy, clever. He lives the good life, has a luxurious boat and shady business interests in Indonesia. Being married to an Indonesian helped there. He throws his weight around in both countries. He's practised at exploiting people, pulls them into his circle by taking them to the races, nightclubs, and so on, finds out how they might be useful, and plays on their weaknesses. Enough?'

'Yes, I get the picture. It's beginning to make some sense now,' Donald said. 'Jo's problems started when Immigration asked your lot to lower her security clearance to stop her nosing around Operation Fishnet – they didn't want an outsider blowing the whistle on their irregular methods. However, when ASIO was called in, they ended up revoking her authority to access any classified material. What you're telling me confirms what Mujo now suspects. ASIO and the federal police had reason to fear that if Jo uncovered Operation Fishnet, she and Mujo would be able to work out that Pike, a gunrunner for a ballsed-up operation relating to Croatian terrorists, had been given permission to people smuggle as part of an immigration sting.'

'Yes, and by that time Pike, the slimy bastard, knew who was corrupt on the waterfront and in the federal police. That was our doing, unfortunately. We let one of our former agents loose with a list of customs officers vulnerable to blackmail.'

Donald sucked that piece of information in, and said nothing about having a copy of that list.

'There was no going back,' Larry continued. 'I can see there would be a lot of people wanting to stop a curious university researcher from finding out any of this. Not enough to kill her, though, I wouldn't have thought. From what you say, Rowan never had access to real information. But none of this has come from me,' he said, eager to return to his golf.

'No, I'm not asking you to go on the record. Mujo and the whistle-blower in Immigration have given me enough to ask others the right questions. And yes, there are still questions about why Jo was killed. Had she been left alone, no one would have been any the wiser about all the dirty secrets. How inept can your mob be?'

'Hey, I'm out of it now. We had a job to do, but in the end, I couldn't really tell the terrorists from their pursuers. Corruption is endemic and stuff-ups are common in the protective agencies. Some of us found it difficult to keep doing the right thing.' He bent down to concentrate on his shot.

'I really appreciate your frankness,' said Donald, shaking Larry's hand. 'You've been generous with your help. Enjoy your golf.' Donald turned to leave, and stopped. 'Oh, just one more thing. Did you ever come across Mad Max – Max Peacock, I mean?' Donald thought a guess that they were the same person was worth a try.

The retired spook sprung upright. 'Be careful, mate. Throwing names around like that could land you into trouble,' with which statement he prepared to drive.

Donald and Rusty now had a complete story on everything but the specifics of how and why Jo had died. It was time for Donald to confront Alec Brown.

'I need to meet you,' Donald said to Alec Brown when he finally got through the ASIO switchboard. Knowing what he did, Brown might well spit out the rest. 'The ABC is ready to go to air with a story connecting two of your operations to your man Fish,' was all Donald had to say for Brown to agree to meet.

They met in the small manicured park across from Brown's building dotted with benches and garbage bins under a few shade trees.

Donald had picked up some sandwiches in Civic and handed a brown paper bag to Brown as they walked. 'We may as well share a sandwich in the sun, so people looking out of windows can get excited when I hand you a brown paper bag! I hope you eat cheese and ham.'

'Yep, thanks,' Brown said, peering into the bag, ignoring Donald's attempt at humour. 'Now, what's this nastiness you want to talk about?'

'I want to know how and why Dr Jo Rowan died,' Donald said. 'Nothing nasty, just the truth. And I think you can tell me.'

'She killed herself, they say.'

'They do, indeed,' Donald replied, 'and it's the "theys" that I want to know more about. I'll tell you what I know, and then you might tell me where I've gone wrong, or what you want me to forget. The latter might be up for negotiation. In the meantime, let's be clear that everything I've found out is with a media investigative team, under embargo. I can sanitise it by agreement if you give me the whole story.'

'Talk away. It's a free country,' Brown invited grumpily, though Donald detected anxiety.

'We know about Rexi Pike, known as Fish to Operation Picnic and Operation Fishnet. We know he has you guys, his federal police handlers, and Immigration over a barrel. He's more than the people smuggler unmasked in the media. He's linked to a web of waterfront corruption and was already a big-time smuggler when he was taken on. We also know that an AFP guy who stuffed up and shot someone he shouldn't have in Darwin is indebted to him for a false witness statement.'

'You know it all, then,' said Brown matter of factly, though Donald knew that he must have been startled. No mention had been made so far of the file Mujo gave Jo the night she died, the one with the statement about how Bozin had been shot. For all the world, it didn't exist. Just how worried was Brown becoming?

'We know more, though,' Donald said. 'He managed both his own smuggling activities, and those he did "officially" – if illegal operations can be official – using ASIO data on the identities of corruptible customs officers. But there is something we don't know.'

'Thank God for that,' Brown squawked sarcastically.

'What we don't know,' Donald went on unfazed, 'is whether these people were never "suitable" for employment as customs officer. Were their background checks deliberately falsified by ASIO? The press could be forgiven for suggesting such a plausible scenario, especially as we have a copy of a list of officers proven vulnerable to blackmail. Although I must protect my source, I can tell you that it originated from an ASIO file.'

Brown kept walking, took a bite of his sandwich and screwed up his face in disgust. He said nothing, and Donald went on.

'Funny thing is, some of those codgers are happy to speak out now they've retired. Perhaps you don't want ASIO to get the credit for Mad Max's key role in the operation, the part which guaranteed Fish's smuggling success.'

'You are a smart arse, an arsehole,' Brown said, turning his back on Donald.

'What happened to Jo Rowan?' Donald insisted.

'She killed herself,' he answered.

'Did I forget to mention that Fish threatened to come to Canberra and cause havoc when he was told that you'd failed to stop Rowan's work in the department, and that Op Fishnet was to be suspended until she finished her report? Hmm, the hold Fish had over the cop in Darwin, his handler – Mitch Ormandy, wasn't it? That's the same man who ordered a people smuggler's boat to be burnt and, as the coroner was told, had been put in charge of the police investigation into Rowan's death?'

Brown turned to face Donald, his eyes red with anger, 'You…'

'Why are you protecting Ormandy, Alec?'

'Ormandy doesn't need protecting, you idiot.'

'Fish was in Canberra, I'm reliably informed, on the night Jo Rowan died. But you know that. Your people were watching him. Then again, who was watching Jo? One of your lot? Someone was.'

'You've said enough. What is it you want?'

'I'll tell you. The coroner has been told that ASIO had a tail on Mujo Zukić when he was with Jo just before she was murdered, and he saw CCTV evidence that someone was following her. Trouble is, the police think it was one of your men. They don't know about Fish, or his presence here that night, or Ormandy's role as his handler. Zukić's movements have been accounted for, but those of his tail have not. You and your officers must be on top of the list of suspects. Jo's book became a real problem for you, didn't it? She detailed your efforts to ruin her reputation and your failed attempt to convert her to your cause. Then she's found dead. Come on, help me out here. This is about Fish – Rexi Pike – I'm sure. I'm trying to help you help yourself.'

'That's enough, you prick,' Brown interrupted. 'We're not licensed to kill. It's not ASIO's policy to execute people.'

'No. No killing, just an unbridled power to make others do your dirty work. Isn't this where you tell me the end justifies the means?'

Brown threw the rest of his sandwich and lunch bag into a bin. His palpable rage pleased Donald. He sat down on a bench while Donald sat smugly beside him.

'What I will tell you about is Operation Fishnet,' Brown said at last. 'It's mostly known now, or it'll be pieced together by the media from Rowan's book, and what came out at the inquest. So, the deal is this. I give you a heads up on information that will soon be in the public arena. But you leave the past alone. Leave Operation Picnic out of it. Leave Ormandy's shooting of Bozin out of it. Drop any thought of implicating ASIO in customs corruption. We had one corrupt officer, only one. He'll be dealt with. You can't touch that.'

'Oh, but I think I can,' threatened Donald.

'No, you can't. We'll slap a notice on you. Identifying a former intelligence officer is an offence. If there's corruption on the waterfront, it can be dealt with as a current or long-standing problem. But national security demands that past operations stay secret.'

'National security, be buggered. That's code for protecting your own arses. But, okay, give me what you can.'

'You're not taping me, I take it?' Brown first asked.

'Taping you without authority? So that you can skin me alive? You have to be kidding,' Donald laughed. 'What I am certain of, though, is that you're wired and recording everything. Go ahead, for all the good it'll do you.'

'Fish has left the country,' Brown said. 'He's unlikely to return. You are not to make a connection between him and Operation Picnic, or mention the Croatian link. I'm authorised to tell you what you want to know about the current operation. That should satisfy you and it's sensational enough to keep the press happy. The police investigations ordered by the coroner will fill in the gaps in the ABC's story. I'll tell you what I know about Dr Rowan's death, off the record. Then we'll discuss what you can use and what you can't. Will you honour that?'

Donald nodded.

'We had nothing to do with Rowan's death. Fish might have played a role, but he didn't do the deed. He has arranged for people to be roughed up in the past, but to our knowledge he's not a killer. We suspect that the night's events got out of hand. Something went wrong. We were too late to stop it.'

'A stuff-up! What on earth happened?' Donald asked, though not convinced that Brown was telling the truth.

'Because of Fish's threats, we had a man watch him. Yes, Fish was in Canberra, but he was with his family at the time Rowan died. We had our regular man watching Zukić until he left, his normal tail, nothing to do with Fish and Operation Fishnet. It was Rowan's bad luck, or idiocy, to meet up with Zukić that night. When Zukić left Rowan and returned to the hotel, our man's job was finished. He went back to his vehicle. He sat in it jotting down some notes. When he was about to leave, he saw Rowan's car driving out of the car park. Someone was in the passenger seat, leaning up hard against her. It wasn't Zukić. Our guy rang us on his car phone. We told him to follow her vehicle. It turned into the yacht club entrance and parked up hard against the bushes. He parked and went in on foot with a torch. He saw Rowan's cabin light come on. The passenger was leaning towards Rowan, who was facing straight ahead. Then the passenger started screaming at her. He was waving something around. Looked like a gun. Our man started to run towards her car.'

'Fucking hell,' was all Donald could manage.

'But Rowan's passenger turned to look at the torch beam, and she lashed out at him, and there was a shot. The killer got out of the car and ran into the bushes. Our man went to Rowan rather than pursue him. It was clear she was dead and he went back to his car and phoned us for more instructions.'

Donald noted Brown's mention of a struggle. There had been no evidence of that. He let it go in favour of a different tack. 'Did he call the police, ambulance?'

'No. We asked him to wait for our back-up.'

'Why am I not surprised? And…'

'We cleaned up.'

'You what? Why?'

'We couldn't afford for this to come out.'

'For what to come out?' There was only one answer. 'Because you knew who the killer was, didn't you?'

'That's your conclusion.'

Donald's mind worked overtime. Who would they clean up for? The light dawned. 'It's your Mad bloody Max. Max Peacock! The gun fence and list flogger.'

'You know no such thing. Our first job was to interrogate Fish, in case he was involved. Whether or not we could prove he was involved, we had to cover quickly, in case.'

'Bullshit. You knew it was something to do with him, or Peacock. Either way, you had to hide what happened and you made it look like suicide. You were there yourself, weren't you? Finding that poem was a bonus, wasn't it? Did you screw it up for effect? You stuffed up there too, another mistake, like the gun. You planted a gun that couldn't have killed her.'

'It was a Glock, one Fish was likely to use. In case suicide didn't stick, we needed to put Fish in the frame, to keep him quiet.'

'You idiots. The killer walked calmly back to his car and drove off while you guys were wiping prints and covering your arses. You let him get away!' Donald was outraged. 'And you left Jo there to rot until she was discovered. You people are feral. Take the law into your own hands. I detest you.'

'Don't get high and mighty about our morals. I'm telling you because you'll get your answers anyway, and the police, under the coroner's direction, will investigate and get the killer.'

'Will you help them, or will it be me suggesting that the killer was former ASIO officer Max Peacock?'

'The killer will be found without your help, and no link will be made to ASIO. I advise you to wipe the name Max Peacock from your mind,'

Brown retorted. 'He has civilian status, and ASIO will deny all knowledge of him. You already have the story about Fish's association with us. You have what you want. The three things you can't have are Operation Picnic, Peacock's leaking of our information, or our clean-up job in Rowan's car. It'll come out that the killer turned it into a suicide scene.'

'But you knew what Peacock was up to,' Donald protested. 'ASIO fed him that list of customs officers to crank up Operation Picnic. You didn't rein him in while Fish was still engaged in an intelligence operation. And on your watch, this ex-ASIO officer operated on the black market, and killed an innocent citizen to keep his enterprise going.'

'She was in the wrong place at the wrong time. Fish would only have wanted to frighten her – get her out of the department. Max was willing to do the roughing up – he had the most to lose if Rowan exposed the waterside story.'

'What? And he went too far?'

'Our intention was to stop Fish from harming Rowan. We failed. Fish knew we would watch him, and joke, we're his alibi. We believe Max followed Rowan and pounced when she was alone, but he was sprung by Zukić's tail. He panicked, Rowan apparently put up a fight, and the gun went off, or he finished the job and ran. It was a shambolic fiasco.'

'And what about Fish? Why didn't you arrest him?'

'Suits us not to. He'd deny it, and tell his own story. It would undermine the agency, and the AFP, and compromise future operations.'

'And now that the coroner has put his foot down, you're prepared to let the AFP take the blame for an incompetent and incomplete investigation into Jo's death?'

'That's their job. They'll play along rather than expose the covering up of a botched operation. You've got plenty of information on the Fishnet Operation. You don't need to go back into history and unravel Operation Picnic. Anyhow, as I said, we can stop you.'

'How will you stop Fish talking, though? His smuggling operations are over and he'll be mightily pissed. Promise him yet another job?'

'That's our business. Not yours.'

42

November 1992

Brooke had invited Greg, her dear neighbour, to join them. Rocky and Rex greeted him with wagging tails as he came through the front door. Donald was uncorking a bottle of red.

'Good timing.' Brooke greeted him with arms open and a kiss on the cheek. 'Fifteen minutes till we see what Quentin Dempster and his team have made of Donald's and Rusty's material.'

The ABC news was winding up with sport, the weather to come.

Brooke pulled a home-made pizza from the oven, a thin base of basil pesto-smeared Lebanese wrap piled high with chicken and fresh asparagus. Melted cheese dripped onto the dish. 'Just something to keep you going.' Brooke collected knives, forks and napkins to place beside a stack of plates, saying, 'You might need these, too. I think I overdid the topping, so it's not exactly finger food any more. The dogs will appreciate any droppages.'

Greg turned to the television. 'Shh, here's the promo for the *7.30 Report*.'

They pulled in chairs, Donald turned the sound up. It had been pre-recorded and included snippets from Donald's earlier interview and clips from the cameraman who accompanied Rusty to Darwin, as well as a new and extended interview with whistle-blower James Pratt, still a silhouette.

Donald had warned Brooke that the program would cover only half the story. He had told her some of what he had learned from Brown, and the justification for keeping some material out of the public arena. She was disappointed and a bit taken aback, wondering if the paranoid thoughts she had entertained on her return from Yugoslavia might be justified. Had Donald been complicit in agreeing to censor the material? Yet what he told her made sense.

'Will it ever come out?' she wanted to know. 'Why do there have to be any secrets? Have you kept good notes, in case it might one day?' she had asked. Questioning Donald at length left Brooke reasonably satisfied with what he had been able to bring into the public domain. After all, the story going to air being revealed was the one that mattered so far as justice for Jo was concerned. The truth was out that she had been killed, tragically and totally unnecessarily, as a consequence of a complex chain of events that reflected badly on intelligence agencies. The stigma of suicide had gone.

A whole lot of things made sense to Brooke now. Why the director-general of security tried to stop distribution of Jo's book. The revelation in its postscript of the efforts to keep her from finding out anything about Operation Fishnet – ASIO's action to withdraw her access to Immigration's files, and then its ultimatum that she agree to spy on her boyfriend or suffer a blighted career – raised suspicion about ASIO's role in her death. No wonder they wanted her murder to appear like suicide. Not only did they want to cover up their links to corruption and ineptness of their intelligence operations, they could not afford to be implicated in the murder of innocent citizens. Justice Arnold, who had presided over the attempt to stop Jo's book, heard none of this, just a bunch of trumped-up reasons.

Nor, she realised, was ASIO then interested in what Mujo knew about Pine Gap, or anything else. Asking her to spy on him was a gambit to compromise her. Had she accepted the deal and returned to Immigration with her security clearance reinstated, she would never be able to disclose what she had learned there. A classic tactic: if you can't get her out, bring her in closer, where she can be watched and controlled. Well, it hadn't worked. Jo had refused the offer to join team ASIO, and the tribunal upheld her right to return to the department to finish her report anyway. So Operation Fishnet would pause until that happened, and with it Fish's and Mad Max's criminal rackets. Fish and Mad Max were not happy. Or so it was presumed.

No one had yet explained what might have happened to Mujo's file on Bozin's death. Perhaps Max saw what it was and passed it on to Fish. Ormandy could not afford to upset Fish so long as Fish was keeper of evidence that Ormandy shot Bozin in the back.

The ABC program disclosed what it legally could. Quentin Dempster introduced the story by revisiting aspects of the whistle-blower's earlier story; an Immigration intelligence operation that went badly wrong when an Australian boat owner, now known to be Rexi Pike, was 'officially' engaged to provide information about people smugglers; and that Pike turned out to be an active people smuggler himself. He handed over to the story's main reporter:

> The *7.30 Report* is now able to reveal that this intelligence operation permitted Pike and corrupt customs officers to continue to profit from his illegal activities. In a further development we have learned that Pike and one of his associates are wanted for questioning in relation to the death of Dr Josephine Rowan, whose death was initially thought not to have been suspicious.

An unidentified officer of the Department of Immigration – James Pratt, as Brooke and Donald knew – described how an informant, Pike, had become angry on hearing that Operation Fishnet was being suspended. Dr Rowan was a researcher who had been 'disciplined' for showing interest in the operation's files, but had been allowed to return to the department. The whistle-blower became worried about what Pike might do, and reported his behaviour to a senior ASIO officer.

The program switched to fuzzy CCTV footage and it was explained that the coroner had studied it and accepted that it showed Dr Rowan being followed up to the time of her presumed death. Extracts from police evidence were read out revealing that Dr Rowan and her boyfriend, a Yugoslav national, were under ASIO surveillance during Operation Fishnet. The coroner's call for further police investigations to answer Fishnet's many unanswered questions was given in full. The reporter went on,

> And there are certainly many questions to be asked. *The 7.30 Report* has discovered that Pike had been smuggling contraband into this country for a decade before he was engaged by Australian authorities in Operation Fishnet.

Brooke was pleased that history had been slipped in. It was enough to suggest that the authorities, if they had not known, should have. There was an image of Rusty interviewing a former customs officer, electronically disguised and telling in a distorted husky voice how he had been 'persuaded' to turn a blind eye when Pike's boats docked in Darwin. The reporter continued,

> But Pike has somehow left the country without being apprehended. We invited the officer leading the investigative team to appear on the program and explain why Pike was not apprehended. Our invitation was declined but we were provided with a statement informing us that 'there was insufficient evidence to apprehend Pike on any charge.'

'What a bugger,' Brooke said out loud, 'that the ABC can't say that Pike wasn't arrested because he'd received an undertaking that he would not be prosecuted.'

Some dramatic footage followed. An ABC reporter was filmed approaching the front door of Pike's house in suburban Downer. A woman opened it and on seeing the camera, tried to close it, calling out, 'I don't know where my father is. Back in Indonesia, I expect.'

The program wrapped up with the reporter concluding that 'Corruption on the waterfront is one thing. Murder to cover it up, is another.'

As the story faded out, Dempster stated that a spokesman for the Federal Police Commissioner had confirmed that police enquiries were in train to find Dr Rowan's killer. In the meantime, Dempster reminded viewers, 'A commission of inquiry is scheduled to commence next month on Immigration's irregular methods of identifying people smugglers.'

'So what about Fish?' Brooke asked Donald. 'He goes scot-free? And Mad Max the murderer? Will they get him, without more help from ASIO?'

'If he killed her,' Donald said.

Surprised, Brooke and Greg said in unison, 'If?'

'What else do you know, Donald?' Brooked asked.

'There were no signs of a struggle, were there, Brooke? And it seems too convenient that both Max and Pike seem to have disappeared. More troubling is Ormandy's involvement in the police investigation.'

'Surely, he took over to cover up for Fish and or Max?'

'But think about it: he didn't owe Fish anything, if Fish gave an honest statement about how Bozin came to be killed.'

'Well, from what Bozin's wife told me, it probably wasn't in self-defence at all. Ormandy was trigger-happy, and he could have bribed Fish to concoct a tale.'

Greg was studying Donald closely. 'What is it, Donald? Do you think Fish and Max are fall guys, and ASIO is behind this?'

'I don't know. Brown seemed to be protecting Ormandy and Fish. They all have something to hide and reason to stick together. When agendas go pear-shaped, it's difficult to work out who'll win and who'll lose when the truth comes out.'

Brooke and Greg listened while Donald talked, quietly staring into his glass.

'ASIO is generally the winner. The bigger the stuff-ups, the greater is the need for more personnel to cover them up. ASIO's insatiable appetite for resources is pandered to by politicians. They're victims of a protection racket. If a brave prime minister says, "No more money", a terrorist act will occur, accompanied by the head spook's words "I told you so". We'll never shed our shadows.' He looked at Greg. 'If I had to guess, Max will be the fall guy. I think that Fish will be kept warm by Australian intelligence. Told to stand by in Indonesia, and that he'll be looked after. They can afford to sacrifice Max.'

'Fish would be standing by for what?' Brooke was incredulous.

'There's an election due next year. If ASIO wants Labor to lose, I wouldn't put it past them to instruct Fish that he's free to send as many leaky boats across to Broome or Darwin as he wants. Whether their passengers get here or drown on the way doesn't matter. On the other hand, if the not-so-bright "small picture" cowboys decide that Labor should stay in power, they will pressure him to hang off till after the election. Mark my word, more boats will come, and Fish will be in business until...'

'Until…?' Brooke waited.

'Until he's found dead in a back alley in Indonesia.'

The chooks had been put to bed. Another bottle of red wine, Greg's contribution, was opened and emptied. Greg had declined to stay on for a bowl of soup. He picked up his coat and shook Donald's hand by way of goodbye. His eyes were sad as he kissed Brooke goodnight. She knew he wanted only her happiness, but they both knew that something of their friendship would be lost if Donald stayed in her life.

Brooke whispered in his ear, 'You're a true friend, Greg. Thank you.' She said out loud, 'See you next week for a game of chess? Life goes on, you know?'

Greg buttoned up his coat and walked to his truck.

The open fire lived on. Brooke and Donald took a large bowl of soup and toast to the bedroom and, propped up by pillows, snuggled into the doona. The bedroom's double louvre doors opened into the living room and they watched the flickering firelight. Donald had left his toothbrush at Brooke's after his last stay. She smiled at his confidence that she would invite him back.

Juggling soup and dropping toast crumbs, they giggled. Then more seriously, 'To Jo,' was the toast, and they talked, ate, and toasted Jo again.

Brooke left the bed to turn off the kitchen lights. Donald followed her with the empty bowls and wine glasses. Back in bed, Donald saw tears running down Brooke's cheeks. He wiped them with his fingertips and brought her body close, hugging her tightly. She knew that he, too, was trying to cope with a roller coaster of mood changes. She had experienced anger, disbelief and frustration during the evening, as well as relief, and a moment of joy with Donald.

This mix of emotions poured into a frenetic, urgent act of lovemaking. That is, until Brooke broke out into a guffaw when runaway breadcrumbs reached her buttocks. Laughter and tears; happiness and sorrow. Brooke could see that their intimacy was not the romantic perfection of Jo and Mujo, but it was good, very good.

Donald grasped her hips from below, trying to ignore prickly toast crumbs. He cracked up with laughter and they started again, teasing each other playfully until the rhythm of their bodies took control and they were spun light years away from a world of badly run intelligence agencies and corrupt greedy men who wormed their way into the murky world of spies. So many lives ruined or changed forever in the name of national security. Jo was Operation Fishnet's unintentional by-catch. It was Brooke's last negative thought before consoling herself with the fact that because of this human tragedy she was getting to know Donald.

ASIO Headquarters, Canberra, December 1992

'All things considered, we got out of that pretty well, boss. The nasty bit was having to clean up after Fish and Max.'

'You think we got out of it well, Alec? The woman's dead. And we're implicated.'

'That is unfortunate, but dying was the best thing she could have done for us.'

His boss, Thurmond Kingfisher, wasn't impressed.

Brown spread his hands nervously. 'Max Peacock can be found, charged and locked up for a while and, better still, we're rid of that pest Fish for a bit. He won't set foot in Australia as long as a conspiracy-to-murder charge is possible.'

'No qualms about Max being convicted of a murder he didn't commit, huh?' Kingfisher's eyes bulged and he was red in the face.

'What do you mean?' Alec asked. The debriefing was not going to plan.

'I'm disappointed, Alec. I've supported you all the way in this matter and now you're not being frank with me. Do you think Max will take the whole rap for Rowan's murder lying down? If his sentence is too harsh, he'll spill everything, and take you down with him for the murder.'

'But, er, you know he killed her.'

'Ormandy's no fool. He's an experienced cop. There was no evidence of Rowan being roughed up. Max is rough as guts, but no more a killer than Fish. This is your chance to tell me what happened. Get it off your chest and then we'll talk about how to handle it.'

'Boss, Max would have killed her, I swear. I saw him. He's up for attempted murder, at least. Who'd believe him if he tries to blame me? If I hadn't tried to stop him, she wouldn't have seen me. It was an utter balls-up.'

'Go on.'

'I followed them when I saw him in her car. When they pulled in near the yacht club, I watched and waited. It was all I could do. When he put a gun to her head, I had to stop him. I ran up shouting and shining my torch on him. He didn't react so I drew my gun and told him to lower his. He turned and said, "Brown, fuck you." She turned to look at me and said, "Brown! Thank God you're useful for something." Max freaked, and said, "Shit, she knows you. You'd better do something," and kept the gun on her head.'

'Oh, you fucking idiot, I can see it coming,' Kingfisher put his head in his hands.

'What would you have done?' Brown said.

'Go, on. Finish your apology.'

'I shouted, "I'm not going to do anything. You are." He yelled back, "No, I'm not here to kill her, just rough her up. Let me out of this," or some such.'

Thurmond Kingfisher looked at Brown with hardening eyes, as Brown continued.

'Cool lady. She said, "Have you two reached a consensus then? Can I go and leave you to argue it out?" So I put my gun to Max's head, and said, "Do it, do it now, or the bullet goes through both your heads." And he did.'

'So with a gun to his head, you made Max shoot her?'

'Cleanest way out.'

'Nice work, Brown, you bloody fool. At least your story matches Max's.'

'You've found Max?'

'Of course we've got Max. We're now trying to clean up after two incompetents.'

'Oh, fuuuck. I never meant any of this to happen.'

'We've done a deal with Max. You'd better listen, so your story matches.'

'Christ.'

'After Rowan's death, we soon made Fish tell us where to find Max. We brought him in and spelled out his options if he ended up on a murder charge. And he will, given the coroner's findings. Max only wanted to scare the shit out of Rowan, keep her from spreading what she knew about that list of customs officers he'd been flogging, and the Berettas Fish smuggled in. The goal for Max and Fish was to keep their operations going.'

'What'll he say if he's arrested?'

'He'll make up a story about wanting her to keep quiet about a Yugoslav sting to catch Croatian terrorists, which is true – leaving us out if it. He'll say she struggled and the gun went off. You'd better hope he won't mention your involvement. He knows he can't prove you made him do it. He'll say he panicked, swapped guns, and made it look like suicide. He'll try to get his charge downgraded to manslaughter.'

'That's still a gaol term,' Brown said.

'With good behaviour remissions, he could be out in four years or less. On the other hand, if he talks about his previous history and his fraudulent use of customs files, and misbehaviour at ASIO, corruption will come into it and his sentence will be doubled. It's not in his interests to go down that path.'

'Will he say Fish put him up to it?'

'We hope so. He has to explain why he came with a second gun, the one found in Rowan's car. We told him we'd left a clean Glock behind. So he'll say that while Fish ordered him to kill Rowan, he only ever intended to rough her up. When the Beretta went off, he made it look like suicide, planting the Glock, just as Fish had directed.'

'So, while Fish has an alibi, he's not in the clear.'

'Right. The plan was for Rowan to be accosted while we were watching Fish at home with his family in Downer. They had to wait until Zukić was out of the way and Rowan gave them the opportunity by going to see Zukić the night before he left. Max followed and lurked around the Hyatt until he saw Zukić leave Rowan's car and return to the hotel. He forced his way into her car as she was leaving.'

'Right,' said Alec, 'and Fish presumably believes Max will implicate him, so he has to leave and stay away in case Max is arrested.'

'That's the story, and we'll all go with it,' Kingfisher said. 'Fish's hold over Ormandy has been weakened. When Ormandy was searching the car, he found the Yugoslav report on the Bozin shooting. That's why Ormandy covered for you. Without that report, no one will ever revisit what's an old case. Ormandy is a useful cop and we don't want to lose him.'

Brown was struggling to absorb the web of threads he was enmeshed in. 'Well, at least I've convinced Donald Fenchurch that there are things he must keep to himself. Without my even mentioning Max, he concluded that Max is Rowan's killer. I doubt if he'll revisit that thinking.'

'Hmm, you took a risk telling him so much. He'll know we let Fish go for a reason. Think he doesn't know that Fish will be waiting for clearance to send another boat?'

'So? He can't prove anything. Anyway, what's our thinking on that? Do we keep Fish on the drip? Let him bring in a couple of leaky refugee boats before next year's election. Make sure we run him, not vice versa.'

'Labor demands no boats before the election. A trickle of boats suits the Liberals, but if they win government, they'll want the boats to stop. Either way, we're well placed to argue for more funding.'

Kingfisher dropped his head and a relieved Brown sensed that the conversation was coming to an end. He was wrong.

Kingfisher lifted his head to address Brown again. 'But there are still loose ends. First, the Immigration whistle-blower, Pratt.'

'He wouldn't have been a problem if Ormandy hadn't foisted Fish on them. Wish we'd known about that complication earlier. Ormandy should have told me about Fish's involvement in Operation Picnic before he used me to get Pratt to block that woman's promotion. Anyway, I can deal with Pratt.'

'You, Alec, have done enough. It'll be me getting a team on to it.' Kingfisher was staring at Brown now, his pupils like pinheads. 'You are to lie low for a while. You will be taking a holiday.'

'Boss? Am I a loose-end too?'

'No, just protecting you.'

'Protecting yourself, you mean.'

'Now, now, don't be like that. Just remember that Fenchurch is still out there with a head full of information. He's very much a loose end. Could cause significant trouble.'

'He's knows he can't. I'll manage him.'

'No, Alec, you won't. You are about to take a long Asian holiday. Keep an eye on Fish, at least till the election. I'll call you if he wriggles too much, or gets too cocky. You just might have to tidy things up over there.'

'I'm out in the cold?'

'Off now. I have phone calls to make.'